D0424346

DO NOT ASK

ELAINE WILLIAMS CROCKETT

Copyright 2017 by Elaine Williams Crockett

All rights reserved. No part of this book may be used or reproduced in any manner whatsoever without written permission from the author except in the case of brief quotations embodied in critical articles and reviews.

Do Not Ask is a work of fiction. Names, characters, businesses, organizations, places, events and incidences are either the product of the author's imagination or are used fictitiously. Any resemblance to actual persons, living or dead, events or locales, is entirely coincidental. ISBN (Print) 978-1-54391-043-8 (Ebook) 978-1-54391-044-5

Acknowledgements:

My sincere thanks to Dan E. Krane, Ph.D., Professor of Biological Sciences at Wright State University, whose consulting company, Forensic Bioinformatics www.bioforensics.com, reviews DNA testing results from hundreds of court cases around the world each year. He is a pioneer in the development of tools and approaches that make forensic DNA profiling more reliable and objective, and I owe him a tremendous debt for his advice about DNA analyses and how DNA evidence is presented in court.

A big thank you to Charles L. Hall, Ph.D, Maryland State Terrestrial Archeologist with the Maryland Historical Trust, who provided advice about archeological terminology and the legal requirements for working on archaeology sites and the reporting of human remains. Charles, I think you must have the most interesting job in the world!

I owe Thomas C. Hill, Esq., Pillsbury Winthrop Shaw Pittman LLP, Washington D.C., a debt of gratitude for taking time out of his busy schedule to read all of the courtroom scenes and then provide invaluable feedback. Tom, you have my sincere thanks.

My first readers: My wonderful husband, Don Crockett, and step-daughters, Shelley Crockett and Alyssa Crockett. Thank you for taking the first bite of the apple, as sour as it must have been, and for proposing such wonderful ideas. Judge Christine O.C. Miller for an amazing review of the manuscript and whose insight and knowledge made the story so much better. And Jon and Betsey Rosenbaum to whom I owe a similar debt of gratitude.

Robert D. Paul, Esq., General Counsel to the U.S. Federal Trade Commission, 1985-1988, I thank for being such a good friend over the years and for avidly supporting my writing career.

And a special thanks to Pintado, who put a face to this story: *Book Cover Design by Pintado, pintado.weebly.com*

For my parents, grandparents, and all who came before.

"What's past is prologue."

The Tempest, (Act 1, Scene 1), William Shakespeare

CHAPTER 1

Where the lane to Blackhall skirts the house and the borders of flowers fall away, the locust, lilac, and crepe myrtle paths lead to the high cliff, where I will hold my precious babies in my arms and plunge into the sea.

My name is Josephine, John Rideout is my husband, and Blackhall is our home. The year I met John was 1773 and John's situation was precarious. Before the Revolutionary War, John was the Secretary to the British Governor of Maryland, but when the War began and the Governor was ousted, John lost his position of power and influence and became someone whose political views were under constant suspicion. Despite his situation, I fell in love with John. He was a wildly handsome man, powerful and strong, thick black hair, steely blue eyes, and he had inherited the olive skin the Rideout men are known for. I was a shy, plain woman but the heiress of a well-respected family, and I see now that I was John's way back to prominence.

Not long after we married, John used part of my fortune to build Blackhall and moved us to this grand Georgian mansion in the deep shade of overhanging willow trees along the Chesapeake Bay. John said that Blackhall would keep us from the prying eyes of the Committees of Safety whose local militias confiscate properties of suspected Royalists in the area around Annapolis. In this way, John said, we would survive the Revolutionary War with our fortune intact.

Yet, John spends most of his time not at Blackhall but at our house in Annapolis. The rumors about John's life in town reached my ears soon after our marriage, and before long, I knew about the women he beds and his gambling vice that decimates my fortune. Yet, after discovering his deceits, I still loved him, and I thought I could survive the whispers and the scandals, and if it came to it, even the poverty that looms ahead.

After our second child, Samuel, was born, I was happy for a while. When Samuel arrived, John became a loving and contented husband. We were a family and Blackhall was a beautiful refuge from the rest of the world. During the day, we took picnics with our children under the weeping willows, and in the evening, John and I would walk arm in arm through our gardens, fireflies blinking about us, while he flirted with me like we were still courting. But when we returned to Annapolis, I discovered...

"Wow! This is so cool! Did she really kill herself?" Eden Hines asked, eyes wide with delight, as she twirled around, waving the old piece of parchment at Davis Rideout and glancing at her identical twin sister, Echo Hines, who was preening and applying cherry-colored lipstick in front of an antique Chinese Chippendale mirror.

"Please put that back," Davis said, annoyed that Eden was digging through desk drawers and rifling through old books in the walnut-paneled library. Leaning against the antique desk, Davis looked like the prep school product that he was, dressed casually in a lightweight navy cotton sweater, a pair of blue jeans, and brown deck shoes, no socks. With his dark hair, blue eyes, and olive skin, Davis possessed a remarkable resemblance to his ancestor, John Rideout, the subject of the suicide note and whose portrait hung just down the hall in the grand gallery. And as with John Rideout, the assignation tonight with two beautiful women was a typical night in Davis's life, or at least it had been, until he'd married Reed.

Eden sipped her martini and handed the yellowed parchment to Davis, her eyebrow raised in a question mark.

"Yes, she jumped off the cliff with her baby, right here at Blackhall."

"How high is the cliff?"

"High," Davis replied, frowning as he examined the parchment under light pouring from the bronze desk lamp. "This is so curled and torn." He hoped Reed wouldn't notice this new damage to the already mangled document. Surprisingly, Reed had become interested in Blackhall's history.

Echo rushed over, eyes like saucers. "Who killed herself?"

"One of my ancestors," Davis said.

"Why?"

"We don't know. The rest of the letter was lost."

"No kidding?" Eden stuck her nose in the parchment.

"The other son was in Annapolis when Josephine went crazy." Davis shrugged. "I guess that's the only reason I'm here."

Eden looked at Davis from under smoky, hooded lids. "Well, thank God for that," she said, moving into the crux of his arm, slipping her hand under his sweater, and running her fingers up his back. "We'd hate to miss out on all the fun tonight."

Davis laughed at Eden's comment. Davis had been thinking about Eden and Echo all week, anticipating this carefully arranged tryst in the countryside. The Hines twins, as they were known, had been on the Washington, D.C., social scene ever since graduating from Brown University last year. Dressed tonight in short, white silk dresses and lit by the moonlight filtering into the room, they looked like the classical beauties of ancient Greek art, women with long, loose twists of thick blonde hair, high cheekbones, and perfect alabaster skin.

Eden slid onto a heavily tasseled dark-green velvet sofa in the library and crossed long, slender legs. This vantage point provided an excellent view of the French doors on the opposite side of the room and the Chesapeake Bay just beyond. All around Eden, the trappings of Davis's country house, the famed Blackhall estate, radiated a luxurious tableau. Fine period antiques, heavily carved mullion windows, and the famous baroque mask carvings representing the Four Winds, each dominating an entire quarter of the library ceiling, attested to the wealth and privileged history of the Rideout family.

"Maybe I'll sit here and watch the two of you play together," Eden said, with a meaningful glance and nod at her sister who quickly grabbed an overnight bag leaning against the door.

"Look what I found," Echo exclaimed, holding the bag over her head.

Davis ignored Echo, slipped the ancient parchment into its polyester sleeve, and returned it to an archival insert in the walnut box on his desk. He picked up a Baccarat crystal decanter of Bombay Sapphire and poured some gin into a tall glass, reminding himself what years of experience had taught him—to display some indifference when women came on to him. He'd found that a certain degree of detachment increased the tension that naturally existed during sex. In fact, it drove some women crazy, even made them beg for it.

Not that these two weren't already in the palm of his hand.

Echo plopped down on the sofa beside her sister, cupped her chin in her hands and sulked.

"How did you two escape your detail?" Davis asked.

"Who?" Eden asked, distracted by her image in a mirror. "Oh, them," she sighed. "We told them to get lost."

"Does your father know about that?"

She flipped her hair. "He can't do anything about it. We're twenty-two and free as birds."

"You fly around by yourselves?"

"Better than being in bed with the Secret Service."

Davis smiled. "Somehow, I didn't think you would mind that."

"Ugh. Not with Secret Service agents." She wrinkled her nose in disgust.

Davis and Reed had been introduced to the twins at a White House state dinner where Eden and Echo had happily chatted away with Reed, striking up what seemed like an instant friendship. At least that's what Davis thought until a couple of days later when he received an explicit phone call from the twins asking if he'd like to meet them at some discrete location *to screw* as they had so delicately put it.

These girls weren't shy. Neither was Davis who had upped the ante by replying that making a sex tape might be fun. Eden and Echo had conferred and giggled in the background before coming back on the phone and agreeing. He couldn't believe his luck. He loved that kind of thing, although it was something he'd never propose to Reed, the mother of his son.

"Your house is so awesome," Echo said, gazing at the plasterwork on the ceiling. "And the road up here was so long I thought we were lost!"

Eden raised her eyebrows. "Actually, this place is sorta spooky," she said, craning her neck, looking beneath the gloss of wealth that hid a desperate need for repairs. Wallpaper flapped under expensive paintings and water stains bled dark and angry like open wounds that refused to heal.

Davis shrugged. "It could use some renovations."

"Well, I love it," Echo said emphatically.

"Come here, darling." Eden slid across the empty space on the sofa and put an arm around Echo. She gently parted her sister's lips and met her mouth, and in the moonlight, they began slowly French kissing, looking like white marble goddesses caressing each other.

Davis swirled some ice in his gin and tonic as he studied the gorgeous twins making out on the sofa, wondering what he had done to deserve such a gift. Just watching the twins was giving him an erection that was straining against his jeans. He needed to pace himself. A long night of trophy sex was ahead.

He'd been faithful to Reed, at least more or less, for the entire year they'd been married. He loved Reed and of course, he loved their baby, little Samuel. But monogamy had proven to be exactly what he'd dreaded and the reason he'd never before married—a painfully bland diet. He needed variety. All men did. Women didn't understand because they couldn't separate sex from emotional attachment. But he certainly could.

And anyway, he reasoned, Reed would never find out.

Davis opened the library's French doors to the night and strolled onto the terrace. Over the Chesapeake Bay, the moon hung like a lantern, a faint red staining its edges, an effect caused by light bending off hexagonal ice crystals suspended high in the atmosphere. It was a magnificent sight, with the moon sitting just off the shoulder of Jupiter.

He glanced at the caretaker's cottage. Good. The Little Cottage was dark and Henry's car was gone. A movement in the trees caught his eye and he squinted into the night. Almost looked like a woman walking along the cliff. Henry would've said it was Josephine Rideout back from the dead, searching for her baby, but it was simply a willow branch swaying in the fog that had begun drifting up from the Bay.

Davis felt a soft hand on his back. "Davis, aren't you interested in us?" Eden whimpered behind him, sounding like a three-year-old asking for a candy bar. Davis turned around, the glass in his hand wet with condensation. Eden and Echo were both naked and standing at his elbow.

"Come here." Davis pulled Echo to him with one hand and kissed her, tracing the wet glass over her nipples and down her tummy to her groin before he let it drop to the rug. Echo gasped as a current of electricity shot through every nerve in her body. Davis moved his hand down to explore the crease between her legs. She moaned and melted into him, moving against his hand, until he finally laid her down, her beautiful alabaster body sinking deep into the soft cushions of the velvet sofa.

Eden knelt in front of Davis and looked up at him with a sly smile as she tugged at his belt and slowly unzipped his jeans. Eden's slow, deliberate movements made Davis even more excited, and his erection was throbbing as Eden slid her fingers into his shorts and took him into her mouth. Davis sighed. Damn. It was so exciting to be with someone new and two at once ...

As the baroque masks observed them from the ceiling, and a video camera from a corner, all thoughts of Reed and everything else important in Davis's life quickly slipped away. And he and the two beautiful daughters of the President of the United States became a tangle of limbs. But the bliss was not to last for long. Before the night was over, death would strike at Blackhall.

CHAPTER 2

Two Days Later

I had no idea my son-in-law had engaged in a threesome with the President's daughters. I guess had I known, I wouldn't have been all that surprised. Davis had been my law school roommate at Harvard twenty-five years ago, so I knew all about his women and then there was that little problem last year when he'd gotten my twenty-one-year-old daughter pregnant. Of course, Reed had propositioned Davis, but their thirty-year age difference made that seem beside the point.

No. That day, June 3, the day that trouble began heading my way like a jail door slamming shut, Davis was the last person on my mind. It was a blistering hot summer day, the kind of day I found myself running from shade to shade in an otherwise empty street. The month of May hadn't been too bad. In May, the stove was just beginning to heat up. Washington D.C., was south of the Mason-Dixon line and part of a subtropical climate that extended all the way south to Miami, Florida, and just like in the deep south, June and July were awful. In June and July, humidity soaked the air but the month of August was the worst. That's why Congress went into recess then. In August, you could wring water from your clothes.

It was just about as hot at the United States Supreme Court where I was the newest Associate Justice—Justice Warren Alexander.

"We need to consider the entirety of the trial record," I said, searching the faces around the table in the Supreme Court Conference Room for signs of agreement. Some of the Justices were attentive, ears perked high, faces pointed toward me. Others appeared to be fascinated by motes of dust floating through the air. "The majority opinion sifts through the trial record like it's panning for gold."

7

The opinion's author, Chief Justice Bannister Brown, glared at me, eyes blazing. I ignored him. I'd tried and hadn't gotten the votes I needed from the other Justices so my gambit was quite unusual, especially at this late stage in the game. Brown didn't like it. I didn't care. The word 'justice' from the Latin root 'justus' meant 'upright and just' and I took my new title seriously. I was looking at one of the most egregious prosecutorial abuses on record.

"Simpson was almost executed," I said. "He was weeks away from the electric chair and five prosecutors in that office hid exculpatory eyewitness and blood evidence for twenty years." Heat rose in my face. "As if that's not enough, Louisiana courts overturned four convictions because of Brady violations in that same office and you're saying that doesn't add up to an actionable pattern because the other violations didn't involve blood or crime lab evidence?" I tossed my pen on the conference table, frustrated. "We need to hold these prosecutors accountable. If it weren't for the Innocence Project, Simpson would be dead."

Chief Justice Bannister Brown cleared his throat. "An impassioned argument, Justice Alexander. One I'm sure my colleagues will take to heart." Brown scanned the room and smiled dismissively. Some of the faces smiled back in support of the Chief. All of the Justices shifted in their chairs.

"Let's vote," Chief Brown said. "In favor of issuing the Court's opinion as written?" Brown called the names of the Justices, beginning with the most senior Justice in the room. One after another, five voices said, "Aye." I'd lost the argument.

It was the ivory tower syndrome. Most of the Justices had begun their careers in academia, where poverty and drugs never entered their world. I'd begun my career in the real world, at the U.S. Attorney's Office. That hadn't been gritty enough for me, so I'd quit and joined the FBI where I felt I was making a difference getting the scum off the street. But I was just as passionate about unethical prosecutions, and in my opinion, the Simpson case was an atrocity because the last time I checked, the inscription above the Supreme Court entrance was–*Equal Justice Under Law*–a specific reference to our criminal justice system. We were, after all, the Court of last resort.

I snapped out of my thoughts as noise filled the room, a rustle of clothing, papers being stacked and shuffled, coughs and groans and creaking of old joints as some of the more ancient Justices struggled to their feet.

Number of Justices: Nine.

Answerable to: No one.

Removable by: The icy scythe of death.

Heady stuff. I stood and headed toward the door, anxious to leave. I was meeting my law clerks for coffee and I'd had enough of my colleagues for the moment.

Chief Justice Brown looked at me. "Tut. Tut. Just a minute. Before we adjourn," he said in his ponderous voice, "I want to announce that I'm assigning United States v. Clark to Justice Alexander to write the majority opinion. There will be a memo to that effect issued later today." He smiled at me.

I was surprised. United States v. Clark was a political hot potato and Chief Brown typically authored the Court's most important decisions, especially in cases like this one, where it was necessary to maintain a fragile coalition of Justices. This was indeed an honor, especially since, as the newest Justice, I was assigned menial tasks such as getting coffee for Conference and answering the imposing wood door when anyone knocked.

"Have a good day, everyone," the Chief said, dismissing us.

In the cafeteria, Jake waved me over to where my clerks were sitting. They were all so different. On the shelves of a book store, Lilly would've been in the mystery section, a rare combination of beauty and brains, a gorgeous dark-haired Harvard grad who was as unpredictable as a gypsy telling fortunes on a roadside. Amy, a Yale graduate and a firebrand women's rights advocate, was a self-help tome, *How to Shatter the Glass Ceiling*. Jake was the stud in a romance novel, a strapping blond-haired, blue-eyed, self-professed *woman magnet*, who probably kept a ruler by his bed. And Todd was pure Dickensian, a young Bob Cratchit toiling away at his desk, never complaining, a wordsmith quietly penning the perfect turn of a phrase every time.

Jake pushed a cup of steaming coffee at me.

"Thanks."

"What a year," Jake said, leaning back in his chair, grinning wide. "Did you think it would be so partisan up here, Justice A?" he asked, referring to the political split that divided the court.

"Hmmm. It seems more like …" I searched for words. I was beginning to think my efforts were being wasted.

"What?" Heads turned to me, expectant.

"Like I'm Sisyphus and the Court is the boulder."

They laughed but I wasn't joking.

Lilly looked at me through thick, dark eyelashes. "Justice A., tell us about Switzerland."

Only Supreme Court Justices and school children had the summer off. Most of the Justices were going to give speeches or relax on some remote mountaintop in Aspen or Gstaad. I was going to use the opportunity to hunt down a criminal I'd tangled with the year before. Not that I was about to divulge that bit of information to my law clerks.

"Claire and I have rented a small villa," I said.

"Someone said it was a *second honeymoon*," Lilly said, sing-songing her way through the last two words.

Something I'd promised Claire. "We're going to renew our vows," I said, a bit self-consciously. "But first we're going to stop in Bangor, Maine, to visit a friend, Sheriff Johnson. It'll be good to get out of this heat and humidity."

Lilly raised one eyebrow, looking slightly wicked. She lowered her voice to a sultry octave dripping with sex. "So, you're going to Bangor as soon as possible."

"*Whoa* …" a long murmur of risqué amazement arose from my other law clerks, all wide eyes and surreptitious glances in my direction. Jake spit some coffee.

"What? What's wrong?" Lilly asked, her voice back to normal, smiling innocently, pretending to be all sugar and spice.

Lilly made me nervous. She'd been flirtatious all year but for the past few weeks, she'd been circling me like a plane coming in for a landing. I didn't need any trouble in my marriage, so, I'd done what any intelligent man in my situation would do—I'd ignored it. The end of the term was nearing and Lilly would be gone soon enough, off to a big law firm. I had to give her credit, though. She had a lightning-quick mind that made her the most valuable member of my team.

Someone tugged at my elbow. "Justice." I looked up. My secretary, Dorothy, was peering at me from behind horn-rimmed eyeglasses attached to a metal chain knotted around her neck. Her brows were knitted together and her lips pursed into a tight little circle. She leaned into my ear. "Ruth is in your chambers and there are a bunch of other FBI agents with her."

Dr. Ruth Jacobson was a psychiatrist and the Section Chief of the FBI's Crimes Against Adults Group, known in common parlance as criminal profilers. I hadn't seen Ruth in months. There was no reason for her to be here. My blood pressure spiked.

I scraped back from the table and started back to my chambers. Dorothy trailed behind—thick body, stick legs—looking like a little wren hopping along. "Honestly, Justice, they look like they're ready to draw a bead. Be careful," she added, her tiny shoes clicking staccato on the marble floor as she strived to keep up. I shook my head, wondering where she got these ideas.

In my chambers, I pushed through FBI agents milling around Dorothy's desk and opened the door to my inner sanctum.

"Hot outside?" I asked.

Ruth had pulled her mass of brown hair into a thick ponytail. Her white linen pantsuit looked like a rumpled grain sack, a victim of Washington's humid clime. But despite the need for an iron, she was dressed very conservatively today. Unusual, because for some unknown reason, Ruth had adopted a bold, leopard print wardrobe as her own peculiar fashion statement. It was quite distinctive among the sea of government employees in dark, serious clothing. It was also oddly endearing.

I pulled up a chair for her. "Sit down." I put my hand on her shoulder. "Would you like something? Coffee? Tea? Valium?" I laughed, trying to lighten the atmosphere.

"You're coming with me," she said.

The hell I was. Ruth's world consisted of murderers, sexual deviants, and drug dealers but mostly murderers. I straightened my red tie and grey suit, purposely settled deep into my desk chair, crossed my legs and frowned. "What's the problem?"

"The President needs you right away."

I drew back. "Me? Why?"

"We have to hurry. I'll fill you in on the way."

I had never seen Ruth so wound up. Something awful had happened. Despite a gnawing in my gut that I was making a big mistake, I dug myself out of my chair and followed her out the door.

CHAPTER 3

I leaned into the black leather seat of the FBI van speeding up Pennsylvania Avenue, last in a caravan of shiny black cars, red lights flashing, sirens blaring. Strings of school kids, wearing identical red tee shirts so their teacher could easily round them up, turned and stared to see if the President was coming through.

I wondered whether Ruth would ever accept that I was no longer an FBI agent. We'd worked closely together at one time but that was eons ago. She still asked me to consult on high-profile cases. Informally and off the record, of course. It was one thing when I was a Judge on the United States Court of Federal Claims. That was a relatively obscure court. The Supreme Court was different. A case that Ruth worked on could wind itself through the appellate process and land on my desk.

Ruth's work required exacting analyses and with my legal training, we'd made a good team. Fortunately, I suspected she'd find an equal partner in her new fiancé, Jeffrey Pennypacker, a renown Scotland Yard Detective, who was about to join her in the States to work alongside her at the FBI.

"Eden and Echo Hines are missing," Ruth said.

I took a deep breath. *So, that was it.* "How long?"

"Two days," she said, frown lines branching across her forehead. "We're working against the clock. When Eden and Echo didn't show up for work Monday morning, their boss became worried and contacted the President. He sent an aide to their house. The twins were gone."

"Any witnesses?"

"Some former classmates from Brown University stopped by Eden and Echo's house Saturday evening. The twins told them they were on their way to the Eastern Shore to meet some men. The friends don't know who the men were or where they were meeting. We reviewed video from the Bay Bridge cameras and the twins' car did not cross the bridge."

"The only access to the Eastern Shore," I muttered.

"Essentially. Both girls left their cell phones at their house. There's nothing there and nothing in their computers that would provide a clue. We found a traffic camera on New York Avenue showing their car heading west about 7:30 in the evening. After that, we weren't able to track the car, even through satellite imagery. And their car is old and doesn't have GPS."

"Where was the Secret Service?"

"The twins dismissed their Secret Service detail. Legally, they can do that."

She was right. There was no law requiring the President's family members to accept Secret Service protection. The same law that authorized protection for the President's family also let them opt out.

"The President begged his daughters to keep their detail," Ruth said. "He had the head of the Secret Service talk to them, warn them about the dangers, but they wouldn't listen."

"What about burners?"

"There's no record of them buying burner phones, although that's our working theory. It's like they wanted to disappear. The President is worried out of his mind. That's why he asked for you. You found Reed after she was kidnapped last year."

I shook my head and looked out the window at the buildings rolling by, soaring grey monuments interspersed with modern towers stacked like Legos. Messengers on bikes wove in and out of traffic, delivering the last of the day's parcels, cognizant that rain clouds were gathering on the horizon, as dark and swirling as the muddy Potomac River. I turned back to Ruth. "That was a completely different situation. I knew who took Reed. You have nothing."

"I might if I can get your input."

Ruth's eyes had sunk into the hollows. Her left eyelid drooped like it always did when she was tired. I wanted to touch her arm and tell her everything would be okay, she would find Eden and Echo safe and sound. *A lie.*

"Did their friends know anything else?"

"They said the twins were wearing short white dresses and rhinestone high heels. A Gucci overnight bag was in the back seat of the car. Then the friends clammed up, claimed that's all they knew. I knew they were lying and I told them the twins' disappearance was a national security threat and I could have them waterboarded."

"I bet that had them singing," I said.

"Like a choir. It seems that Eden and Echo wanted to live out their sexual fantasies without getting into serious relationships but they were afraid men would blab about hookups with the President's daughters and that would hurt their father's chance for re-election. So, they decided married men would be ideal sex partners because they wouldn't talk, for obvious reasons. That's why the twins didn't want Secret Service around."

"Married men don't like witnesses to infidelity," I said.

"Here's the real kicker. It appears they chose men at random."

"The twins were heading to a hookup with men they didn't know?" I was amazed they would be so reckless. And I thought Reed was a handful. I looked around. We were speeding along Massachusetts Avenue, long past the turnoff to the White House.

"Where are we going?" I asked.

"You'll see."

At the Naval Observatory, the sirens died and our caravan fell away. "We don't want to alert the press there's a problem," Ruth said.

We turned north and flew up Reno Road, by beautiful old homes shaded by centuries-old trees, and crossed into the Cleveland Park area of Washington. An almost supernatural hush hung in the air, broken only by the occasional drone of a lawn mower. The area reeked of country club money.

"You're not gonna believe this," she added.

We pulled into a side alley, negotiated a few bumpy potholes, and stopped beside a garage attached to a small bungalow. There were no other FBI agents around, no crime scene tape. The engine shut off.

"Is this their house?" I asked.

"Yes." She jerked her head toward a large, tree-filled front yard where a man in overalls was potting geraniums. "He's FBI. His job is to keep everyone away."

The gardener looked up and nodded solemnly at Ruth, then shoved a trowel into a bag of potting soil.

I clicked my seat belt open. "Place looks small." The house was white with black shutters. A row of trim boxwoods bordered its base. Very neat and tidy. What women would call cute.

"It's two bedrooms."

We slid out of the van. The day had turned dark. Black, foamy clouds roiled overhead and tall elms swayed, shedding loose leaves to the wind. The temperature had dropped twenty degrees. I buttoned my jacket.

Ruth opened the back door with a key. I hesitated.

"Don't worry, we've already processed it."

A mountain of dirty dishes languished in the sink and a pile of clothes was growing mold by the washing machine. The place smell like a boys' locker room. "Has someone ransacked this place or is it always like this?"

"The President says it's always like this. After we searched the house, we put everything back like it was. What you see is how they left it. Follow me. I want you to look at something."

Off the kitchen and down a narrow hallway were two bedrooms. We walked by one bedroom set up as an office and into the other one. Drawers were open, shoes tossed about, and dozens of teddy bears—feet up, arms splayed—were scattered across a king-size bed like victims of a mass attack.

"Notice anything unusual?" Ruth asked.

"Maybe they're used to sleeping in the same bed. They are twins."

"Oh, c'mon. Grown women?" She shook her head. "Look at Mr. Love Bear." She pointed at an enormous black bear sitting in a corner. He must've been five feet tall, a red satin heart sewn rather sweetly onto his chest.

I picked him up. "This one?" He was tattered around the edges and one paw was ripped open. "Love Bear's had a hard life. And he's very lumpy."

Ruth unzipped Love Bear's back and dumped items on the bed. Sex toys, dildos, chains, leg bars, and black bondage strips came pouring out.

I raised an eyebrow. "The twins have a hobby." Then I noticed some flash drives mixed in with the sex toys. "You've looked at these, right?"

"Yes. They're all blank."

"Odd that they're in with these ... other things."

Lightning flashed. A boom followed and a sheet of rain hit the window like a hail of bullets. We'd gotten inside just in time.

"Isn't it? And there's something else." Ruth walked to a chest and pulled out a drawer crammed with everything from empty chewing gum wrappers and hair bands to light bulbs and old receipts. "I didn't find a lot, although this could be interesting." She thumbed through a small book, located a page and handed it to me. "It's Eden's diary."

"Does it say who they were meeting?"

"No, but look at this." She jabbed at a page where Eden had written 9500, underlined it in black ink and drawn a big star by it. Directly under that was the figure 1140000, also starred and underlined in black.

"What do you suppose that means?" she asked.

"I don't know. It was written the day they disappeared so it could be important." I looked around the room. "You see these numbers anywhere else? In their computers or phones?"

"No. Just here."

I handed her the diary. "Take it to your crack de-coders at the FBI."

"You mean the same people who spent two years trying to decipher the lyrics to *Louie Louie* until someone had the brilliant idea of walking over to the Copyright Office and looking them up?"

"Definitely a low point in the history of the Bureau." I snatched the diary back and examined the figures. "Wait a minute. What if 9500 is $9,500? Think about it. Sex with married men and blackmail go hand-in-hand."

She laughed. "You can't be serious. You think the President's daughters are blackmailing married men?"

"Stay with me. Let's say, hypothetically, the girls have ten men on the string for $9,500 a month each. That's $95,000 a month total and exactly $1,140,000 a year, the second figure in the diary. And $9,500 a month is just under the $10,000 deposit a bank has to report to Treasury."

"What about a SAR?"

"Suspicious Activity Report? Not only could wealthy men pay blackmail, their banks would be accustomed to withdrawals and transfers of large amounts of money. If nothing looks unusual, a bank won't file a SAR with Treasury." I waved my hand at the bed. "And look at all these sex toys. Why so many? It's almost like they're stage props. And the flash drives. Some video cameras can record directly on these. Which makes me wonder if the twins are filming their adventures."

She looked at me like I had gone nuts. "Let me get this straight. You think the twins are not only blackmailing wealthy men, they're using sex tapes to do it?"

"It would make more sense with their dropping their Secret Service detail. They wouldn't want witnesses to their criminal activity. And why would they leave their cell phones behind? They didn't want an electronic footprint of where they were headed. Why? I think that's the question you need to be asking."

"But blackmail? They're the President's daughters. They have enough money."

"Maybe they don't think so."

Ruth shook her head. "We haven't found any large sums of money deposited into their bank accounts."

"Keep looking," I said.

"The night the girls disappeared ... are you saying the twins met someone they're blackmailing?"

"Or maybe they were setting up other victims and something went wrong."

"That's crazy." She sank back. "I think." She narrowed her eyes. "Realistically, how likely do you think that is?"

I shrugged. "Maybe sixty/forty but definitely worth considering."

She weighed what I said. "If that's the case, and that's a big *if*, what about all that money? What happened to that? You think they're smart enough to hide that?"

"From what I've seen? I think they're too smart for their own good."

CHAPTER 4

Lilly stood over Dorothy's desk, anxious to see whether Justice Alexander was available for an appointment later that afternoon.

Dorothy checked Justice Alexander's schedule. "Hmmm, let's see. Tomorrow morning at 8:00 is the earliest he has available," she said, looking Lilly up and down.

Lilly was used to people inspecting her body. "Nothing before that? Justice A. left me a phone message that I was to write the first draft in United States v. Clark and I need to speak with him."

Lilly had already begun working on the case and she needed to clarify a central fact. The opinion was a Chinese puzzle of interlocking pieces. If one piece didn't fit, the entire puzzle fell apart. It was best to get any clarifications as she went along.

Dorothy gave Lilly a sad little face. "Sorry, the Justice has left for the day."

"Already?"

Dorothy looked over her shoulder. "He left with the FBI," she whispered.

Lilly felt a little charge go through her. "Really? What's going on?"

"I didn't ask. He said he'll be back later." Dorothy gave Lilly an officious look. "He didn't know when. Maybe around 7:00." Dorothy hesitated. "You could talk to Chief Brown, if it's that important."

Lilly nodded. "Okay, thanks." She drifted back to the small office she shared with Justice A.'s other law clerks. Amy was hunched over a mountain range of legal books, deciphering some ancient legality, trying to mold it into new currency. Todd was nose deep in his computer and Jake was on the telephone, probably chatting with a girlfriend from the tone of his voice.

Jake looked up and winked at her. Lilly rolled her eyes. Would he never leave her alone? Someday, Jake was going to trip over his own dick. Lilly did a couple of barre stretches, then placed her palms flat on the floor in an exercise routine she'd perfected for breaking up the long days at the Court. Sliding into her chair, she swiveled for a view through the window near her desk, her thoughts returning to Justice A.

That FBI thing was pretty exciting. Justice A. looked like an FBI agent—cheekbones sharp as knives, close-cropped hair shot through with grey, kind eyes that smiled even when he didn't, features that matched his integrity, as though his personality was chiseled into his face like the Presidents on Mount Rushmore. And his body! He had a runner's build, strong and lean. Even though he was old, fifty-one, he looked exceptional for his age. She'd heard some of the other clerks say he ran in the annual Marine Corps Marathon. She could believe it.

She loved it when he called her into his chambers to discuss legal issues. She felt closest to him there, in that small room where he worked in his shirtsleeves, the room that smelled of his aftershave. Her mind would race through legal arguments while she imagined undressing him. Even dreamed about it. Get him out of those red ties and grey suits he always wore. God, he must've had a hundred red ties—fat red ties, skinny red ties, red striped ties, but always red. Same with his suits, a profusion of grey— plain grey, grey pinstriped, grey plaid, but always two-piece and always grey. But that was the Christmas wrapping. She wanted the gift.

But he'd never shown interest in her, never once looking at her in that way men always did. Not a total surprise at the staid institution but so disappointing. Especially that time she'd been wearing a tiny skirt, turned her back to him, and bent over from the waist to pick up a pen. When she'd straightened up, he'd been looking out the window! She tapped a fingernail against her keyboard and stared off into the distance. What the ... nothing like that had ever happened to her before.

Maybe it was her imagination but after that he seemed to talk about his wife more. And now the term was coming to an end but she wasn't done yet. She had a plan. And part one was already in effect.

****

I glanced at my watch. Right about now, Ruth would be entering the Oval Office to brief the President. I was back at the Supreme Court where I took the elevator to the second floor. The chime sounded and I walked into the hallway, a wide formal corridor of smooth Sylacauga marble valued for its pure white color. The massive hallway echoed in an empty end-of-the-day feeling. It was a little after seven and the support and technical staff had already left. There were a few isolated noises, the swoosh of a printer, the clacking of a keyboard, some soft music drifting into the hallway from the offices of a few law clerks who were still in the building, hunkered down, anxious to finish their tasks and leave to meet friends for drinks and dinner.

I walked by Dorothy's desk and into my chambers, paneled in American quartered white oak. A fireplace was centered directly across from my desk and on one side of the room, a large bookcase contained every Supreme Court opinion dating back to 1791 when West v. Barnes was rendered in a procedural matter. My law degrees and bar memberships crammed every inch of one wall and a photo of President Hines administering the oath of office, my wife Claire standing beside me, sat on a nearby credenza. Claire looked beautiful. Most sentimental to me was a large crystal eagle Claire had given me on my first day at the Court. It held pride of place on my desk.

But what really dominated the room, the first thing a person noticed when entering my chambers, were two 6 x 8-foot colonial-era portraits of a man and a woman dressed in the elegant, dark clothing of the period. A recently retired Justice had left the portraits behind and while I initially thought little of the paintings, I had come to admire the dignified strength of character these two projected to the world. A plaque underneath identified Colonel and Mrs. Bertrand Ewell. And from the wall, they presided over my chambers, just like the office I held, sober and grand and a constant reminder of the solemn nature of the responsibilities I had assumed.

I placed my rain-soaked jacket over the back of a chair and unknotted my tie. The night loomed ahead and I'd already called Claire from the van and told her I would be late. I'd bought a day-old ham sandwich from the neighborhood deli and as I tore through the square container of cardboard and cellophane, I thought about Echo's name. I'd been thinking about the name all day and not just as the name of the President's daughter. Echo was an unusual name and could be a wry comment on being a twin, although something else about the name was familiar, something I should remember and hadn't been able to place.

I was chewing when it finally came to me. Quickly wiping my hands, I grabbed the phone and called Ruth. "Have you briefed the President?"

"Yes, I'm on my way back to Quantico," she said.

"I just thought of something that could be helpful. Do you remember the Greek mythology of Narcissus and the wood nymph, Echo?"

There was a momentary silence as she realized what I was getting at.

"You're right," Ruth said, an undercurrent of excitement running through her voice. "Echo fell in love with Narcissus who saw himself in a pond and fell in love with his own image."

"I'm wondering if Echo is actually a nickname that reveals something about the twins' relationship. The twins shared a bed. Like you said, that's not normal. What if the twins are like Narcissus, romantically in love with their own images? And in their case, that would be each other."

"That would be the most interesting case of narcissistic personality disorder I've ever heard of."

"You're the psychiatrist, so you tell me, but the way I remember it is that narcissists choose partners who the world sees as exceptional."

"Yes," she said. "It's classic objectification of the sex partner. A narcissist's ego is wrapped up in their partner and for a woman the thinking would be that if Mr. Big Shot sleeps with me, I'm also wonderful and powerful."

"And where would Eden and Echo meet men who were exceptional? The White House. Think about it. Senators, movie stars, athletes. You should check out the White House guest list."

"That would give us a suspect pool," she said, thinking out loud. "But if that's right," she continued, "the men they've targeted are not merely wealthy, they're also high-profile, men whose images are everything and who might kill to protect themselves. And if Eden and Echo really did manage to conceal their contacts, we may never find them ... if they're still alive."

"Not very encouraging, is it?"

"No."

"Try to get some sleep, Ruth."

I hung up and stared straight ahead at the life-sized portraits on my wall. Colonel Ewell and his wife looked concerned. They should be. The twins were in way over their heads.

✶✶✶✶

Lilly exited the Foggy Bottom Metro and walked into Georgetown, a historic 1.172 square-mile town founded in 1751, annexed by the City of Washington in 1878. The brick sidewalks were deserted, night had fallen, and dim street lamps stretched light over quivering puddles left by the storm.

Lilly slowed to peer into a few of the brightly lit homes, stopping at a white house on O Street where she always lingered for a moment on her way home from work. The Georgian mansion was set back on its lot, secured by a spiked, black iron fence. A heavily-pillared, two-story porch jutted onto a lush side yard where Lilly had often seen parties spill out from the house, Chinese lanterns glowing across the lawn like private moons.

But tonight, everything was quiet, the house in a slumber. On the second floor, a large shadow in the kimono sleeves of a bathrobe crossed a window. Another shadow, a shorter feminine one, appeared and the lights blinked off like a door closing shut.

Lilly adjusted her shoulder bag and moved on. At Wisconsin Avenue, the small, smart boutiques had closed for the day, only CVS and a smattering of restaurants still open. Everything was eerily quiet, everyone in for the night. No one walking home late at night, like she was. She wished she hadn't stopped at that bar in Union Station to wait out the rain. She'd had too many margaritas and now, her brain was awash in sand.

She crossed Wisconsin Avenue, dodging a few cars that sprayed thin curtains of water, and walked straight into a tunnel of darkness. For some reason, the street lamps were out on this side of Georgetown, the only light, a few strands of yellow seeping from behind richly-draped windows. She glanced around, thinking she'd heard a noise. She stopped and listened. Nothing. She hurried on, picking up her pace, her shoes uncertain on the knobby brick sidewalks.

There were fewer houses on this block, a hazy moon outlining the hulking shapes, black and shrouded by menacing looking trees. She never liked this street. Too many trees crowding the sidewalk. Too much land, yards too deep, places to hide and jump out. A low-hanging branch scraped her face and shook rain across her shoulders. She heard a footstep behind her. Her heart began racing and she broke into a run.

At her apartment building, she fumbled with her keys, shards of metal that wouldn't fit the lock. Damn! She took a deep breath, heard a noise. *Another footstep.* She tried the lock again, breathed a sigh of relief. She was inside her building. Her apartment was twenty steps away. She flew through her door and slammed it shut behind her, double-bolted it, and shoved the chain into the slot. *She was safe.*

A knock. She cautiously cracked the door and frowned. "What the hell?" she said, irritated. "You scared me and anyway, what are you doing here? I told you I wasn't interested!"

CHAPTER 5

Slowly, the news about the President's daughters started to leak out. CNN aired a short piece about a potential problem at Eden and Echo's house and showed several police cars and one FBI van positioned like barricades in front of their bungalow. The overt presence of law enforcement meant Mortich was going to go public. Soon.

I turned off the TV in my chambers and returned to my work, trying to concentrate when a strange noise started coming out of the west. It had begun far away, like a long roll of thunder over Fairfax County and it was heading this way—fast, loud, ominous. Suddenly, they were on top of us, hundreds of them, right over the Supreme Court building.

Dorothy ran to the window. I looked over her shoulder. *Whump-whump-whump.* Air Force HH-80 Pave Hawks search and rescue helicopters blacked out the sun like a biblical plague, the helicopters all pitched forward, heading east. The blade slap was deafening. Just as quickly, they were gone, leaving a wake of silence as startling as the initial assault.

I clicked on my TV. FBI Director, Allan Mortich, and other law enforcement officers were squeezed together at a podium, their eyes darkly, fiercely determined despite the news Mortich had just announced.

Presidential daughters Eden and Echo Hines missing.

I spotted the leopard print blouse before I saw her face. Ruth was at Mortich's side, jammed up against his right shoulder.

"No, we don't know anything more than that," Mortich said. "Yes, I'll repeat my statement. Eden and Echo Hines left their house Saturday evening and have not been heard from since. There is an indication they may have traveled to the Eastern Shore. The twins were driving a 2005 black

Porsche Boxster, license plates DA 5145. If anyone has seen this car or these young women, please call the FBI at ..."

"You knew about this, didn't you? That's why Ruth was here." Dorothy glowered at me.

"I couldn't say anything. The FBI had to decide when they needed the public's help."

She bit her lower lip. "What do you suppose happened to those poor lambs?"

"I don't know. And it's apparent to me that Ruth doesn't either."

That wasn't entirely true. I knew the FBI hadn't received any ransom demands, terrorist chatter hadn't yielded any clues, and Ruth had no other leads. Those were the only reasons the FBI would appeal to the public at this stage in the game. But I didn't want to relay that information to Dorothy because it meant there was little chance of finding the twins alive. The hard fact was that Ruth needed a break. After the news conference, Ruth would be inundated with leads, and if she were lucky, one or two would steer her to critical information.

Dorothy started to say something.

I held up a finger. "I want to hear what Mortich's saying."

"I will not be taking any questions about the President's daughters," he said. "Because of national security concerns, we cannot share any more information than we've already given. However, I have one more announcement. As of 5:00 tonight, Route 50, East and West, will be shut down to all traffic from the District of Columbia line to the foot of the Bay Bridge. Anyone planning to use Route 50 after 5:00 tonight must take an alternative route."

A murmur swept through the press. This was a headline in itself. Thousands of people who worked in Washington lived in Annapolis and Route 50 was the main artery between the two cities. A shut down would cause an immediate exit from offices and jam local roads.

The reporters broke into a frenzy of questions.

Mortich rapped the podium for quiet. "I can only answer one person at a time so if we can do this in an orderly fashion, we'll get through more questions. Yes, Jim," Mortich said, pointing at a reporter, who asked a lengthy question in a mumble no one could hear.

Mortich turned to the camera. "I'll repeat Jim's questions. First, why are we shutting down Route 50? We're shutting it down so the military can conduct an extensive air and ground search for Eden and Echo Hines. Second, when will Route 50 re-open? By 5:00 tomorrow morning, in time for rush hour."

Dorothy started jabbering in my ear. I knew she would prefer to spend the day speculating about the twins' disappearance and it wasn't our problem. We had work to do and I would have to set an example.

"Dorothy, have Lilly come in here."

"She's out sick."

"Then tell Jake I want to see him."

For the next few hours Jake and I managed to get some work done. We were about to wrap up for the day when Dorothy rapped on my door. "General Fontaine is on the phone."

I grabbed the receiver. "Hey Mike, how are you?"

"As you can imagine, things at the White House are not good."

Naturally, the situation at the White House was tense and a large portion of that tension was squarely on Mike's shoulders. He was the President's National Security Advisor. I'd met him through Ruth, who occasionally sat in on National Security Council meetings at the White House.

I leaned back in my chair. "Is that why you're calling?"

"Look out your window. There's a van waiting for you."

I swung around and peered through the glass. A shiny black van with gleaming chrome wheels and government plates idled at the curb. Two Secret Service agents stood on the sidewalk, dark sunglasses staring at my second-floor window.

The military search, now a call from the President's National Security Advisor. It would be interesting to see what was going on.

"I'm on my way."

CHAPTER 6

President Hines was anchored behind his desk, the same desk JFK had used, a massive stump of timber from the ancient British frigate, *The HMS Resolute*. Behind the President, the last shafts of sunlight melted into a red haze over the Rose Garden, the sun glinting one last time before sinking behind the tree line.

The President struggled to his feet and shook my hand, looking nothing like the man who'd administered the oath of office to me just a year ago. His bearing was normally precision military, his clothes always crisp, starched shirt, neatly knotted tie. Today, his clothing was disheveled, his shoulders sagged, and his trademark, round tortoiseshell eyeglasses hung askew like an off-kilter frame.

His hand trembled as he tapped a cigarette from a pack and lit up, a vice rumored in public but only seen in private. "I begged Eden and Echo to keep their detail." Smoke wafted into his eyes. He angrily waved it away and a tear slid down his face. "They wouldn't listen to me. Maybe their mother could've done something if she were still alive. I don't know." He laughed bitterly. "They're so headstrong. They were always impossible to discipline. Even as children."

"Could this be terrorist related?" I asked.

"It's possible," he said, choking on his words. "Although there's no chatter like we would expect." The President turned to General Fontaine. "Mike, fill him in."

General Fontaine's uniform was a thick patch of stripes and gold stars gleaming under the light. He exhaled, the first time he'd moved since I entered the room. I couldn't imagine the kind of pressure he must be under. From my time spent with Mike, I knew there was little that could bother this man. His credentials were impeccable, West Point, former Supreme Allied Commander Europe. The best of the best the military could produce.

"We're waiting to hear about the results of the helicopter search," General Fontaine said, his face expressionless as a block of wood and just as hard. "It's possible their car ran into a ravine—"

The President cut him off. "Just a minute, Mike. Here's Dr. Jacobson."

A Secret Service agent escorted Ruth in. She looked at us gravely. "We were flooded with calls after the press conference and we've already had a break in the case. A man named Frank Newman said he saw Eden and Echo headed east on Route 50 Saturday evening, this side of the Severn River. They startled him because they were so pretty. He thought they were the President's daughters but the light was fading and when he looked closer at the car, figured he was wrong, that they wouldn't be driving an old car with two big dents in the bumper, even if it was a Porsche. Newman liked the twins' looks and blew them a kiss. They blew him off with a finger each."

Ruth turned to the President. "Sir, does that sound like something your daughters would do? The finger thing? I need to verify Newman's statement."

"Yes," the President said, sounding irritated. "That sounds like them."

"Good, because Newman described the twins' Porsche accurately, right down to the gashes on the left rear bumper. We know Eden and Echo didn't cross the Bay Bridge, so that gives us approximately thirty miles where the twins could've turned off 50 East. It's a large area, lots of roads, lots of shoreline properties and big estates, many of those belonging to important people."

Ruth looked at me. "And that ties in with your theory that the twins may have been meeting important men who were recent White House guests."

"How many men are you looking into?" I asked.

"First estimate? At least seventy-five."

I whistled, shocked by the figure. "That many?"

"It's a big Navy area, Annapolis being so close by. There's a lot of brass around there, active and retired."

"You've taken a drone overhead? Look for disturbed ground?"

Ruth shot a glance at the President. "We did that yesterday. Unfortunately, a lot of the area is heavily forested."

"And your search with the helicopters?" I asked.

"There's no sign of them."

The President cleared his throat. "Justice Alexander, I know you found your daughter after she was kidnapped last year because of your profiling skills and I need your help."

I went silent.

Ruth and Mike exchanged glances.

"Not officially," the President continued. "It won't interfere with your duties at the Supreme Court. You'll be in an advisory role." The President lit another cigarette, sucked the smoke deep into his lungs and exhaled. Threads of smoke joined a grey stack overhead. "FBI Director Mortich is on board," he added.

I shook my head, trying to find the right words. "Sir, I empathize with what you're going through. However, the entire FBI is at your disposal and they have the knowledge and skill to find your daughters without any assistance from me."

The President glared at me.

I put my elbows on my knees and studied my shoes. Although a year had passed since Reed was kidnapped, my heart still raced when I thought about her ordeal. I knew exactly what the President was going through— terrified, trying to figure out where his daughters were, wondering if they were still alive. I'd been lucky. I'd found Reed. Unfortunately, that didn't mean I would be able to find the President's daughters.

"Is Echo your daughter's birth name?" I asked.

The question took the President by surprise. He looked stunned, then exasperated. "I'm not sure what that has to do with anything." He sighed.

"She talked me into letting her legally change her name for her 18th birthday. I never did like the damn name," he muttered.

So, maybe I was onto something after all but the Supreme Court was another consideration. "I'm afraid there's no precedent for a Supreme Court Justice to become actively involved in a missing person's case," I said.

"I'll personally talk to Chief Justice Brown," he said.

How could I say no to a man that desperate? "All right."

The President extended his hand. "Thank you, Justice Alexander."

Poor bastard. If my blackmailing theory was correct, there was little that I could do.

CHAPTER 7

Ruth and I consulted frequently over the next few days, without any measurable results. Another day had passed and I was headed home, thinking about the case and wondering about Claire. I hadn't seen Claire for three days. Seen her awake, that is. Claire had been working late at her law firm while I'd been doing the same at the Supreme Court. I'd been going to bed about eleven, and around midnight, I'd half-wake and hear her tiptoe into our bedroom. When I left for the Supreme Court at six-thirty, she'd still be asleep.

We'd talked on the phone and agreed that we'd both get home at a decent hour and have dinner together. I arrived first at our house, which was on 31ˢᵗ Street, just above Q in Georgetown. It was an old white farmhouse built circa 1790 when the land around it was still planted acreage. By Georgetown standards, ours wasn't a large house, certainly not a mansion like most of our neighbors. It was the honest simplicity of the house that appealed to me. White picket fence and Amish-plain on the outside. Large, sunny rooms on the inside, original fireplaces throughout. I'd come up in the world.

I'd started life in Wyoming in a little tumble-down house slanting to one side, a jack under the house preventing a complete collapse. A carport was out back, a fancy term for a metal frame. Nothing in our part of town was known to thrive, certainly not the people who lived there, only the dandelions and thorny weeds that grew wild and free and choked off what little grass dared raise its head. By the time my mom got home from working two jobs, it was dark and I have early memories of peeking through a hole in the screen door, the light of a kerosene lantern on our steps, my mom behind an old, rotating blade mower, fighting through the prickles, the heat, the night.

My parents divorced when I was three years old and I never saw my dad again. By the time I was ten, I'd developed a chip on my shoulder the size of a log house, and I'd begun smoking pot behind the old schoolhouse and stealing cigarettes from the local Mom and Pop. My Uncle Jim was a no-nonsense rancher two counties over and he had a remedy for my afflictions. He set me loose in his bullpen where I soon discovered that other critters were a lot angrier than I was. After being bucked around for a while by some very irate bulls, Uncle Jim rescued me and said it was time to channel my anger into shouldering hard work and taking pride in what I could achieve in the world. Otherwise, he said, I'd end up in a pen with animals far more dangerous than his bulls.

I thanked God every night for my Uncle Jim.

I heard the front door open. Claire was home. I poured some scotch and waited.

"Claire?"

I heard the door again. Claire came into the room. "I was unloading the car. I stopped by Safeway and bought some steaks."

"Need help?"

"Just finished," she said, sliding onto the sofa, sweeping her skirt underneath her, a movement as elegant as her lithe figure. Tonight, she was wearing a red suit. Her thick, dark hair skimmed her shoulders and my diamond ring glittered on her hand. She turned down the lamp and dark shadows washed over her skirt and pooled at her feet. She kicked off her heels.

I lifted my drink, ice clinking against the glass. "Want some? Oban."

"No, thanks."

"I hate seeing you work so late."

"We're in litigation all week. A deficiency matter."

Claire had just been named one of the ten best tax attorneys in the Washington metropolitan area. I was proud of her although I wished we spent more time together. Work-a-holism was the scourge of Washington and the disease had hit our home particularly hard.

She pulled her legs under her. "Between our schedules, I never see you anymore," she said, a smile playing on her face. "You're just a big lump under the covers."

"This lump is busy at the Court."

She grew serious. "You don't seem happy there."

"It's frustrating. I want to get things done. And the Court is such a contrast to working with Ruth."

She raised a perfectly arched eyebrow. "Don't tell me you're working with Ruth again."

"The President asked me to help find his daughters." I saw her face. "It's only an advisory role." I sipped at my scotch and shook my head. "Working with Ruth is such a contrast to the Court. With Ruth, decisions are lightning fast. At the Court, I practically have to beg the other Justices for a one-on-one meeting."

"Why's that?"

I smiled ruefully. "Their nap time gets in the way."

"Oh, come on." She laughed, tossed her hair.

Smiling, I set my glass down and walked over to the sofa. "The other Justices give new meaning to the phrase *dead on your feet*." I laughed. "Yesterday, I had to help one of them back into his casket. I had to find a step ladder and everything." I was on a roll.

As I sat down, Claire gave me a little punch in the gut.

"Hey." I gathered her into my arms and snuggled into her. "Seriously, do you remember JFK's brilliant put down of Washington?"

She laughed again. "No, but I'm sure you're going to tell me."

"He said, Washington is a model of southern efficiency and northern charm."

"Actually, Senator Warren Magnuson said that first."

I kissed her neck. "You're too smart for me. That's why I love you, but believe me, the Court personifies that."

"Give it a chance. It's your first year." She hesitated. "Can you talk about the Hines case?"

"No. Everything's confidential."

"Those poor lambs."

That phrase again. What was it with that? Some nursery rhyme I'd missed out on? Most people assumed Eden and Echo were innocent victims going about their own business when the bogeyman jumped out and grabbed them. And why not? They were known for serving soup to the homeless in South East and tutoring disadvantaged children from Anacostia. But the hard fact was that completely random victims were rare.

She put her arms around my neck. I loved being this close to her, inhaling her perfume, soft as velvet.

"Want me to make dinner?" I offered.

"It's late to eat." She made a move for my Oban.

I playfully held it behind my back. "Thought you didn't want any," I said.

She slid a finger down my chest and looked up at me. "Hmmm. You know I do."

I put my arms around her and we kissed. She knew all my moves, clumsy as they were. Luckily, she loved me anyway.

CHAPTER 8

When I entered my chambers the following day, Dorothy was on the phone. I stopped by her desk for my mail and she cupped her hand over the receiver.

"Has Ruth called today?" I asked as I picked through my mail.

"Not yet."

"Tell Lilly to come into my office."

"She's still sick."

I frowned. "Really?"

"But I do have someone on the phone who wants to talk with you. Your daughter."

I shut the door and draped my jacket over the back of a chair.

"Reed?" I heard traffic noise in the background and knew she was probably on her way to their estate in Anne Arundel County, Maryland. Reed was spending a lot of time out there, mostly on the weekends.

"I wanted to let you know I'm driving out to Blackhall with Samuel. And Daddy! You should see him in this little outfit I bought. He looks so cute! Like a little baby sailor."

"Is Davis with you?" Davis spent most of his time flying around the world in his private Gulfstream, carving out deals, buying companies and re-selling them for massive profits. *Houses, cars, private planes.* That was Davis's world but he hadn't gotten through life as easy as his price tags would suggest. I should know. We'd bonded in law school over late night beers at Cambridge taverns where we'd discussed everything from painful childhood memories to the theory of Original Intent.

"He left for Hong Kong Saturday evening."

"He's opening another office?"

"Uh-huh. And checking out new factory sites. Samuel! Ouch."

"What happened?"

"Samuel hit me with a rattle. Damn. I have a bump on my head."

"I worry about you all alone at Blackhall." And now, Reed was spending more time at the estate, moving ahead with plans to renovate the old rock pile. I suspected she'd been watching too many PBS shows about life at English country manors.

"Don't worry. Henry will be there."

"Henry?" I laughed. A burglar could kill Henry with a slap to the face. A big guard dog would be more effective.

"Why are you laughing?"

"It's not because I'm happy—"

"Daddy, did you hear about the President's daughters? Isn't that awful?"

"That's exactly what I'm getting at. No one knows where they are. And there you are, all alone at a big estate in the middle of the country. I worry, especially since you had those break-ins last year."

"That's why Davis built that huge wall and anyway, it's just a bunch of kids. Nothing's going to happen. I promise I'll be careful."

"Call me if the slightest thing is out of place or if you hear any strange noises."

I heard an extended sigh. "I'll always be your little girl, won't I?"

"I certainly hope so."

I hung up, knowing I was probably too protective of Reed. That's what Claire said and what Davis thought. But neither one had gone through what I had.

Reed's mother, Joanne, had been killed in Nantucket when we were on the island celebrating our tenth wedding anniversary. I'd given Joanne a diamond eternity ring. I couldn't really afford it on my FBI salary. It was the one time I'd made an exception to my rule of never overspending. The ring was beautiful, ten perfect diamonds.

When I left the next morning to bring Joanne some breakfast from a coffee shop, someone came into the room and took the ring. Joanne fought back and was shot in the head. I'll never forget seeing the fear frozen on her face, the knowledge she was about to die the last thing she ever knew. I'll never forget closing her eyes with my fingers, and I'll never forgive myself for leaving her that morning, for not finding her murderer, for not killing the son of a bitch.

Immediately after Joanne's funeral, I found Reed behind a locked bathroom door, a trickle of blood seeping under the wood frame. I smashed the door in with two wild, desperate kicks. The hard smell of blood flooded the room. Reed had slashed her wrists. She was nine years old.

Being an FBI agent wasn't conducive to being a single father with a daughter who was distraught and desperately needed my attention, and shortly after, I'd accepted an appointment to the United States Court of Federal Claims where I could work a nine to five schedule. A few months later, I met Claire, we married and things eventually improved, but once you see your child bleeding out on a bathroom floor, you never, ever, stop worrying.

✸✸✸✸

Blackhall was a magnificent house befitting its perch, a high promontory overlooking the Chesapeake Bay. Pooh-poohing it as a "small hunting lodge," much as the king of France referred to Versailles, John Rideout had constructed a lighthouse of prestige that beaconed the wealthy to his shores for fancy dress balls held after the British were decisively routed in 1783, when Rideout was comfortably in the clear, his politics no longer under suspicion.

Rideout built the center portion of the manse in 1775 and soon after added two identical additions, one in 1777, the other in 1778. When the first addition fell short of his vision, he'd indulged himself to tear it down and try again, determined that the façade properly reflect the grandeur of the plaster and woodwork that would decorate its perfectly symmetrical rooms.

That was the family lore that Reed had found easy enough to verify at the Maryland Historical Society, where she located a small announcement in the May 15, 1777 edition of the *Maryland Gazette*.

> *Wanted: Master masons, carpenters, and joiners to rebuild mansion house of John Rideout, Gentleman, Anne Arundel County. Men of character and ability will meet with interest by applying to William Paca, Agent, 186 Prince George Street, Annapolis Maryland.*

John Rideout's extravagance had resulted in an extraordinary home and Reed had fallen in love with its architecture. And while the old bones retained John Rideout's vision of 18th century beauty and elegance, even Reed could see it needed significant repairs, especially the roof. The library was the only room that didn't leak.

Davis didn't think much of the house. Reed wasn't sure why, something about his childhood that he wouldn't talk about, and he'd ignored urgent repairs, letting the old mansion fall into a disgraceful state of decay. At her urging, he'd finally agreed to restore the property and let her be in charge of the renovations. Mostly to get her off his back, she thought.

She didn't care. She was excited about the renovations. This was a chance to prove herself with Davis and with Daddy. Neither one seemed to think she was capable of much and that hurt her feelings. Just because she was blonde and beautiful and looked like a swimsuit model didn't mean she didn't have a brain. She would show them.

Reed turned onto Blackhall Lane. For the next five miles, white fencing zipped by, the sunlight filtering through morning fog as the sun rose towards noon. She drove on, through a dense forest until a newly completed rampart across the headland came into view, a massive ten-foot-high field-stone wall that enclosed four hundred acres of ancestral land.

The new wall, the first in a series of slated improvements, had taken thirteen months and two hundred men to build. After its completion, some of the locals became upset because portions could be glimpsed from boats on the Chesapeake Bay. The wall became controversial, sides taken, and the local newspaper ran a story, *Rideout's Great Gall.* Not that Reed cared. You couldn't please everyone. But the newspaper called attention to a vacant mansion in the middle of nowhere and the break-ins had continued.

She stopped at the imposing iron gates and punched in an elaborate code of numbers and symbols. The sharp spikes obediently swung back, then slammed shut with a resounding clang. A half mile later, she spied the three-story Georgian mansion known as Blackhall soaring above the Chesapeake Bay, the middle section towering over the additions on either side like a mother gathering her children against the ravages of the sea.

Further view of the house was blocked by an allee of trees on the hard, steep climb up the hill. At the drive's crest, a vast green lawn unfurled to a precarious cliff at the water's edge and the lane hooked around the house to the formal entrance. A dizzying view of the two-hundred-mile-long estuary stretched from east to west.

Reed stopped under a grove of weeping willows, their long slender branches jerking through the grass like fingers searching for something in the ground. She lifted little Davis Samuel Rideout II into her arms. What a chubby little thing he was! He wiggled his toes, batted his eyelids, pink and translucent in the sunlight, and made a little baby gurgle. *So cute.* She kissed his forehead and wrapped a tiny blanket around his shoulders.

Wait. Henry's car was parked by the Little Cottage. Good. She needed to talk to him about her renovation plans. Henry was a valuable source of knowledge because both he and his father had grown up on the estate. And Davis was very fond of Henry. She knew that for sure because despite the break-ins, Davis had insisted upon keeping Henry on as the caretaker. What Davis had left unsaid was that without Blackhall, Henry had neither a job nor a home. That was just like Davis. People didn't realize how generous and caring he was. It would have been terrible to put Henry out of a job.

The huge skeleton key rattled in the ancient lock. The cylinder clanked and the door squeaked open, revealing a magnificent entrance. In the center of the fourteen-foot-tall ceiling, an enormous gilded plaster phoenix clutched bolts of lightning in its claws. *A masterpiece.* She'd asked Henry about it. He'd said that a phoenix is a bird reborn by rising from the ashes of its predecessor. Appropriate, she thought, for the restoration the house was about to undergo.

An awful smell hit her nose. Drat. Samuel's diapers were in the car. She ran back outside, toting the baby with her, as Henry came meandering out of the stable toward her. Henry's hair was a frost of white and deep craters lined his face, pocked and tough as cured leather, features so age-encrusted that he seemed as permanent as the earth and the moon. He shielded his eyes from the sun with giant hands that had labored on the estate for decades, hands the color of rich delta soil. Henry was an African-American born on the land on which he stood. He often joked he hadn't moved more than a mile in his lifetime.

"Mrs. Rideout," he said in a Tidewater accent that turned time into *tam* and oyster into *arster.* "I didn't hear your car."

"Henry, would you mind holding Samuel for a minute?"

"Not at all, he's such a cute little tyke." He wiped his hands on a pair of grease-stained overalls, took the child, and winced.

"What's wrong, Henry?"

"Doc says it's arthritis. Had a lot of it lately." Henry cradled the baby in his arms and smiled down at the boy. "Oh, my. Looks just like his daddy."

"Doesn't he? Everyone says that."

Henry bounced the child up and down. "Why, I remember when his daddy was just this size. 'Course, that was a long time ago. Before age snuck up on me."

Reed smiled. "I have to get his diapers from the car." She opened the trunk.

Henry leaned forward, leaving the scent of hay and engine oil on the air. "Can I get any of that?"

"I'm going to bring the luggage in later. Right now, I just want to get Samuel changed and set up in his crib."

"I'll carry him up to the house for you."

Reed smiled at Henry fondly. "That would be nice."

They walked to the house together and Reed settled into the master bedroom and changed Samuel's diaper but something still smelled horrible. "Do you smell that?" she asked Henry who was setting up Samuel's crib. "It can't be his diaper."

"Yes, but I don't know where it could be coming from."

"I think it's downstairs. Could you watch Samuel for a minute?"

Reed flew down the stairs and followed the smell to the library. "Henry!" she screamed.

CHAPTER 9

This was Reed's second call today. Somehow, I was expecting it.

"Daddy, we've had another break-in!"

I knew this was going to happen. Didn't she realize that Henry was too old to guard that huge estate?

"And the smell in here," Reed said. "I can't describe it. It's horrid, like some sort of rot combined with bleach."

"Take Samuel and go to the Little Cottage with Henry. Someone could be in the house. Then call the police. When they get there, have them go through the place, room by room and closet by closet." I drummed my fingers against my desk, thinking. "I'll drive out there. I'd feel better knowing you weren't alone."

I grabbed my jacket and stopped at Dorothy's desk. "Tell Chief Brown I'm going to miss Friday Conference."

Dorothy's mouth fell open. "Conference is sacrosanct."

"Yeah, well, he'll have to do without me today."

"Everything okay?"

"Reed's estate in Anne Arundel County was broken into again. I'll be back on Monday."

****

When I arrived at Blackhall more than two hours later, Reed and the baby were huddled with Henry in his cottage. The cops still hadn't showed. I took matters into my own hands. It took only one phone call from a Supreme Court Justice for the police to arrive less than five minutes later, pounding on Reed's front door.

They went through the entire house and checked for signs of theft and damage and for anyone who might be hiding inside. They also helped me scour the basement for the source of the smell Reed was complaining about. Henry confessed to spilling bleach the previous week when he'd been cleaning the kitchen, so that solved the problem of the bleach smell. But there was another, overpowering smell of decay. It was obvious that a large animal, maybe a raccoon, had crawled under a floorboard and died. Unfortunately, it must have holed up in a space with no obvious access because we never did find the carcass.

I joined Reed and the officers in the hallway. Officer Stapleton stumbled a couple of steps backwards and let out a loud whistle. "Jeez … $200,000 for a piece of glass?" He pushed his cap to the back of his head.

"A piece of crystal," Reed corrected him. "And the $200,000 was donated to Smile Train. It's a charity that provides cleft surgery for children in poor countries."

"I'll be," Stapleton said, shaking his head. "Okay. I've never heard the like but let me write that down." He clicked his pen. "Tell me again."

Reed put her hands on her hips and peered over the officer's pad of paper. "A decanter is missing. It's called a Revelation Baccarat Crystal Decanter. It's a deep blue color and looks sort of like a giant sapphire. Oh, and the tip has diamonds and sapphires. They came from a famous jeweler in England. Gerrard. And the decanter is heavy, about twenty-five pounds."

"You said your husband actually uses it?"

"Yes, for gin."

"Lady, how the heck can he even pick it up?" Stapleton and his partner, Jones, a rotund cop with pink cheeks, laughed heartily.

"Well, he can. He works out."

Stapleton gave Jones a nudge. "I would work out too if I had a glass of good gin at the bottom of my barbell." Both cops laughed vigorously, their bellies jiggling.

Reed shook her head. "Please, officers. Take this seriously."

"Yes ma'am, we're just having a bit of fun." Stapleton cleared his throat. "It would help if you could provide us with a photo of the decanter. We'll take it around to the pawnshops and alert the stores to keep an eye out. Pawn shops are where most of the stolen goods in this area end up."

"Daddy, could you run off that photo and article I brought up on the Internet?"

"Sure." I retrieved the photo from the library where Reed had just installed a new computer and printer.

"Was there anything else missing, Mrs. Rideout?"

"No. Is that odd?"

"Burglars want valuables that are easily transported. I'm surprised they didn't take your new computer." Stapleton's shoulder crackled with dispatch information. He ignored it and turned to Henry. "And Mr. Turnbull? It's Henry Turnbull, right?"

"Yes, sir."

"You didn't hear or see anything?"

"No, sir. No, I didn't." Henry held his cap in his hand.

Stapleton scribbled in his notebook. "What was the last time you went through the house?"

"Last Friday. I think it was in the afternoon, yes, in the afternoon."

"And you've been here all week?"

"All week." Henry looked around a little nervously. "I'm the caretaker, so I'm almost always here."

Reed butted in. "How do you think they got onto the grounds?"

Officer Stapleton puckered his mouth. "I'm not sure, ma'am, but I'm sure about one thing. You need to install additional security measures. This is a big place for Mr. Turnbull to guard by himself. I would suggest a perimeter system for the house. At the minimum."

"What does that mean?"

"In general? Closed-circuit monitors and electromagnetic cables buried in the ground that can detect intruders on the property. There are a host of other measures you can also take."

"We need more security?" Reed asked, incredulous.

Stapleton smiled indulgently. "Ma'am. With all due respect, if you're going to keep $200,000 bottles of gin in an unoccupied house, you need more security."

Henry looked at the floor.

Reed reached out and put her arm through Henry's. "Thank you, officer. Henry and I will consider that."

I handed the photo of the decanter to the police.

"Thank you, Justice Alexander. As I said sir, we'll get right on this." His mouth was a thin, straight line of concentration.

I held out my hand. "Thank you. I appreciate that you have a difficult job to do."

"Yes, sir. Thank you, sir." He tipped his cap at Reed. "We'll show ourselves out, ma'am."

Reed rested her head on my shoulder. "Thank you for driving out here, Daddy."

"You're welcome."

"Mrs. Rideout," Henry said, "I'm going back to my cottage. I'm feeling a little tired."

"Are you okay, Henry? Can I get you anything?"

"No, no, I'm fine. I just need a nap. Too much sun, I guess."

Reed hesitated. "Well, okay. Call me if you need anything."

"I will. Thank you." Henry put his cap on and ambled out the door.

When he'd gone, Reed turned to me. "Do you think he's okay?"

I nodded. "Yes, he's fine, but the police are right. You can't expect Henry to protect the estate by himself. He's too old."

"Henry needs the job and a place to live."

"I'm not suggesting you turn him out on the street. Let the poor guy retire. Doesn't he deserve a pension by now? How old is he? Seventy-five? Eighty?"

"He says he wants to work but I'll talk to him."

"No matter what, you have to secure this place for Samuel's sake. A big mansion is enticing to burglars. It's like a woman wearing a fifty-carat diamond ring to the shopping mall. People are going to notice and be tempted." I plopped down on the sofa and yawned.

"You look tired," Reed said. "We'll eat early."

While Reed scrounged around in the kitchen, I strolled onto the terrace that overlooked a vast lawn shaped like a baby grand piano. The giant curve of the instrument was the grassy sweep to the cliff that dropped a hundred feet down to the water. The rectangular space above the keyboard was where the house sat. And in the small s-curve was the terrace where I stood, the only spot on the lawn with seating directly above the waves.

A footstep. "Let's have dinner out here," Reed said behind me. "Get away from the smell in the house."

"Great idea." Most of the windows in the house hadn't opened in years, but I'd managed to hammer some open in the library, the room with the strongest odor, and while the smell was gradually abating, it was still unpleasant.

Throughout our meal, Reed chattered on, excitedly bombarding me with her plans to renovate the house and replace the dilapidated stable. Davis's parents had raced thoroughbreds in the 1960s and Reed wanted horses at Blackhall again. She also wanted to add a swimming pool and tennis courts. As darkness fell, the soft patter of her voice began to mingle with the waves sloshing against the rocks below and I began drifting off. A finger poked me in the side.

"You're not listening."

I jerked awake. "Of course I am," I said, miraculously managing to repeat her last sentence back to her.

"Your eyes were closed."

I yawned loudly. "Sorry, I'm dead." I stood up.

"Okay." She gave me a quick hug. "Goodnight, Daddy."

I climbed the staircase to the second floor where the hallway walls were packed floor to ceiling with paintings of racehorses, a remnant of faded Rideout glory. My bedroom was decorated in dark-green wallpaper, some sort of floral pattern with sprigs of white lilies that once had been cheerful but had since given up on life. Several heavily stained chairs were clad in matching green fabric, dirty yellow batting popping out of the seams like an animal partly gutted.

For some reason, the room gave me a feeling of foreboding, the same as I'd experienced in my law enforcement days when I walked into a field and spied the medical examiner's tent over the next rise. Maybe it was the furnishings that spoke of decay. Or perhaps the air in the room that smelled as stale as old shoes, almost as if the room had been trapped in its own world for decades behind a closed door.

I tried to pound a window open with my fist, but as in the library, the windows were glued shut by centuries of paint. I whacked at a window again and to my relief, the sash finally shot up. Wind blew into the room, hitting my face and ruffling my hair. A storm was moving in. In the distance, lightning flickered across the black sky, providing a glimpse of clouds trailing tendrils of rain. I took a chance and left the window open, then tunneled under the comforter and fell into a deep sleep. It seemed like mere seconds before I was awakened by the frantic screech of willow trees clawing the house like they were trying to get in.

The storm was upon us. The wind was torrential, rain slashed at the windows, and thunder boomed and crashed. I closed the window and drifted off again—until about three in the morning, when I was bolted awake by Reed's banshee screams from hell.

CHAPTER 10

I ran down the hall, my heart thumping like a hammer pounding nails. Lightning flashed, illuminating Reed in the giant canopied bed. She was on her back, clawing at a naked man straddling her. From Samuel's crib rose a wild, primitive wail. I looked around for a weapon, grabbed a lamp and hoisted it over my head.

"Davis!" Reed gasped.

"Stop it," Davis yelled. "You're hurting me!"

"I thought you were an intruder. You had your hand over my mouth!" Furious, Reed hit him with a pillow.

"I didn't want you to wake Samuel," he said, flopping back on the bed, exploring the damage to his face.

Disgusted, I dropped the lamp and headed back to bed.

****

The rest of the night was uneventful and the next morning, I decided to make breakfast for Reed and Davis, even though I was pissed at Davis for scaring everyone in the middle of the night. As I rummaged around the kitchen for a frying pan, I realized just how dilapidated the house had become. Nothing in the kitchen had been updated for a good fifty years. The floor was linoleum, scuffed and permanently stained with traces of fossilized food. The cabinets were old, scalloped-edged boxes of wood straight from a carpenter's primitive saw, and the kitchen's mid-century rusting appliances were completely out of place in a house built in 1775.

However, the most serious problems were in the basement. When I was searching the basement with the police, I'd noticed there was no telephone connection into the house from the county. Exactly why, no one could fathom. The rest of the infrastructure was also a disaster. The furnace was about seventy years old and ready to blow. The wiring in the basement was so ancient, it was amazing the lights stayed on. Reed was right, the house needed a renovation and not just a superficial fix.

Davis sauntered in while I was flipping some eggs over easy.

"Your face looks like a cat landed on it," I said.

He winced and touched the deepest scratch. "I should've called from the plane."

"She's on edge."

"The burglary? She told me. No wonder I got such a thrashing." Davis opened the refrigerator door and peered in.

"Do you always buy $200,000 decanters?"

Davis stared at me, unbelieving. "We paid that much for that thing?"

I nodded.

"Jesus," he said, shaking his head. "Your daughter knows nothing about saving money."

"And you have a lot of other expensive items in the house. Bottom line, you need to get serious about security. Hire professional guards. Put motion detectors around the grounds. It would put her mind at ease."

He laughed. "It would put *your* mind at ease. No one's interested in this crappy old house except a couple of kids looking for electronics to pawn. And I just built that wall. That outta keep the devil himself out."

"Didn't work this time."

"I think Henry left the gate open. He's getting forgetful."

"Terrific," I scowled.

He placed his hand on my shoulder and examined the contents of the skillet. "How 'bout making some eggs for me?"

"These are for you," I said, flipping them onto a plate and shoveling some bacon next to them.

"Thanks, Dad."

"You're a riot."

Davis laughed. He knew I wasn't comfortable with the idea that my law school roommate had married my daughter. Of course, there hadn't been a lot of choices when he'd gotten her pregnant. And that had been a surprise because I'd had no idea they were dating and if I'd known, I would've been furious. Davis had stepped over the line and things between us had been tense ever since.

Davis sat down at the kitchen table and began chomping down his breakfast. "What else is new?"

"I guess you heard about the President's daughters."

Davis shoved some food around with his fork. "When I was in Beijing, I saw something about them missing. Surely, they've turned up by now."

I sat down, shook out a bowl of cereal, and poured some milk. "No one's seen them since Saturday evening."

Davis dropped his fork. "Saturday? That's when they disappeared? And no one's seen them since? God."

We sat in silence for a few minutes.

He pushed back from the table and tossed his napkin on the table. "You know, I think I'll talk to Henry about that security system. You're right, it's time I jumped on that."

"You haven't eaten your breakfast."

"My stomach's acting up," he said and left the room.

A few minutes later, Reed came into the room. "Davis just walked by me like he didn't even see me."

"I think he caught a stomach bug in China."

I looked out the window as I washed the skillet. Davis was talking to Henry. I was glad Davis was finally getting serious about security, but Henry looked like he was resisting the idea. He was furiously shaking his head.

****

The President's National Security Advisor, General Mike Fontaine, fumbled with his collar and pricked his finger on a straight pin the cleaners had left in his shirt. Damn it. He reached for a tissue and held it tight until the bleeding stopped.

He was nervous. The FBI had no new information about Eden and Echo Hines and the President was a wreck, demanding Fontaine work longer and longer hours, even though terrorism had been ruled out and the case was firmly in the hands of the FBI. Fontaine suspected that the President, who had begun staying up all night in the hope his daughters would walk through the door, simply needed the support of someone being nearby. His wife had died a few years ago and Eden and Echo were his babies.

Tonight, Mike had begged off the bleak vigil because Annabelle had insisted on going to the Kennedy Center. He looked around the vast foyer of their newly built antebellum home. White marble floors glistened like an ice rink. Palms sat squat in black urns, looking like plumed sentries guarding the bottom of the wide staircase. Annabelle was a socialite with vast reserves of family money that afforded them a lifestyle unheard of for most military types.

And she never let him forget it. In turn, he'd become obsessed with her faults, nitpicking at her, complaining when she forgot an RSVP or gained a few extra pounds. But since Eden and Echo's disappearance, he'd realized he'd be crushed if anything happened to Annabelle.

He slipped his tuxedo over his shoulders and admired his profile in the hallway mirror. Still trim and fit after all these years. His posture was straight, his hairline holding firm, and his precision-angled crew cut was level enough to land a fighter jet. He flicked a piece of lint off his tuxedo, walked over to a table, reached for a large black velvet box and fingered it. He had a peace gift for Annabelle.

Footsteps. He turned on his heel. Annabelle was gliding down the sweeping staircase, wearing a long red taffeta dress. "Anny! You look amazing!"

She looked shocked. "Moi?" She twirled happily as realization set in. Her skirt rustled over the white marble floors. "You like?"

"You know I love you in red, baby." He smiled, took her in his arms and whirled her outward, the full skirt swirling and wrapping back around with a soft swoosh.

"Whyyy, Michaelll! What's gotten into you?" she asked, her southern drip soft as honey.

He pulled her to him so their lips touched. "Just want you to know how much I love you, baby." He produced the box.

She batted surgically enhanced eyes and gasped. Was she was feigning surprise? Why else would he tell her not to wear a necklace tonight?

"Oh, how wonderful!" Her eyes glistening, Annabelle opened the box and almost fell to the floor. In the box was a beautiful diamond necklace. It was something only worn by movie stars.

He was thankful she liked it. No, he could see in her eyes that she loved it. He smiled. He was determined to do everything in his power to make Annabelle happy and fall in love with him, all over again.

CHAPTER 11

First thing Monday morning, Chief Brown knocked on my door.

"Everything okay at that big estate your daughter owns?" He smirked.

I looked up from my desk. "What? Oh, yeah. She had a burglary. We had to call the police."

"Well, glad to see you back. I moved Friday Conference to 3:00. That's 3:00 *today*. I hope your schedule allows for it."

I stared at Chief Brown. He was a brilliant man although socially awkward. His saving grace was a towering intellect that had landed him a position of tremendous power and influence. Unfortunately, during his rise to power, he'd ignored his body, and he was now so obese that his stomach was indistinguishable from his butt.

"I'll be there." I got up and squeezed by him and asked Dorothy to have Lilly come into my chambers.

"See you at 3:00," the Chief yelled over his shoulder as he waddled out of my chambers.

"I'm not sure she's here today," Dorothy said. "Let me see."

"Is she still out sick?" I was getting irritated. If she was still out, I'd have to give United States v. Clark to Jake and he was already knee deep in alligators.

"I'll find her."

I waited and continued to work. Someone rapped loudly on my door.

"I'll be right with you," I said without looking up. Out of the corner of my eye, I saw an apple core whiz by me and hit my wastebasket with a bang that rattled the metal container around on its edges. I looked up, annoyed.

Jake was at the door. "Oops, sorry Justice A., didn't know it would be so loud." Jake sprawled into a chair and smiled at me, knowing I gave him leeway because I identified with him, a kid whose family had lived in a cardboard box on the outskirts of Detroit, a childhood rougher than mine. But Jake was smart and ambitious and with a scholarship to the University of Michigan, he'd pulled himself out of poverty.

Jake's Achilles heel was women and there he walked a fine line. His eyes burned through women's clothing and issued invitations to bend over his desk. Sometimes, I even saw him lusting after Dorothy and that was just sick. But Jake never said anything that could land him in trouble and looking wasn't a crime the last time I checked the books.

"Sir, I know you're expecting Lilly but Dorothy can't find her."

This was damn irritating. Where the hell was Lilly? I tilted back in my chair, took off my reading glasses and rubbed my eyes. "Okay Jake, what do you need?"

"Psst … Justice Alexander." Dorothy was at the door. I held up a finger to Jake. "Just a second." I looked at Dorothy expectantly.

"Lilly's nowhere to be found. She must still be sick."

I frowned. "She's been sick a long time. Has she been calling in?"

"She's been texting, but no one's heard from her today."

"Texting?" I had a bad feeling. How many days since I had seen her? I quickly calculated. Five days. A long time.

"You tried calling her?" I asked.

"Yes. No one answers."

"Someone needs to drive over to her apartment and check on her. Maybe she's seriously ill and needs medical attention."

"I'll go," Jake volunteered.

I hesitated. There had been some sort of tension between Jake and Lilly lately. "I'd better go with you. Dorothy, get me her address."

At Lilly's building, the thick steel door looked impregnable. We rang Lilly's bell. No answer. We tried the bell marked *Super* but it was the middle of the day and again, no answer. Jake and I waited, hoping we could follow someone into the building on their vapor trail. We sat on a low brick wall until a guy with a bag of groceries arrived and we caught the edge of the door as it swung shut behind him.

Lilly's apartment was at the end of a dark hallway. We knocked loudly and waited. Jake and I exchanged concerned looks, fearing the worst. I kicked the door in. Lilly's keys were on a credenza by the door, like she'd just walked into her apartment.

"Lilly?"

Dead silence.

We looked in the living room. Empty. Jake and I made eye contact and silently made our way to the back of the apartment. The bedroom door was closed. Not a good sign. I slowly pushed it open. Lilly wasn't there. I'd arrived hoping to find her, now I heaved a sigh of relief.

We searched the place thoroughly, looking for signs of blood or a struggle but everything seemed to be in order.

Except that Lilly had vanished.

✷✷✷✷

Jake and I divided up a list of area hospitals and morgues and began calling without success. Within the hour, we'd driven to the Ward 2 police station on Idaho Avenue and reported Lilly missing. While we were there, a patrolman broke into the conversation I was having with the captain behind the desk.

"Can I see that photo?" he asked.

I showed him the photo from Lilly's LinkedIn page.

The patrolman scratched his chin. "I saw her in Georgetown. Maybe five, six nights ago when I was walking my beat. About 11:00 at night. She was sorta staggering."

"Staggering?"

"Yeah, and when I crossed the street to see if she was okay, she took off like the devil himself had spit in her hair."

I turned back to the captain. "See. Something's wrong. Lilly is fearless."

"Okay, we'll get a unit over there."

I went with them and showed them the apartment, explaining the broken door as we entered.

They asked all the right questions—was there any evidence of foul play, was Lilly's behavior consistent with her established pattern, etc., etc. And they filed all the right reports into all the right systems—the Washington Area Law Enforcement System and the National Criminal Information Center—and issued an area-wide alert. They also began a house-to-house search in Lilly's neighborhood and organized a press conference where I would appeal for the public's help in locating her.

Back at the Supreme Court, I picked up the phone to inform Ruth about Lilly's disappearance. It had been a few days since we'd consulted about Eden and Echo, so I needed to get an update on their case. I was also hoping Ruth could throw some resources our way, although I knew it was unlikely because every FBI agent available was looking for Eden and Echo.

"Is there any evidence that Lilly is in imminent danger?" Ruth asked.

"She was running for her life."

"You just said the cop didn't see anyone following her."

"Yes, but Lilly's keys are in the apartment. She wouldn't go anywhere without those," I said, trying to add a sense of urgency.

"Could be an extra set. Did you see any blood, signs of a struggle?"

"Ruth, listen to me. This might be connected to the Hines case."

"What? Do you have any evidence of that?"

"No," I reluctantly replied. "But you said you have nothing new in the Hines case. Maybe this is a lead."

"You know I can't divert assets away from the President's daughters without a good reason. I don't have to tell you about the politics in the Bureau. For now, work with the Washington cops. They're good."

The D.C. Police had been good so far but like most local forces, they had limited manpower and unless they located Lilly right away, I knew they'd grow weary of investigating a missing person's case without some evidence a crime had been committed. I didn't have a single drop of blood. I had a feeling this was going to be a long and difficult case that would require the FBI's resources and expertise.

I hung up. As I was mulling over my options, Dorothy slid into my chambers and hovered over my desk.

"Not now," I snapped.

"The Chief wants to talk to you. You missed Conference."

"Jesus Christ." I glanced at my watch. "Screw him. Bring me Lilly's personnel file." I needed to contact Lilly's mother who lived across the country in California.

"Mrs. McCleary, I've reported Lilly's disappearance to the police and they need to ask you some questions. Could you give them a call—"

"What kind of questions?" She sounded terrified.

"Just the usual questions. Whether she has any medical conditions, whether there are any relatives or friends she might be visiting, whether Lilly has any tattoos or scars—"

I heard a great rush of breath. "They didn't find a body, did they?"

"No ma'am, these are just questions that could help the police find her."

"You don't think Lilly's dead, do you?" she sobbed.

I felt awful for her. "Mrs. McCleary, let's not get ahead of ourselves. I'll be working with the police and I promise I'll stay in touch and call you the second I hear any new developments. We'll find her."

Before the conversation ended, Mrs. McCleary told me she was a widow confined to a wheelchair and Lilly was the only light in her life.

I couldn't have felt any worse.

I picked up a pen and absentmindedly fiddled with it. I had a close rapport with Jake and Todd, but my instinct was to keep a certain amount of distance from my female law clerks. I used to think that was a good thing, even a necessity in Lilly's case. Now, I was beginning to wonder. I didn't know anything about Lilly's personal life at all. I only knew about her achievements and there were many.

I paged through Lilly's personnel file, reviewing the astonishing accomplishments she'd managed to rack up in her life—Radcliffe Phi Beta Kappa, Harvard Law School Law Review Editor, D.C. Circuit Court of Appeals Law Clerk to Judge Ray Vandervan. She'd gone through Radcliffe in three years, so she'd jammed all that into seven short years. Pretty damn impressive.

I needed to question my law clerks. I thought Amy was the most likely to know about Lilly's private life and I started with her. It turned out that Amy knew less than I did. She knew little about Lilly's personal life and the only Court case they'd discussed lately was United States v. Clark. Same with Jake and Todd. They knew nothing. Nada. Zero. Zilch.

I spoke with Jake last.

"What was going on between you and Lilly?"

"What do you mean?"

"She seemed annoyed with you."

"I didn't notice anything," Jake said.

I wondered if he was being honest with me. "Is Lilly dating anyone?"

"Not to my knowledge."

"Has she mentioned anything unusual?"

"No."

As Jake got up to leave, I had another thought, one about Lilly's career. During the past few months, I'd had several phone calls from partners in big Washington firms interested in hiring Lilly at the end of the term. I knew most of the partners personally and I'd given Lilly stellar recommendations.

From our conversations, I was certain Lilly had received offers from all of them, although I had no idea which firm she'd signed with.

"Do you know, Jake?"

He shook his head sadly. "Afraid not. Lilly's pretty private."

That would turn out to be an understatement. I would soon discover that Lilly was an enigma.

CHAPTER 12

The next morning, I was the first one in the office, and as usual, I was carrying a chocolate donut and a cup of coffee. The newspaper had already been delivered, and I set my breakfast on Dorothy's desk while I unfolded the paper.

WHY ARE BEAUTIFUL YOUNG WOMEN DISAPPEARING IN THE DISTRICT?

I kept reading, rooted to the spot. The story broke the news of Lilly's disappearance and commented on how unusual it was for affluent, professional women to disappear off the face of the earth. Two photos dominated the front page, one of the President's daughters smiling broadly, their arms wrapped around each other. It was the same photograph that had been plastered on the front page of every newspaper in the country since the FBI made its announcement. And now, Lilly joined the twins in a lineup no one wanted to be in.

So, three beautiful women were splashed across the front page. Three women who looked like super models with luxurious manes of hair, perfect white teeth, and beautiful bone structure. Was that the common denominator? Could be. I'd seen it before.

I flipped to the inside and scanned to the end of the article. It gave an update on the search for the President's daughters and cited an unnamed law enforcement source who said the cases could be related.

I was the unnamed source. I had hand-fed the information to a reporter friend. She was always looking for the next big story and I was anxious for Lilly's case to get some publicity. More importantly, I had convinced the reporter to frame the story in a manner that would start an earthquake at the White House.

I looked at the clock in my chambers. 7:30. I plopped down on the brown leather sofa near my desk, pried the lid off my coffee, and washed the donut down my gullet.

A knock at my door. I motioned to Ruth. "Come in, I was expecting you."

"You saw the paper," she said, falling into a chair, propping her feet on my coffee table, looking as exhausted as I've ever seen her. "The President called Mortich at six this morning," she said. "He's demanding that I look into whether the two cases are linked."

I shrugged. "He has a point. Prominent young women don't just fall off the grid."

She narrowed her eyes. "I know you're behind that story, so I hope to God you're right about a connection to Lilly. Anyway, I'm here to ask questions."

"Start with me. Dorothy and my law clerks don't drag themselves in until 8:00." I stopped dead. Ruth's face was a pasty white that belonged on a cadaver. "You look awful. Can I get you some coffee? I'll call downstairs and have some brought up. How about a donut or some yogurt?"

Ruth nodded and sat up straight. "A donut and coffee would be great."

While I made my call, she pulled out a pad and pencil.

I hung up and looked at her. "Okay. Ask away."

"When did you last see Lilly?"

"Same day we were at Eden and Echo's house. Jake says she worked late that night although I didn't see her. So, you'll have to talk to him for specifics."

"But everything seemed normal?"

"Far as I could tell," I said.

"You can't think of anything at all unusual?"

"No."

"You were one of the best agents at the Bureau. What's your theory about why Lilly disappeared?"

"I have absolutely no idea," I said, sipping at my coffee.

"First thing that comes to mind?"

I shrugged. "Maybe it was retaliation for my helping the FBI with the Hines case."

"An interesting thought but how would anyone know you helped us?"

"Good question because again, I have no answer."

I rolled out of my chair, extracted a sheet of paper from a drawer, and handed it to her. "Here's something else," I said. "Yesterday it occurred to me that I didn't know which law firm Lilly had signed with. She interviewed with four of them. Here's a list. They're all in Washington and they all offered Lilly terrific jobs with big bonuses and interesting work. It seems she turned them all down."

"Is that strange?"

"I think so. It's customary for a firm to call me before offering one of my clerks a position and no one else did. Just those four firms."

I heard a knock. Chief Brown stepped into the room a few feet, looked at Ruth and back at me. "I won't stay. I just wanted to see if there's any news about Lilly."

"Nothing yet."

"Well, let me know." He shook his head sadly. "I hope this isn't going to reflect badly on the Court in some manner."

What an ass.

I turned back to Ruth. She struggled out of the chair. "I'll see what I can dig up," she said.

CHAPTER 13

Ruth stood back, raised her hand against the blinding sun, and noted the number of windows staring back at her. The apartment building where Lilly lived sat on the corner of R Street and bumped up against 35th. It was a tall, three-story building built in the 1930s, one of the only Art Deco structures in Georgetown, known for its Federal and Victorian architecture.

"Okay, you two," she directed a couple of new agents, "circle the building and see if there are any security cameras." She scanned the front of the grey stucco building. There were several apartments and all the inhabitants would have to be interviewed. A big job. She sighed. She'd been getting three hours sleep a night. Max.

Tim reported back. "One trained on the alley."

"Good. You have the keys?"

He jiggled a mass of metal in front of her. "Yep."

"The Super lives in the building?"

"Affirmative, boss."

"Go talk to him about that camera. It could tell us a lot and I bet it's on a loop, so we need to stop it from erasing. Now." The agents trotted away. "Wait up! Then start knocking on doors. You know what the questions are. What are Lilly's habits? Does Lilly have any regular visitors? Have there been any strange people hanging around the building?"

Tim butted in with a smile. "Boss, we were at the Academy."

Ruth grunted. She didn't like working with young, new agents. They were brash and thought they knew everything but she was stuck with them. She needed her more experienced agents to continue working other aspects of the twins' disappearance while she tried to establish a link with Lilly.

She shouted after the agents, "And follow up with anything that sounds promising!"

Ruth examined the building's front door. It was heavy riveted steel that could take a rocket. At the top of three concrete steps was another locked door. To the right and all the way down a gloomy hall was the entrance to Lilly's apartment, 2G. A long crack splintered the door jamb. Warren was right, he'd kicked it pretty hard.

She slipped on disposable gloves and booties, walked inside and took stock of the surroundings, getting a feel for the place. Her first impression was that Lilly was a neat girl. Either that or someone had cleaned up. It was a corner apartment, nice and sunny with a lot of windows. The air was stuffy although there were no unusual smells. She took some photos.

The furnishings were what Ruth would expect from a young professional—a white sofa on hardwood floors, a green palm nearby, wilted and dying from lack of water, but nothing knocked over, no signs of a struggle, nothing obviously out of place.

A mirrored coffee table sat in front of the sofa, and off to one side, an ornate white mirror rested on a walnut sideboard. Ruth got down on her knees and searched under each piece of furniture, then opened the drawers in the sideboard. On another wall, a low bookcase ran the length of the room. She looked behind it and pulled several frames out from the wall, then eased them back into place.

A kitchen, small yet functional, was adjacent to the living room. Ruth cracked the refrigerator. It contained fresh food consistent with Lilly being gone for less than a week. The dishwasher was empty, the dishes washed and put away.

Down the hall, Lilly's bedroom contained a walnut bed, an antique armoire, another palm, also on the verge of death, and a large window. *Finally.* Something of interest. The window overlooked an alley where a dumpster occupied a permanent spot. Three cars were parked nearby and in the space of a few minutes, at least two cars had driven by. A busy alley with a direct view into Lilly's bedroom if Lilly left her curtains open.

The curtains were open now.

Rear Window.

Had Lilly had given someone a show while undressing at night? Maybe someone had watched her and became obsessed with her. Sex offenders were everywhere. Georgetown wasn't exempt.

Ruth pivoted and spotted three photographs on the mirrored dresser, all of Lilly and Warren together. Here was a woman with a serious crush on Warren. Not surprising. It had happened before. At the Bureau. She sighed. But he'd never noticed and maybe it was just as well.

Ruth picked up one of the photographs, a formal portrait taken at the Supreme Court, Warren and Lilly in front of a brightly lit Christmas tree, Lilly in a red dress that matched Warren's red tie. My God. Lilly's hands were wrapped tightly around Warren's waist and she was actually hugging him! Warren looked stiff and frantic, like he wanted the nearest exit. Behind them, a party was going on. Wreaths and holly and a Santa handing out gifts. Claire was off to one side, frowning.

The other two photos were candid shots of Warren and Lilly laughing together in his chambers, Warren behind his desk, wearing a bemused smile about something Lilly had just said, Lilly with a beam of white teeth, a carefree moment that captured Lilly's youth and beauty in all its glory. Ruth paused and picked up the photograph and squinted. Lilly reminded her of someone she knew, but who? *Claire.* Lilly was a younger version of Claire. Why hadn't she seen that before?

Ruth looked around the apartment but didn't find any other photographs. Strange. Most beautiful women have photographs of themselves everywhere. Something about that wasn't right. There was an old adage—

Men desire women and women desire to be desired.

Yeah, that pretty much hit the nail on the head. And a photograph was a beautiful woman's proof of her desirability.

Ruth shook her head. Why no photographs of boyfriends? Was Lilly too busy to date? Ruth was aware that Lilly's life was mostly work and little play, with not much time for socializing, still ... that seemed odd. It would also be too bad. A boyfriend would be a lead. It wouldn't be the first time a boyfriend was why a woman had gone missing. She heard a loud knock on the apartment door.

"We have a tape," Tim said.

"Good. What about witnesses?"

"Not many people home right now. We've already done the rounds."

"How many people did you talk to?"

"Seven."

"Seven? That's all? Anything promising?"

"No. I'll come back tomorrow. More people will be around on a Saturday."

Maybe the kid was worth something after all. "What's your name again?"

"Tim, but everyone calls me Jonesie."

"Okay, Jonesie, pull the names of all the registered sex offenders in the area. Right now, though, go outside and see if you can locate any other security cameras in the area. Go five blocks in all directions. Report back ASAP. And there's a dumpster in the alley. Secure it."

Ruth returned to the bedroom and began shifting through a mirrored chest, hoping for a clue. She held up a low-cut sheer bra and matching sheer panties and looked at the labels. French designer. Expensive stuff, some with the price tags still attached. Ruth whistled low. Lilly had spent some big bucks on expensive lingerie. That wasn't particularly unusual for a woman of Lilly's age although it did suggest a certain level of sexual activity inconsistent with Lilly not having a boyfriend. Ruth took more photos.

She turned her attention to the windows in the apartment. They were all the same style, small panes of glass encased in metal and long, thin handles that locked tight when pulled in the horizontal position. Ruth didn't find any broken glass or other signs of tampering and the handles all worked perfectly. No signs of a break-in.

Ruth finished by doing a thorough search in the rest of the apartment, bookcases, closets, shelves. There was nothing suspicious and nothing indicating where Lilly had gone. Ruth noted that Lilly's computer was in the living room but didn't see her cell phone. Ruth stripped off her booties and gloves.

There was a voice at the door. "Ready boss?" It was Jonesie.

"Yeah. Any other security cameras?"

"No."

"And you secured the dumpster?"

"Yep. And told the Super not to let anyone touch it."

"Good, let's go. After you and your partner talk to the other tenants, report to me. For now, I'll get a forensics team in here to process this place."

CHAPTER 14

I sent the opinion in United States v. Clark to Chief Justice Brown's computer. The Chief had mandated that all work product be electronically transmitted, his effort to wrangle the Court into the technology age. Amazingly, most of the Justices still didn't use email and didn't understand texting, preferring to communicate with each other by hand-written memos on heavy ivory paper delivered by an aide.

With my judging duties over for the term, I was free to do some further investigating on my own. I still consulted with Ruth periodically about the Hines case but her investigation into Lilly's background hadn't turned up any common denominators with the twins and she'd informed me the FBI was dropping that angle. And that left the D.C. Police to continue the investigation into Lilly's disappearance.

The police had done what they could. They'd held a press conference where I'd appealed for the public's help. They'd thoroughly searched Lilly's neighborhood and reviewed the security camera in the alley but found nothing suspicious. Through her computer, they'd located an old boyfriend who said Lilly had become serious about someone else, but who, he didn't know. Most disturbing was that the police hadn't been able to trace the texts that Dorothy received from Lilly.

But after that initial spurt of activity, the police had left Lilly's case languishing like an old dog left out in the sun. I was hoping to pick up on something they'd missed and I headed downstairs to review video from the cameras that scanned the side of the Supreme Court building.

One of the Supreme Court security guards set me up in a small room where I fast-forwarded until I spotted Lilly the last day she was at work. She left the building through a side entrance at 9:05. The camera lost her a block away walking north toward the metro at Union Station. I left five minutes later. Jake left after I did. He was the last one out until security guards changed shifts at midnight. No one else left or entered the building until personnel began arriving the next morning. Lilly walked away alone and unharmed.

However, there was an unaccounted for two hours between the time she left the Supreme Court and when the cop saw her in Georgetown. I walked over to Union Station to see if anyone had noticed her. The bartender at the Thunder Grill said he'd noticed her. Not only was she beautiful, he thought she'd had too many drinks for her own good. Perhaps someone had followed her home.

That was a general fit with Ruth's idea that someone may have watched Lilly and determined her schedule. We both agreed the motivation for taking Lilly could be sexual assault. It was a disturbing thought but I couldn't dwell on. Emotions were luxuries in criminal investigations, distractions that clouded judgment and my job was to find her. And for that, I needed a clear head.

My next job was to question the Super at Lilly's building. Auggie was waiting at the building under fluffs of white clouds. He couldn't have been more than twenty-five years old, a young lad with the rumpled look common on Ivy League campuses—tan kakis and a wrinkled blue shirt with madras lining, sleeves rolled up, a woven leather watch band on his wrist.

"Sir," Auggie greeted me, politely offering his hand, giving me a winning smile. "How can I help you?" He looked at me with crystal blue eyes from under a mop of brown hair.

I liked him immediately. "So, Auggie Custis?"

He chuckled. "Yeah, it's actually Augustine Washington Custis but that's a mouthful. Everyone calls me Auggie."

"Are you a descendant?" I searched his face, suddenly curious if I could picture this young kid in colonial garb and a powdered wig. I couldn't.

"From Washy Custis, Martha Washington's grandson who lived at Mt. Vernon with Martha and *The Great Man*, as they called George."

Meeting a descendant of one of the first families was unusual although not unheard of in Washington. While it was often said that native Washingtonians were a rare breed, the truth was that some of the early families had never left.

"My daughter would be interested in meeting you sometime. She's become interested in history."

"I'd be glad to meet her." He smiled pleasantly.

I looked up at the building. "Of course, as I said on the phone, I need to ask you questions about Lilly."

"Let's sit down," he suggested, motioning to the low brick wall where Jake and I had waited a week earlier.

"I'm not sure how much I can help you," he said. "I've already talked to the FBI."

"I may have a different take on something." I smiled.

"Well, I'm not around the building all that much. I just got my M.A. from Georgetown and I work part time at Branham's Coffee and Beans on Wisconsin Avenue until I find a full-time job." He motioned to the building behind us. "Being a Super gives me a place to live rent free." He grinned. "Thankfully, the building is in pretty good shape and the small stuff, I can address on the weekends. I learned some handyman stuff from my grandfather. He's a lawyer. Isn't everyone? But work-shopping is his hobby. If there's anything I can't handle, I call in the professionals."

He laughed again, crinkles forming around his eyes. "In fact, I do that most of the time. The building's owner basically wants someone responsible to report any problems. My name probably helped me get the job but, hey, I'll take it," he shrugged, "because living in Georgetown rent free and being able to walk to campus is a fantastic deal." He stopped short and scanned my face. "I'm afraid I've rattled on about myself and you want to know about Lilly."

"Do you know her?"

"I know her to see her. We don't have much interaction, though. She's never complained about anything breaking in her apartment, like a water pipe. I saw her when she moved in last year. We said hello and I helped her carry in a few boxes but she had movers so I told her to call me if she had any problems with the apartment and I headed off to class. She seems nice. I was surprised to hear she's vanished." He paused. "She works for you at the Supreme Court?"

"Yes. Did you ever see her with anyone?"

"No, can't say that I did."

"Anything else you can think of?"

"Nope, but I'll be glad to call you if I remember anything."

"Here's my number." I pulled out a business card.

Auggie seemed to be thinking. "You know, there is something else. About a month or so ago, some kids from the school across the street started hanging around the alley behind the building."

"School kids?"

"Yeah, then some older guys started joining them. Really rough-looking characters. A few weeks ago, they were smoking weed in the alley near Lilly's window. I remember wondering how safe it was for her with them around but I didn't see them again and I forgot all about it."

"Did you tell the FBI about them?"

"No. You think it could be important?" He looked hopeful.

That fit in with the scenario Ruth and I thought was possible. Usually, the most obvious scenario was the correct solution and this fit with what we knew.

"Could be."

Auggie produced a list. "Here are the names and telephone numbers of everyone in the building, like you wanted." He pointed at a name. "You might want to talk to Tabitha. I think she knew Lilly."

I stuck out my hand. "You've been a great help, Auggie."

"No problem. I love helping the Feds." He grinned.

I smiled. Without Auggie's family, the Feds wouldn't exist.

CHAPTER 15

Reed floated downstairs in tight pink jeans and a black tee shirt, her blonde hair flowing long and loose around her shoulders. She loved it here at Blackhall where Samuel was protected from crazies who might want to kidnap and hold him for ransom. She shuddered, thinking about her ordeal last year, determined that Samuel would never go through the same thing.

She glanced at her watch. Ten on the dot. Where was he? She'd left the gate open like he'd asked. The doorbell rang and through the archway into the foyer, Reed caught a glimpse of Harrison Smith. She was surprised. Harrison looked young on his website but his reputation was so well established that she thought those were old photos. But he looked just like the pictures—curly blond hair, a deep tan, light blue shirt, white pants over a youthful athlete's physique. A tennis star … holding a large white box tied with a pink bow.

Reed stared at the gift. "Oh! Mr. Smith. I, I don't know what to say," she stammered.

"Please call me Harrison. And don't worry, Mrs. Rideout. This doesn't obligate you in any way. It's just a small present from an admirer." He reached out and kissed her hand.

"Come in." Reed awkwardly withdrew her hand and escorted Harrison through the large foyer and out the back door to the terrace where they sat under a canopy of weeping willows rippling in the breeze, rustling low like old women whispering.

"Is Mr. Rideout here?" Harrison asked, pleasantly.

"No, he's never here so it's just the two of us," she said, immediately regretting her words. *Help is miles away.* But Harrison was an architect not a kidnapper. She needed to calm down.

"Isn't Mr. Rideout interested in the renovation?"

"Not really." She tucked a piece of blonde hair behind her ear. "It's my project. So, I would be your boss."

"That sounds delightful. Please, open the box, Mrs. Rideout. I think you will be surprised." His smile was a brilliant white.

Reed unwrapped a pink construction hard hat with her name stenciled in purple letters. "How cute!" she exclaimed. "And pink is my favorite color. But I can't accept this, Mr. Smith."

He looked downcast. "It's Harrison and please, Mrs. Rideout, consider it a gift. No strings attached. I know how much you do for the children of this county. I see your photo at charity events all the time. No matter what architectural firm you decide to go with, it's a well-deserved gift from someone who admires your commitment to the community."

"Oh, well," Reed said, flustered.

"Here, let me put it on for you." He lifted the hard hat over her head, snuggled it down and fastened the strap. "There, you look beautiful."

She looked around. The helmet made her feel nervous, like a football might be headed her way.

He smiled and picked up some large scrolls of paper he'd left nearby. "May I? I've brought some architectural plans to show you my vision for the estate."

Reed pulled off the hard hat. "But I haven't shown you around yet."

Harrison looked wistfully into the distance. "I'm actually familiar with Blackhall. I visited here a long time ago with my uncle. Mr. Rideout's parents were still alive and even though I was a small boy, I've always remembered the house." He sighed. "It's beautiful," he blushed, "and it's what motivated me to become an architect."

"Your uncle knew the Rideouts?"

"My uncle was an interior designer. He did a room or two for the Rideouts. The gentlemen's and the ladies' drawing rooms."

Reed gasped. "Really? Because those are my two favorite rooms. Although we never spend time there and I don't know why. I'm hoping you can help me with the flow of those rooms and still retain the integrity of the house." She paused. "Although I love the way the rooms are decorated," she added.

"Then, let's start there." He grabbed his papers and tucked them under his arm and headed for the gentlemen's drawing room where he directed Reed's attention to windows framed with wood that undulated in curves and dips.

"Do you know why this room has no draperies?" Harrison asked.

Reed shook her head.

"My Uncle wanted to keep this room true to its history. You see, since this was the gentlemen's drawing room, any draperies would've been ruined by the smells and dirt from the rank green tobacco used in the 1700s. The ornately carved window architraves are the decorations and make draperies unnecessary."

Reed was dazzled. Harrison's knowledge was so impressive.

"It's extraordinary that an undulating theme was executed in wood. That's virtually unknown in period Colonial architecture. This room belongs in a museum."

Harrison took Reed's elbow and walked her across the hall. "Now. The ladies' drawing room. You will notice that this room is restrained in its trim and plasterwork. There are some grapes and sheaves of wheat carved in wood and attached to the plaster, but the framing is simple and the trim and plasterwork are painted a virginal white. The architect's idea for this room was to convey the quiet and elegant nobility and good character of the ladies of the family."

Reed's mouth was practically agape with awe.

He smiled. "I think I can draw up some plans to help with the flow between these rooms and the rest of the house. A connecting arcade would be true to the period. We can replicate the Palladian style windows found in the library. That will provide light to the interior and we can line the walk with works of art to draw the eye forward to the next painting, and therefore, to the next room. That would make exploring the drawing rooms an event and they would become enticing, even irresistible." Harrison paused, looking concerned. "In general, though, it's important to remain as true as possible to the house's original footprint."

"You know so much about early houses!" Reed gushed.

"I was at Yale, American History and Architecture and Design." He held a finger in the air. "Now, in regard to the house's dependencies, we should be able to change the configuration of the grounds as long as we stay a thousand feet from any wetlands. Did you know, Mrs. Rideout, that an octagonal racing stable originally stood on the grounds?"

"Octagonal?" Reed looked stunned. "I didn't know a stable could be octagonal."

Harrison pulled out a roll of paper from the batch he'd been carrying around. "Here's a copy of the original 1775 plan."

Reed crowded in. "My God, it is octagonal. And it has two stories!" She pointed at the architectural rendering. "And round windows." Reed was floored. "I've never seen anything like it."

"The plans are quite extraordinary, aren't they Mrs. Rideout?" Harrison looked deeply into her eyes like they were long lost soulmates.

"Please. Call me Reed," she stuttered, feeling flushed.

"*Reed*." Harrison looked away dreamily.

She stared at him. The way he said her name sounded like the soft patter of rain.

He turned back to the drawings. "Well, *Reed*, these are the plans I envision for such a beautiful chatelaine's home. I think we should reconstruct the original stable. Tear down that rotting pile of wood that's out there now. It's an eyesore. Just think how stunning it would be to have an octagonal stable as the first thing a visitor sees upon entering the grounds. It would be the only one like it in the entire region, maybe the entire United States."

They talked the rest of the morning. All of Harrison's plans blew Reed away. They discussed adding a swimming pool connected by a path to tennis courts on the west side of the house, plans to renovate the kitchen, and add more bathrooms. Harrison presented sketches and she couldn't imagine anyone creating concepts that seemed to be more historically accurate while being so evocative, beautiful, and most importantly, functional, all at the same time. Davis would love it! And Daddy would be so impressed.

CHAPTER 16

I rose early and headed toward R Street where Auggie had arranged for me to talk with a number of tenants in Lilly's building. My walk took me up 31st Street and past Tudor Place, an 1815 Federal manor originally owned by descendants of Martha Custis Washington, Auggie's umpteenth great-grandmother. At R Street, I turned left and walked by the red brick Civil War era home of Ulysses S. Grant, then at the corner of R and Wisconsin, I passed townhouses carved from the sprawling old mansion once owned by Evelyn Walsh McLean, the owner of the Hope Diamond from 1911–1947. A ten-minute walk. Two centuries of history.

I was at Lilly's building.

It seemed that no one living in the building knew Lilly other than to nod at her until I knocked on Unit 3D. A slender young woman about Lilly's age cracked the door and peered through a latched chain. She blinked several times before recognition flooded her eyes. She giggled nervously.

"Oh, hi," she said, unchaining the door. "You must be Justice Alexander. Auggie said you'd be coming by. He's worried about the women tenants. Told us to be careful."

"Good advice."

"I'm Tabitha Stevens. Come in."

I entered a sun-filled space of large green plants and Lucite furniture.

"Please sit down," she offered. "Auggie said you're looking for information about the woman in 2G? Lilly McCleary?"

"Do you know Lilly?"

"Not really. I would see her in the hallway and we'd say hello but that was it."

"Did you ever see her with anyone? Maybe a man?"

"I did!" she said, her face lighting up. "There was a guy. Dark hair, good build, although I have no idea who he was."

"Did he seem like a boyfriend?"

"Maybe. It's hard to tell. I did see her with him a few times."

"And this was recently?"

"Yes, a few weeks before she went missing."

"Do you remember anything about him? Age? Weight? Height? Distinguishing characteristics like scars?"

She giggled. "Scars, that's funny." She fiddled with a strand of hair, thinking. "He was tall, average weight, nice-looking. I'm not sure how old he was, maybe late twenties or early thirties, about her age."

"Could you ID him if you saw a photo?"

"I think so."

I gave her my business card and asked her to call me if she saw him again.

I thought the man Tabitha described must be connected to Lilly's disappearance because no one like that had contacted me or Lilly's mother to express concern and ask what the police were doing to find her. Finding him was number one on my list.

I walked the perimeter of Lilly's building, looking for something, anything, unusual. Immediately, something jumped out at me. At the end of the alley was a large French Creole plantation-style house hidden behind a ten-foot-high, white fence and equally tall stalks of bamboo. On the lawn, lush magnolia trees dripped huge white blossoms across the walk leading to the front door. The house, which must have been beautiful at one time, was now old and forlorn, its windows opaque with curtains drawn shut like long-formed cataracts.

A curtain moved on the second floor. I pushed the doorbell, stepped back and kept my eye on the window. I had a bad feeling, like someone was hiding inside, watching and waiting for me to leave. I walked the side yard.

The curtains appeared to be old bed sheets and every window was covered. I made a note to check property records and see who lived there. Anyone in the house with a good pair of binoculars would have a direct view into Lilly's bedroom window.

✶✶✶✶

Back home, I went to the on-line Sex Offender Registry at DC.Gov, hoping the address of the "bamboo house" would pop up but there were only four sex offenders in the immediate area and none who lived in Georgetown. I tried Google and discovered the house was owned by a Mrs. Olivia Trego. At Intellius.com, I was able to ascertain that Mrs. Trego was a ninety-year-old widow. No wonder she hadn't answered the door. She was probably infirm or maybe afraid to open the door to a stranger. Another dead end. One that brought me back to square one.

Someone put a hand on my shoulder. I jumped. "Claire."

"You're jumpy." She laughed.

"I was so engrossed in what I'm doing that I didn't hear you."

"What *are* you doing?"

"Trying to find information about Lilly's neighbors. I talked to some of them today. One of them saw Lilly with a man who I bet had something to do with her disappearance."

Claire sat down. "I need to talk to you about my litigation schedule. The other side keeps asking for continuances. I'm afraid we might have to cancel our trip to Switzerland."

I kissed her on the forehead. "It's all right. We'll do what we need to do."

Secretly, I was relieved. I didn't like the idea of leaving town until Lilly had been found. And I was going to speed along the investigation. I picked up the phone and called Tabitha.

"Tabitha? I'd like you to meet with a sketch artist to draw up a composite of the man you saw with Lilly. I'm going to ask the police if they will call another press conference and request the public's help in identifying him."

CHAPTER 17

Reed was going to throw the first shovel of dirt! She was so excited. Davis knew about the renovations to the house but not about the dig. This would surprise Davis for sure! She'd secretly spent months on the project with Archeology Associates, a private firm that had completed preliminary work at the Maryland State Archives, researching land records, census data, wills and probate inventories, all useful information for understanding the context of any objects they might uncover at Blackhall.

Davis was in Taiwan for two weeks and before he'd left, he'd said, "Go ahead and finalize architectural plans but before the actual construction begins, we have to locate the systems coming into the house. Do not start tearing up the grounds!"

She'd smiled and nodded. Archeology Associates had pulled all the information and knew which areas to avoid. The archeologists also knew where to look for interesting old artifacts. Where the old summer kitchen used to stand was of particular interest. The archeologists told her that was an area where colonial-era trash and broken objects might be buried. It would be interesting to see if any treasures could be unearthed at Blackhall that would shed light on its first residents, John and Josephine Rideout.

She gave herself a mental hug. This would show Davis how creative she was! It was the perfect complement to go along with the renovations and with any luck, she'd have some interesting historical objects to display in the renovated house. She was keeping the dig a surprise from everyone, even Henry, her usual collaborator.

She had let a new friend in on her secret, though. Harrison. He was such a dear. She couldn't resist telling him. Harrison had been fascinated but said he was overseeing construction that day. Too bad. It would've been fun having him here, keeping her company. They had so much in common.

She took a sip of coffee as she waited in the library for the workers to arrive. She'd dressed in navy blue shorts, a red tee shirt, and running shoes, ready for what she supposed a dig would entail—dirt and worms and icky stuff. She was set! But it was getting late. She glanced at her watch, frowning. Where was everyone?

Some loud thumps sounded like car doors. Cradling her coffee, Reed rushed to the library windows and peered out. At least eight vans from Archeology Associates were in the driveway. Reed had written a big check to put maximum manpower into this project. She wanted to complete it before Davis returned from Taiwan, show him what she could accomplish on her own. Archeology Associates had informed her that was going to be difficult. Dirt had to be troweled by hand and shifted for tiny objects, it was time consuming, something that couldn't be rushed.

Yawn! Reed had written another check. Even so, Archeology Associates had made no promises. Oh, well, she didn't want to think about that now because here they were, ready to begin! She smoothed her hair, secured it into a ponytail, and hurried out to meet them.

Something fluttered in her peripheral vision. A cyclone of motion. Henry had popped out of his cottage, hopping on one foot, pulling on a shoe. "What's going on?" he yelled from across the lawn, his forehead a mass of wrinkles.

What was with Henry? Reed smiled, trying to reassure him. "Don't worry Henry. We're just going to do a little digging around the grounds to see if we can find some old artifacts that belonged to Davis's ancestors. It will be fun!"

Henry rushed over, raised both hands and began flopping them around, shaking them furiously. "No! No! You can't do that, Mrs. Rideout!"

The entire crew had departed their vans and were standing around, some leaning against their vehicles, arms crossed, all of them looking at her, seemingly amused at the scene in front of them. She looked at them, embarrassed, and turned back to Henry.

Her smile had vanished. "Why not?"

Henry started shaking. "I … I … uh … uh … Davis said—"

"Oh that! Don't worry. We've already pulled the permits and we know where all the underground systems are located. We won't touch them." She threw her biggest, brightest smile at Henry, hoping that would calm him down.

Henry just stood there, mouth agape.

She gave him a big hug. "Henry, you worry too much."

The dig went ahead, on schedule.

CHAPTER 18

It was noon when I arrived at Quantico. The first thing I noticed was a red rash slashed across Ruth's cheek.

"What's wrong?" I asked.

"Psoriasis."

"Since when?"

"Last year. It flares up with stress."

Little wonder. Two weeks had passed since the twins' disappearance and the FBI had become a laughing stock. The media couldn't understand how the President's daughters had simply vanished. And it wasn't just the American media. All around the world, reporters were questioning the FBI's investigative tactics.

Ruth walked over to her desk and picked up a sketch. "Here's Tabitha's composite drawing," she said.

My heart sank. The image was too generic to generate any real leads. "This looks like a cartoon." I stared at Ruth, stunned. "I was hoping for something that would have the public calling in with an ID."

"Me too," she said.

"I still think these cases could be related. Three high-profile women disappear from Washington in the same week. How often does that happen?"

"I told you we investigated their backgrounds. Lilly has nothing in common with the twins. No common acquaintances, no work contacts, not even a shared spinning class or a mutual love for hamsters. Look, you're the best agent I've ever known but I need something solid to keep going down that rabbit hole. Have the police come up with anything?"

"No. They have a missing-person case without a body or a crime scene."

"You've just described the Hines case," she said.

I thought she'd just proved my point but there was no sense arguing with her. "Okay," I said, exasperated. "I'm here to help so let's get on with it. Fill me in." I plopped down in a chair.

She walked to a white crime board filled with photos and time lines. "Basically, nothing's changed although we have a better grasp of the twins' early movements. They didn't cross the Bay Bridge, and that means they weren't traveling to the Eastern Shore."

"They were spreading disinformation?"

"That's my theory and that would fit with your blackmailing scenario. They didn't want anyone knowing what they were up to and not just the Secret Service. It's logical they'd want to keep the victims' identities secret from one another."

"You're saying they were on their way to meet one man, not two?" I asked.

"Right."

"That makes sense. It would be safer for them if things got rough. They could gang up on one man. Where does that leave you?"

Ruth walked over to a map of the Annapolis area and traced a black magic marker along Route 50. "The only solid lead we have is the information we received from Joseph Newman, who saw the President's daughters driving east."

"Anything else come of that?"

"We've developed a few more details." She circled a spot in red. "Newman left Route 50 at Exit 23 so that means Eden and Echo exited somewhere between there and the Bay Bridge. The twins could've driven into Annapolis but roads through Annapolis have security cameras and the twins weren't spotted on any of them. So, we know they drove past those exits." She crossed the exits off with the magic marker.

"And no one else has come forward?"

She smirked. "Just the usual kooks and publicity seekers. Newman is the only credible witness. The President's daughters simply vanished off the face of the earth and Newman was the last person to see them." She frowned. "Unfortunately, he has an alibi for the rest of that night."

"What about the profile we generated?"

"It still seems promising. We had some excitement about a couple of retired brass living near Annapolis. Both are wealthy men who'd recently attended White House functions."

"Oh, yeah?"

"Uh-huh. One guy was a retired admiral, an Admiral Tyler who lives on Gibson Island. He seemed particularly suspicious. He'd been at the White House for a military awards ceremony and he was seen chatting and laughing with Eden and Echo afterwards. Several guests told us that Eden rubbed her body up against him in a suggestive manner and the Admiral burst into a huge smile and whispered something into her ear."

I smiled. "Sounds like a case of middle-age libido to me."

"It does in retrospect because he had an alibi." She impatiently waved her hand at an area much closer to the Bay Bridge. "Now, the other man was a retired general, a General Rosenbaum who lives in a mansion fronting the Severn River. He recently consulted with the President on the use of drones in foreign conflicts and stayed for an informal dinner with the President and his daughters. He also had an alibi. And those were my two best leads."

"So, now you're back to randomly questioning the other seventy or so men you targeted as potential suspects?"

"Yes, and none of them feel right."

"Intuitively?"

She nodded, scrutinizing the map of Annapolis and the surrounding area. "Without some leads, I might as well throw darts at that map."

"You're still going with the blackmailing theory?"

Ruth began pacing. "Yes, because it fits most of the facts. The President isn't independently wealthy like most politicians so the twins may have seen blackmail as a way to supplement their income. The problem is that I have no evidence of blackmail. Forensic audits of their finances haven't dredged up any unusual financial activity—no off-shore bank accounts, no bitcoin accounts, and the twins' lifestyle is consistent with their earned income. They do have that Porsche but it's an old, second-hand car the President bought for them on the cheap. There's no expensive art in their house, no extravagant vacations to exotic places. In short, the twins aren't living large like I'd expect of two flush blackmailers. On the surface, everything is completely normal. So, I need to look outside that box."

I nodded, sympathetic. "And you have no crime scene that could yield footprints, clothing, or blood."

"Which means, basically, I'm at a complete loss."

All of her pacing was starting to make her office heat up. "For God's sake, sit down," I said. "How can you pace in here? It's so damn hot."

"Yeah, I know." She fanned her blouse. "This office is too hot in the summer and too cold in the winter."

"Turn the thermostat down."

"It won't do any good. The controls have been overridden by heartless bureaucrats at GAO."

Her phone rang, surprising us both. It was FBI Director Mortich and he was yelling.

"Two graves have been found at Blackhall, an estate near the Bay Bridge in Anne Arundel County, Maryland. Some asshole is posting photos on the internet. Get out there. Now!"

CHAPTER 19

Icy fingers gripped my throat. *Blackhall?* This must be some sort of sick joke.

Ruth stared at me. "Where have I heard that name before?"

"That's where my daughter lives."

"What the hell is going on?" Her eyes swept my face.

"Ruth, we don't know it's Eden and Echo."

"Who else could it be?" Ruth grabbed her gun and quickly arranged for an FBI helicopter.

While she was doing that, I called Reed's cell phone. No answer. I jumped out of my seat. "I'm going with you."

"No." She was out the door.

I grabbed her arm and dug in my fingers as she rounded the corner. "I need to know my daughter's okay."

Ruth let me fall in step with her. "I didn't know Reed had a home out there," she muttered.

"It's been in Davis's family for a long time. Centuries."

"I didn't run across his name during my investigation." Her eyes were dark.

"It's not in his name. It's in a family trust owned by a corporation."

"And you didn't tell me?" A barrier had been thrown up between us. "Davis fits your own profile!"

"He's never at Blackhall. Reed is the one who loves the place." Still, the idea that Davis would meet the President's daughters for sex would be just like him. And the criminal profile I'd pieced together practically indicted him.

A wealthy, prominent man with a house near the Bay Bridge. Someone who'd been a recent guest at the White House.

I crammed into the helicopter with Ruth and another agent. The chopper lifted straight up with a deafening roar that blocked out further conversation. Another chopper trailed just behind. The town of Dumfries, Virginia was below us and within minutes, we were soaring over tiny roads winding through miles of green farmland and thick forest in the Maryland countryside.

I wasn't sure what to think. I had always wondered whether Claire and I had made a mistake in encouraging Davis and Reed's marriage when we found out she was pregnant. It was what Reed wanted and it seemed like the right choice even though I was afraid Davis would make a lousy husband. After all, I was the one who'd shared a dorm room with him at Harvard Law School.

That was a year I hadn't gotten much sleep. Night after night, Davis would sneak another beautiful girl into our room, and night after night, I would adhere to the time-honored roommate creed and shuffle off to the Law School Library where I slept on an old leather sofa. After all these years, I still remembered the lump in the center cushion.

You'd think the hours Davis kept would have exhausted him. That never happened. Davis always showed up in class, bright-eyed and armed with brilliant, precise legal analysis. Everything was so easy for him. In contrast, I was a shy, awkward kid from the wilds of Wyoming, insecure and out of my depth at Harvard, both scholastically and socially. I'd admired Davis as a first-rate legal mind and envied him as a dashing libertine whom I secretly desired to emulate. But even then, I knew I wasn't cut out for juggling multiple girlfriends and I now chalked up my wishes to the vagaries of youth. Much later as Reed's father, Davis's proclivities had taken on an entirely different meaning. But Claire and I had vowed not to interfere in their marriage, no matter what, and maybe that was the wrong decision.

The pilot landed the chopper on Blackhall's lawn. A dozen red trucks with the words Archeology Associates scrawled in enormous white script crammed the driveway. Reed was sitting on a large rock, staring into the horizon. Henry was standing next to her, chewing his fingernails. Nearby, the archeologists were wearing protective gear, silent and grim and engrossed in their find.

Reed flew into my arms. Sweat dotted her brow. "I don't know what's going on. They said they found two bodies and I had to stay back." Reed looked at the helicopters and her knees gave away. I barely caught her. "Does the FBI think it's the President's daughters?" she gasped.

A man approached us. He was tall, muscular, and roasted brown from long hours in the sun.

Ruth unhooked her sunglasses from her face, folded them with a click, and stuffed them into a pocket. She flashed her badge. "FBI. Your name?"

"Tom Corbin, President of Archeology Associates."

Ruth's mouth was small and twisted. "I need you to step back, Mr. Corbin, and take all these people with you." She waved her hands at him.

Corbin looked over the top of his sunglasses. "What's the problem?"

"Sir, this is a crime scene."

Corbin started laughing. "Then the killer is long gone because these remains are eighteenth century."

Christ. We'd flown out to an archaeology dig that had stirred up some old bones.

"Sir," Ruth said, glancing around at the other FBI agents, their faces twitching with anger and disappointment, "why are you digging here?"

"Mrs. Rideout wanted to survey the grounds to see if we could find artifacts dating to the early use of the property by her husband's family. We ran ground-penetrating radar in this area and saw signs of soil disturbance but we had no idea we'd stumbled upon some old graves."

"Are you sure they're old?" I asked. "Wouldn't the bodies be decomposed by now?"

"Not with this cliff's soil and drainage. And we can tell the difference between ancient and modern remains by the context of deposition, including the condition of the body. Also, we have some coins from the 1780's, probably dropped by grave diggers."

"Can you identify the remains?" Ruth asked.

Corbin rubbed his chin. "We have two skulls that appear to be females. Men generally have thicker, heavier skulls. And the temporal line also indicates they're females. We'll know more after we do DNA testing on the teeth." He adjusted his cap and squinted. "They could be women from the Rideout family. That would be consistent with some pearls we found with the remains. We're not sure if the pearls were from a necklace because pearls were also used in the hair and on gowns but their presence makes it clear these were high-status women."

Ruth jutted her chin out. "If they were such important people, they'd have tombstones."

"No, it wasn't unusual not to have markers. It was the same at President James Madison's graveyard. Madison was also one of my projects," he said proudly, his chest puffing out. "It took us years to sort through all those graves and determine who was who. Some people were buried on top of others, just like here, and almost all of those early graves were unmarked, just like these."

Ruth looked deflated.

"We've contacted the County States Attorney, like the law requires," Corbin added. "Also, the Maryland Historical Trust." He smiled at Ruth and looked over his shoulder at the other archeologists who were staring at them, anxious for Ruth to leave so they could resume their work. "A representative from Anne Arundel County should be here, shortly." Corbin smiled at Reed. "Mrs. Rideout, expect some media attention. These finds are rare."

I sat down by Reed. Hard. Black dots swam in front of my eyes. I'd never been so relieved.

"Oh, for God's sake," Ruth muttered. "Sir, we're going to do our own DNA testing. I want you to coordinate with my forensic team."

Ruth spun around and stalked over to the archeologists who were standing around, eyeing the FBI agents. "Okay," she yelled at them, "who's the jackass who's posting photos?"

Two college age boys began studying their toes.

"You two!" Ruth yelled, her face crimson. They looked at each other and hesitated. She yanked them by their collars and grabbed their phones out of their pockets.

"Give them a break, Ruth," I said. "They're kids."

"Yeah, we're kids," said one of them. He smiled and nodded at me, grateful I'd come to his rescue.

My daughter spoke up in a tiny voice. "It's my fault," Reed said. "I wanted to surprise Davis by finding some old relics."

"Well, you certainly surprised me." Ruth sighed heavily. "Does Davis know the Hines twins?"

"What? No. I mean ... we met them at a state dinner although he doesn't really know them. Why?" Reed asked.

"Is he home?"

"He's out of the country but he'll be back tomorrow morning."

"Tell Davis I'll be back here. Tomorrow. At noon. We're questioning all men with a certain profile. It's routine but I need to ask Davis where he was the night the President's daughters disappeared." Ruth was talking to Reed but glaring at me. She scowled and pointed her finger in my face. "*You* can find your own way back." She turned and climbed into one of the helicopters.

I stayed at Blackhall that night. The twins weren't in that hole but when Mortich said bodies had been found, I'd had a terrible realization. The figures 9500 and 1140000 in Eden's diary with big stars drawn by them were actually numbers and asterisks—9500*1140000*—the code for the gate at Blackhall.

CHAPTER 20

Should I have informed Ruth about the code? Yes. Instead, I convinced myself it could be a coincidence, even though I didn't believe in coincidences but at the time, I told myself I did. And that was my dilemma the next morning as I walked into the library where sun was streaming through the room's southern facing windows.

Reed was on the green sofa, frowning, and Davis was standing nearby, wearing an impeccably tailored Italian linen jacket, looking like one of those old-fashioned movie stars who wore smoking jackets and had whippets following them about all day.

He stared over Reed's head and blew cigarette smoke into the air.

I'd walked into the middle of a raging argument.

"What's going on?" I asked.

He glared at Reed. "I botched a multi-million-dollar deal and flew all night because some old bones were found in my front yard."

"I didn't ask you to hurry back," Reed huffed.

"You were screaming that dead bodies had been found in our yard. What was I supposed to do? Let you handle it by yourself?" He snuffed out his cigarette in an ashtray.

I heard a helicopter overhead and looked out the window. Ruth was back and an agent I didn't recognize was with her. He tilted his head back and scanned the mansion. He was young and built solid. My guess was a Navy Seal background.

I turned around. Davis had left the room to answer the door. I could hear snatches of conversation as they came back down the hall.

"Hi, Ruth," I said.

"Warren." Her voice was like an ice dagger. "This is Tim Jones. We call him Jonesie."

Jonesie's eyes were glued to Reed. Not surprising. Reed's beauty had attracted a lot of attention over the years. Some of it unwanted. Particularly scary was a stalker in college who'd stolen into her sorority. He'd taken a photograph album and panties. The photos, he'd mailed back to her one by one. The panties, he'd kept.

Ruth was addressing Davis. "I'm sure you've heard—"

"Yes," Davis said, "you're questioning men with property in this area who were recently at the White House." Davis sank into the green velvet sofa, leaned back into the deep cushions and crossed his legs. "What do you want to know?"

"Well, I guess the first thing would be—where did you get those scratches?" Ruth peered into his face.

Davis seemed surprised. "These?" he asked, pointing at his face. "Reed thought I was an intruder."

"When was that?"

"About a week ago."

"They look serious."

"Reed is my little wildcat." He smiled.

Ruth looked at Reed for confirmation.

She nodded. "I thought Davis was a burglar."

Ruth turned back to Davis. "I need to ask you where you were Saturday, the first of June."

"Oh, yeah, that's the day I flew to China. Reed and I had an early dinner in Washington and I left our house about 7:00. I went to my office in Georgetown and worked there for an hour, then drove out here to pick up some documents I needed."

Reed swung her head around. "I didn't know you came out here."

"I'd forgotten some papers." He patted his pockets, looking for a cigarette. "I stayed here for a bit, watched the Tommy Woofer show, then left for BWI. I got there about 1:30 in the morning. My pilots were waiting. They might remember the exact time. We took off for Hong Kong right away, about 1:45 or so." Davis leaned forward, took a pen from a table and scribbled a note. "Here's their information. Contact them, if you want." He lit a cigarette and waved a funnel of smoke from around his face.

Ruth studied the information. "Tommy Woofer?"

"Uh-huh."

"Who was Tommy's guest that night?"

"I don't remember."

"Really? You remember everything else from that night." Ruth glanced at her notes and her eyes widened. "And in amazing detail."

Davis shrugged and flicked some ashes into a tray.

"Do you remember flying out of BWI?"

"Of course," Davis snapped.

"Why BWI?"

"You know why. Reagan National doesn't allow private planes."

She tilted her head. "One in the morning is pretty late to fly, isn't it?"

"One-thirty and I can sleep on the plane. There's a bed. So, late works fine for me. I do it all the time. And it's better with traffic between Washington and the airport."

"And you never saw the Hines twins?"

Davis laughed. "That's ridiculous."

"That's your official statement? *That's ridiculous?* Or did you not see them?"

"I did not."

"Was there anyone else here at Blackhall the night the twins disappeared?"

"Henry is usually here. He's the caretaker. You can talk to him."

"I'll get him," Reed said, digging herself out of the sofa.

✳✳✳✳

Henry carried the smell of freshly-cut grass through the library doors. He quickly made eye contact with Davis who gave him a fast smile and a reassuring nod.

Ruth shifted her attention to Henry. "Mr. Turnbull?"

"Yes ma'am?"

"Please sit down."

He eyed his grass-stained pants. "I'm good standing. Don't want to get the chairs dirty."

Ruth flipped some pages in her notebook. "Okay." She smiled at Henry. "I need to ask you a few questions. I guess you have a TV out here?"

"And a computer. In the Little Cottage."

"The Little Cottage? What's that?"

"That's the cottage I live in. It's little—"

"I should've known." She swung her torso around and eyed the chair beside her. "Please sit down, Mr. Turnbull. The chair will be fine."

Henry perched on its edge.

"Now, since you have a TV, I guess you know the President's daughters have disappeared."

"Yes, ma'am. Terrible thing." Henry shook his head.

"Yes, it is. We have reason to think the girls drove out this way, perhaps to one of these big estates on the Bay. And I need to ask if you saw either of them the night they disappeared, Saturday, June 1st."

"Sure didn't."

"Were you here that night?"

Henry stole a glance at Davis. "I went to Biggy's Bar. It's just this side of Annapolis."

"See anyone there you know?"

"No, ma'am."

"What time did you arrive at Biggy's?"

"About 10:00. Left about 2:00."

"That's pretty late, isn't it?"

"For me it is."

"Any reason for that?"

"Just felt like getting out."

"Mr. Turnbull, has anything unusual happened around here during the past few weeks?"

Reed broke into the conversation. "Someone stole an expensive crystal decanter from the house."

"Which day?"

"Sometime before that next Friday, the day I drove out here. Isn't that right, Daddy?" She turned to me with big eyes.

"There have been some burglaries out here," I said. "Seems to be a bunch of teenagers breaking into big mansions when they think no one is around."

"Did you report the burglary, Reed?"

"Yes." Reed scrounged through a desk and found a copy of the police report.

"Mr. Turnbull? Do you have anything to add?" Ruth asked.

Henry glanced at Davis who frowned.

"No, ma'am."

CHAPTER 21

After dinner that night, I followed a shaft of yellow light spilling from the library doorway. Peaceful in his crib, Samuel swatted at a blue and yellow butterfly mobile bouncing up and down over his head. Once in a while, he would smack his lips, wildly kick his legs and wave his tiny hands. Reed was curled up on the green sofa, clutching a book. A floor lamp streamed light over her shoulder and reflected off the white pages, illuminating her face like a spotlight in the dark room.

I stood in the doorway. "Don't you ever get lonely out here?"

After her kidnapping, Reed had become increasingly withdrawn, afraid of crowds and people she didn't know. She said the gates at Blackhall protected Samuel from potential kidnappers, and perhaps that was her motivation, but self-imposed isolation was common among kidnapping survivors. I'd seen plenty of it during my stint at the FBI. The problem was that Post Traumatic Stress Syndrome, if unabated, could develop into Post Traumatic Stress Disorder, a chronic and crippling condition. The only symptom Reed didn't seem to have was extreme agitation.

She smiled softly. "I have several girlfriends who drive out from Washington. They think the house is awesome. And Samuel keeps me company. Then there's Henry ... so there are people around all the time."

"I would feel isolated."

Since Reed had been held captive for only a few days, I thought she'd be able to work through the aftermath fairly quickly. I was wrong. I needed to talk to her about seeing a mental health professional although now was not the time.

She returned to her book.

The library's French doors were open to the night and I walked onto the flagstone terrace and leaned against the stone balustrade, pitted from centuries of wind and weather. On the horizon, the moon was an orange ball hovering over the tree line. To the south, the lights of Annapolis flamed like a red brush fire. And in the distance, an occasional plane silently dipped into BWI.

No matter what Reed said, the break-ins last year had escalated and while the police had questioned some teenagers, they hadn't arrested anyone and that bothered me. I wanted to talk to Davis about the security system again, see what the status was, and leave for Washington.

Stuffing my hands into my jacket, I strolled down to the edge of the cliff. The smell of flowers filled the night and I stood there for a few minutes, watching the moon dance on the water, before starting back to the mansion. In the Little Cottage, a dim light poked through a torn curtain, throwing a silhouette against the window. It was Henry. He moved the curtain aside and Davis stepped from the direction of the old stable, looking like a shadow lurching toward the cottage door, furtively glancing over his shoulder before ducking inside.

Henry turned a light on and I could see them through a window. Henry was holding a red box. He lifted the lid, pulled out a sheet of paper, and handed it to Davis.

I watched, remembering how they'd silently communicated with each other during Ruth's questioning. Something was going on. The way Davis and Henry were acting … the code to the gate in the twins' diary. I suspected Eden and Echo had been with Davis at Blackhall the night they disappeared. And that scared me to death.

****

Davis hadn't been inside Henry's cottage since Henry's wife, Susannah, died five years before. Moonlight flooded through a gap in a curtain drawn and hooked over a crooked nail pounded into the window frame. Spider webs drifted from the ceiling, floating like spun sugar. A fireplace should've brought a warm feeling to the room but it was a cold, empty cavity grown black with soot.

A cold empty cavity, Davis thought, bitterly. That would've summed up his childhood with his parents, a distant, uncaring mother and an alcoholic father who everyone called Old Paul to distinguish him from a cousin called Young Paul. Davis shook his head, thinking about all the times he'd fled to the Little Cottage.

Davis had hated the mansion and all the things associated with it. The only good memories of his childhood involved Henry and Susannah. Henry taking the rein of Pudding the pony when Davis was six years old and teaching him to ride. Henry and Susannah driving Davis into town for ice cream at Friendly's on sweltering summer evenings. Henry giving him someone to run to when Davis's father was angry, a swinging belt in his hand.

But Old Paul would storm away when Davis hid behind Henry, who always refused to turn the tyke over. "Goddamn, some day, boy!" Old Paul would yell, but he'd always back off. That is, if Henry was there. In his prime, Henry had been big and strong and broad-shouldered and Old Paul was afraid to tangle with him. Davis would never forget hiding behind Henry, trembling and wrapping his little arms around Henry's legs, which at the time had seemed big as tree trunks, and the feeling of overwhelming relief when Old Paul returned to the mansion where he continued his day of drinking whiskey and rye.

Then there'd come the day Davis still thought of as *The Day*. A turning point. Davis's sixth birthday. Old Paul had just thoroughly whipped him. *Happy Birthday, son*. Davis finally broke loose and fled into the yard, wailing for Henry to save him, Old Paul just behind, chasing him with a flying belt. Henry saw them. Something in Henry's eyes changed. Like a key turning an engine over, a roar came out of Henry like no one had ever heard.

Old Paul froze. Henry flew through the air and landed on him with an awful thud. Old Paul's head smashed into the dirt. *A terrible silence.* Davis thought his father was dead. Another short scuffle and Henry yelled,

"If you ever touch Davis again, I will bash your brains in and if I don't manage to kill you, I'll tell Lorraine about you and Pauline!"

Lorraine was Davis's mother and Pauline was a sleek-looking blonde who'd been coming around to look at racehorses. Old Paul turned bright red, and spitting and coughing, managed to drag himself to his feet. Davis was terrified. He was in more trouble now. Instead, Old Paul turned and slunk into the house. Henry the hired hand had won. It was an unthinkable outcome. Old Paul never touched Davis again.

After that, Henry began spending more time with Davis, taking the boy on walks in the woods, teaching him to appreciate the beauty of the Chesapeake Bay, the largest estuary in the United States and home to numerous inhabitants—bullfrogs, sturgeon, striped bass, eels, and rainbow snakes. It was Henry who pointed out osprey, ducks, and the occasional bald eagle. It was Henry who taught Davis about wild plants in the area, including different types of grasses, wild celery, and rice that provided food and habitat for fish, crabs, and waterfowl in the shallows that stretched along the shoreline.

Davis was shipped off to Choate at the age of thirteen. He loved the school and spent the summers working in Wallingford, coming back to Blackhall for the holidays, avoiding the mansion as much as possible, spending most of his time with Henry and Susannah in the Little Cottage, exchanging gifts, getting caught up, laughing together. Henry and Susannah were always interested in what he was doing, his goals in life, the girls he dated.

At age eighteen, Davis left for Stanford, shuddering as his parents firmly latched the great door of the mansion behind him, their eyes staring blankly through the window like he was a stranger who'd happened by for a handout. It was Henry who drove Davis to the airport. It was Henry who stood at the gate, a tear in his eye, full of pride at all the things Davis was accomplishing.

And later, it was Henry who led Davis home again. By that time, Davis had accumulated a fortune and Old Paul was on the verge of bankruptcy. Davis had hesitated about helping his father back to solvency and

Henry had stepped in with gentle encouragement, saying that families were like the willow trees at Blackhall—the branches were tender shoots trembling in the wind but their roots were remarkable for their size, toughness, and ability to endure.

"Henry, listen to me," Davis said, looking him in the eyes. Henry looked scared. "Henry. Now, listen carefully. That was the one and only time you will ever, and I mean *ever*, talk to the police. Got it? They will be back and they are going to try to isolate you and get you to talk. You tell them you want a lawyer. Do not say any other words. I want a lawyer. Period. Okay?" Davis searched Henry's eyes.

Henry nodded.

Davis patted Henry's back. "Good."

Henry struggled to his feet. "I need to show you something." Henry opened a storage closet in the back of the cottage, stood on a stool, and pulled down a battered red box with a heavy brass clasp. There was a yellowed piece of thick parchment inside.

"Look at this," Henry said, poking a wrinkled finger at the document.

Davis started reading and slowly sat down. He looked up at Henry. "This is the rest of Josephine Rideout's suicide note. Where the hell did you find it?"

"High up in that closet on the back shelf."

"I wonder how it got there," Davis muttered.

"Don't know but it's been there a long time."

Davis read further and wiped sweat from his forehead. "Did you read this?"

Henry put his hand on Davis's shoulder. "Yes, son, I did."

Davis griped the arm of his chair, his knuckles turning white. "Do you think this is what happened?"

"I don't like to think so, but I told you I seen Josephine Rideout walking along the cliff. She's making trouble, yes she is."

"Don't start with that stuff. Josephine has been dead for centuries."

"Ain't never stopped her yet."

Davis ran his hand through his hair. "Jesus Christ."

"Now, we can't go mentioning this to anyone," Henry said.

Davis nodded thoughtfully. "You're right. This remains between the two of us."

****

I heard the front door scrape open, then close with a clunk. A few seconds later, Davis appeared in the library doorway, frowning. He sat down heavily across from us and pulled a pack of cigarettes from his pocket. He'd been smoking a lot, much more than usual.

He eyed me.

"How's the security system going?" I asked.

"I've already spoken with Tech Security."

I wanted to pull Davis aside, away from Reed, and ask why his gate code was in Eden's diary. But he'd just given Ruth his statement. He wasn't about to tell a Supreme Court Justice—family or not—that he'd lied to the FBI. And he wasn't about to tell me he'd cheated on Reed. I'd have to investigate on my own. I glanced at my watch. It was after midnight. "I'd better get home."

Reed stood. "Daddy, are you sure you don't want to stay the night?"

"No, I have to get going. Claire's expecting me."

CHAPTER 22

FBI Director Mortich paced the floor of his office. He stopped, put his hands on the windowsill and observed the rain sweeping down Pennsylvania Avenue. Through churning dark clouds, a red light atop the Washington Monument blinked a warning to a caravan of three military choppers swooping down to transport the President.

"God Almighty. The President is off to Camp David. Poor bastard." Mortich twisted around to look at Ruth. "What about the DNA results?" Mortich ran a hand through his hair, a blanket of steel wire. Sprouts of hair broke through the skin on his hands like new shoots through soil. A few strays jutted from his ears. It was inevitable that he was the butt of a long-running joke in the Bureau about being walking proof of Darwin's theory. Not that anyone would dare say that to his face.

"The skulls found at Blackhall are old," Ruth said. "The DNA shows they were probably sisters but they're definitely not Eden and Echo Hines."

"You informed the President?"

"As you requested, sir."

"You said something about a smell at the house?"

"I talked to the police who investigated the decanter stolen from the Rideout estate. They said the house smelled like a dead animal but when they talked with me, they agreed it could've been the aftermath of decomposing bodies."

Mortich ran the pad of his hand over the back of his leather chair. Behind his desk, rifles and guns were displayed in a dark mahogany bookcase. His prize, center stage, was a long sword, blood ossified on the blade, used in the Revolutionary War by one of his ancestors who'd fought alongside General Daniel Morgan at Saratoga. "The point is," he said, "dead animals are common in the countryside. What about Turnbull and Rideout? What did they say?"

"Turnbull said he was at Biggy's Bar in Annapolis from 10:00 to 2:00 in the morning. I checked. The security camera outside the bar confirms Turnbull left at 2:00 on the dot."

"And Rideout?"

"His wife confirms that he left his house in Washington for his office in Georgetown about 7:00. He says he worked in his office for an hour. We were able to confirm the time he left the District by picking up his car on traffic cameras. He says he drove to Blackhall, ostensibly to pick up some documents. We have no reason not to believe that. And his pilots gave his arrival time at BWI at 1:30. Security cameras at the airport and flight logs confirm their statements."

"Do you have anything else?"

"No."

"So, you have a dead animal. Congratulations." He shot her an angry look.

"Sir—"

"Give me one reason why Davis Rideout would kill those girls. It doesn't make sense."

"I looked into Rideout's history in Annapolis. He has a wild reputation that started as a teenager. And after his parents died, he was known for having sex orgies at the estate."

"Are there court records about the orgies? Police reports to back up the stories? Divorce records with actual proof attached as evidence?"

"Well, no."

"We need a hell of a lot more than gripes from pissed off husbands to take on someone like Davis Rideout, and oh, let's not forget his father-in-law, Mr. Supreme Court Justice." Mortich scowled and jabbed a finger in Ruth's face. "That's money and political power. With those types of resources, you'd better have an iron-clad case."

Ruth started pacing the room. "Rideout recently met the twins at a White House dinner. He has a secluded estate on the Chesapeake Bay. There was a decomposition smell of some sort at the estate. He's the type of man the twins were interested in, good looking, accomplished, rich … married. Rideout fits the profile."

"A few days ago, you were questioning the profile."

"I was wrong."

Mortich threw his hands in the air. "Which time? See, you're not even sure now. What would Rideout's motive be?"

"We think there were restraints, sex toys, in the Gucci bag. Things went awry—"

"So you say."

"Please sir, hear me out. I suspect Rideout tied the restraints too tight and the girls choked. He panicked and covered up the crime."

"Rideout's a lawyer. A smart lawyer. Why would he be stupid enough to cover up an accident and make things worse?"

"He'd be facing involuntary manslaughter. Minimum. There's no way he'd avoid jail time. And there's the scandal aspect." Ruth sighed. "There's something else. I'm not sure what to make of it but Warren Alexander didn't tell me Rideout had a house near the Bay Bridge even though Rideout fit his own profile."

"Did he explain why?"

"Says it never occurred to him but I think he was protecting his daughter's husband."

"You think he would stick his neck out that far?"

"She's his daughter."

Mortich nodded thoughtfully. "What about this Henry Turnbull character? What's his background?"

"Family has a history with the Rideouts. His father trained horses for Paul Rideout, Davis Rideout's father. Turnbull is the caretaker at Blackhall and he has one prior arrest for a bar fight."

Mortich gave Ruth a withering look. "Find out more about Turnbull," he said. "If Davis Rideout murdered Eden and Echo Hines, he hopped on a plane before he had time to clean up his mess. If that's the case, Turnbull helped him. Jam your knee into Turnbull's throat, threaten him, tell him he's going to be charged with Murder One, tell him anything that will make him talk. An old man like that doesn't want to spend his golden years staring at a jail cell wall. And, Dr. Jacobson …"

"Yes?"

"I know you wanted Alexander on board but it's time to stop being so Goddamn trusting."

CHAPTER 23

I was holding the newspaper. On page one was a photograph of Reed and Davis standing in their front yard, archeologists behind them clustered under a tent that shaded the old Rideout graves. The headline read: *Unusual Discovery of 18th Century Graves.* Reed looked sunny and fresh, a brilliant white smile displayed for the camera. Davis was gritting his teeth, looking sullen. He didn't want to be in the photo.

I needed to forget about Davis and Eden and Echo for the evening. Tonight was the law clerks' going away party. Jake and my other clerks had suggested we cancel because of Lilly's disappearance, but the party was a Court-wide event and everyone would be there, all the Justices and all of their law clerks. I thought my clerks would eventually regret missing the last function of the year, so I'd insisted that we all appear and make an effort to be social.

It was six-thirty and the party would start at seven in the Supreme Court Grand Reception Room. Photographers would be circulating among the guests, and my clerks could have their photos taken with the other Justices and have the chance to say goodbye to the other law clerks. A buffet and a decent assortment of wines, followed by desert, would be served. Nothing too expensive, but nice.

I'd just spoken with Claire who was on her way over from her law firm. I was about to head down the hall and get an early glass of wine when the phone rang. It was Tabitha.

"I'm glad you called," I said. "I wanted to remind you about the press conference tomorrow morning. I'll see you there with the composite sketch. Nine o'clock, sharp."

"Actually, Justice Alexander, that's why I called. Did you see that guy in the newspaper, the one out in Maryland with the old graves in his yard?"

"You mean Davis Rideout?"

"Yes, that's his name."

I tensed. "What about him?"

"He's the guy I saw with Lilly!"

I sucked in my breath. "You said the guy you saw with Lilly was her age."

"Well, gee, the guy's buff so he looks young in person. Y'know, his physique and the way he carries himself, but that's his face. For sure."

I must've blanked out because the next thing I remembered was Tabitha saying, "Hello? Are you still there?"

"Yes, Tabitha, I'm still here."

I don't know why I was so surprised. Davis and Reed had attended the annual Supreme Court Christmas party as my guests and I vaguely remembered seeing Davis talking with Lilly.

I went ahead with the press conference the next morning. The D.C. Police Chief and detectives working on the case made an appearance. I reminded the public that Lilly was still missing and asked anyone with information to please call the District of Columbia police. But, now, there was no reason to publicize the composite drawing. The bottom line? I needed to confront Davis.

****

Lucy Diamond's fingers trailed down Davis's naked body and began stroking his cock, exactly how he liked it, but he remained at half-mast. She moved to his balls, cupping them, fondling them in her hand, hoping that would excite him.

A sudden jerk against her shoulder and Davis rolled away from her. "Damn it," he said, looking down at himself.

Lucy fluffed her long blonde hair and pulled silk sheets over their naked bodies. "Don't get so upset. It happens to everyone." Lucy leaned back on the pillows in the antique French bed and studied the rock crystal chandelier dripping glittering sprinkles of light over their bodies. Her apartment was only four rooms in the French Quarter but because the ceilings were tall and the rooms were large, Lucy had been able to decorate in an elaborate way that made it look like the inside of a mansion.

"Not to me," Davis snapped, eyes closed, fists clenched.

"Are you worried about something at your company?"

"No." He threw his legs over the edge of the bed and fumbled for a pack of cigarettes in his jacket. He'd been smoking way too much. It was starting to affect his health. Maybe that's why he couldn't get it up. *Jesus.* He crumpled the pack and tossed it into a wastebasket.

"You're traveling a lot," Lucy said. "And now you're going to Cambodia. All that jet lag would get to anyone."

He glanced across the room to Lucy's full-length mirror and studied himself. He was carrying bags under his eyes. The emotional toll was getting to him. He didn't know how much longer he could go on this way. He was desperate to forget about Eden and Echo. They haunted him day and night and now they were following him from bed to bed.

He lay back down. "I flew down here just to see you," he said, flipping the sheets back so he could see Lucy's body. Beautiful. Breasts round as melons, flat tummy, skin as pink and translucent as fine porcelain. If anything could focus his attention, it was Lucy's luscious shape. He traced his hand down her side, admiring her hourglass figure. His finger slid over her tummy toward the v between her legs.

"You did?" She wiggled toward him on the bed.

Davis grabbed Lucy's hips, pressed against them and felt heat rush through his groin. He looked down. Nothing. *Christ.* "Yes, you. I miss you." He slid his arms around her and held her close. "Do you like New Orleans?" Maybe if he kept talking, Eden's and Echo's faces would fade into the shadows.

"It's okay, not as exciting as Washington, though. I may move back."

"How's your job with Senator Thompson?"

She giggled. "I think he's more interested in my body than the body of politics." She paused. "Honestly? The political scene here is boring and he's an old, fat letch. He's disgusting. I hate him."

Davis laughed. "Other than that, how was the theater, Mrs. Lincoln?"

"What?"

He smiled. "Okay, what *would* you like to do?"

She sighed. "I'm still thinking about that." She twirled a lock of hair around and around. "You'd think I'd know by now, wouldn't you?"

Davis gave her a deep kiss. "If you move back to Washington, I could buy a house for you."

"Don't tease me," she said, poking a finger into his chest.

"I'm not. I miss you." He was being honest with Lucy. He did miss her. Unlike Reed, she had no expectations of him.

"What about Reed?" she pouted.

"She couldn't know."

He swallowed hard and his face started burning. *Reed ... Eden and Echo ... and his lies to the FBI.*

It wouldn't be long before the FBI found out what had happened. It would be impossible to hide it forever and then he'd go to jail and little Samuel would grow up without a father. Reed would divorce him and turn Samuel against him. And he wouldn't blame her because it was all his fault. All of it. And here he was ... with Lucy instead of Reed.

He'd fled his marriage the moment he said *I do*. Work, travel, other women. If he was honest with himself, he knew it wasn't so much about Reed. Deep down, he was worried about Samuel. Davis's heart sank, thinking about the possibility of repeating his father's mistakes, perpetuating a cycle of anger and violence, and Samuel ending up hating him the way he'd hated his own father. He couldn't face that. And now, he was going down a chute straight to jail.

"Are you okay?" Lucy peered at him. He was white as the sheet on the bed.

"Yeah." He swallowed hard.

"What about getting some dinner?" she suggested. "There's a great French restaurant on the corner."

He gagged, dived for the wastebasket and heaved.

Lucy jumped up, pulling the sheets with her. "Oh, my God!"

He came up, gasping for air, hoping it was over. He tried to stand but collapsed back onto the bed. "Give me a minute. I'm okay."

"No, you're not," she said, peering into the wastebasket. "There's blood in your vomit!"

Davis couldn't catch his breath. "I think I have an ulcer," he said between pants.

Lucy started pulling her clothes on. "I'm taking you to the emergency room."

"No! I'll see a doctor when I get home."

CHAPTER 24

After a day of shopping and lugging Samuel around, Reed was glad to be back at Blackhall. She shut off the car's engine and clicked her seat belt open, immediately noticing that the mansion's front door was open. Henry wouldn't leave it that way.

Something was wrong. She hurriedly unstrapped Samuel from his baby seat and carted him up the stairs. A funny smell hit her nose. Pungent, smoky. My God. What was going on? She rushed down the hallway. All the doors and windows were wide-open. Behind her, someone was talking. She spun around and spotted Henry in the library, waving a bundle of smoking leaves, the smoke drifting into the corners of the room and along the ceiling.

Henry kept repeating, "I cleanse this room of all spirits and ghosts. I cleanse…"

Reed was so transfixed by the scene that she almost dropped Samuel. "Henry! What are you doing?"

Henry turned to Reed. "Oh! Mrs. Rideout. This is sage. See the smoke floatin' out the windows? It's taking the bad spirits to the light where they'll find God."

"What bad spirits?" she asked tentatively. She thought Henry had been acting strange lately.

"Mrs. Rideout," he said, waving the bundle of smoking sage. "Bad things don't happen in places by accident." His eyes grew wide. "There's evil spirits in here relivin' their lives. My Grandma said spirits do that sometimes." He shuddered, remembering his Grandma's crinkled face and cunning grin, squatting in her garden in a raggedy nightgown, mixing potions in an old tin can. That woman knew too much of bad things.

And worse, she'd told him he had the gift.

"Our family came off a slave ship right here in Annapolis harbor centuries ago and they brought knowledge of spirits with them that they passed down, all the way to my Grandma herself."

"What do you think happened here that was so bad?" Reed whispered.

"Long ago? Josephine Rideout killing her baby. More recently?" He hesitated. "That's hard to say, hard to say." He shook his head, looking sad. "But I've seen Josephine Rideout in her long green dress like she'd just stepped out of that old painting in the gallery, yes I have. She walks along the cliff edge, looking for her baby."

Reed's mouth fell open. "The woman who lived here in the 1780s?"

"Yes, ma'am."

"You're freaking me out."

"I'm sorry, Mrs. Rideout."

She slid into a chair and wiped some dribble from Samuel's chin, thinking. "Henry, do you believe in synchronicity?"

"Don't know what that is."

Reed bounced Samuel up and down in her lap. "It's a theory. You said bad things don't happen in places by accident. Synchronicity is sorta like that. It's hard to explain although the general idea is that life is not a series of random events, that people experience connections with personal meaning and they have no way to explain how the connections come about."

"That sounds right to me."

She sighed. "Daddy says there is no such thing as coincidence. He says that if I had spent any time in law enforcement, I wouldn't either."

He smiled patiently. "Oh, I don't think that's coincidence you're talking about, Mrs. Rideout. Sounds to me like your soul is attractin' people and places into your life. And none of us know how to explain that, now do we? That's one of God's mysteries."

Reed was deep in thought. "Henry, there's something that I've been meaning to mention that's been bothering me. Sometimes I get up in the middle of the night and there are spots of liquid on the floor. What do you think that is?"

Henry scratched the side of his face. "Could be a leak in the roof. Or could be something my Grandma called ectoplasm. She told me all about that, yes, she did. Y'see, spirits can leave behind slime when they're trying to manifest themselves."

Reed's eyes popped wide. "Are you serious?"

"Ain't for nothing that I'm cleansing this house!"

"Are you sure?"

He stopped to face her. "I've seen it myself, Mrs. Rideout, yes I have. When I was a little boy. My Grandma was in the middle of a cleansing when—splat! A spirit got her, right on the shoulder. I remember it like yesterday." Henry spread the fingers of his left hand and his voice grew low and eerie. "An electric charge hit the room. I saw sparks flyin' off her fingertips. Saw it myself, yes, I did. The spirits need electricity to reveal themselves." He nodded for emphasis.

"God, that's awful," she said, her mouth turning down as she sat motionless while Henry continued waving the sage. She finally spoke. "Henry, did you know the floorboards creak at night? They sound like long groans or more often, bird-like chirps. It's creepy. Do you think that has anything to do with spirits?"

He smiled kindly. "Oh, that's normal. That's just old floors. Ain't nothing to worry about, Mrs. Rideout."

"When I'm in bed?"

Henry scratched his chin. "The floors could be making noise when it gets cool at night. Temperature changes can make the seams buckle open when it's cool and close up again when it gets hot. These old floors do that."

"This is different." She stared at him as he paced back and forth with the sage. "Are you listening?"

He smiled patiently, placed the smoking bundle in a glass bowl, and sat down beside her.

"You see, I keep dreaming about birds," she said, a look of concern creeping into her eyes. "It'll be in the wee hours of the morning and I'll be dreaming about a flock of geese flying right over my head. I see the sun, it's very bright, then I hear the birds flapping and feel the breeze from their wings and I wake up, and I'm aware I was dreaming but I'm scared to death because I know the noise I heard wasn't a dream. It was real, it was the floorboards creaking and someone is going to be walking across the floor toward me. But there's no one there." She wrapped her arms around Samuel. "It scares me."

He patted her shoulder. "Now, now. You shouldn't worry about that, Mrs. Rideout. The living can't get in here to hurt you. There's no reason for you to be afraid of them. It's the dead you should be afraid of."

CHAPTER 25

Reed burped little Samuel against her shoulder, trying to forget her conversation with Henry about dead people and creaking floorboards. She shuddered. *So creepy.*

Samuel smiled at her, a great big baby grin, and she burst into a smile and clapped her hands. She lived for these moments and she kissed Samuel's warm cheek before putting him down in his cradle for a nap, the same cradle that rocked Davis when he was a baby in this very house.

She had a couple of babysitters on call but so far, hadn't hired any full-time help, although Davis had suggested hiring two nannies, one for the day nursery, another for the night. That way, he'd said, they could finally get a decent night's sleep. Reed had snapped back that she was not about to hire two little temptations to flounce around under his nose. Davis had laughed like that was some sort of great joke but she knew better. She knew Daddy was right when it came to Davis and women.

She sighed. All she ever wanted was a family and someone to love. For most of her friends, that wasn't enough. All of her girlfriends had big careers. They had so much to offer the world, so much more than she ever would have. She remembered how relieved her father had been when she'd graduated from college. She wasn't the smartest person in the world and she'd barely gotten into a college, a small, struggling school on the west coast. The lowest ranked college in the country. But her acceptance had occasioned a big celebration at home!

Her major had been physical education. She was quite a talented volley ball player but that hadn't translated into a paying job. She'd been lucky to score a job as a television correspondent with CBS through one of her father's friends. The producers said she was a natural, the camera loved her, but she was also expected to do investigative reporting. She was at a loss about how to go about that and was hesitant about asking for help, which was interpreted as being lazy, and when people started whispering about nepotism, her chances of remaining at the station quickly dwindled.

And where did that leave her? Out in the cold. She knew her blonde, ethereal type of beauty wouldn't last long. So, for her, more than for other women, it was imperative to find a man when she was young and her beauty was still fresh because truth be told, she needed someone to take care of her. She wasn't proud about that but she didn't have to be brilliant to be realistic. And when Davis proposed, her dream had come true! The most eligible bachelor in Washington had married her and now she had everything she ever wanted. She had a handsome husband and a beautiful baby and hopefully, they'd have another baby soon. They were working on it.

✦✦✦✦

That night, Reed felt an odd sense of trepidation as she undressed for bed. She slipped into pink silk pajamas, tucked Samuel into his crib, and climbed into the same bed that John and Josephine Rideout had slept in, an old Colonial four-poster with an elaborate, blue and white silk canopied top that depicted—of all things—birds in flight. Everything in this room was thought to have been the same as when Josephine occupied it. The fireplace mantel that was taller than most men, the oriental rugs rumored to be priceless, the old cherry wood chests and dressers, silver jars on a table. Josephine had probably chosen everything herself.

That idea, which never bothered her before, now crawled under her skin like a wriggling worm, and she tossed and turned for a long time before finally drifting off. But like previous nights, her dreams were once again filled with the cries of approaching birds. Right over the house. A wedge of geese, a raft of ducks, a pitying of turtle doves. So many birds! Wings blocked the sky! Flapping wings, so close, right in her ear, so much noise! Her head began swirling. Danger! Danger!

She gasped, woke up with a start. Complete silence. She was sure someone was in the room. She quietly swung her foot over the bed and touched something wet on the floor. Ick! She jerked her foot back, flipped on the bedside lamp, and waited while her eyes adjusted. She leaned down and squinted. On the floor was some liquid. Damn. It *did* look like slime.

A little spark zapped her wrist and static billowed her pajama top. Electricity. Just like Henry said! She froze, certain that Josephine Rideout was in the room. *Her room.* Nothing moved. The only sound, Samuel cooing in his sleep.

After a few minutes, Reed bent over and looked under the bed. No one was there. *The closet.* Shit. The old door was slightly ajar. She grabbed a poker from the fireplace and tiptoed across the room. Holding the poker above her head, she opened the closet door. Her clothes stared back at her. She yanked them back. Nothing. She returned to the canopied bed, pulling Samuel's crib closer and checking the battery in her cell phone, making sure it was charged in case she needed to call Henry.

She sank into the pillows but was soon seized by a strange and over-whelming desire to look at the portrait of Josephine Rideout in the grand gallery. She threw back the covers, slipped into the hallway, and flipped the hall switch. It didn't work. Damn. The circuit breaker. *Again.*

The moon was a slit of light on the staircase and she floated down the passage to the kitchen where she grabbed a flashlight. She clicked it on. The batteries were low, and the light was a dim yellow, just enough to guide her to the grand gallery and the ancient portraits hanging on the walls.

The flashlight flickered across Josephine's face like candlelight at a dinner party. Josephine was wearing a large emerald ring and a green silk taffeta dress with a low-cut bodice and white lace cuffs that fluttered loosely over her fingertips. Josephine was an heiress and everything about her reflected her upbringing. Her back was ramrod straight and her shiny brown hair pulled into an elegant knot behind delicate diamond earrings. And her hands ... the artist had perfectly captured the translucent skin on Josephine's hands that were as white as the hands of a ceramic doll. These were hands that had never seen the sun, fine little blue-veined hands that belonged to an exotic bird, not a flesh and blood woman.

Behind Josephine stood her husband, John Rideout, full of pomp, a notorious *bon vivant,* the initiator of many an adulterous affair. His resemblance to Davis was uncanny, although his expression was different, even sinister. The little boy, Daniel, wrapped his arms tightly around Josephine's waist as he pouted and peered from the canvas. A baby in white lace bounced on Josephine's lap, smiling happily. He didn't know his fate. Henry had told her the baby's name was Samuel and he'd died when Josephine jumped off the cliff, clutching him in her arms. One hundred feet. Ten stories. An instantaneous death.

Reed shivered. She remembered the first time she'd stood in front of the portrait and how she'd identified with Josephine, a young mother with a philandering husband, but that was before she knew Josephine had killed her baby. And what was the likelihood of Josephine's baby being named Samuel like her own son? It was disturbing. She looked out the window at the vast Chesapeake Bay, ever-changing with the weather and the light. Tonight, it was a slick sheen, quivering and menacing, a black drink silently waiting for prey.

For Josephine to contemplate killing her baby, then to actually jump off that cliff with him! John Rideout must've done something terrible to provoke such a drastic act although they would never know what because the portion of Josephine Rideout's suicide note explaining her actions had been lost long ago, sealed in another time like flecks in a snow globe.

A long groan upstairs, right over her head. Then, a bird-like chirp and another. Her heart stopped. Someone was walking across the floor in the master bedroom.

Josephine!

Josephine was alone with Samuel. Reed flew up the stairs, tripped on the hem of her pajamas and fell, scraping her hands on the wood floors. A black shadow disappeared into the wall at the end of the hall. Frantic, she picked herself up and rushed into the master bedroom, to Samuel's crib. He was blue.

Samuel was dead!

Her heart gave away. She grabbed Samuel. He cried out. Her knees buckled with relief and she barely caught herself. Samuel had just been sleeping soundly and his color, a trick of the moonlight. She clutched him to her chest and exhaled, her heart pumping wildly. Damn. She'd given herself an awful fright and holding him tightly, she staggered to the bed, her nerves jangling like keys on a chain.

She collapsed into the deep pillows, rocking Samuel, snuggling him into the crook of her arm and kissing his sweet little cheek, her eyes wet with tears, relieved that her baby was safe, determined that Josephine would never get to them again.

CHAPTER 26

A few days later, two teenagers illicitly rock climbing along Blackhall's cliff wall spied something strange. It was a human arm sticking out of the ground, looking for all the world like it was waving at them to come take a closer look. Animals had dug up a body.

Law enforcement descended. Ruth was among the first to arrive. The area was roped off and the FBI's best forensic technicians began processing the crime scene. It had been three weeks since Eden and Echo Hines disappeared and advanced putrefaction made the corpses unidentifiable, but the short white dresses tossed on top their naked bodies left little doubt as to their identity. Any lingering uncertainty was squelched when a Gucci overnight bag was found smashed and torn beneath them. All of their S&M toys were still inside. The President's twin daughters had been found.

✴✴✴✴

Mortich was concerned about the President's mental state. The President's eyes were crazy, threatening—*bullets loaded into a chamber.* The President was trying to control his rage but any pressure on the trigger …

Mortich tapped the fingers of his left hand. "We have a crime scene, the autopsy results are in, and the FBI lab is treating this like JFK's assassination. We'll get some solid forensics."

"Did you find semen?"

"Do you really want the details, sir?" Mortich asked.

"Yes." The President clenched his fists, held them both to his mouth like he was trying not to scream.

"There's sperm. It's at the FBI lab right now. Hopefully, we'll get a DNA profile."

The President nodded as the information sank in. "What's the likelihood of that?"

"It's been almost three weeks. However, sperm cells are slow to degrade in a dead body. If we do get a profile, we'll run it through CODIS."

The President glared at him through tortoiseshell glasses. "How long before we know something? *Anything!*"

Mortich involuntarily flinched. "Soon," he said.

"Cause of death?"

"Eden had one fracture on the back of her head. Consistent with a blow or perhaps a serious fall. Echo was stabbed in the heart."

"Stabbed. Are you sure?" The President's face filled with rage and purple blood.

"Yes, sir."

The President stood and picked up an oversized photo of his daughters smiling and laughing as a golden retriever licked their faces. He clutched the photo to his chest and closed his eyes tightly, a steady stream of tears escaping his eyelids, sliding to his chin, dripping onto his starched shirt.

"I'm sorry, sir," Mortich softly.

The President kept his eyes closed. "You'd better get the sick bastard who did this to them," he said quietly.

Mortich had seen it all in his forty years in law enforcement. The President was a ticking time bomb.

The President stumbled back to his chair and sank deep, hunched over, hugging the photo, rocking it back and forth.

"Sir," Mortich said, "a search warrant for Blackhall is being drawn up even as we speak."

The President didn't respond. He just stared at the photo of his daughters and traced a finger over their faces.

Mortich left and walked down the hallway. A loud, long wail broke the silence. Mortich paused, then kept on walking.

****

Henry stood on a rise overlooking the spot in the forest where Eden's and Echo's bodies had been discovered. A white tent covered the crime scene, technicians fluttering inside the canvas like moths caught in a lampshade.

An agent came out of the tent and spotted Henry. "Hey you! This is a restricted area!"

Henry turned and threaded his way back up the hill, through pockets of groaning willow trees. A willow branch caught the wind and lashed his face. Henry stopped, his cheek stinging. Made him think back decades ago, to his grandmother's purple-veined hand tugging and pulling him as he dragged his little legs in protest. She'd taken him to a graveyard on a hill, under a cluster of old elms where small, broken twigs laid on the ground like gnarled fingers snipped off.

It had been scorching hot, dead still, until they entered that small gated cemetery where dozens of crows screeched and cawed, gathered together like they had something important to discuss. Opening that gate opened a door to another world. Wind stung his eyes, ruffled his hair, whipped his shirt up off his belly and flew in his face, smothering him in a vortex that sucked the air from the bottom of his lungs. *Spirits,* his grandma had said. *Show respect, son.*

Henry continued the climb up the hill to the mansion. When he reached the top, he spotted Reed in the distance, dressed in a long white dress, standing at the edge of the cliff. Little Samuel was in her arms. *God almighty.* He broke into a sweat, rushed down the lawn to where she stood, slowed, and walked the remaining few paces.

"Mrs. Rideout?"

Reed turned. "Oh, hi, Henry," she said, her hair fluttering in the wind. She tucked a strand behind her ear.

"Are you okay, ma'am?"

"Yes."

"Well, I seen you down here and with the bodies being found and all …" Henry spotted dried tear tracks on Reed's face.

She looked out over the water. "I'm fine Henry, just getting some fresh air."

"Okay. I didn't mean to disturb you. I'd best be on my way."

"Henry?" She looked at him through thick strands of blonde hair.

"Yes?"

"Would you stay with me for a while?"

"Of course."

She slid her small hand into his giant one and together they stood and looked out over the water, Henry in his old overalls, Reed in her white dress, and little Samuel in a tiny red jumpsuit.

CHAPTER 27

I was in my chambers when the news came. The President's daughters were dead. Found buried on Davis's property. Of course, I felt awful for the President. I also feared the worst for Davis. He didn't know what was about to hit him.

Claire and I raced out to Blackhall. Reed met us at the front door and stumbled into my arms. "Davis is in Cambodia," she said, her voice shaking. "His plane has a mechanical problem but he'll be back in a couple of days."

I wondered whether Davis would return. Cambodia didn't have an extradition treaty with the United States.

I sat Reed down in a chair and looked straight into her dazed eyes. "A search warrant will be executed for the house and surrounding land. Soon. Maybe tonight. More likely, first thing in the morning. The house and property will be torn apart. It isn't a place for a baby. You need to take Samuel and move back into Washington."

She nodded at me stoically.

I cancelled our long-anticipated trip to Switzerland. Claire helped Reed pack. The plan was for Reed, Samuel, and Claire to leave for Washington first thing in the morning. Henry, too. The FBI would kick everyone off the estate during the search. So, that's how it progressed. Everyone else left for Washington long before the crack of dawn. I stayed, hoping to speak with the agents and ameliorate any serious damage to the property.

The FBI soon arrived to execute their warrant. Ruth was with them. As I'd expected, she ignored me. She directed the agents to the main house where they started an initial walk-through, videotaping each room, taking photographs of potential evidence, entering descriptions into a photo log, and sealing and labeling items before toting them to a waiting truck. The technicians meticulously examined each room and tested everything for blood evidence. In the library, luminol revealed a large stain on the rug that looked like a massive blue cloud. Someone had tried to clean up blood, a lot of blood.

The FBI uncovered most of the incriminating evidence the first day. For example, the car. When the agents entered the stable, a whoop went up like I'd never heard. Sitting in the stable was the twins' old Porsche everyone had been desperately searching for. And that's how the day went, one find after another.

I finally left Blackhall at midnight, right after the FBI had informed me they'd be working through the night.

****

I checked into a sorry little motel on Rte. 50, just off Blackhall Lane. The room's carpet was a deep brown like horrible accidents were the norm. I went to bed with my socks on. Finally, I fell into a sleep so deep it felt like a coma, only to be rudely awakened by a phone call from Chief Justice Bannister Brown.

"Hmm ... Warren," he said. "Such disturbing news about the President's daughters. Such a tragedy."

"It certainly is."

I rubbed my eyes and struggled to wake up. Blinding headlights pulled into a parking space outside, illuminating the room. My watch said 1:10 a.m.

"And the most incredible thing is that you seem to be in the middle of it."

"Middle of it?" Now I was alert.

"The Hines twins were found on your son-in-law's estate!"

"Your point?"

"How do you think that makes the Supreme Court look? And now, you're acting as liaison with the FBI for your son-in-law."

"There's nothing unethical about what I'm doing."

I heard a car door slam and drunken voices raised in song, *"Fifty-two bottles of beer on the wall ..."*

Brown lost his cool. "It's ... it's ... a conflict of interest."

"There is no conflict of interest. This is not a matter before the Court."

Brown's voice hardened. "Let me warn you. It could be."

"That's what recusals are for."

The door adjacent to my room slammed and I heard someone yell, *"June bug!"* A woman giggled.

"Recusals are problematic," he said. "I didn't want to bring this up but some senators have been talking about impeachment proceedings. Against you."

"Your point?"

"What do you think my point is? You don't want to taint your family with that scandal. And that's not all. I've been watching you all year, all the Justices have, playing footsie with your girlfriend."

"Girlfriend?" My head started buzzing.

"Lilly McCleary. Your law clerk. Who, I will remind you, is now missing."

"What the hell are you talking about? Lilly and I aren't involved."

"I tried to keep the affair private, for the Court's sake, while you dilly-dallied with her, although I didn't like it. Very unethical. And now, with the spotlight thrown on your son-in-law and Lilly still missing ... well, I can't keep a lid on it forever. It's only a matter of time before someone will talk. Maybe one of your own law clerks. Thank God we know where the rest of them are. And what a shame when your wife finds out. Of course, all of this could be avoided if you resigned from the Court."

What a jackass. "I don't know what kind of game you're playing but I'm not going to be threatened by you." I hung up.

Someone pissed next door, the toilet flushed, and a man's voice said, *"June bug, spread those purdy legs. Here comes papa!"* There was a loud crash as someone landed on the bed. The woman started laughing and shrieking.

I pulled a pillow over my head and prepared myself for a sleepless night.

✶✶✶✶

Chief Justice Bannister Brown set the phone in the cradle on President Hines's desk. "There. That's what you wanted."

"Thank you, Bannister."

"I only did it because of our history together."

President Hines raised a glass of cognac. "Yes. A toast. To Princeton."

"To Princeton," Bannister agreed, studying President Hines who had acquired the disheveled appearance of an old man. He was now so thin that his shoulders looked like wire hangers holding up empty clothes. His hair had grown thin, slick, and oily and his eyes, wild and furtive.

"Shouldn't you be getting some sleep, sir? It's after midnight."

The President ignored the suggestion. "Ah yes. Princeton. Seems like yesterday," he said, draining the cognac.

"To get back to Alexander," Brown said. "There's nothing else I can do."

"What about that affair with his law clerk?" President Hines scowled.

Chief Brown stirred uncomfortably in his chair. "I don't know, sir. That affair with his law clerk is just a rumor. Our law clerks work long hours. They need a release. I suspect the rumor is idle speculation on their part. Sort of like a game, really." Chief Brown was worried. He was walking a fine line. The President had grilled him about Alexander and Brown wanted to be honest with the President but Brown also needed to protect the Court's reputation. Future scholars would refer to Brown's reign as Chief Justice as *The Brown Court* and even the whiff of a scandal could reflect on his good name.

The President eyed the bottom of his glass and poured another round of golden-brown liquid. "I was begging for Alexander's help and he knew where my girls were all the time." He pointed a finger in Brown's face. "Alexander's son-in-law killed my children and I'm going to make Goddamn sure they're both strung up! And you, my friend, are gonna help me."

CHAPTER 28

"Henry, this will be your room," Reed said, smiling at Henry who was looking around, open-mouthed, suitcases in hand. The bedroom in the Rideout's Massachusetts Heights mansion was furnished with antiques. Yellow satin draperies pooled onto the floor and a black marble fireplace dominated one end of the room. Through a door, Henry could see a matching black marble bathroom fitted with walls of beveled mirrors and another fireplace for frosty winter morning bathing.

Henry shook his head. "Me-oh-my. Mrs. Rideout, this is too grand for the likes of me."

She put her arm around Henry's shoulders and gave him a little squeeze. "Nothing is too good for you, Henry. I just want you to be comfortable."

He seemed to consider that. "Well, what kinds of jobs can I do around the house? Make myself useful."

"What about relaxing for a change? The house is brand new. There's nothing to fix." She picked up a remote and pointed it at the fireplace. "Here's something you might like. A flat screen TV." She pushed a button and a painting over the mantel slid back to reveal a sleek black box.

"This is all so different from Blackhall." He shook his head. "Don't get me wrong, Blackhall's nice but it's old and we don't have flat screen TVs."

"That's not all," she said brightly. "We have a tennis court and a swimming pool." She crooked her head to one side. "Actually, I don't know what you like to do in your spare time. You'll have to tell me and whatever it is, I'll make sure it's available for you."

"Thank you. That's awful nice, yes, it is," he said, setting old suitcases on the plush white carpet.

She smiled at the tattered brown leather vessels, incongruous in the swanky room. "I'll let you unpack, settle in. Dinner is at seven. I moved it up for you because I know you like to eat early. I have to go downstairs now and talk to the cook."

His eyes widened. "You have a cook?"

"We live a different life here." She laughed and rolled her eyes. "Davis's life." She headed toward the door. "We're having steak, your favorite."

He sat down on the bed and started fiddling with the remote.

✶✶✶✶

The second day of the FBI search dawned wet and dreary. Knots of grey clouds tumbled in a brisk wind skipping off the water. While other agents deployed to small dependencies dotting the grounds and divers scoured the depths of the Chesapeake Bay, Jonesie and Ruth started for the mansion.

"Dr. Jacobson!"

Ruth whirled around. Robertson, the agent in charge of searching the shoreline, came running up to her. "You need to see something."

Ruth and Jonesie followed Robertson through deep brush and into a dense, verdant forest. "Where are we going?" Ruth asked, as she slipped on a crop of moss-covered rocks.

"You'll see," he said, thrashing through the undergrowth.

A mile or so later, they came to a clearing. Ruth could make out traces of an old path leading to the cliff edge.

"Look over the edge," Robertson directed.

Ruth inched closer, spied two dilapidated wooden handrails buried under weeds and brush. She peered down. She could make out the skeletal remains of an old staircase crisscrossing the towering cliff face, ninety feet in height.

"How old do you think the staircase is?" she asked.

"Turn of the century, 1900 or earlier."

"What's it doing way out here?"

"Could've been access to a boat dock that's washed away. This is the only place on the property with beach access. The staircase has obviously been forgotten. Can't see it from the cliff or the shoreline unless you're practically on top of it."

"Think it would take any weight?"

"We tested the bottom rungs. It can take the weight of a man but I wouldn't want to climb it. It's rickety and several rungs are missing, two, three at a time. Too much weight could pull it off the cliff, snap it like a rubber band."

Ruth exhaled, looking at the white caps swirling far below. "Hmmm. Any footprints in the sand?"

"No. The tide washes everything away."

Ruth looked off into the distance. On the Chesapeake Bay, some Coast Guard boats surrounded several small motor boats. "What the hell? Is that the press?"

"Yeah. They're trying to get to the crime scene but the Coast Guard is keeping them at bay." He smiled.

Ruth smiled back at his little joke. Very clever.

✶✶✶✶

Day three of the FBI search and Ruth and Jonesie were in the mansion, searching for the entrance to the attic. There had to be one. They could see the fan-shaped windows at the top of the house. Now, how to get up there?

In a guest bedroom, they finally spotted something hopeful. The wood floor had fresh scrape marks leading to a highboy chest shoved up against the back wall. Jonesie pushed the chest to one side and behold, there was the attic door.

"I wonder why…," Jonsie said.

"It can't be good," Ruth replied. "No one closes off an attic." She pulled the old iron latch up, peered in. "Look at this." Ruth pointed to a broom at the foot of the steps. The straw was dark red, almost black. Looked like dried blood and a trail of it continued up the stairs.

They drew their guns and ascended the stairs, quiet, nerves on edge. The steps were steep, almost straight up. Old insulation dangled from the ceiling, heavy with spider webs. Ruth spit cobwebs from her mouth.

At the top of the stairs, Ruth scanned a vast sea of old furniture coated in centuries of dirt and grime. She kicked aside a broken chair and wound her way through the debris. Old frames that once held paintings were discarded in a corner. The rest of the furniture was cracked, old, and chipped, and most of the larger pieces had a leg or two broken off. Didn't look like anyone had been up here in years.

Except for the blood.

They followed the trail to the small fan-shaped window where a large chest sat. As they got closer, a smell began seeping into the room. The chest lid was smudged, like someone had recently handled it. Bits of straw, matted with blood, stuck to the floor. The smell from the chest became awful, unmistakable.

Ruth looked at Jonesie. "Stand back," she said, her heart racing. "This isn't going to be good." Ruth pulled on some plastic gloves, bent over, and flipped the latch.

Shit. She threw her arm across her nose and violently jerked backwards. Inside the chest was a dead woman. Bloated and black. Face unrecognizable. Powdered lime everywhere. Jonesie doubled over and barfed.

****

Later that day, Ruth conferred with Mortich.

"Does Alexander know about the body?" Mortich asked.

"No, sir. Alexander had returned to his motel and didn't come back to the estate."

"You think it's his law clerk?"

"The physical description matches Lilly McCleary, about five foot eight inches tall, long black hair, small boned, and the clothing matches what she was last seen wearing."

"Okay. Identifying this third body could give us a common denominator among all three women. We'll get forensics but because of where the bodies ended up, it would be odd if the same person didn't commit all three murders."

"Yes, sir."

"Has your investigation into Lilly McCleary's disappearance uncovered anything that could implicate Justice Alexander? Rideout isn't the only one with access to Blackhall."

Ruth hesitated. "No, sir."

"Okay, this development stays confidential. This new victim is our now our best investigative tool into all three deaths."

CHAPTER 29

As I'd predicted, Davis was the lead story on every political talk show in the nation, both radio and television, the subject of false reports, imagined scenarios, and scandalous innuendos.

"Rideout's a sex machine who lured the President's daughters into his lair at Blackhall. And his wife ... what a fool she is!"

People believed the stories, and after hearing them repeated time and again, began to believe that Davis killed Eden and Echo Hines. The twins were found on Davis's property and proximity equaled guilt. Innocent until proven guilty was an antiquated, noble concept destroyed by twenty-four-hour news programming.

The press, energized by soaring ratings, dug up a number of women who'd participated in orgies at Blackhall. The stories started slowly. First one, then two, and then the floodgates opened, thanks to Sandra Norris, a famous feminist attorney known for unearthing women who lived on the fringes of society and portraying them as innocent victims of wanton male aggression. In this case, a few prostitutes came forward, high-end call girls who could've been fashion models. The other women were more sophisticated and just as gorgeous.

Within days, it became an unending parade and dozens of beauties flooded the cable news shows. Exactly why was unclear. The value of their interviews seemed to be pure titillation. None of them could say Davis did anything to them that wasn't consensual. They simply wanted their fifteen minutes of fame. And the public wanted to hear their stories. Boy, did they ever.

What did Sandra get out of it? A lot. She exchanged legal represen-tation for royalties from book contracts, an arrangement that netted her far more money than the fees she could reasonably charge upfront. And her forays into the public conscience bolstered her legal practice because she was good at what she did. She carefully rehearsed each woman and they all had stories, most relating to Davis's orgies at Blackhall, that not only rang true but most likely were true. The result? The public was clamoring to see Davis hanged.

****

The stink of jet fuel filled the cavernous hanger at BWI where Davis's private jet was about to roll in. A chauffeur and black van waited nearby. I was standing by the van's door. I had a lot of questions for Davis. And I wasn't the only one. Ruth and Jonesie were also there.

"You should know," Ruth said, "that we found an old staircase leading from the shore to the top of the cliff on Davis's property. It was overgrown with vegetation and rotting out, although it could hold some weight. That may be how those burglars are getting into Blackhall."

Our conversation was interrupted by the whine of the jet. Blinking red, green, and blue navigation lights rolled toward us. The ground marshal guided the silver bird in and the jet engines died down.

I heard another roar from the direction of the terminal. Hordes of reporters were jumping up and down at the windows, a pack of animals smelling meat just beyond their reach, clawing, pacing, desperately search-ing for a way to get onto the tarmac. There was a police line trying to control the reporters but it looked thin and the police had their hands full.

The ramp descended and Davis jogged down the stairs. His jacket was soaking wet with perspiration. His mouth was drawn tight. I'd never seen Davis scared before but he was. Scared. Now.

Ruth rushed him.

Davis backed away. "Can't talk to you, Ruth, on the advice of my counsel."

And there was nothing Ruth could do about it.

Davis's chauffeur opened the door to the van.

"Let's jump in," Davis said, putting his arm around my shoulder.

"I have my car here."

"I'll have someone come back for it. C'mon." He managed a small smile.

The master of the game was about to be cut down to size. Events were out of Davis's control, something he'd never experienced before. I wondered how he would handle it. More importantly, I wanted answers.

Davis eased into the back and I took the spot across from him. The van jerked forward and he pushed a button that windowed off the driver. As soon as it clicked shut, I turned on him.

"I want to kill you," I seethed. "I can't believe you dragged my daughter into this mess."

"Okay. Let's get this over with," he said. "I had absolutely nothing to do with Eden's and Echo's deaths. I have no idea who killed them."

"Taking the Fifth, huh?"

"No. I don't know anything."

"Well, why were they at Blackhall? They were found on your property. Can you really look me in the face and deny seeing them there?"

"On that, I will take the Fifth."

"Goddamn it, Davis. This isn't a game."

Davis flashed anger. "You don't think I know it? I didn't have anything to do with the murders. And I don't know what happened."

"Are you shitting me?"

"No."

"That's all you're going to tell me?"

"That's all I know."

"Nothing?"

"Nothing."

"Who's your attorney?"

"Jerry Arnett." Davis cracked the window and sunlight glinted off his face. We were zipping along the Washington-Baltimore Parkway through a tunnel of trees and yellow and purple wild flowers. Two press vans caught up with us and jockeyed for position on the road, trying to pass and snap a photo of Davis. One came rearing up beside us, a camera raised. To no avail. Davis closed the tinted window.

"I'm sorry," he said softly.

"Tell that to your wife," I growled.

Davis melted deeper into the seat. The leather seemed to swallow him up and it occurred to me he'd lost a good ten pounds.

"You lied to the FBI about the twins and then, there's Lilly."

Davis frowned. "Lilly?"

"I have an eyewitness who saw you with her. Goddamn it. You were sleeping with her. And now, she's disappeared. Just like Eden and Echo. That's what the FBI calls a pattern."

"For God's sake, I had nothing to do with Lilly's disappearance. She's my new associate."

I stared at him. "What? Why didn't you tell me?"

"Since when do I report to you?" He hesitated. "Maybe I should've said something to Reed but I was afraid she would think … look, Lilly said she wanted to learn about mergers and acquisitions so I offered her a job. It was an easy decision for her. Three hundred thousand at a law firm versus eight hundred thousand plus stock options working for me." He glared at me, his self-righteousness returning. "Why shouldn't I hire her? You were always going on about how brilliant she is." He reached into his jacket for a cigarette, jammed one into his mouth and lit up. "And I didn't fuck her," he mumbled, the cigarette perched on his lower lip. "I keep my business separate from my personal life. I've had bad experiences in the past."

Now, that I could believe. "Why were you at her apartment?"

Davis fumed. "I saw her downtown a few weeks ago, standing at a bus stop. I gave her a ride home. Later, I dropped off a contract at her apartment."

It was difficult to believe Davis would personally drop off a contract unless he'd used it as an excuse to put the moves on Lilly. But the immediate problem was that the Hines twins had been found dead at Blackhall and Davis was the logical suspect. It didn't look good for him.

Davis opened the sun roof. The smoke coiled into a thin wisp that swirled out of the car like smoke up a chimney.

I could hardly contain my anger. "For God's sake," I hissed. "Eden wrote the code to Blackhall's gate in her diary the day she disappeared. That puts them at Blackhall with you. You've already admitted to being out there that night. The FBI hasn't figured out what the numbers mean but they will. It's just a matter of time."

Davis looked visibly shaken. "I had no reason to kill them."

"The FBI thinks Eden and Echo were blackmailing married men with sex tapes. The FBI's going to say they demanded money from you and you murdered them."

"Christ."

I averted my eyes and looked out the window. There seemed to be nothing else to say. We stared at the landscape of trees flying by, and once in a while, glanced at each other. In silence.

We entered the gated walls of the Massachusetts Heights limestone mansion and the driver killed the engine. The door rolled back. Reed stood in the driveway with bloodshot eyes and furrowed brow, holding little Samuel who looked so innocent that it tore my heart out.

Reed transferred Samuel's weight to her left hip and threw her other arm around Davis and began crying. He stayed in her arms, tears streaming down his face. Samuel started bawling. Reed and Davis rocked each other, both reluctant to let go. I was amazed. Reed had forgiven him. I wasn't sure whether to be proud of her emotional maturity or afraid for her naiveté.

****

Over the next few days, the press established a tent city outside the Rideout home. The Massachusetts Avenue Heights mansion was ground zero. Reporters climbed over the wall and rushed the house, tried to ram doors and pry open windows. Anything for a story. The media hysteria far surpassed anything the country had ever seen, and the police had to take over, establish a militarized no-go zone, and assume a full-time presence. Police cars barricaded the entire block. Helicopters flew overhead. It was flat out war and only designated family and friends were allowed across enemy lines. The Rideouts had been found guilty, locked up, and the key thrown away, all without a trial.

CHAPTER 30

I dragged myself into the Supreme Court building to stow away the crystal eagle and other personal items on my desk. Since the term was over, I didn't expect to see anyone except the security guards, so I was surprised to see Jake in the clerks' office, packing a box.

"Jake! It's good to see a friendly face."

He followed me into my inner office. "Sir, I'm sorry about everything your family is going through." He grimaced. "And the media ... I couldn't believe the battering ram."

"No one could." I sat down in my high-back leather chair. "Sit." I motioned to an opposite chair.

He plopped down. "I can't stay long. I dropped by to pick up the extra shirts I kept here."

"Have you started your new job yet?"

He grinned. "First, I'm going mountain climbing."

"Really?"

"In Nepal. Some law school buddies are going with me. We've hired Sherpas and everything."

I laughed. "Wonderful. Sounds exciting." I found myself wishing I were going with him.

Jake grew serious. "Sir, I wasn't expecting to see you here but now that I have ... well, there's something I should tell you." Jake blushed a deep red and ran his fingers nervously through his blond hair. "God, I don't know where to begin. Maybe I should leave." Jake shook his head and struggled to his feet.

"Jake," I said sharply. "Sit down."

He studied my face. "There have been rumors all year long—"

"About?"

"About you and Lilly," he said, cringing.

I exhaled. "Relax. Chief Brown has already informed me."

"He has?" He looked surprised.

"Yes, I told him there was nothing to them."

Jake looked skeptical like I was trying to put one over on him. "She was always flirting with you."

"That was Lilly. It didn't mean anything." I smiled at Jake.

He blinked. "Justice A., I didn't want to say this …"

"Go ahead."

"Lilly said she was sleeping with you."

I leaned forward in my chair and fixed on him. "Impossible because it never happened."

"Well, I don't know," he stammered, looking like he wanted to disappear, "but that's what she said."

I held my fingers to my temples against the raging pulse of blood pounding through my head. A grenade had gone off. "Lilly is a beautiful woman but there's nothing between us."

"You've been good to me, Justice A. You didn't have to bring me over from the Court of Federal Claims. I know that. You had your pick of a thousand lawyers who wanted to clerk for you. That's why I feel obligated to tell you Chief Brown asked me what I knew about you and Lilly."

"Okay …"

"I told him what she said."

I narrowed my eyes. "Which was what, exactly?"

"That you two were having an affair. And Justice A., I don't think I'm the only one she told."

I nodded, stone faced.

"Well, I should go," Jake said nervously. "I hope I didn't upset you, Justice A. I just want you to be prepared."

I stood. "Thank you for being up front with me."

We shook hands. I stared at Jake's back as he left. So, Chief Justice Brown was gathering his arrows and this one was in his quiver.

I glanced up at the paintings of Colonel and Mrs. Ewell. They looked worried. They should be. The Court was the final arbiter in difficult and serious cases, including those involving sexual harassment and other sexually related issues. For the system to work, the public needed faith in the character of the Justices who decided those cases. A scandal could shred the moral fiber of the Court and shake its august foundation, and that was something the Chief wouldn't tolerate.

✳✳✳✳

Chief Brown had called a meeting. I was looking forward to it. It was time to put the rumors about me and Lilly to rest.

I made my way through the Supreme Court corridors, into the Chief's chambers, larger and more imposing than mine, but with the same dark wood paneling and fireplace. This was the Chief's entire world. The Court was his hearth, his home, and his legacy and he was willing to protect it at all costs. I was expecting a rough ride.

The Chief was holding a hand mirror and gingerly adjusting his few remaining strands of hair into a nest on top. A Fitbit was strapped to his wrist. That was new. I certainly hoped he'd assumed some sort of exercise routine because I'd heard rumors about serious health problems, a shame for someone only sixty years old.

I coughed.

He jumped. "Oh, I had something in my eye," he said, turning bright red and pulling an eyelid down. "There, got it." He pulled out a drawer and quickly dumped the mirror in.

I sat down and he began wagging a chubby finger at me.

"You do understand that I have to look into any rumors of impropriety at the Court," he said.

"I wouldn't expect less," I agreed.

"The bottom line is that the Supreme Court can't have Justices going around banging their law clerks."

That was a sentence I never thought I would hear.

The Chief was steaming, his face flushed. "There's a bill in Congress right now that would require us to adopt a version of the Code of Judicial Conduct. However, we're not like other courts. Article II of the Constitution creates only one court and that's the Supreme Court of the United States." He leaned forward with sharp little teeth, bared like a dog. "The idea! Subjecting us to a written ethics code! It's completely antithetical. Our integrity has always been above reproach and as long as I'm Chief, it always will be!" He took a big breath. "And your law clerk, Jake Larson, has told me quite a tale." He hesitated.

I waited. I was going to make him say it.

Chief Brown's face turned from red to a deep scarlet. "Well, basically, Lilly said she was having an affair with you and I have to look into any allegations of misconduct."

"Why now? You said you've known about the rumor all year."

"That's irrelevant!"

"I'm sure this has nothing to do with the Hines case," I said sarcastically. "Look, I can't speak for Lilly. I have no idea why she would say that."

Chief Brown tapped his foot impatiently. "So, explain the situation to me. From your point of view."

"Lilly liked to flirt. It was a sport with her, like big game hunting."

"She wanted to bag a Supreme Court Justice?" Chief Brown raised his eyebrows.

"I don't know. She flirted with a lot of men."

"You're the only one Lilly said she was having an affair with." He drew his head back and looked down his nose at me. "And frankly, your story isn't convincing."

I stood up and leaned over him, seething. "I'm not here to answer to you like a schoolboy. I'm here so you have the truth."

He picked up a stack of newspaper clippings from his desk and shook them in my face.

"And another thing. I don't like all this publicity. Newspaper interviews, press conferences. You keep putting Lilly's name out there and some snoopy reporter will find out about your affair. And that's going to reflect badly on my Court!"

I headed toward the doorway. "Do what you have to do," I said over my shoulder. "And I'll do what I have to do."

"Think about your wife when she finds out about you and Lilly," he yelled at my back. "And public impeachment? My God, man. Save everyone the embarrassment and resign!"

I slogged down the hall, to my chambers and slumped into my desk chair. I didn't dare look at Colonel Ewell and his wife. I already knew they were disappointed in the way I'd handled Chief Brown. I'd let my temper get the best of me. And the Chief was right. In contrast to Lilly's tale, my denial rang hollow because I had everything to lose—career, marriage, reputation. It made me sick.

CHAPTER 31

"The blood on the broom matches the body in the attic," Jonesie told Ruth. "The killer used the broom to sweep away his footprints. And he probably wore gloves."

"What about DNA?" Ruth asked.

"There's no match in the system. But we've submitted Lilly McCleary's toothbrush for DNA comparison and those results should be back soon."

"Toxicology results?"

"Clean. Unlike Eden and Echo who had Devil's Breath—"

"Scopolamine? The drug that puts victims into a compliant trance?"

"Yep. First used by South American tribes to convince the widows of dead chiefs to be buried alive with their husbands. And our victim was stabbed to death but not with the same weapon that killed Echo Hines. It's unclear whether she was raped. The body was too decomposed to make that determination. The medical examiner gave the time of death as several days after the Hines twins died."

"Okay," Ruth said. "You've given me the differences. Let's determine the commonalities besides the obvious—the ages of the women and the location itself. Don't overlook anything. It would be awfully strange for three bodies to end up at the same estate and the cases not be connected."

"Okay, boss."

"Remember, this information remains strictly confidential." Ruth stared Jonesie down. "Got it?"

"Got it, boss."

****

"Ruth! What do you know about this?"

Ruth looked up from her desk, startled to see FBI Director Mortich standing in the doorway to her office at Quantico. What the hell was he doing way down here? He should be in Washington. This could be trouble.

Mortich flashed a piece of paper in front of her face.

"What's that?"

Mortich pushed Jake Larsen's statement under her nose.

"Oh, that." Her throat swelled tight. "Warren would never have an affair with his law clerk."

Mortich twisted his mouth and glanced around Ruth's office. His gaze landed on Ruth. "Damn, I'm hot."

"Welcome to my office, hot in the summer, cold in the winter." He was calming down. Thank God.

Mortich picked up a book, Ruth's famous tome on criminal profiling, *Criminal Psychosis and Symptomatic Behavior*, now a standard reference work in law enforcement. He examined it, turned it over and back again, held it out like he was reading the back blurb. "I wasn't talking about your office," he said quietly, eyes focused on the book.

She nodded, subdued.

"That statement," he said, his voice starting to rise like the blare of a horn, "the one you're holding in your hands, was given to me by none other than the President of the United States. I was called into the Oval Office this morning, told that the statement was given to the FBI weeks ago and we hadn't done a damn thing about it. I had no idea what the President was talking about. How do you think that made me look?"

Ruth looked straight ahead. "Not good, I suppose."

Mortich reared back and hurled Ruth's book into the wall, leaving a large hole in the wallboard, just above a coat peg. He turned back to Ruth.

"Yes, not good," he seethed, his face a brilliant scarlet. "The DNA isn't back yet, but you and I both know that the body in Blackhall's attic is Lilly McCleary. And you didn't think to tell me that Alexander was having an affair with her? I specifically asked you if you had any information that would implicate him in her disappearance!"

He leaned over Ruth's desk. "Damn it. You let your friendship with Warren Alexander cloud your judgment! I'm ordering you off the McCleary case!"

He stormed out.

****

Ruth slumped in her chair, suddenly spent. She looked across the room at a small mirror she'd hung by the door to check her teeth for food. She looked old, worn to a frazzle. Not even her leopard print scarf lifted her spirits. And it was her favorite one. She pulled it off, stuffed it in her drawer, wondering what was the point. She'd be packing up her office before long.

Mortich was right. She'd let her friendship with Warren affect her judgment. She'd left Jake's information out of her report because she knew it was wrong. When she'd interviewed Warren's law clerks, Jake had blurted out:

Lilly and Justice A. are having an affair.

Ruth had laughed in Jake's face. She knew Warren a lot better than Jake did. She'd worked with Warren for years and he had the highest possible ethical standards.

****

That afternoon, Charles Hunt grilled Ruth. "So, Justice Alexander was the person who reported Lilly missing?"

She fiddled with her collar. "Yes."

"And you didn't think that was an alarm bell?"

"Not in this case," she huffed.

Ruth was sitting at a table. She was on one side, Charles Hunt and Ginger Baker on the other. Charles was clean-shaven, his hair trimmed short, a stereotypical FBI agent with rippling muscles and a flat stomach that could deflect steel. Ginger had freckles across her nose and voluminous red hair flowing down her back. She could've been a sexy calendar pin-up model wielding a Glock as a prop. Instead, she and Charles were the new FBI agents assigned to Lilly's case. Out of the Academy a few years, they had a reputation for partnering together, being ambitious, and working long hours to solve the most difficult cases the Bureau could throw at them. Ruth was there to fill them in about Lilly's investigation but the meeting was turning into an inquisition.

Charles Hunt sorted through some papers. "That should've been ringing like a five-alarm bell because of this statement that didn't exactly see the light of day." He held it out in front of him. "I'll read it," he said, nodding at Ruth. She knew what was coming.

"Justice A. and Lilly were having an affair."

Charles looked at Ginger. "That's Jake Larson's statement. Lilly told him about her affair with Alexander. Lilly should know. She was on the receiving end of his dick. And Ginger and I talked to Alexander's other law clerks earlier today. It seems that Lilly flaunted the affair. Everyone knew about it."

Ruth remained silent.

"Why would they lie?" Charles opened a file. "Here's a photo of Lilly." Charles's eyes widened and he handed the photo to Ginger. "With Lilly's looks, I find their statements easy to believe."

"I knew no one would understand."

Ginger gasped. "Are you saying you buried Larsen's statement on purpose?"

"I'm interested in justice, not in arresting innocent people."

"That has nothing to do with hiding information," Charles said. "The body at Blackhall is undoubtedly Lilly McCleary. The estate is gated and Alexander is one of the few people who has access to the house. The information you hid is highly relevant."

Ruth stirred in her chair. "Jake Larsen doesn't know Warren ... I mean ... Justice Alexander like I do."

"It isn't just Jake Larsen."

Ruth was silent. The surveillance tape was next. She braced herself.

"And there's this surveillance tape from the Supreme Court building. Ginger and I have reviewed it. Lilly McCleary leaves alone through the side door and Justice Alexander leaves through the garage five minutes later. You didn't think Alexander might've followed her home?"

More silence. The atmosphere in the room was beginning to feel like a wake. For Ruth's career.

"And your file on McCleary's apartment ..." Charles sorted through the file and pulled out a large sheet of paper. "Here's your drawing of the layout." He twirled it around so she could see it clearly.

Like she didn't know it by heart.

"Your report says there were three photos in the apartment, all of McCleary and Justice Alexander together." Charles flipped through the file. "*Whoa.* I see we have the photos." He held up one of them. "McCleary is draped all over Alexander. Does that make sense if he's merely her boss? And you found a lot of expensive lingerie." His hand landed on some 5 x 7 glossies and his eyes bulged. "And here we have the lingerie. More holes than fabric. Makes me blush." Charles shook his head. "I don't get it, Ruth."

"What?"

"Why didn't you turn this case over to someone objective?"

"I am objective."

Charles flung the photos under Ruth's nose. "Oh, yeah? Lilly McCleary didn't wear those bras and panties to clean her toilet! There's only one reason to wear that type of lingerie and no jury's gonna believe Alexander turned her down. He's on the ugly side of fifty, she's a young, hot knockout. And I don't know ..." Charles rubbed his chin. "It looks like Alexander went to McCleary's apartment when she didn't show up for work. Jesus, that's smart. That gives us a reason to find his fingerprints, hair, and other fiber evidence in the apartment. Of course, as a former FBI agent, he knew his search of Lilly's apartment would establish a reasonable connection to forensics that could've otherwise implicated him."

"That wasn't the way it happened," Ruth said. "Lilly had been sick for days and when she didn't answer her phone, Justice Alexander thought she might need medical attention. That's why he went to her apartment. It was completely innocent."

Charles and Ginger stared at her.

Ruth slumped in her chair, knowing Charles was right. The information in that file pointed directly at Warren. Murder suspects had been convicted on less. Juries didn't like married men whose lovers turned up dead and the evidence made it look like that was exactly what happened. Warren had just become the prime suspect in Lilly's case.

CHAPTER 32

Ruth entered Jenny Barton's office at the FBI's crime lab. Although Mortich had pulled Ruth off the McCleary case, she was still on the Hines case and she needed information.

Jenny looked up from a stack of papers. "Hey, Ruth. I bet you're here about the DNA results from the Hines women."

"I also need information about the DNA recovered from the body we found in the attic at Blackhall."

Jenny frowned. "I didn't think you were still on that case."

"So, word has gotten around."

Jenney shrugged. "You know how it is. Short answer, we don't have those results back yet. Although, I do have good news." Jenny smiled broadly. "In the Hines case, we have a match and not just any old match. This guy's DNA is rarer than a raw steak."

Ruth groaned at the joke.

"Seriously, it's nothing short of amazing—"

"Give me the details."

"We found a degraded mixture of DNA, most of which is clearly the victim's—"

"There was foreign DNA in only one woman?"

"The semen sample from Eden Hines was too degraded to analyze."

"Okay—"

"So, we have Echo's DNA and a minor contributor who is the source of the semen sample. And, get this, we found a 9 at D3."

"That's unusual?"

"Hell, yes. We've never seen that before. So, we thought the D3 9 was an artifact of some sort."

"Interesting."

"Interesting but not evidence. We had only 9 core loci but because it's such a high-profile case, we ran the sample through CODIS without the D3 9 because we didn't think the D3 9 could be real." Jenny laughed. "Amazingly, there was a perfect match to this guy's profile and—get this—he also has a 9 at D3! Just to confirm the match, we did a 16 locus Y-STR test. He matches at all 16 loci." Jenny shook her head and smiled. "This is one of the best matches I've ever seen."

"What's the random match probability?"

"Better than one in one trillion. We've nailed the bastard who killed Eden and Echo Hines."

****

The FBI had informed Jerry Arnett that Davis would be arrested within the hour. Reed was beside herself, had called crying and begging me to come over. The press knew something was up and they were salivating as the cops opened a barricade to let me pass. A block down, at Davis's house, U.S. Marshals Service vans were stacked up the driveway like storm clouds on the horizon. The limestone mansion's timbered front door creaked open. U.S. Marshals shouted at me with open, angry mouths. "Stay back! Stay back!"

A platoon of Marshals poured out of the mansion, jostling a man between them. Reed followed closely behind, sobbing. The man's head was down, his hands in front of him, in cuffs. I had braced myself but not for what I saw. Henry was being bundled out of the house, tears streaming down his face. I've never seen anyone who looked so guilty. Davis was right behind him, no handcuffs, no officers propelling him along. He spotted me and hurried over.

"I'm going with Henry," Davis said. "Jerry Arnett is going to meet us downtown."

"What the hell is going on?"

"The FBI thinks Henry killed Eden and Echo Hines."

The U.S. Marshals continued to fast-walk Henry down the drive. They pushed his head down as they shoved him into the back of a van.

Davis jerked his head toward Reed. "Your daughter needs you." He hurried off and drove away, his car following Henry and a line of silently flashing red and blue lights.

The press jumped into their cars and followed. Within minutes, the media's tent city had been abandoned, their equipment packed up and moved downtown. Henry was the story now and they were hot on his trail.

****

I had stayed at the mansion. It had taken awhile but I'd finally gotten Reed calmed down.

Davis walked through the door and Reed jumped up. "How's Henry?"

Davis folded her into his arms. She began crying. "It's okay. He's all right. Jerry Arnett met with him for an hour and I told him I'd be back first thing in the morning and that we'd get through this together."

"Henry wouldn't hurt anyone!" Reed sobbed.

"I know," Davis said. "But we have to deal with the facts. The grand jury has issued an indictment. Henry's been arrested for felony murder. That's a done deal. Now, we have to get him the best defense possible and get him back home."

"What's the evidence?" I asked.

Davis looked white. "Let's sit down." He guided Reed to the sofa and collapsed beside her. "They told Arnett the DNA matches."

"DNA from what type of evidence?" I raised my eyebrow.

"I don't know."

"Something's wrong." I'd questioned a lot of killers in my lifetime, serial and otherwise, all up close and personal, and the idea that Henry was one of them was insane.

CHAPTER 33

The black alabaster walls in Arnett's office reflected our shapes like gauzed mirrors as Davis and I moved about the conference room at the crack of dawn. Arnett's gut hung over the table, his belt slung down around his hips. A young, worried-looking assistant came in juggling multiple cups of coffee and passed them around, avoiding our eyes. Arnett grunted a "thank you" in return.

I would later learn that two attorneys in the firm had resigned that morning because Arnett had agreed to represent Henry. No one wanted to be associated with Henry's defense and the firm was sure to lose clients. The press had already declared Henry guilty.

Arnett put his hand on a stack of papers relating to Henry's case. "It's looking bad." Arnett stared at me. "And strangely, you're part of it. After your daughter was kidnapped last year, Congress amended 18 U.S.C. to make murdering a member of a federal judge's family a federal offense. And while they were at it, they did the same for murdering a member of the President's family."

"So, they're going to try Henry in federal court."

"Yes."

"Have you seen the lab results from the DNA?"

"No."

"I want to see them when they come in," I said, even though I wasn't familiar with DNA interpretation. When I'd left the FBI, DNA was in its infancy.

Arnett stared at me with cold, reptilian eyes. "What are you doing here, anyway?" he demanded. "You're a Supreme Court Justice!"

"I've interviewed hundreds of killers and I'm convinced that Henry is innocent. I'm not going to stand by and watch an innocent man being railroaded. I'm offering you my help."

"And the Supreme Court?"

"Let me handle that."

I was no longer concerned about Chief Brown and his threats of impeachment. It was Chief Brown's stance that the Supreme Court was exempt from an ethics code. So, I'd decided to let Brown live with the consequences because he couldn't have it both ways. Without an ethics code, a presumed extra-marital affair wasn't an impeachable offense. And barring a moral or ethical cataclysm on my part that would land me in jail, I was pretty much free to do anything I pleased, including participating in Henry's defense. And that was my plan—to exonerate an innocent man.

Arnett's eyes warmed up. He nodded his head agreeably. "All right. Maybe I can use your help."

"I want to be at the defense table, too," Davis said.

Arnett grimaced. "Not a good idea. Your face is everywhere. The jury will view you as the sex addict who started the whole mess."

Arnett pointed at me. "Okay, partner. I want to push the trial date up as soon as possible. The longer Henry stays in jail, the more the public will see him as being guilty."

That was one trial strategy. Another strategy was delay, delay, delay. However, Arnett's proposed strategy was part of the O.J. Simpson defense, and I had to admit, it was effective in that high-profile case.

"This isn't simply a trial of Henry's peers," Arnett said. "This is a trial of public opinion. No matter what jurors say, they're influenced by publicity. If you're going to have a media circus, you'd better be the ringmaster because when a juror tells you they haven't heard anything about a big case like this one, you can be sure they're lying."

"I guess it wouldn't help to seek a change of venue," Davis said.

Arnett snorted. "Of course not. The entire country is being saturated with publicity. Sides are being chosen, ninety-nine percent of it against us, and time is of the essence. We need to get a jury sequestered. We'll have to patch our case together on the fly. I like to work with several investigators and a couple of good ... no, make that ... brilliant ... a couple of brilliant lawyers. Any more and the team gets too clumsy for me."

Davis frowned. "More isn't better?"

"Too much infighting. Lawyers like to argue." He laughed loudly. "Who would've thought it?"

He had a point. O.J.'s dream team had quickly turned into a scream team. "What's the evidence?" I asked.

"When the DNA from the semen sample was run through CODIS, Henry immediately popped up as a cold hit."

"DNA from semen?"

Arnett nodded.

That was hard to believe. A seventy-eight-year-old man raping two young women? I guess it was possible. "Why was he in the system?"

"Henry was in a bar fight ten years ago."

"Was he convicted?"

"No, the charges were dropped. There's a serious question whether Henry's DNA should've been expunged from the database. I could argue it's inadmissible but, at this point, the Government has sufficient evidence to get a search warrant for Henry's DNA, so I'd be wasting ink and paper. Oh, and his DNA was also on the car's steering wheel."

I thought for a moment. "What about Davis? Has he been implicated?"

"Davis was exonerated early on despite the gobbledygook the Feds were feeding me. They do that sometimes. Their form of a fishing expedition to see if he knew anything and would rat out Henry. But the Feds estimated the twins' time of death by the absorption of food in their stomachs, matched that against the time the girls left the house, when their friends saw them eating celery and carrots. The time of death is inconsistent with

Davis," Arnett paused and nodded across the table at Davis, "inconsistent with Davis being at Blackhall. He was at the airport by 1:30. Of course, there's also the DNA match to Henry. And that's the clincher."

So, the target was Henry and Henry alone. We were deadly quiet. Davis examined his coffee dregs.

"What did they say was the random match probability?"

"Prepare yourselves because that's the worst part."

We looked at him expectantly.

"One in one trillion. Henry has some sort of rare DNA that's never been seen before." Arnett grimaced. "The Feds are bringing out the big guns and they're planning to shoot Henry out of the sky."

****

The President was scanning newspapers at his desk. Turnbull's DNA matched the semen samples. Thinking about it made the President want to throw up. He couldn't wait for the trial to begin.

Mike Fontaine walked into the Oval Office. The President barely noticed.

"Ahem, Mr. President?"

President Hines glanced up and jabbed his finger at the paper. "Have you seen this, Mike?"

"Yes, sir."

"That sonafabitch better fry!"

"May I make a suggestion, Mr. President?"

"What?" the President snapped, returning his eyes to the newsprint.

Fontaine shifted his weight. "I was thinking, sir, that it might be better if there was no trial."

The President looked at him like he was crazy. "What the hell are you talking about?"

"Some problematic things will come out at the trial. Your daughters' predilections, for one. We've managed to keep their, huh … activities under wraps until now. Unfortunately, the trial will bring out all the messy details. Not only embarrassing to your family, it could kneecap your re-election prospects. It's a lot of scandal for the public to stomach."

The President scrutinized Fontaine. "There's nothing I can do about it. Turnbull has to pay."

"What if Turnbull killed himself in jail? That would be justice and the unpleasant details would never come to light. Case closed."

The President looked suspicious. "What are you suggesting?"

Fontaine smiled innocently. "Why nothing. I'm just saying it would be high on my wish list, if I were you. Everyone knows he's guilty. His DNA match is one in a trillion. And your constituents would be thrilled. If Turnbull doesn't get the death penalty, he could be living on their dime the rest of his life."

The President took a moment, swung his chair around and gazed out over the Rose Garden. "Hmmm. I see what you're saying." The President was quiet for a few minutes before turning back to Fontaine. "How would one do that without getting caught?"

CHAPTER 34

Henry stumbled into the small room at the E. Barrett Prettyman Federal Building, gingerly touching a bruise under the white stubble on his face.

"How did that happen?" I asked, pointing to his cheek.

"Fell in the middle of the night."

"Are you sure?"

"Yes, sir, yes, I am."

Arnett snapped his litigation case shut and stacked some papers into neat rectangles. He looked at Henry. "Henry, I need to go over the charges against you to make sure you understand everything."

"Yes, sir."

"Let's focus on the basics. First, since it's a federal crime to murder the daughters of the President, you will be tried in federal court." Arnett took a deep breath. "The U.S. Attorney has filed a number of charges against you, murder, kidnapping, lying to the FBI. The list is endless and I'm not going to go over every charge, there may be more coming down the pike, so suffice it to say that at this point, we should focus on the big enchilada— First Degree Murder under 18 U.S.C. sections 315 and 1751, which make it a federal crime to kill a family member of an incumbent President. If you're convicted on that charge, you can get the death penalty." Arnett added in a sympathetic tone, "You do understand?"

"I understand I'm in a lot of trouble."

"I'm afraid so. You're going to be arraigned tomorrow, here, in U.S. District Court in front of a magistrate judge. At the arraignment, the judge will advise you of your rights and read the charges against you. Then, you'll enter a plea—"

"Not guilty."

"Well, yes. The judge is certain to deny you bail because of the high-profile nature of the case. So, you'll remain in the custody of the U.S. Marshals Service. They'll secure you at an undisclosed location. Not here, somewhere else. Even I won't know where you're going until tomorrow."

"Why's that?" Henry frowned.

"Because of the public interest."

"You mean I'm gettin' death threats?"

"It's nothing to worry about." Arnett grew quiet. "Are they treating you well? If anyone is mistreating you here, I can file an emergency motion to have you—"

"No, no. They're treating me fine. But wherever they take me, I want to be in Washington, close to the Rideouts, yes, I do."

Arnett looked perplexed. "Okay, I guess that's important to you. It shouldn't be a problem. They won't want to transport you over long distances because of security concerns." Arnett paused to see if Henry had any questions.

None.

Arnett picked up some papers and adjusted the bifocals on his nose. "Let's go over the evidence against you. The prosecution is claiming your semen was found inside Echo's vagina."

Henry's jaw dropped to the floor and he started shaking his hands in front of him. "Oh, no, no, that can't be! The only woman I've ever been with is my wife and she's been dead near on five years."

Arnett looked over the top of his glasses. "DNA doesn't lie, Henry."

"Neither do I. I swear on a stack of Bibles from here to heaven that I never touched them!"

"Henry, I have to be honest with you. And I need you to be honest with me. DNA is the gold standard. It's pure science. That's why juries love it. It alleviates their concern they'll convict the wrong person."

Henry looked terrified and a tear ran down his face.

Arnett pondered the list in front of him. "Now, another problem is that the twins' car was found in the stable at Blackhall and your DNA was found on the steering wheel. Perhaps if you can't explain the semen, you can explain that." Arnett waited for Henry to reply. There was a long, pregnant pause.

Henry wiped sweat off his brow and shifted his feet under the chair.

"I need to know so I can properly defend you." Arnett waited patiently.

"I'd have to start at the beginning," Henry said.

"Good. Take me through the entire day and into the next week."

Henry glanced at me, uncertainty creeping into his eyes. "You're Mrs. Rideout's father. Maybe I shouldn't say anything in front of you."

"Don't worry. I know all about Davis and his hookups."

"You do?"

"Yes."

Henry exhaled. "Okay, then. Davis told me he was going to have a little party with two women. I was used to him havin' women out to the house. But that was before he married Mrs. Rideout. And this time, I protested." A tear wobbled in the corner of Henry's eye. "You see, Justice Alexander, I think so highly of your daughter. She's been wonderful to me and she's such a good momma to that little baby. So, I asked him if he knew what he was doing. He told me not to worry, Mrs. Rideout would never know."

Henry ran his hand through his hair. "Well, sometimes there's no talking to him, so I went to Biggy's Bar and stayed there until I was sure Davis and his women had left."

"Did you have anything to drink?"

"Just soda."

"What happened when you got home?"

"I saw a strange car sittin' in the driveway so I thought the party was still going on and I headed off to bed. The next morning, the car was still there and I decided to check things out. No one answered the door and I went in and found them. The President's daughters! I couldn't believe my eyes, but it was them." Henry wiped tears from his face. "I didn't know what had happened and I was scared and panicked. All I knew was I had to clean up as fast as possible and hide the car. Someone was gonna come lookin' for *those* girls, that was for sure!"

"So, you cleaned up the crime scene?"

Henry bobbed his head up and down. "Good as I could. Took a long time, though. And then I was faced with the bodies. Oh God ..." Henry closed his eyes and collapsed into sobs.

Arnett scrapped his chair closer to Henry. "Take a deep breath."

Henry looked heavenward and clasped his hands in prayer. "God forgive me! I got a wheel barrel from the barn and took them down to the estate boundary, where it's walled off. Later, when Mrs. Rideout started talking about digging up the ground all around Blackhall ... well, I thought about moving them off the property but the idea of diggin' them up made me Godawful sick."

"What about the twins' car?"

"I put it in the stable."

I leaned forward. "Why in the world didn't you just call the police?"

"Because I was afraid Davis would be blamed! I had no way of contacting him and askin' him what happened. And I couldn't call up Mrs. Rideout and say—There's some naked dead girls out here. You have to understand, I thought ... well, I don't know what I thought." Henry started bawling great big, fat tears. "I had to make a decision and I guess I made everythin' worse. And I feel awful about that but Davis is like a son to me and I was trying to protect him, like I've always done. And when my Susannah was dying of cancer, Davis was so good to us. He spent hundreds of thousands of dollars on her medical bills. The best doctors, the best hospitals. He even paid for her funeral. I would do anything for him."

Henry was sobbing but I saw something knowing and dark in the depths of his eyes and I had an epiphany like God had opened the heavens and shouted at me to pay attention. I sat my reading glasses on the table and looked Henry straight in the eyes. "Henry, you know who killed Eden and Echo, don't you?"

He was quiet for a moment. "Yes, sir, yes, I do," he said in a voice so low I could barely hear.

"Who?"

"Josephine Rideout."

I frowned. "Who's that?" I looked at Arnett who shrugged.

"The woman in the long green dress in the portrait gallery. I've seen her."

My mouth dropped open. "You mean Davis's ancestor? The one who built Blackhall?"

"Yes."

"Henry, you know that's impossible. She's dead. Don't you mean you saw a woman?"

"No, sir."

"Then what are you talking about?"

"It's just that ... well ... I mean, Josephine is the only one who could've done it. I'm just sure it was her. She's a tortured soul, that one is."

CHAPTER 35

The FBI issued a statement exonerating Davis. And when Henry's DNA results were leaked to the media, the sheer magnitude of the one-in-a-trillion match sealed his guilt in the public's eye. At that point, Davis should've been relegated to a footnote in history, but Davis was handsome and wealthy and he intrigued the nation. And it was true that Davis was inextricably linked to the facts of the case, so the press didn't let him off the hook. He was too valuable to be dropped from the story. His movie-star looks and suave manner kept the cable channels on the air, the public buying newspapers, and money flowing into the coffers of both. So what if some of the stories were outright false? The media didn't care. Cold, hard cash was the air they breathed.

Tommy Woofer, host of Tommy Woofer Late Night, speaking low and urgent: "Confidential sources have informed me that Henry Turnbull is merely the canary in the coal mine."

Woman with overly botoxed lips and the skyline of New York in the background: "*Ab-so-lute-ly!* The Feds have charged Turnbull so he'll testify against Davis Rideout!"

Tommy Woofer looking nervous but excited: "Just to make sure the record is correct, Rideout hasn't been arrested or accused of a crime."

Botox lips rolling her eyes: "*Oh, pull-eease.* We all know they were in it together!"

Tommy Woofer, smiling (wink wink): "To protect against legal liability, we'll refer to Rideout as Henry Turnbull's employer until he's arrested."

Botox, guffawing. "That won't be long!" she yelled, her lips so puffy they ate up the entire screen. "Mark my words!"

And that was one of the more favorable shows I'd seen.

I turned to Jerry Arnett and he clicked off the TV.

"That seemed objective," I said sarcastically.

"That's why we need to get a jury sequestered. Talk about tainting the jury pool."

"Use it as grounds for appeal."

"It's going to be an uphill battle. See, even you have Henry convicted."

"I have?"

"Of course. You're already focused on an appeal."

Arnett pushed a document across the table. "You wanted to see this."

"So, the prosecution finally sent the DNA Report." I had started reading up on DNA and I grabbed the report and started flipping through it, anxious to read the details. "We need to file discovery requests for the lab notes and the Genetic Analyzer electronic files. If we're lucky, we might spot improper lab procedures or inconsistent results."

Arnett slapped me on the back. "Way ahead of you. Already filed." Arnett raised his arms over his head, stretched and looked around his office. "Oh, man. It's after midnight. Let's get outta here." He reached for his jacket. "Can I drop you off?"

"You're in Georgetown, right?"

"Just a few blocks from you."

"Thanks."

We went down the elevator to the garage. Our footsteps echoed in the vast concrete cavern, and in a corner, a leak dripped like the ticking of a clock. We walked past rows of empty spaces to a reserved spot occupied by a low-slung car with a red paint job that shined like a pool of water.

I ran my hand over the hood. "Nice car. Ferrari, right?"

"Yeah, one of the perks of ninety hour weeks." He shook his head. "Sometimes I wonder if the stress is worth the toys." He laughed. "Until I get in my baby, here."

The Ferrari roared to life. Arnett revved it a few times, grinned at me, and shot the car up the ramp. The engine was powerful and hungry for the road. We were going for a ride.

At the top of the ramp, Arnett slammed on his brakes, barely missing a figure in dark clothing. My head grazed the windshield, my seatbelt caught and flung me backwards. Dozens of lights flashed in our faces. Damn. A horde of reporters prowling around in the dark.

And that's how our photograph appeared in the newspaper the next day, two reckless, joy-riding attorneys in Arnett's flashy red sports car who'd spent the evening callously plotting the exoneration of the most reviled man in the United States—Henry Turnbull—the man accused of killing the President's daughters.

****

The President was furious. On page one was a photograph of a startled Jerry Arnett in his red Ferrari, zipping out of his parking garage after midnight. Justice Alexander was in the passenger seat. Obviously, they were working together to prepare a defense for Henry Turnbull. It was time to act. The President picked up the phone and called General Fontaine.

CHAPTER 36

Jerry Arnett and I had divided up duties. I was still pursuing my theory that Eden and Echo had blackmailed married men, and I needed to find some of their victims and get them on the witness stand to show the jury that several men had a reason to kill Eden and Echo.

Fortunately, everything I knew about the twins validated my original profile. As narcissists, Eden and Echo needed a man who held an important position in the world. As women, they needed a man who was good-looking so they wouldn't be grossed out during sex. And as blackmailers, they needed a man rich enough to pay their demands. Davis had been a perfect target.

I recalled my conversation with Ruth. She had interviewed two recent White House guests, both retired military. And that's when it hit me. The twins wouldn't care if their targets were guests at the White House. I needed to expand my search to anyone they came into contact with and that included men who worked at the White House.

And one man fit all the criteria—General Mike Fontaine. He was one of the most important men in the administration, he'd kept himself in impeccable shape, and he was rich. He was also good-looking, maybe not as good-looking as Davis, although for the twins' purposes, he'd more than do. Yeah, Mike would've made a terrific target and I wanted to find out more about him.

One of the first rules of the FBI was *follow the money*. Because of Mike's position at the White House, he was required to file a Government OGE-278 Financial Disclosure Form that detailed his assets in excess of $1,000 and transactions of the same amount. If the twins were blackmailing

Mike, his transactions should reflect, in some manner, the twins' demands for substantial amounts of cash.

I filled out an on-line request at the U.S. Office of Government Ethics' website for Mike's last two disclosures. Within the day, I had the information spread across my desk. The value of Mike's assets had remained virtually unchanged from the previous year, a reflection of a bad year on Wall Street. And he'd listed only one transaction, a $9,000 purchase of stocks. I wasn't certain what I was expecting to see but there was nothing useful there.

I dug deeper. In addition to various news stories about Mike's influence at the White House, I found magazines with dozens of photographs of Mike and his high-society wife, Annabelle, at various parties and galas around town. I flipped through the pages. There they were, flashing Cadillac-grill smiles at the French Embassy after the White House Correspondents' Dinner, and just a week later, hobnobbing at a British Embassy garden party with Prince Charles, Mike in full regalia.

The magazines contained some juicy tidbits, mostly snide remarks about various embassy hosts, but nothing pointing to Mike as being involved with Eden and Echo. So, I implemented my favorite investigative tack, one cherished by old detective novels, and the approach that had always gotten me the most results—*cherchez la femme.* I focused on Annabelle.

Reading about Annabelle propelled me into another world, one I knew nothing about. It seemed that Annabelle was famous in a gossipy sort of way. Her father had been some sort of silver tycoon from Mississippi and she'd inherited a lot of money, some spent on a recently built antebellum mansion.

I went back over the photos I'd collected and organized them by date. That's when I noticed something unusual about Annabelle. I compared the dates again. After the twins were murdered, there was something distinctly different about Annabelle but I couldn't put my finger on it. Then, I saw it! The evidence was right in front of my eyes.

I immediately called Ruth.

****

Mortich cleared his throat, signaling his staff to be quiet. "The DNA results on the woman found in Blackhall's attic have come back, confirming what's been obvious all along. She is Lilly McCleary, former law clerk to Justice Warren Alexander."

Mortich scanned the room, looking each agent in the eye. "If anyone leaks this information to the press, to their friends, or *even mentions it to their family dog*, I will ferret you out and hunt you down like a mad hound and you will never work again, not for me or for anyone else. *Ever!* I can do that."

He looked around to make sure his threat had sunk in. It had. "Okay. Our job is to do a thorough investigation into who killed Ms. McCleary and our best investigative tool is to keep her murder under wraps for now. Only the murderer knows she's dead, how she died, and where he put her body. I want you to question the D.C. Police involved in McCleary's investigation, see if they've come up with any new leads. I also want you to re-interview McCleary's neighbors, her co-workers, and most importantly, Justice Warren Alexander. Do not tell Alexander that we found McCleary's body. Lock him into a timeline first. Maybe he'll hang himself with his own words. He's our prime suspect in her death."

"What about Davis Rideout?" an agent shouted from the back.

"He was out of town at the time of Ms. McCleary's death, which was about two days after the twins were killed."

Someone mumbled, "Turnbull wasn't."

"Turnbull's DNA wasn't found on McCleary and there are other differences. Eden and Echo Hines were drugged before they were killed and buried on the grounds. McCleary wasn't drugged and she was dumped in the attic. Also, the murder weapon was different. Echo Hines was killed with a knife, Lilly McCleary with a screwdriver. More importantly, Turnbull had no connection to McCleary, whereas, it was widely known that Warren Alexander was having an affair with her. She confirmed that with her co-workers, so we're not talking about a rumor. We're talking about a fact.

We think she insisted he get a divorce, things turned ugly, and Alexander disposed of her body at Blackhall before he knew the twins were killed there and the house would be a focus of law enforcement."

No one said a word. Mortich clapped his hands loudly. "All right. We have a job to do!"

Ruth began to leave the room and Mortich pulled her aside. "Don't screw this up. You're in this briefing only because you need to know what evidence we've separated out from the Hines case. However, if you mention any of this to Alexander, if you even wink at the man, you're out of a job."

"Yes, sir, but there may be another angle to the Hines case. Justice Alexander called me with some interesting information about General Fontaine."

CHAPTER 37

The days seemed to grow hotter as the summer progressed although that could've been heat accumulating in my body as I internalized concern about the upcoming trial. Time was getting short and suddenly, I'd had another interruption.

My secretary, Dorothy, exhaled, blowing her bangs off her face. She was dressed in elasticized blue jeans and a brown tee shirt, looking overwhelmed as she scanned the dozens of empty cardboard boxes piled at our feet.

Auggie stood in the doorway to Lilly's bedroom, hands in his pockets. "Thank you, Justice Alexander, Mrs. Davenport." He looked embarrassed.

I put my hand on his shoulder. "Don't worry. Someone has to take charge of her things."

"I didn't know who else to call."

"It's fine," Dorothy said, her voice hitting a high note that would break a wine glass. "We'll have this wrapped up in no time." She rubbed her hands together, pretending to be excited about packing up the sad remnants of someone else's life. I thought she was going to do a damn jig.

"The police released the apartment weeks ago," Auggie said, "and I thought we could let it sit until Lilly returned but the building's owner said he didn't know when that would be and he's losing rent and wants to get it on the market. I talked to Lilly's mother and she can't pay the rent or movers—"

"I know," I said. "She's in a wheel chair. We'll get these things sent to her."

Auggie looked around uncomfortably. "Unfortunately, I have to take off. I have the morning shift at Branham's."

I smiled. "Go. We're fine. We'll lock up behind us."

"Okay, well thanks." He started out the door. "It's terrible though, isn't it?"

"It is."

"You think they'll ever find her?"

"Eventually, the police usually do."

"Okay. You have my phone number in case you need me." He started out the door.

"Auggie?"

"Yes?"

"Thanks for taking care of Lilly's things."

"No problem."

The door shut behind Auggie. He had been too polite to say so, had tactfully skirted the subject using euphemisms, but we all knew that Lilly was undoubtedly dead.

****

On my way home, I stopped by Reed's house. I wanted to see how she was holding up. She'd been through a lot and although the press no longer surrounded her house, she'd sounded depressed the last time we talked. I found her opening mail in a small study. She smiled, crooked her finger, and pointed out the window through a patch of green trees glinting in the sun, ruffling in the breeze.

"Look at this."

I walked to the window. "What?"

"Henry put in rose bushes."

Along the wall by the swimming pool were newly staked, neatly spaced trellises. "My God, he did. I'm surprised you had him plant rose bushes."

"Why?" She pouted. "I couldn't get him to play tennis."

"I mean that I didn't think you liked roses."

She shrugged. "He wanted to and he needed something to do." Her shoulders slumped. "What will happen to him?"

I hugged her. "He'll be okay. Jerry Arnett meets with him and he has a psychiatrist coming in every day. His spirits have improved."

"Will Jerry Arnett be able to get him off?"

I laughed. "Arnett's a powerhouse, the best criminal defense attorney on the East Coast, maybe the entire country."

Reed shook her head. "I don't know."

✳✳✳✳

What she did know was that Davis could telegraph what he wanted to do to a woman from fifty yards. Reed remembered one evening at a fancy restaurant, Davis glancing at another table where a ravishing raven-haired beauty was dining with her husband. Davis had ordered an expensive bottle of wine and excused himself. Halfway into a glass, Reed realized that Davis had been gone a long time. She whirled around. The dark-haired beauty's chair was empty. Reed exchanged looks with the woman's husband, an unspoken suspicion crossing the room between them. When Davis returned to the table, his face was all splotchy-red. Reed took his hand. He jerked it away but he couldn't hide the smell. Cunt.

Right then, she'd been faced with a decision. She could file for divorce or fight for her marriage. Although she'd been as hot as boiling oil, she'd decided to fight but now ... Reed choked back a sob. She'd tried her best to forgive Davis but she couldn't. Davis was still sampling the produce when they'd already been through the checkout line!

And two of those melons belonged to Lucy Diamond, one of Davis's old girlfriends. Reed seethed, just thinking about her. Davis had sworn he wasn't seeing Lucy anymore but Reed knew better. Just because Lucy was in New Orleans didn't mean she was out of his life. Too many late-night calls he said were business. Voices too low, laughter too sexy. That wasn't the way business was conducted, anyway not any business she knew. And there were more women. Many more.

It was Davis's animal magnetism that attracted them. He was like a black panther, a dark and dangerous force no woman could tame. Not even her. She sighed, discouraged. She would never be enough for Davis. No one woman ever would be.

****

Reed found Davis on the sofa in front of one of the two massive walk-in fireplaces that dominated their living room. Giant beams of wood, like timbers from some ancient Viking ship, peaked in the center of the ceiling. Enormous windows were framed in mahogany.

Reed had attempted to give the house a chic old world look to replicate the feeling at Blackhall where acquisitions had been collected over generations. But no matter what she did to the rooms, she could never get them to match Blackhall's intimacy. Strange that two houses about the same size could feel so different. Strange that she was focused on decorating when her life was crashing down around her.

"Davis."

Davis looked up. "What's wrong?"

She shoved a flash drive in front of Davis's face and he turned pale.

"I found this at Blackhall," she said. "I bet you've been looking for it, haven't you?"

Davis studied Reed's eyes. "Where was it?"

"Behind the library sofa." She choked back a sob. "You know, it's one thing to know you're cheating on me but ... to see it with my own eyes."

Davis stood and tried to put his arms around Reed. She pulled back.

"Reed ... Reed. I love you."

"I tried to overlook your affairs, but I can't! You've been cheating on me the entire time we've been married!"

He looked at the suitcases behind her and his shoulders slumped. "You're leaving me," he said flatly.

"And I'm taking Samuel with me." Reed put both hands to her eyes to hold back the tears but they came anyway. "You don't love me!"

Davis put his arms around her. She started pounding her fists into his chest.

"I do. I do love you, Reed. Those girls didn't mean anything to me."

She jerked away from him. "Those girls are dead!"

He hung his head. "I ... I ... don't know what to say."

Reed started for the door.

"Wait! Just ... please stay."

"I need some time by myself."

"Reed, please don't," Davis winced. But she was gone.

✦✦✦✦

Davis sounded nervous on the telephone. "We had a fight. Reed left for Blackhall. Just to get some space."

I knew there was more to that story. What had he done, now? Probably something to do with a woman.

"Did you have that cliff staircase torn down?" I asked.

"Yes, last week."

"I don't understand why you didn't you do that years ago. That could be how those burglars are getting into your house."

"Don't be ridiculous," Davis said. "No one would climb that thing. It's a death trap."

"How about those motion detectors we talked about?"

"They're on order and she has that huge wall." Davis exhaled loudly. "You worry too much. She's safe, much safer than we are in Washington.

And it's good for her to be away from the city, the press, and the constant news about Henry."

"She really cares about him."

"She really does. He's been her constant companion at Blackhall."

"And with Henry in jail, she's all alone. I think you should hire some security guards."

****

Sevier joined his lawyers. "What about the murder weapon?" he asked. "What's the status on that?"

His top lawyer spoke up. "The FBI sent divers into the Chesapeake Bay, searched the Blackhall property thoroughly, went through the mansion and the cottage, emptied the kitchens, the tool sheds, the barn, and tested anything that could be the murder weapon. Nothing matched."

Sevier pulled at his chin. "There were no knives at Blackhall?"

"None the right shape. The FBI took a bunch of other things too, wire cutters, blades, tested everything. They think Turnbull tossed the murder weapon off the Bay Bridge. We'll never find it."

"I'd feel a lot better if I could present the weapon to the jury."

"We've got Turnbull's DNA."

Sevier rubbed his hands together. "A one-in-a-trillion match. Okay. This will be fun!"

CHAPTER 38

I'd met with Charles Hunt and Ginger Baker to go over the statement I'd made to Ruth about Lilly's disappearance. I was glad the FBI was pursuing Lilly's case but surprised at their aggression towards me, going over my statement time and again from every possible angle, only letting up after three hours.

But I couldn't think about that now because today was day one of the trial. Reporters from the three prime-time news stations and the three highest-rated cable news channels filed into the building, loud and boisterous, anxious for the show to begin. Right behind them were the first-in-line ticket holders who had stood outside in a drizzling rain since four a.m.

The courtroom itself was a large room paneled in blond ash. A large seal of the United States was attached to the wall behind the judge's chair and the American flag hung loose from a nearby stand. As with all courtrooms, it conveyed a sterile efficiency that carried neither emotion nor forgiveness.

I'd been a judge for so long that I'd forgotten what it was like to be on the other side of the bench. Two words—nerve wracking. The power in the courtroom rested firmly and completely with the person wielding the gavel, in this case, Judge Horatio Greene.

Judge Greene had made a number of pretrial decisions, including one that allowed a single TV camera in the courtroom because of the public interest in the case. He'd also informed the trial attorneys that he wouldn't tolerate any shenanigans in his courtroom. I believed him. He ran a tight ship and his reputation was tough. What I didn't believe was that our defense team was fully prepared to go to trial.

God help us, everyone.

✴✴✴✴

Bailiff: All rise. The U.S. District Court, Criminal Division, is now in session, the Honorable Judge Horatio Greene presiding.

Judge Greene entered the courtroom from the Judge's robing room. He was a handsome African-American man of about sixty years. His salt and pepper hair was pulled into a low ponytail and three silver rings and a silver bracelet, all inlaid with onyx, adorned his hands. He walked to the bench and sat down with the regal bearing of an African king.

"Everyone but the jury may be seated," Judge Greene said. "The bailiff may swear in the jury."

The bailiff stood in front of the jury box. "Please raise your right hand. Do you solemnly swear that you will render a true verdict and a fair sentence as to this defendant?"

A chorus of *I do's* preceded a swish of clothing as the jury settled into their seats.

Judge Greene addressed the jury. "Ladies and gentlemen of the jury. As you have been informed, you will be sequestered during this trial and I caution you not to talk to anyone, not even your fellow jurors, about the evidence until both sides have presented their case and you begin your deliberations. At that time, you will decide whether the testimony and other evidence establish reasonable doubt to acquit the defendant or prove the defendant guilty of the various crimes as charged. Right now, the trial will commence with opening statements. I caution that what you will hear in the opening statements is not evidence. It is merely an overview of each side's case. The actual evidence will be presented during the trial itself and you must base your decision as to guilt and innocence on that evidence and only that evidence."

Judge Greene looked at U.S. Attorney Bill Sevier. "Is the prosecution ready?"

Sevier stood. "Yes, your Honor."

Judge Greene pivoted to the defense table. "Is the defense ready?"

Arnett stood. "Yes, your Honor."

"The prosecution may give an opening statement."

U.S. Attorney Bill Sevier walked toward the jury, both arms stretched slightly out to his sides palms up, a welcoming embrace that disguised an old trial attorney trick—*Nothing in my hands, nothing to hide, just an honest bloke you can trust.*

Sevier leaned against the end of the jury box, friendly but not too close. "Ladies and gentlemen of the jury. On June 1, Eden and Echo Hines, the daughters of the President and the late Mrs. Hines, visited Blackhall, an isolated, grand estate sited on the tidal lands of the Chesapeake Bay. Eden and Echo Hines were twins. They did everything together. They attended college together. They served food to the poor together. They tutored disadvantaged children together. And that night … that fatal night … they died together. They were at Blackhall to visit its owner, Mr. Davis Rideout."

Sevier paused a full five seconds to let the visual he'd just described set in. "The twins, Eden and Echo Hines, had met Mr. Rideout at a White House dinner. Mr. Rideout's reputation is infamous and sordid. We don't know what Mr. Rideout said to lure these innocent, young women to his estate but his covert intentions were to have sex with them. Things did not go as he planned. After Eden and Echo Hines arrived at Blackhall, the twins refused his advances. Mr. Rideout was furious and drove off to the airport where he departed on a business trip to China, leaving the twins vulnerable and alone at his house."

Sevier's voice hardened. "*Shortly after Mr. Rideout left for the airport,* the estate's caretaker, Mr. Henry Turnbull, came home from a disreputable establishment called Biggy's Bar, located on the outskirts of Annapolis. When Mr. Turnbull drove up to the estate, he saw a light in the mansion. Mr. Turnbull was the caretaker at the estate, so he investigated and what did he find? He found two beautiful girls alone in the house. And what did he do? He raped them. Then he killed them. You might ask how Mr. Turnbull was able to subdue and restrain two healthy, young women. Simple. A drug known as Scopolamine. It's also known as Devil's Breath and the Zombie Drug because it makes victims compliant. But at some point, the drug began to wear off and Eden broke free and fought back."

"Mr. Turnbull shoved her!" Sevier shoved an imaginary victim. "Eden's head slammed into the fireplace mantel and her skull cracked like an egg. She died instantly. Henry Turnbull then turned on Echo Hines. She wasn't lucky enough to die right away. Turnbull pulled a knife and stabbed her through the heart!" Sevier rapidly pumped his arm in gruesome stabbing motions. "Time and time again!" Several women jurors flinched.

Sevier's demeanor grew calm again. "Hatefully. Mercilessly. Heartlessly. Then what happened? Henry Turnbull panicked and tried to cover up the crime. He hid the twins' car in the stable and he buried their bodies in the woods."

Sevier held up his finger. "We will prove that Mr. Turnbull was the only person with the motive, the opportunity, and the means to kill Eden and Echo Hines. More importantly, Mr. Turnbull's DNA matches the semen sample taken from Echo Hines and also matches DNA found on their car's steering wheel. And DNA evidence, ladies and gentlemen of the jury, is definitive, scientific proof that is utterly unimpeachable. Thank you."

The jurors looked like they wanted to applaud. I had to admit, it was quite a performance. I was hopeful that Arnett would match it, live up to his own hype.

Judge Greene looked down from the bench. "Mr. Arnett?"

"Your Honor, we will present our opening statement after the Government rests its case."

I didn't think it was smart to leave the jury with such a visceral presentation without telling our side of the story. Judge Greene had addressed the jurors for a reason. Research showed that about eighty percent of jurors lock in their verdict immediately after hearing opening statements.

Judge Greene furrowed his brow. "Very well," he said, "the prosecution may call their first witness."

"The prosecution calls FBI Section Chief Dr. Ruth Jacobson."

Ruth walked down the aisle, wearing a navy pantsuit with a leopard print scarf discreetly tucked into her collar.

Judge Greene looked at the bailiff. "Please swear in the witness."

The bailiff faced Ruth. "Please raise your right hand. "Do you swear to tell the truth, the whole truth, and nothing but the truth?"

"I do."

Sevier began his questions. "Dr. Jacobson, did you interview Henry Turnbull about the murders of Eden and Echo Hines?"

"Yes, I did."

"Did Mr. Turnbull say where he was the night they were killed?"

"He said he was at Biggy's Bar outside of Annapolis."

"Were you able to verify that Mr. Turnbull was at Biggy's Bar that night?"

"Yes."

"How were you able to do that?"

"I examined Biggy's security tapes."

"And what time did Mr. Turnbull leave Biggy's?"

"The tape shows Mr. Turnbull left Biggy's at 2:00 in the morning."

The prosecutor picked up a small black box and showed it to Ruth. "Is this the video-tape from Biggy's Bar that shows Mr. Turnbull exiting the building?"

Ruth examined the FBI label glued to its side. "Yes, it is."

"Your Honor, I request that Government's exhibit #1 be admitted into evidence."

"Now, Dr. Jacobson, how long would it take for Mr. Turnbull to drive from Biggy's Bar to the Blackhall estate?"

"About thirty minutes."

"Thank you. No further questions."

"Do you care to cross-examine the witness, Mr. Arnett?" Judge Greene asked.

"No, your Honor."

"The prosecution may call its next witness."

"The prosecution calls Dr. Jordan Marsh to the witness stand."

"Dr. Marsh, please recite your credentials for the court."

"I am a Forensic Pathologist for the State of Maryland. I have a medical degree from the University of Maryland—"

"Your Honor," Arnett interrupted, "defense will stipulate to Dr. Marsh's credentials."

Sevier nodded. "Dr. Marsh, can you tell the court the estimated time of death for Eden and Echo Hines?"

"I determined that they died sometime after 3:00 the morning of June 2nd."

"And what is that determination based on?"

"On the known time of their last meal and the digestive process of the contents of their stomachs, ascertained during the autopsies I performed on their bodies."

"And was a drug test also administered?"

"Yes."

"And what, if anything, did that test reveal?"

"Eden and Echo Hines were both subdued with a drug known as Scopolamine."

"Does Scopolamine have a street name?"

"Yes, it's known on the street as Devil's Breath or the Zombie Drug."

"Please tell us what Scopolamine does."

"It puts victims in a hypnotic state."

"Thank you, no further questions your Honor."

"Mr. Arnett, do you wish to cross-examine?" Judge Greene asked.

"Yes, your Honor."

Arnett straightened his tie and faced Marsh. "Dr. Marsh, is the drug known as Scopolamine commonly available in the United States?"

"No, sir."

"Would you say that it's rare? Even exotic?"

"I don't know your definition of exotic," Dr. Marsh said.

"Well, have you come across it before where it's been used to subdue a victim?"

"In the autopsies I've performed? No."

"In other countries, is it more common for criminals to use Scopolamine to subdue victims?"

"I believe it's used in crimes committed in South America, sometimes in Europe. It seems to be their date rape drug of choice."

"And in this case, how was this drug administered to Eden and Echo Hines?"

"In powder form. We found traces of it in their nostrils."

"And how did the powder get into their nostrils?"

"It appears the powder was blown into the victims' faces and they involuntarily inhaled it."

"So, Eden and Echo Hines were administered a powdered form of Scopolamine. Yet, the FBI did not find any Scopolamine or any trace of Scopolamine on Henry Turnbull or at his residence, did they?"

"I believe that's correct."

"So, we are to believe that this old family caretaker somehow procured this rare, powdered Scopolamine, kept it handy just for the day the President's daughters showed up so he could rape and kill them and knew how to use and dispose of the drug, all without leaving any trace of the powder on his person or his possessions?"

"Objection!" Sevier sputtered. "Argumentative!"

"Sustained."

"No more questions, your Honor."

Judge Greene looked at the clock on the wall. "It's getting late. We'll pick up in the morning. Court is adjourned for the day." He slammed down his gavel.

****

The President turned to Chief Justice Bannister Brown. "What the hell is going on? Now, Alexander is part of Turnbull's defense team! Can't you get the man disbarred?"

Brown stretched his neck. "Sir, by itself, having an affair is not a basis for disbarment. If it were, there'd be no attorneys left." Chief Brown was angry at the President for hectoring him and furious at Alexander for using the lack of a written ethics code as carte blanche to do as he pleased, including representing Henry Turnbull, an action that brought the Brown Court under even greater Congressional scrutiny. "I need him to resign," Brown said.

"He's not going to resign," the President huffed. "You would have to force him out."

"Any of the other Justices would resign," Brown muttered.

"He's not like the other Justices. He's … different," the President said.

Which made Brown wonder what Lilly had seen in Alexander. Alexander may have graduated from Harvard Law School but the man had attended a public high school. What kind of education was that? And that unfortunate Wyoming connection. No wonder he had no social skills. But it seemed that women were attracted to Alexander in a lewd, physical way. Chief Brown snorted. "Did you know that Alexander's father was some sort of rodeo circuit rider who deserted his own family?"

"Circuit rider? I heard that his father was the rodeo clown," the President said.

"Clown?" Chief Brown started laughing, tears streaming down his face. "Oh, my God! That's too good. I hadn't heard that although I knew his uncle was a rancher. Alexander said he shared a sleeping bag with a Navajo

Indian on a cattle drive. He told me himself. Just threw the information out there, like that was normal behavior." Brown wiped tears from his eyes.

"Are you kidding?" The President shook his head.

"The man grew up like a boxcar tramp," Brown said. "And with that background, what kind of intellectual gravitas can Alexander bring to the Court? I work with the man and I can tell you—none. It's a travesty that he's on the Court."

"I wonder how he got into Harvard," the President mused.

"I think that was about the time Harvard started putting an emphasis on diversity."

The President raised his eyebrows. "*White trash* is now a legally protected class?"

They roared with laughter. But something had to be done about Alexander. White trash or not, he had street smarts and he wasn't going away.

CHAPTER 39

Two o'clock in the morning and Jerry Arnett sank deeper into the bucket seats of his Ferrari parked outside the Uptown Tap House on Connecticut Avenue. He was waiting for a mysterious informant and he was getting discouraged. The man had called two hours ago, requesting a meeting in the restaurant's parking lot and he should've shown by now.

A shuffling noise behind the car. Startled, Arnett swung his head around. Just a guy taking a short-cut through the lot. He watched in his rearview mirror as the man jumped into a large black SUV and drove off.

Arnett had almost dismissed the caller as a kook until the man had started talking about a Revelation Crystal Decanter that had been stolen from Blackhall. That was something not known to the public. The caller claimed to have the decanter in his possession and information about who'd stolen it. If Arnett could present evidence to the jury that placed a burglar at Blackhall the night of the murders, that could be a game changer, raise reasonable doubt as to who killed the twins.

Arnett looked at the time again. A little after 2:00. He listened. The sound of cicadas rose, banked, and fell in an endless primal pattern. No other sound. The caller wasn't going to show. It was time to head home. Reluctantly, Arnett revved the Ferrari and headed west on Massachusetts Avenue. Near the Brazilian Embassy, he made a left-hand turn, his headlights picking out the grainy, black asphalt as he sped down the incline to Rock Creek Parkway. He didn't see the black SUV pull close behind him.

Arnett took two curves and downshifted at the bottom of the hill before merging onto the parkway. To his left, a horrible screech and—bam! He slammed on his brakes but his car kept moving sideways. The black SUV had crashed into the driver's side and was pushing him off the road.

Blood drained from his face. *Shit!* He tried to control the Ferrari. A bridge abutment came hurtling at him. He gripped the steering wheel and turned it with all his strength but it was useless. His car was no match against the powerful beast. He braced himself.

****

At 2:45 a.m., on a lonely stretch of Rock Creek Parkway, Jerry Arnett's bright red Ferrari was found wrapped around the base of Lauzun's Legion Bridge. Arnett lived alone and no one knew why he'd been out at that time of night but it appeared he was on his way home because the accident happened a few yards from the P Street entrance into Georgetown. Jerry Arnett was 50 years old. Jerry Arnett was dead.

The patrol cop who'd happened on the scene found Arnett hanging from his seat belt, eyes wide open, gasping for air. Arnett grabbed at the policeman with a grip shocking for someone who was dying and practically ripped the buttons from the officer's uniform. The cop cut through the seat belt and tried to administer CPR but by the time Arnett was on the ground, it was too late.

****

"Yes, Mr. President," General Fontaine said. "Arnett lost control and hit the bridge. Nasty business."

The President sucked in his breath. "You didn't have anything to do with that, did you?"

"Sir, the U.S. Marshals were moving Turnbull every night. It was impossible to take him out because my people could never set up a plan for going in. And, sir, we discussed—"

The President shot to his feet. "We discussed Turnbull, not Arnett!"

"Calm down, sir."

The President ran his hand through his hair. "*Christ.* Turnbull murdered my daughters but Arnett … what have you done?"

"Sir, with Arnett out of the way, we're assured of a conviction and no one will dare take over Turnbull's case. The Judge will have to appoint a public defender and I'll make sure the only ones available are just out of law school."

"How the hell could you do that?"

"It's not as difficult as it sounds." Fontaine smiled. "I did this for you, sir. One day, you'll be grateful."

✶✶✶✶

A shock wave reverberated through the legal community. Attorneys whispered among themselves. Hadn't they warned Arnett not to take Turnbull as a client? The White House was a dangerous adversary.

I know I was suspicious. "The newspaper reported two sets of skid marks. It looks like someone ran him off the road."

Henry shook his head sadly. "Does he have family?"

"Not in town. He has a nephew in Iowa who is flying out to take care of the arrangements."

A tear ran down Henry's face and he wiped it away with the back of his hand. "Bless his soul," he said. "He was a good Christian."

That wouldn't have been my first thought about Jerry Arnett but it was probably Henry's highest compliment. "Okay, Henry, we need to address that you are now without counsel."

"The Judge will declare a mistrial," Davis informed Henry.

"No. I think Judge Greene will forge ahead," I said.

Davis stirred in his chair. "You think anyone will want to represent Henry after what happened to Arnett?"

"No. That means the Judge will appoint a public defender." I turned to Henry. "Henry, if you want a public defender, fine. There are some good ones out there. However, it's difficult for any attorney to be dropped into the middle of a trial. It's like being dropped into a bucket of ice. On the other hand, I'm familiar with the case and the evidence."

Davis saw where I was going. "Your experience is as a prosecutor…"

"A good prosecutor prepares as though he's going to argue both sides of a case."

"Why would you want to do that?"

"I'm already involved." I looked Henry squarely in the face. "And I wouldn't be if I thought you were guilty."

"What about the Supreme Court?" Davis asked. "Chief Brown is already hopping mad about your involvement."

"That's a different battle."

"Do you really want to push Brown on this? You can do a lot of good on the Supreme Court."

"I have that under control."

Davis looked at Henry. "What do you think, Henry? Sounds like a pretty good offer to me."

Henry smiled. "I'd sure be grateful, Justice Alexander."

CHAPTER 40

"Your Honor, this is outrageous!" U.S. Attorney Bill Sevier roared.

Judge Greene peered at him from behind rimless spectacles. "It would be helpful, Mr. Sevier, if you would articulate your objections."

"The Code of Conduct for U.S. Judges prohibits them from representing clients in court."

"Supreme Court Justices aren't bound by an ethics code," I said.

"Your Honor," Sevier said, "ethics aside, the jury's gonna associate Justice Alexander with the Supreme Court and that will be prejudicial to our side."

Judge Greene swirled in his chair. It creaked. "Justice Alexander's been sitting at the defense table all this time and I haven't heard a peep from you."

"That's, that's different," Sevier sputtered, his face looking like a sack of red apples.

"You're saying the jury didn't recognize him when he was sitting at the defense table but they will the minute he jumps to his feet?"

"Of course not. Most people don't know a Supreme Court Justice by sight. But you'll be calling him by name!"

"Alexander is a common enough name," Judge Greene sniffed. "There's no reason I have to refer to him as Justice Alexander. I will refer to him as Mr. Alexander. Now, are you satisfied?"

"No!"

"Counsel. Lower your voice."

"I apologize, your Honor."

Judge Greene removed his eyeglasses and twirled them in his hand. "Your objection is noted, Mr. Sevier, but it was best brought at the beginning of the trial. Now, I have additional concerns. For one thing, I have a duty to the taxpayers. Hundreds of thousands of dollars of tax money have already been invested in this proceeding. It would double the cost to declare a mistrial and start over. I know you think I can magically find a replacement for Mr. Arnett just like that," Judge Greene leaned in and snapped his fingers in Sevier's face, "however, the most experienced lawyer in Mr. Arnett's firm has never handled a death penalty case, whereas Justice Alexander has. Then, of course, there's the pesky little problem that no other attorneys want to take this case. I wonder why that is," he said sarcastically.

"With all due respect your Honor," Sevier said, "a public defender would be required to represent Mr. Turnbull."

"Someone who isn't versed in the case? At this point in the trial, that would hardly make for a vigorous defense. Mr. Sevier, if Justice Alexander is brave enough to take this on and Mr. Turnbull is satisfied with his new counsel, you are just gonna have to live with it."

"Thank you, your Honor," I said.

"You're dismissed," Judge Greene said with a wave of his hand. "All of you."

I jumped in. "Your Honor, there's another matter that needs the court's attention. Now that Jerry Arnett has died under suspicious circumstances, our DNA expert has withdrawn from the trial. He's receiving death threats and he's terrified."

Judge Greene pondered my words.

"Even before Arnett's death, our expert witnesses started getting death threats the minute we hired them. The Hines trial is an emotionally charged case, my client is the most hated man in America, and anyone affiliated with the defense automatically becomes a villain. I suspect your gag order is being violated for use against us."

Judge Greene puckered his mouth. "How many times has this happened?"

"Three times."

Judge Greene looked at Bill Sevier. "I have a gag order in place that precludes the release of witness names. If their names are placed into the public domain, that not only threatens their safety, it makes providing a proper defense impossible when Mr. Turnbull has a constitutional right to a fair trial. Do you care to comment, Mr. Sevier?"

Sevier looked flabbergasted. "Your Honor, the U.S. Attorney's Office would never participate in the harassment of a witness."

"Yet, these witnesses' names are being released by someone. I'm not saying you are harassing anyone, Mr. Sevier, but it seems you have a leak in your office."

Sevier put his hand over his heart. "Your Honor, it isn't us!"

Judge Greene was silent for a few minutes. "Justice Alexander, find a new DNA expert and Mr. Sevier, since you are in charge of your office, you will be held in contempt of court and face significant jail time if this happens again." Judge Greene punched his finger at Sevier. "I will not have an expert witness intimidated and a man denied a right to a fair trial in my courtroom! Do you understand me?"

"Yes, your Honor," Sevier said meekly.

CHAPTER 41

When I took over Henry's case, the other lawyers in Jerry Arnett's law firm had shoved Henry's files at me, said *adios amigo* and slammed the door behind me. I'd heard laughter and cheering on my way out.

My study at home was now Litigation Central. I had so many papers in the room, it looked like I was mapping battle plans for the Normandy invasion. My files covered the red sofa, blocked the fireplace, and spilled down the hallway. Claire had suggested setting up road cones.

I was deep into the DNA report when the doorbell rang. I tried to stand up. The chair came with me. I had molded into the Goddamn chair! Visions of myself as an old man flashed through my head—all bent over, the undertaker breaking my back to get the coffin closed. I needed to get back on the running trail before my body atrophied into a U-turn. I shook the chair loose and it clattered to the floor. Hobbling down the hallway, my knees creaking like old hinges, I wondered why I was bothering—it would be a journalist on the other side, looking for a new bone to chew.

"Jake!" I couldn't believe my eyes.

Jake was standing on my doorstep, looking amazingly fit and deeply tan. His time in Nepal had changed him from a frazzled-looking law clerk into a buff-looking movie star.

"Justice A." He held out his hand and displayed gleaming white teeth. It made me realize how long it had been since anyone outside my immediate family had smiled at me. I grabbed his shoulders like he was my only friend in the world. "Come in. Has it been a month already?"

"More," he said as I led him to my war room. He surveyed the scene— the computer logged on to WestLaw, the litigation briefcases overflowing with case law, the post-it notes on my desk lamp, scribbles of last minute thoughts about how I wanted to present evidence to the jury.

He flinched. "I heard you were taking over Turnbull's case. Hard to believe there's this much material. A lot for one person to manage."

"Sit down. Can I get you something to drink?" I cleared a chair.

"No thanks," he said, still glancing around the room. "Actually, I can't stay. I stopped by to volunteer my services."

I lifted my head, thinking this was too good to be true. "You want to join the defense team?"

"It's hardly a team," Jake snorted. "You need help."

"You should know what you're getting into before you make the offer."

"It's—"

"Jake, listen to me. Jerry Arnett pushed for an early trial date and since his death, the other lawyers and investigators have quit the case. It's up to me to find new investigators and with the rumors about Arnett's death, that's proven to be impossible. Also, there are still people to be interviewed and it's all on me." Jake started to interrupt and I held up my hand. "As I said, there are suspicions about Arnett's death and that's something you should consider. Your safety could be at risk."

"You think Arnett was murdered?" He looked shocked.

"It's possible. Bottom line, I think you should sleep on it before you make a decision."

Jake straightened his shoulders. "I don't need to sleep on it. I'm in. Mountain climbing in Nepal was not exactly safe."

"What about Davidson and Davidson? They may be unhappy about the publicity. Arnett's firm was ecstatic to get rid of Turnbull."

"I don't start for another two months." Jake grinned. "C'mon! What else am I going to do with my time?" He grew serious. "You were there for me Justice A. when I needed you and now, I'm returning the favor."

I studied him. "Are you sure?"

"Yes."

I decided to take him at his word.

"Okay," I said, opening my desk drawer, grabbing a house key and handing it to him. "You may need this because this is the only place where I can keep these files. And I need you to start as soon as possible. While I find a new DNA expert, I want you to go out to Anne Arundel County and interview some witnesses."

I'd been granted a miracle. Jake was a damn fine lawyer and would be a tremendous asset.

★★★★

That night, I decided I was a fool for ignoring what had happened to Jerry Arnett. I called the Supreme Court Police, the first time I'd ever asked for their protection. They were at my house within minutes.

CHAPTER 42

Reed had returned to Washington because of Henry Turnbull's trial. And that had begun to make him angry. Real angry. But she was back. About time! She couldn't treat him like a nobody. The President's daughters had made that mistake. He'd been in the mansion, looking for things to steal, when Rideout arrived, then the President's daughters. He'd crouched in a closet and peered through the keyhole while Rideout had his go at the girls. After Rideout left for the airport, the girls had tarried behind. How unfortunate for them.

He always carried a stash of Scopolamine with him, just in case he came across a pretty face on his forays into local mansions. But the twins had been surprisingly impervious to it. He'd struck Eden across her mouth and she'd fallen and cracked her head and Echo had tried to run him through with his own knife. It was a pleasure tearing his knife from her hands and driving it through her heart. Again and again. In and out. In and out. Like sex. But better. He liked killing. It was an acquired taste and once it had touched his tongue …

He'd started young, killing his grandmother's prized Corgis, experimenting with poison, graduating to snapping their necks, making it look like a fox had killed them on the grounds of her vast estate. But he had to be careful with Reed. He had big plans for her. He needed to bring her along slowly, carefully. So far, she was unsuspecting, like a baby bird cupped in his hands. And he needed to make Reed think everything was normal so he could continue snatching small items to keep him afloat while he figured out how to get the larger, more important pieces out of the house. There were antiques much too valuable to leave behind.

He wouldn't kill Reed … yet. That was his desert, like chocolate ice cream and her baby's kill would be the cherry on top! Right now, he was still on the main course, fulfilling one of his biggest sexual fantasies by sneaking into her bedroom, standing over her, and jacking off while she slept.

He'd been using the cliff staircase to access the house. Dangerous as it was, it was doable for someone in his peak physical condition equipped with some rock climbing gear. But any valuables had to be carted away in his backpack. And he needed the antiques. He was in a precarious financial spot.

Fortunately, everyone accepted him because of his wealthy family, good looks, and accomplishments, including Reed. About the time the cliff staircase had been torn down, *Reed had given him the code to the gate.* Handed it to him herself, written on her very own stationery! Nonetheless, there was a problem. That damn Davis Rideout had hired guards to man the gate and he couldn't drive vans of antiques past them without arousing suspicion. Yes, his timing had to be perfect.

He saw movement in the house. A light came on in the library. He crept over the grounds. There she was! He raised his eyes to window level and licked his lips. The beautiful bird was feeding her baby chick. He liked that.

A noise. He peered into the dark. Was someone coming? A guard on patrol? He whirled back to the window and Reed looked up. *Damn.* Had she seen him? He was cornered, crouched under the window ledge. He'd have to think fast.

****

Reed adjusted her nursing bra and buttoned up her blouse in the library where she'd just fed Samuel. She was about to take him upstairs and put him in his crib for the night when she happened to look up. Plastered against the window was a man's face! She screamed and grabbed her blouse, her heart jumping out of her chest.

She rushed to the French doors and swung them open. "Harrison! What are you doing? You scared me to death!"

"I'm so sorry," he said, his brows knitted together. "You didn't answer the doorbell so I came around here."

"I thought I told you, it's broken," she said, thinking how creepy it was that he'd been looking at her through the window in the dark.

He took her hand and kissed her cheek. "I didn't mean to scare you. I tried to call earlier."

She glanced around for her phone. "I guess I left my phone upstairs."

He smiled. "Lucky that you gave me the gate code. And thank God you did because this place has become quite the fortress." He laughed. "In fact, I just ran into a guard patrolling the grounds."

"Davis's idea."

"A good one. Listen, I was hoping we could meet tonight. I'm going to be out of touch for a few days. My uncle's in the hospital. Nothing too serious but he's having surgery in the morning."

"What happened to him?"

"He fell and fractured his hip. He's getting old, so I guess it's not entirely unexpected."

"I'm so sorry." Reed hesitated. "Is he your uncle who decorated some rooms here?"

He smiled proudly. "Yes. Lawrence Smith. You may have heard of him."

Reed shook her head.

"No? Well, he was quite well known in his day. My mother was his assistant. Uncle Lawrence was an established interior decorator when she graduated from Swarthmore and joined his firm. She was a true talent and also quite beautiful. They worked together on large estates for the crème de la crème of society." He laughed. "I'm a lot like her, I'm afraid."

"Is she still working?"

"Oh no. She died young." He shook his head, sadly. "A hunting accident."

"That's too bad," Reed said, studying Harrison's face.

Harrison smiled. "Please, don't misunderstand. My life has been amazing. My grandfather was in the Kennedy administration. He retired soon after I was born and I spent a lot of time with my grandparents at our ancestral home in Cornwall. Have you ever been to Cornwall? No? Well, it's wonderful, the landscape is so dramatic. And our roots run deep in England. My grandmother inherited a peerage and my great-grandfather was in the House of Lords. I had a wonderful childhood, roaming around their estate, learning to ride, fox-hunting, all the things the English love. And I attended Eton, where I received an amazing education, before coming back here to college."

"What about your father?"

"He was wealthy but my mother died and he was busy pursuing other women, so my grandparents took over. It actually worked out quite well."

"Your family sounds interesting. You should be proud."

"I am, Reed dear, believe me, I am." He sat down. "Listen, I'm glad we could meet tonight and I'm thrilled you're going to be making Blackhall your permanent home. I was afraid," he said, lowering his voice and looking over his shoulder like someone might be listening, "with the murders here and all, you'd change your mind and abandon the place." He frowned. "And to let such a grand house collapse under its own weight would be such a shame."

Reed drew herself up to full height. "No, I'm staying and ... and ..." her eyes welled up, "I'm leaving Davis. So, it's perfect timing."

Harrison reached out and patted her knee. "I had no idea. I'm so sorry." He looked around the room. "Well, don't worry about the murders, the renovation will sweep them away like they never, ever happened."

"Harrison, nothing can change that! That was awful." She shuddered. "I want to ... no, I need to transform this house. Henry is right, it needs to be cleansed. So, I've decided to go ahead with the renovations."

Harrison nodded approvingly. "That's wonderful. Just wonderful."

CHAPTER 43

A black van pulled up to the E. Barrett Prettyman Courthouse and Claire and Reed emerged—two elegant, tall women who looked like their legs had never stopped growing. Reed was dressed in a conservative white suit. Claire had advised her, "Don't wear black in front of the jury" and Reed had taken Claire's advice seriously.

The minute their feet touched the pavement, they were mobbed by news reporters frantically shouting questions. Claire put an arm around Reed's shoulders and anchored a spot on the courthouse steps. Cameras clicked away and a red-haired reporter thrust a mike in Reed's face. "Mrs. Rideout! You're here for Mr. Turnbull's trial. Why?"

Reed pulled off her sunglasses. Silence descended on the crowd. Reed's blonde hair was a tumble of gold in the sunlight and her lips were pink and plump. "I know Henry Turnbull," she said in a voice like raw silk, smooth with occasional catches, "and I'm here to show my support for him. He is a good and honorable man and he could never kill anyone. I completely believe in his innocence. And that's all I have to say. Thank you." Claire grabbed her hand and they bounced up the courthouse steps, pursued by a mob of reporters shouting questions at their backs.

****

I was grateful that Claire had taken a day away from her litigation schedule to accompany Reed and show support for Henry. On the other hand, I'd banned Davis from the courtroom. Arnett was right. Davis had gotten so much bad publicity that physical proximity to Henry could prejudice the jury.

A hush fell as Claire and Reed slipped through the crowd to the seats I'd reserved for them behind the defense table. Reed and Henry hugged.

"Where's Jake?" Claire asked, looking concerned. Claire had been beside herself with worry about me since Arnett's death.

"He's interviewing witnesses. He'll be back tomorrow."

"You're all alone up here."

"I'm in the middle of a federal courtroom surrounded by U.S. Marshals."

Claire chewed her lower lip. "What about the Supreme Court Police? Where are they? They're supposed to be here."

"They're in the gallery in plain clothes. I have more protection than Area 51."

Claire looked around and jerked her head toward the prosecution table. "They certainly look confident," she said as she slid into her seat.

"No kidding." Bill Sevier and his team looked like Wall Street bankers moving in to foreclose on a small family farm.

I was like a donkey without a cart. Sevier had the full resources of the Government at his disposal, whereas I still hadn't been able to scare up an investigator, certainly not one who ever wanted to consult for the U.S. Attorney's Office again. And I would be lucky to find a good DNA expert. As it was, I was scrambling to learn about DNA from the Internet, hardly an ideal situation.

Sevier was on his feet.

The prosecution calls FBI Special Agent Nick Zulauf.

Sevier began his questions. "Special Agent Zulauf, please tell us what you found relating to the deaths of Eden and Echo Hines at the estate known as Blackhall."

"We found Eden and Echo's car parked in the stable and Echo's blood on the rug in Blackhall's library. And, of course, we found their bodies buried on the property."

"And can you tell us the exact location where Eden's and Echo's bodies were found?"

"About a mile east of the mansion."

"Thank you, no further questions." Sevier sat down.

"Care to cross-examine?" Judge Greene asked.

"Yes, your Honor." I jumped up and headed to the side of the courtroom where I retrieved a large aerial photo of the Blackhall property and placed it on an easel.

"Special Agent Zulauf, is this the spot where Eden's and Echo's bodies were found?" I pointed to the photo where I'd marked an X.

"Yes, sir. Where the X is."

"And what is the terrain like in that immediate area?"

"As you can see, it's thick forest."

"Could a person drive a car to the location?"

"Not unless you cut down those trees."

"I offer the aerial view of the Blackhall property into evidence as defense exhibit #1. No further questions." I sat down.

The prosecution calls Dr. Daniel Hallerburg to the stand.

The bailiff swore him in.

Sevier approached the witness stand. "Dr. Hallerburg, would you state your credentials for the court?"

"Yes, I have been Chief of the FBI's Forensic Research Science Unit since 2011. I have a Biology Degree from the University of Michigan and a Medical Degree from Harvard Medical School."

"And have you been able to match the DNA samples found at the crime scene to a suspect?"

"Yes, we matched the sample to the defendant, Mr. Henry Turnbull."

"Please tell the court how you did that."

"We deduced the DNA profile of a minor contributor to the sample and searched the CODIS database for someone with a matching DNA profile."

"And for the benefit of the jury, please tell us what CODIS is."

"An acronym for the FBI's Combined DNA Index System. It contains the DNA profiles of almost 13 million people."

"Thank you. Now. Do you know why Mr. Turnbull's DNA was in the database?"

"I'm unsure of the precipitating factor but I know that Maryland takes the DNA of all arrestees."

"Please tell us how frequently this particular DNA profile occurs in the general population."

"It occurs in fewer than one in one trillion people."

"And how was that random match probability arrived at?"

"The semen sample from the crime scene matches Mr. Turnbull's DNA at 9 Core Loci and exhibits an extremely rare allele, which increases the mathematical probability of the match to one in one trillion."

"Please tell the court about this rare allele."

"We observed a never before seen allele in the semen sample, a 9 at D3S1358. Mr. Turnbull's DNA also has this same rare allele. A 9 at D3 has never been reported in the STR base so at first, we thought it was a mistake until we ran the sample through CODIS."

"Please tell the Court the FBI standards for determining a DNA match."

"The FBI typically requires a minimum of 13 Core Loci, but in this case, the DNA was partially degraded. Nonetheless, we were able to confidently determine alleles from someone other than the victim at 9 Core Loci."

"And what are the minimum loci requirements for the sample to be searched in CODIS?"

"At least 8 of the 13 CODIS Core Loci if combined with a match rarity of at least one in ten million. And the crime scene sample falls within those parameters."

"Did you perform any other tests on this sample?"

"Yes. We used a test kit called a Y-filer in order to get a clean look at the male DNA."

"Why was that necessary?"

"When DNA samples are collected in sexual assault cases, they often contain relatively little male DNA relative to the amount of a female victim's DNA. In effect, the male profile is overwhelmed by the female profile. On the other hand, Y-STRs are found only in male DNA and the female DNA does not interfere with the detection of the Y-STRs."

"And what were the results of that test?"

"The Y-filer test kit generates results from 16 different loci on the Y chromosome. Mr. Turnbull was a perfect match at all 16 loci."

"Can a conclusion can be drawn from the Y-STR test?"

"Yes. It's independent confirmation that Mr. Turnbull is the source of the DNA from the semen sample found in Echo Hines."

"And can a conclusion can be drawn from the results of both tests?"

"The chance that a randomly chosen, unrelated individual would be found to have the same DNA profile found in both the evidence sample and Mr. Turnbull's reference sample is less than one in one trillion."

"No further questions."

Judge Greene turned to me. "Mr. Alexander, do you care to cross?"

"Yes, your Honor."

I stood. "Dr. Hallerburg, I think we need to back up a bit and educate those of us who do not have a Ph.D in science on exactly what you mean when you talk about a DNA profile and a DNA match."

Hallerburg turned to look at the jury. "Since the 1990's, the FBI has been generating DNA at a set of 13 to 15 core short tandem repeat loci. Each locus has two alleles, one inherited from each parent. On an electrophero-gram, these alleles show up as peaks and they can be seen to vary from per-son to person. If there are enough common alleles between the DNA sample and the suspect, that is considered to be a match."

"Please tell the court whether the height of these peaks is taken into account as a part of the DNA analysis."

"It is. The height of the peaks corresponds to the quantity of DNA present in the original sample. Peaks representing alleles from a single per-son are generally expected to have the same height."

"Are there ever problems with DNA samples collected from a crime scene?"

"Yes, as samples age, DNA begins to break down, due to warmth, moisture, or a variety of other factors, and degradation can result in signif-icant loss of the largest DNA molecules within a sample. That's what hap-pened in this case. The DNA degraded and resulted in some peaks falling below a pre-determined height threshold that is considered to be reliable. If peaks are too low, they can't be distinguished from background noise."

"And by background noise, you mean—"

"Air bubbles, urea crystals, or other sample contaminates that affect the testing process."

"I'm going to show you an electropherogram displaying the 15 loci from the DNA sample retrieved from the crime scene and its comparison to Mr. Turnbull's DNA. As you just stated, the FBI submitted 9 of these 15 loci to CODIS. Yet, these 6 loci—the ones from the evidence sample that you did not submit for comparison—show peaks that correspond to alleles that Mr. Turnbull could not have contributed, do they not? His peaks are not in the same position as the peaks in the crime scene sample."

"The 6 loci you reference are unreliable because the peaks are too low in height to be distinguished from background noise."

"You mention pre-determined height levels. Are there any generally accepted thresholds for how high a peak must be to qualify as a real allele, as opposed to simply background noise?"

"Well—"

"Yes or no."

"No."

"Might not other testing labs or experts consider these 6 loci to be of sufficient height to be reliable?"

"Possibly."

"So, the FBI's interpretation that Mr. Turnbull is the contributor of the DNA from the crime scene is subjective, is it not? As you stated, there is no universally accepted height level threshold for peaks and another lab or expert could have excluded Mr. Turnbull as being the contributor of the DNA using your own test results."

"I don't think that's likely, the FBI tests are—"

"A yes or no answer, please."

"Yes, it's possible."

"No further questions."

The press murmured among themselves, shook their heads and took notes.

★★★★

Reed's spirits were high on her drive back to Blackhall. She didn't know anything about DNA but from the reaction of the press, she suspected her father had put a dent in the prosecution's evidence.

Her cell phone rang.

A disembodied voice said, "I saw you in court today."

"Harrison, how are you? You were there?"

"No, on TV. You looked beautiful."

She giggled.

"I was wondering if you'd have dinner with me."

"Where are you?"

"At Blackhall."

She burst out laughing. "I never know where you're going to show up, what you're going to do."

"I know what I'd like to do," he muttered.

"What?"

"Nothing. So, will you? Have dinner with me?"

"I'm driving up Blackhall Lane right now, so why not?"

CHAPTER 44

Chief Brown had requested another meeting but Henry's trial consumed every second of my time. Brown said it was urgent, so I'd agreed to talk on the phone. I was listening to Chief Brown, thinking how much I had grown to hate the sound of his voice when he threw a thunderbolt at me.

"I've had a visit from two FBI agents," he said. "A Charles Young and a Ginger Baker. They're looking into Lilly's murder—"

"Murder?"

"They found her body. They said they talked to you so I thought you knew."

"No. Why didn't they tell me?"

"Maybe because you're their prime suspect!" he shouted.

I heard plastic crack on his end, probably from squeezing the phone too hard.

"Jesus Christ, I can't believe this is happening," he said. "Her body was found in Blackhall's attic during the FBI search. She was killed with a screwdriver a few days after Eden and Echo Hines were murdered."

My head was swimming. Lilly murdered at Blackhall? *The decomposition smell in the house.* Henry said he moved Eden and Echo Hines's bodies out of the house the morning after they were killed, yet the smell of rotting flesh was in the library a week later. The smell of death hadn't been from a raccoon. It had been from Lilly's body. *While I leisurely dined on the terrace.* I almost vomited.

"My God, man," Brown said. "Don't you understand how serious this is? A member of the United States Supreme Court can't be implicated in a murder. I insist that you resign from the Court!"

I'd been prepared to hear that Lilly had been killed—but not at Blackhall. I ran my hand through my hair, reeling from the news and its implications, the most worrisome of which was that my daughter was out there at an estate where three women had been found dead.

****

I called Reed but she didn't answer. I left a message begging her to move out of that house and back into Washington until all three murders were solved. I waited. Nothing. I was ready to put my fist through a wall. I called Davis.

"Yeah, I heard about Lilly," he said. "It's on the news. It's awful. God, I can't believe what's happened out there. Maybe we should shutter the house."

"That's the best idea I've heard in a long time! Davis, I have to ask. Do you know anything about Lilly's murder?"

"Of course not. Have some faith in me."

That was hard. Honestly, I didn't know what to think anymore. "I'm worried about Reed. I can't get hold of her."

"She won't return my calls," Davis said. "She's mad at me. I'm not sure what she's doing. The last I heard she's working with an architect on plans for the renovations."

"Have you met the architect?"

"No, but his name is Harrison Smith. Reed says he comes highly recommended."

"I'm not worried about his credentials. I'm worried about Reed alone at Blackhall. What is it with her and that Goddamn house?" I muttered.

"I don't know. She won't budge. Something about showing her independence. Look, I took your advice and hired security guards. I have twelve guards patrolling the grounds and another eight stationed at the gate, all on different shifts around the clock. No one can get in without the code and going through an ID check with them. I call them every day to make sure she's okay."

That made me feel better and I hung up. I had to prepare for court in the morning but I googled "Harrison Smith, Annapolis, Maryland." His website looked polished and impressive. I clicked on a photo of Harrison at a construction site, looking confident and in charge. He was medium height with curly blond hair, piercing blue eyes, and an athletic build. A good-looking guy.

I wove a path through the papers and files in my study to a small bar under the bookcase and grabbed a bottle of Oban. I poured some of the amber colored liquid and slugged it back. I told myself that Reed was a grown woman. But the guards at the gate were a half-mile away from the main house and couldn't get to her quickly. It wasn't the best situation.

The television was on mute and I happened to glance up. Tommy Woofer appeared on-screen, looking like he'd just won the lottery. A banner scrolled beneath his face.

U.S. Supreme Court Justice Warren Alexander questioned in the murder of his law clerk Lilly McCleary.

I turned up the sound. The first thing I heard him say was "Can this really be happening in the United States?"

Woofer had two guests. One was Ms. Botox lips. "I just knew it! My God! What a family. First, the President's daughters and now, his own law clerk found dead on his son-in-law's estate!"

The other guest was no more constrained in tone. "I'm concerned too, Tommy. What is the status of Ms. McCleary's case? We don't know. It's been buried under Turnbull's trial. If Justice Alexander is a suspect, why has the FBI not pursued him prior to this? Is there favoritism at play? That's not how the system should work."

Botox lips broke in. "And why is Alexander representing Henry Turnbull? I mean, is he a defense attorney or is he a Supreme Court Justice?"

The other guest spoke up. "My big concern, Tommy, is that my sources tell me Justice Alexander was romantically involved with Ms.

McCleary and statistically, we all know that boyfriends are involved in disappearances and deaths."

I was glued to the TV, mortified yet mesmerized, like I was looking into a crystal ball, anxious to ascertain the future but knowing it wouldn't be good. Thank God Henry's jury was sequestered.

Claire came into the room.

"Have you seen this?" I asked her, pointing to the TV.

"I've been watching it upstairs. It's trash. Turn it off."

I reached for the remote. Claire put her arms around me. Thank God she believed in me. And she was right. I needed to turn off the TV. I needed to focus on Henry's trial.

The phone rang. I was surprised to hear Ruth's voice.

"What are you doing?" she asked, her voice low and contrite.

"Right now? Claire and I are watching Tommy Woofer."

"Me too," she sighed. "Warren, you don't deserve this."

"The FBI leaked it."

"No. We think it was the White House."

"Is that why you called?"

"I called to tell you that I know you're a good man and I believe in you."

I was surprised to find myself choking up. "Thank you. It's good to hear your voice ..." I didn't know how to phrase what I wanted to say. "You ..." I struggled for the right words. Ruth meant a lot to me. More than she knew. At one time, after Joanne's death ... but I hesitated about getting involved with someone at work and then Claire had come along. My throat constricted with emotion.

"I'm on your side, Warren. I'll do whatever you need."

I immediately thought of Reed. "If you really mean that, would you see if a Harrison Smith from Annapolis has a record?"

CHAPTER 45

I had a job to do and it was my turn to present our case in court. I began my opening statement, walking along the jury box, making eye contact, but I was receiving a chilly reception from Henry's peers.

"Any person faced with the awesome power of the government is in great jeopardy, even though innocent. Facts are always elusive and often two-faced. What may appear to one to imply guilt may carry no such overtones to another. Every criminal prosecution crosses treacherous ground, for guilt is common to all men." I paused for effect. "That, ladies and gentlemen of the jury, is a quote from the late Justice of the United States Supreme Court, William O. Douglas. Facts are elusive. Appearances are deceptive. Government employees are human and make mistakes. Even the FBI."

I walked behind Henry and placed my hands on his shoulders. "My client, Mr. Henry Turnbull, is an innocent man. He was simply in the wrong place at the wrong time and that has destroyed his reputation, threatened his liberty, and even his life." I walked toward the jury, shaking my head. "The sad fact is that the FBI targeted Mr. Turnbull early on as the primary suspect in the murder of Eden and Echo Hines and never let go *even when the evidence led a bread-crumb trail right to the door of other suspects.*"

As I talked, I watched the jurors. They were frowning. All twelve of them. I thought I'd been effective in countering the prosecution's DNA evidence. Instead, it looked like Henry was headed to death row. I forced myself to remain calm, remembering Churchill's words: *When you're going through hell, keep going.*

"The Hines twins were victims, their deaths tragic. But Mr. Turnbull did not kill them. The Government must prove their case beyond a reasonable doubt, and we will establish that reasonable doubt by showing that several men wanted Eden and Echo Hines dead. But," I pointed to Henry, "Mr. Turnbull was not one of them."

I looked each juror in the eye, at least the ones who would look at me. "As you know, this trial is being called the trial of the century. That's why you have been sequestered. That's not typical in a normal murder trial but outside influences can bring bias to bear and pressure to vote in a certain way. And, like Judge Greene, I'm appealing to you to keep an open mind. The world's eyes are on you, not to convict my client, but to do the right thing. And I am convinced that when you hear the details of our story, you will agree that Mr. Turnbull is innocent and you will acquit him of all charges brought against him. Thank you."

I sat down. Sweat seeped through my shirt and into my jacket. Clearly, I'd gotten through to jurors but in the wrong way. They were shaking their heads no. Only Judge Greene didn't seem to think the trial was over because I heard him say, "Mr. Alexander, you may call your first witness."

I pulled myself together. *"Your Honor, the defense would like to call Anne Arundel Police Commander Anthony Stapleton to the stand."*

Stapleton was sworn in.

"Commander Stapleton. Were you called to the estate known as Blackhall on June 6th?"

"Yes, sir."

"For what reason?" I asked.

"Mrs. Rideout reported a burglary. We've had several burglaries of big mansions in that area."

"Was there anything taken from the estate?"

"Yes sir. An expensive decorative object."

"So, anyone knowing about the contents of Blackhall may have targeted the estate?"

"More than likely."

"And was the burglary the same week the Hines twins were killed?"

"Yes, sir."

"Was the burglary the same night Eden and Echo Hines were killed?"

"It's unclear. It's possible. It was reported as happening sometime during that week."

"Thank you, nothing more."

"Do you wish to cross-examine the witness, Mr. Sevier?" Judge Greene asked.

"No, your Honor."

"*The defense calls Anne Arundel County Sheriff James Arterburn to the stand.*" Arterburn was sworn in.

"Mr. Arterburn, has Mr. Turnbull ever been convicted of a crime?"

"No, sir."

"Then can you tell us why his DNA is in the State of Maryland Database?"

"Mr. Turnbull was in a bar fight ten years ago. He claimed self-defense, his story was backed by several eye-witnesses, and the charges were eventually dropped."

"So, the State of Maryland took his DNA merely as a procedural matter and not because he was convicted of a crime?"

"That's right."

"No further questions, your Honor."

"Do you wish to cross, Mr. Sevier?"

"No, your Honor."

＊＊＊＊

After court recessed for the day, I met privately with Henry. "I'm worried about how the trial is going," I said. "I want you to tell me your entire life story, starting from the beginning. And I don't want you to leave anything out. There's something about this case I'm not understanding."

"Could be a long story."

"We have all night."

"I was born—"

"No. Before that. Tell me about your family. What's their history?"

"Well, my Grandma told me that our family came off a slave ship in Annapolis harbor in 1751 but that's all I know."

"I seem to remember that your father trained horses for Davis's father."

"Yes."

Before we could continue, I got a call from Ruth. "Harrison Smith's full name is Michael Harrison Smith and he's not in the system. However, his company had some financial problems because of the recession. It was touch and go for a while. He barely avoided bankruptcy and he's still not completely in the clear."

"Thanks, Ruth."

"Wait. There's something else. He was working on a renovation when some valuable jewelry disappeared from a client's house. Harrison was accused, charges were filed, but the jewelry suddenly reappeared and the charges withdrawn."

"What do you make of that?"

"I think it could be a worry. That's why I mentioned it."

"Okay. I owe you."

When I turned back to Henry, his eyes were bleary and bloodshot and his neck had slid down his chest. He was losing his will to go on. I gently placed my hand on his back. "Okay, Henry," I said softly. "Let's continue but first, what would you like for dinner? We might as well get some provisions in here."

CHAPTER 46

Reed wiped paint off her nose. She was trying to get on with her life after hearing that Lilly McCleary had been found dead in her attic. It was awful! A total shock! She shuddered just thinking about it.

Her father had called her, begging her to move back to Washington until the murders were solved, but she had more fortitude than people suspected. She was determined to make Blackhall her home, no matter what. Daddy was upset about her decision but the cliff staircase had been torn down and Davis had hired a total of twenty security guards to patrol the grounds and man the gate. Plus, they had that huge wall. Honestly, it was getting ridiculous. What was next—barbed wire? She and Samuel couldn't be any safer.

She was more worried about her father than herself. That horrible Tommy Woofer show! Now, everyone was saying her father and his law clerk had an affair! And worse, that he knew something about her murder. Impossible. Reed had talked to him and he said not to worry, everything will work out. *Everything will work out.* That was her father's stock response to any crisis. Strangely, he'd also said that he'd been trying to call her for days and had left several messages. Something was wrong with her phone. She was going to have to replace it.

She dipped her roller into the paint and started on another wall, rolling the paint on with even strokes. She stood back and admired her work. Robin-egg blue. Perfect for Samuel. He was six months old, time to have his own nursery. And this was one of the few rooms the renovation wouldn't touch. Her phone rang. *Harrison.* "You're here?"

"Yes."

"You have your key?"

She heard him bounding up the stairs.

"I've arrived with provisions," he announced, smiling, showing her the numerous bags he was carrying.

"You're a dear!" More masking tape, extra paint rollers, and drop cloths, all the things she'd run out of but was too paint-soaked to leave the house to buy.

He put his arms around her.

"Harrison, I'm all painty!"

He lovingly wiped a dab of paint off her nose and put it in the middle of his forehead. "Now, we're the same."

"But you have on nice clothes!"

He traced his finger across her paint roller and wiped it on his jacket in a giant X. "Not now." He smiled.

She laughed. "You're crazy."

"Crazy about you," he said, hugging her.

She giggled. Harrison was fun.

"C'mon," he said. "Let's do this together. We'll get it done faster that way." He ripped through the cellophane on a new roll of masking tape.

She hesitated. "Well, okay. I mean, thank you!" Harrison was such a good friend.

✶✶✶✶

I finally received some good news and it was resulting in a heated discussion in Judge Greene's chambers. Ruth and I were at the table, as well as Bill Sevier and an attorney new to the group, Rick Stevenson, who was General Mike Fontaine's lawyer.

Ruth had just presented Judge Greene with an outline of the FBI's evidence in criminal charges that were about to be filed against General Fontaine.

Judge Greene was taking a lot time in studying the file. He eventually looked up at Rick Stevenson. "Mr. Stevenson? Do you have something to say?"

"Yes. These are entirely different cases."

"The charges against General Fontaine are material to Mr. Turnbull's case," I said.

"How soon will these papers be filed?" Judge Greene asked Ruth.

"Tomorrow or the next day."

Judge Greene mulled that over. "So, this will be a matter of public record in a few days."

"Yes," Ruth said.

"Your Honor," I said, "the jury has been sequestered and they will be oblivious to this development, which is crucial to our case, unless General Fontaine takes the stand to testify."

Rick Stevenson seethed. "General Fontaine will take the Fifth Amendment if he's called to the stand. He has no choice because of the indictment against him and that could prejudice his right to a fair trial. General Fontaine has served his country with honor and dignity and doesn't deserve to be paraded around like a monkey on a leash."

Judge Greene pondered Stevenson's arguments. "I understand, Mr. Stevenson. However, I have a man sitting in my courtroom whose life is at stake. I tend to think that's the heavier burden to bear. And," Judge Greene frowned, "General Fontaine will have his own jury and his own day in court. To claim he would be prejudiced by an appearance in this courtroom when the charges will soon be public is not a convincing argument."

"Your Honor," Rick Stevenson pleaded, "General Fontaine's mere appearance in this court will not have any probative value in this matter."

"I think taking the Fifth on the stand will be probative in itself," I said.

"I agree with Mr. Alexander," Judge Greene said. "General Fontaine can testify as he wishes, by giving testimony or by relying on his right under the Fifth Amendment. It's his choice." Judge Greene closed the case file. "I want finality in my courtroom. I don't want an appeal and a retrial because relevant evidence wasn't properly admitted. And there would be an appeal. This information would surely be central to the jury's decision."

"Your Honor," Sevier groaned.

"I've ruled, Mr. Sevier. In my courtroom, I will not keep out properly obtained evidence that could affect the jury's determination as to guilt or innocence. That's why we are here. As Justice Brandeis once said, '*Sunshine is the best disinfectant.*'"

CHAPTER 47

Reed had driven into Washington. Harrison said he had a meeting in Georgetown and thought it would be fun for them to have dinner together at a new French restaurant everyone was raving about, Chez Billy Sud.

She'd hesitated. It was a long drive, an excuse to say no. When she crossed the District line and found herself detouring to Massachusetts Heights, she realized why she'd agreed.

She slowed and craned her neck as she inched by her house. There was a light on in the living room. Davis was home. She wondered what he was doing. She glanced at her watch. Damn. She was late for dinner with Harrison. She stepped on the gas.

Reed turned out to be exactly thirty-eight minutes late. Breathless, she rushed into the small Georgetown restaurant. As she'd expected, Harrison was already seated and nursing a martini. His second one.

"I am so sorry," she stammered. "Traffic you know. It's gotten awful."

Harrison looked through her.

She dropped into a chair and looked around at the delicately painted mint-colored walls and gold-framed French paintings. "This is lovely, Harrison. A wonderful idea."

"Let's order," he snapped. "I'm famished."

When Reed handed the menu back to the waiter, Harrison noticed the emerald ring she was wearing. His jaw dropped. "Is that the ring Josephine Rideout was wearing in her portrait?"

She smiled. "It's amazing, isn't it? A jeweler told me it's an old Colombian emerald and worth a fortune. Davis gave it to me."

"You never wear it."

"I used to wear it, then Henry told me some stories about Josephine and I got sorta freaked out." She laughed. "But I started thinking that wearing it might appease Josephine."

He frowned. "What do you mean?"

"I guess I'm getting superstitious, that's all."

Harrison leaned across the table and took her hand. "Let me see." He studied the emerald, fascinated, turning Reed's hand to catch the light. "It's fantastic," he concluded.

She couldn't help notice that Harrison's mood had shifted from sour to elated when he spied the ring. She took her hand back. "You're really into beautiful things," she said nervously.

He smiled. "Of course. That's why I'm into you, Reed."

She lowered her eyes. Harrison was getting too serious about her. She tried to think of a way to change the subject. "Remember those old graves the archeologists found? The women were young, about my age. The DNA shows they were related, probably sisters. But here's the strange thing, I've checked and there's no record of any women like that in the Rideout family!"

"Reed, Reed," Harrison said, picking up his glass and waving it around, sounding slightly inebriated. "Isn't it obvious? They married into the Rideout family. And I'm sure they weren't happy because women who fall in love with Rideouts would not be happy, now would they? When are you going to leave Davis? He doesn't deserve you. Divorce him!"

"Harrison, that's a big step. I'd have to think about that."

He took her hand, a glimmer in his eye as bright as her emerald ring. "Think about it, darling. You'd get a big chunk of money from Davis and you and I together ... at Blackhall. We'd be the most beautiful couple in Maryland with the most beautiful house in the entire United States. Power, prestige, money ... we'd have it all."

She had no idea how to respond.

✳✳✳✳

But she did have an idea about the old graves and the next day, she returned to the Maryland State Archives. Because wasn't it strange that two women would be buried with coins? Maybe the coins belonged to the grave diggers but maybe not. What if the coins belonged to the women and someone buried them quickly without realizing the women had money on them?

The archeologists said the coins dated to the 1780s and she searched for articles about the Rideouts from those years but found nothing relevant. She tried searching for information about prominent women, preferably sisters, who died during that time and found a 1789 article in the Gazette.

Missing! Misses Thomasina and Theresa Gilbert, daughters of Maryland Governor Thompson Gilbert. Great reward for information.

She stayed at the archives until she was dizzy from scrolling through microfilm. There were several articles about the missing women. Thomasina and Theresa Gilbert were last seen in the area near Blackhall. Their empty carriage and horse were recovered a few miles away. A massive search ensued but Thomasina and Theresa Gilbert were never found.

Reed sat back, shocked. John Rideout looked sinister. But could he have murdered the Governor's daughters?

CHAPTER 48

"The defense calls General Mike Fontaine to the stand."

General Fontaine walked to the stand, straightened his chest of medals, and looked straight ahead with perfect military bearing.

"General Fontaine," I said, "just hours ago you were indicted on two charges of laundering money obtained during the commission of a criminal act."

Murmurs rippled through the courtroom. Fingers flew over iphones.

"Is it true, as the indictment claims, that the criminal conspiracy transpired as a result of Eden and Echo Hines blackmailing you with a sex tape they recorded without your knowledge?"

General Fontaine cleared his throat. "I invoke my right under the Fifth Amendment and decline to answer on advice of my counsel."

Reporters jumped up and ran out of the room. My God! This was too good! They needed to ready themselves for a live feed and analysis of this new development.

"And is it true, as the indictment claims, that Eden and Echo Hines were blackmailing several men? Also with sex tapes."

A loud buzz swept through the courtroom. This was better than O.J. and the white Bronco!

Judge Greene slammed down his gavel. "Quiet! Quiet in the courtroom! If I don't have quiet, I will have the courtroom cleared." He scowled at the gallery and the chatter stopped. "General Fontaine, please answer the question."

General Fontaine spoke into the mike. "I invoke my right under the Fifth Amendment and decline to answer on advice of my counsel."

"And isn't it true that Eden and Echo Hines forced you into holding on to the cash they received from the other men they were blackmailing?"

"I invoke my right under the Fifth Amendment and decline to answer on advice of my counsel."

"And didn't Eden and Echo Hines direct you to convert the money into a diamond necklace when the amount they collected exceeded $1,000,000?"

"I invoke my right under the Fifth Amendment and decline to answer on advice of my counsel."

"And didn't you, as the FBI claims in the indictment, buy a necklace costing $1,225,000 on the black market in the New York diamond district?"

"I invoke my right under the Fifth Amendment and decline to answer on advice of my counsel."

"And didn't Eden and Echo Hines direct you to deliver the necklace to them so they could sell off the diamonds one by one over a period of time, and in that manner, avoid detection of their criminal enterprise?"

"I invoke my right under the Fifth Amendment and decline to answer on advice of my counsel."

"And after Eden and Echo Hines were murdered, didn't you give the necklace to your wife as a gift?"

"I invoke my right under the Fifth Amendment and decline to answer on advice of my counsel."

"And isn't this a photo of that necklace?" I held up a photograph from the Washingtonian Magazine showing General Fontaine and his wife at the British Embassy Ball.

"I invoke my right under the Fifth Amendment and decline to answer on advice of my counsel."

"Your Honor, we offer the indictment against General Fontaine into evidence as defense exhibit #2 and the photo into evidence as defense exhibit #3."

****

After I reassured Henry the trial was going as well as could be expected, I hopped into a Supreme Court Police car for the drive home. In the back seat, I pulled out my iPad and watched the news, like I did at the end of every day. It was a good barometer of how the trial was being viewed by the public. On Fox News, the talking heads were discussing General Fontaine's day in court, dismayed at the news of his involvement with the Hines twins.

I flipped to another station. CNN was reporting that people were staying home from work to watch the trial on TV and others were following the trial from iPads at their desks. The anchor mused that Henry's trial had become a reality show, saying, *"A Supreme Court Justice questioned in his law clerk's death is defending the suspect in the murder of the President's daughters. And the Supreme Court Justice has just taken down the National Security Advisor. Only in America, folks."*

One thing I knew for sure was that, at this point, the entire world was watching. And they had all discovered where I lived. We turned onto my street in Georgetown. Hundreds of people lined the road. Angry faces everywhere. As soon as they spotted the Supreme Court Police car, they ratcheted up the chants. *"Justice for Eden and Echo!"* they screamed, waving placards with the twins' photographs in full color. *Boos* swept through the crowd and everyone rushed out into the street, trying to reach the car to personally give me the finger. Police on horseback were ready. They corralled the mob and held them back as we drove past. And now, a new chant, *"Justice for Lilly!"*

CHAPTER 49

Stars spilled like sugar across the indigo night and the moon floated among silver-lined clouds. It was a mild summer evening and Reed and Harrison sat on a blanket at the edge of the cliff enjoying a gourmet picnic. At first, Reed thought a picnic was a ridiculous idea. But Harrison had gone to a lot of trouble. French bread, gazpacho, jumbo shrimp and crab cakes, chocolate cake and Pouilly Fuisse. A veritable feast. Harrison was so thoughtful. It was everything she loved! And after a glass of wine, she had begun to relax and enjoy herself. And after three glasses, she was feeling very bubbly, like champagne uncorked! She hiccupped, then giggled. She was bubbly!

She giggled again, leaned on her arms and looked back at the house. A mist had come up, thickening into a fog billowing around the base of the home, making Blackhall into a wonderland emerging from a misty dream. Enchanting was the only word for it. She was so happy this was her home. No matter what happened at Blackhall, she would never leave. She would make it her own. No matter what Davis—

A soft cry. She spun her head around. It couldn't be Samuel. He was with a babysitter. "Did you hear a cry?" she asked Harrison.

"No."

"It sounded like a baby but maybe it was the willows. Henry says when the branches blow in the wind, they can sound like they're crying and that's why they're called weeping willows."

Harrison laughed loudly. "That's ridiculous!"

"Henry knows a lot about a lot of things," Reed said, defensively.

Harrison cocked his head. "Hmmm. I concede he's right on one point. The term weeping reflects a broad association with grief. Also, there's extensive folklore, from Japan to Appalachia, about ghosts appearing wherever willow trees grow. More importantly, in Greek mythology weeping willows are sacred to Hecate, often called the Queen of Ghosts because she ruled ghosts, magic, and mystery. She also ruled the powers of nature—birth, life, death."

Reed's eyes widened. "You're so knowledgeable."

He flipped his head. "I did learn something at Eton."

"Oh."

"Have you thought what it would be like to fall off that cliff?" he asked.

"What?" She quickly turned and eyed the precipitous drop, the seawall and rocks so far below, so distant, so small. The crash of the waves suddenly thundered in her ears and the hairs on her arms stood on end. "What a strange thing to say!"

He reached for her and laughed. "You were talking about a baby and I was thinking about Samuel. When he starts to walk, you need to keep him away from that cliff."

"Oh, yeah." She exhaled. Her heart was pumping fast. She was much too tense. She'd begun to realize that happened sometimes when she was around Harrison and she wasn't sure why.

Harrison stretched out flat on the navy and white plaid blanket, looking so peaceful and relaxed. His curly blond hair glowed, a halo in the moonlight. His brown eyelashes were so delicate. Her gaze drifted to his long, lean body, back to his face. He was beautiful, like Gabriel the angel. His looks were such a contrast to Davis's olive skin and cold eyes that made him look just like his ancestor, John Rideout, *the murderer*. Harrison, the angel. Davis, the …

He caught her looking at him. "Come here," he said.

Reed leaned into him and planted a kiss on his cheek, friendly, but not too friendly.

He grabbed her and pulled her on top of him. "That's better."

They were nose-to-nose, mouth-to-mouth, breathing together, each inhaling the breath the other had just taken. She could feel him through his jeans. He was rock-hard. Her head swam with the wine.

"I love you, Reed," he whispered.

She wanted to melt into him but she couldn't. She was lonely now that Henry wasn't around but she didn't love Harrison.

He slipped his hands under the back of her blouse and unfastened her bra. She tensed.

He felt her stiffen. "What's wrong?"

"I ... I can't. Right now, I just need a friend." She blew a strand of hair out of her eye, blinked several times, feeling tears starting to form. "Daddy's right, I've isolated myself. First the kidnapping, then Davis and Eden and Echo Hines ... it's been such a difficult year." The wine magnified her emotions and she started snuffling, thinking about everything she'd been through. It was too much.

He held her close. "Shhh. It's okay, baby. I'm here."

The unexpected sympathy released a floodgate and she began sobbing. "And I think I'm losing my mind! I keep misplacing my cell phone!"

"Oh dear, you do keep losing that phone."

She sniffled. "Have you seen it?"

"No, baby, I haven't, he said, rolling over, feeling Reed's phone deep in his back pocket where he'd placed it earlier in the day after he'd erased all her messages.

"I can't imagine where it is," she sobbed, burying her face in Harrison's chest.

He held her tightly. "I'll take care of you, baby. I'm here. You can count on me."

CHAPTER 50

"The defense calls Mr. Davis Rideout to the stand."

I heard a bang from the direction of the prosecution table. Sevier had pushed his chair back so hard it had tipped over. Gasps ran through the courtroom and journalists ran out of the room to report the development on live TV. No one had expected Davis to testify for the defense and open himself up to questions during the trial.

"Your Honor! May I approach?" Sevier asked.

Judge Greene looked over the top of his spectacles and muted his mike.

"Your Honor, Mr. Rideout is not on the defense's witness list."

"Your Honor," I said. "Mr. Rideout was not planning to testify but last night, he changed his mind. It turns out that Mr. Rideout is our most important witness and his testimony is critical to our case."

"I'll allow it," Judge Greene said.

Sevier glared at me. The bailiff swore Davis in.

I approached the witness stand. "Mr. Rideout, did you see Eden and Echo at Blackhall the night they were killed?"

"Yes, I was at Blackhall with them. They asked me to meet them for sex."

A collective gasp hit the courtroom ceiling.

"How did that come about?"

"They called me a week earlier and said they wanted *to screw*. Their words, not mine."

The gallery moved like one enormous tidal wave. Media types grabbed their iphones and started texting wildly. Other reporters jumped up and ran for the door. Later, I would find out that cell phone service became so jammed it was impossible to get through.

Judge Greene pounded the gavel for silence. "Silence! Silence! If I don't have silence, I will clear the courtroom."

The crowd settled down. Everyone was dying to hear what was next.

"Proceed, Mr. Alexander."

"Thank you, your Honor. Mr. Rideout, did anything unusual happen during your sexual encounter with the Hines twins?"

"They wanted to play around with some bondage. They thought it was fun. Personally, I could take it or leave it."

"Did anything else happen that was unusual?"

"We videotaped the sex. Some people might think that was unusual."

I held up a flash drive. "Mr. Rideout, does this flash drive contain the video you're referring to?"

"Yes, it does."

"Your Honor, I offer the sex tape of Davis Rideout and Eden and Echo Hines into evidence as defense exhibit # 4."

Sevier bounced to his feet. I could see his heart pounding under his suit. "Objection!"

"Approach the bench!" Judge Greene bellowed.

The Judge turned off his microphone and we conferenced in front of him. "What the hell do you think you're doing, Mr. Alexander?"

"Your Honor," I said, "the tape is evidence that Mr. Turnbull was not the source of the semen sample as the prosecution claims. The tape will show that Mr. Rideout had sex with Eden and Echo Hines, that Mr. Rideout was not wearing a condom, and that he did, in fact, ejaculate."

Sevier was about to have a heart attack. "Your Honor, this tape was not on defense's documents list!"

"Mr. Rideout gave me the tape last night. I knew nothing about it before."

"I will allow it," Judge Greene said.

"The tape can't be authenticated!" Sevier yelled.

"Mr. Sevier! Lower your voice. Need I remind you that Mr. Rideout just authenticated it?"

"Under Rule 412, the defense can't offer evidence to show the victims engaged in other sexual behavior."

"Your Honor," I said. "This qualifies as an exception under section (b) of Rule 412, allowing into evidence proof that a person other than the accused was the source of the semen."

"But the tape is highly prejudicial," Sevier sputtered.

Judge Greene jabbed an index finger into Sevier's face. "The prosecution opened this door. It was your theory of the case that Davis Rideout wanted to have sex with Eden and Echo Hines."

Sevier looked confused and desperate. "I didn't introduce evidence to that effect."

"You put forth that theory in your opening statement. It's not up to me to teach you the Rules of Evidence, Mr. Sevier. I suggest you read United States v. Moore in your spare time. And this tape is evidence that proves your point so I would think you'd be thrilled." He glared at Sevier. "I'll let the evidence in. The probative value outweighs any possible harm to the victims who, I will remind you, are now deceased."

"But ... but ... I didn't think the jury would view the girls in the act," Sevier groaned.

"I'm not here to mop up after you," Judge Greene barked. "I've ruled, now sit down!"

The tape was run for the jury. Judge Greene had his own private screen. The audience couldn't see the action, the screen was strategically angled away, although everyone in the courtroom and at home could hear the twins giggling, followed by moans and groans.

A half-hour in, Sevier rose from his seat. He was sweating profusely and asked to approach Judge Greene who ordered the tape to be paused. Judge Greene muted his mike.

"Your Honor, is it necessary to continue this? The jury gets the idea. Haven't they seen enough?"

I jumped in. "No. It's important to run the tape to the end so the jury can see the evidence in its entirety, especially the ejaculation part."

"Jesus Christ!" Sevier said, slapping his forehead.

"I agree with Mr. Alexander," Judge Greene said. "The tape is evidence and I'll allow it to be run in its entirety."

Altogether, the tape ran for more than an hour. Toward the end, the jury looked breathless and dazed.

"Your witness," I said, looking at Sevier. He remained down, too distraught to attempt a cross-examination. When Judge Greene recessed for the day, Sevier stayed at the prosecution table, his head in his hands.

I didn't enjoy putting the twins on display but the tape proved there was something wrong with the prosecution's DNA evidence and I was the only person standing between Henry and a lethal injection. Except for Davis. He'd just admitted lying to the FBI, a felony carrying a long prison sentence, in an attempt to save Henry's life. And, frankly, there was no guarantee his testimony would sway the jury. It was a brave act, an act borne out of love.

✶✶✶✶

The President felt like his hair was on fire. "I want you to arrest Alexander," the President directed FBI Director Mortich. "That sonafabitch just dirtied my daughters! Lilly McCleary was Alexander's law clerk. They were having an affair. Maybe the man killed her. Find out. Get a Goddamn search warrant for his house. Now!"

Chief Justice Bannister Brown broke in. "Mr. President, there's the Supreme Court's reputation to think about. Surely, there must be another way."

"There is no other way."

"Then, keep me out of it," Chief Brown huffed. "I will not be a party to the downfall of my own Court!"

"You're not in it, Bannister," the President seethed. "I'm letting you know as a matter of professional courtesy. If you'd gotten Alexander disbarred like I wanted, you wouldn't be in this predicament, now would you?"

Mortich cleared his throat. "Sir. If I can find enough evidence for a search warrant, I'll have one executed, but no matter what, I will not have the FBI interfere in an ongoing murder trial. The fact is that Alexander is going nowhere. There's plenty of time to do a thorough investigation and put all our ducks in a row. And you don't want to be seen as unduly influencing the FBI. So, just let us do our job. Sir."

CHAPTER 51

Reed was sobbing. Davis had humiliated her on TV. She collapsed into Harrison's arms. He didn't say anything, just rubbed his hand up and down her back and held her. After a few minutes, he stood and swept her into his arms, off the green sofa, and carried her up the staircase to her bedroom where he lay her down on the canopied bed.

He took off his shirt, keeping his eyes on her like she was prey that might get away, unbuckled his belt, and slid off his pants. There was a look in his eyes she'd never seen before. Confident. Cold. In seconds, he was naked and taking off her clothes. Nothing was said. An unspoken agreement had passed between them.

His weight was on her, pressing her deep into the bed. He pushed her legs open with his knee. She wanted to yell out, *wait, wait, hold me for a while.* She didn't and wham! She wasn't ready. It hurt. Like he was slicing her insides with a blade! For a moment, she wondered if he'd inserted a knife. No, that was crazy. No one would do that. She tried to relax. It was impossible.

He panted and panted and pushed and pushed and become more and more frantic. His eyes were closed, intent on his own satisfaction. It was like watching a train roaring by. A huge grunt over her head as he pressed all the way into her, the veins in his neck straining, his hands holding her thighs tightly, and then he collapsed on top of her. It was over.

As if Davis hadn't humiliated her enough.

She wanted Harrison to get off her. She felt dirty, violated. She was still under him. His sweat ran down her face, warm semen oozed in her vagina. She was afraid to move.

Finally, he rolled over, panting. "Oh, Reed," he said, his eyes tightly closed, "that was wonderful."

She got up and ran into the shower, feeling the sting of salt in her tears. She stayed under the water a long time, sobbing over recent events. All of them. Davis … the twins … that awful tape that somehow had already gone viral … and Harrison. She was furious at herself for giving in to Harrison. Shit. She needed to get her act together. And Harrison's actions? He'd taken advantage of the situation. And the way he made love was not how normal men made love. If love was what he felt for her and maybe it wasn't.

Water trickled down her face as she turned off the shower, stepped out onto the rug, and rubbed herself dry with a fluffy towel. Peeking around the bathroom door, she could see her clothes on the floor at the foot of the bed. Harrison was gone. She walked into the bedroom. She could hear Harrison in the bathroom down the hall. She looked for her cell phone. Damn! She'd misplaced it again, and this time, she wasn't going to let Harrison know she couldn't call anyone.

She was so tired. She lay down on the bed. Just for a minute. A cool breeze swept across her naked body and she slid under the sheet. Just for a minute. The next thing she knew, she was jolted awake by a strange noise. Everything was black. It was the middle of the night. She was groggy. How long had she been sleeping? And that noise? Sounded like a bird chirping. Why was she always dreaming about birds? Was Henry right about there being an evil spirit in the house or was someone creeping around?

She noticed a light under the bathroom door. Harrison. He must have stayed the night. So, that was the noise. Harrison walking across the floor. She turned over, ready to fall back asleep when she noticed Harrison's jacket on a nearby chair. A screwdriver protruded from the pocket.

Her brain sizzled like it had been tossed onto a bonfire. Scared to death, she jumped out of bed and ran across the hall to check on Samuel.

✸✸✸✸

The next morning, Reed rose early. Six a.m. She had slept fitfully and she was anxious for Harrison to leave so she was elated he was already up and at the breakfast table.

He had a busy day, he said, and had to get going. She quickly made some scrambled eggs and he chomped them down like he'd never eaten anything better.

"So, Harrison," she said, trying to sound casual, "why do you keep a screwdriver in your jacket?"

"What? Oh, that. I was working on a construction site, put it in my jacket, and forgot about it." He narrowed his eyes and smiled. "What? Do you think I'm a serial killer?" He laughed, held an imaginary screwdriver over his head and lunged at her.

She recoiled. "That's not funny!"

"Okay, okay. I'm sorry. I was just kidding."

"Daddy says his law clerk was killed with a screwdriver!"

"I'm so sorry. I had no idea. Honest." He put his arms around her.

CHAPTER 52

"Call your next witness, Mr. Alexander," Judge Greene said.

"The defense calls Professor Wilson Hammond to the stand."

Professor Hammond was an elegant-looking man dressed in a tailor-made suit and a red bowtie. While he was being sworn in, I scanned my notes.

"Now." I looked up and smiled. "Professor Hammond, I'd like to establish your credentials."

"Yes, sir. I am a Professor of History at the University of Maryland. I specialize in Colonial Era Sociology in Maryland and Virginia, and I'm a certified Genealogist."

Sevier was on his feet. "Objection! Relevancy!"

"Where are you going with this?" Judge Green asked.

"Your Honor, I'm establishing a foundation."

"Keep it relevant, Mr. Alexander."

I turned back to Professor Hammond and placed some documents in his hands. "Professor Hammond. Can you identify these documents?"

Professor Hammond spoke into the microphone. "Yes, I was alerted to these papers by your associate, Jake Larsen. He located them at the Maryland State Archives. They were among some 18th century papers that Davis Rideout's father, Paul Rideout, donated to the state. One of these documents sets forth the history of the Rideout family."

"Please explain what you mean by Rideout family history."

He pointed at a bound folder. "This folder contains the story of the first Rideout in Maryland, Mr. John Rideout, who is Davis Rideout's ancestor.

The other folder," he put on his glasses, "yes, here it is," he said and picked up another group of papers. "This documents Henry Turnbull's ancestry. Mr. Turnbull's family were slaves at Blackhall and at the time, slaves were considered to be property, very valuable property at that. Each birth of a slave added to the slave owner's wealth so many colonial-era families, including the Rideouts, kept close track of slave births. Now... right here," he pointed at a page, "is an entry dated 1781 showing that a house slave at Blackhall by the name of Jade gave birth to a baby boy she named Samuel."

"And why is that important?"

"The house slave, Jade, was Mr. Turnbull's 5th great-grandmother."

Judge Greene frowned. "Counsel! Approach the bench." I stepped forward and Sevier joined me at the bar. The mike fell mute again.

"I've given you leeway, Mr. Alexander, but really, I do not see—"

"Please, bear with me. This is extremely relevant to the case."

Judge Greene glared at me. "You'd better be going somewhere with this."

"Now, Professor Hammond, please tell us how you determined that Samuel is Henry Turnbull's ancestor."

"In John Rideout's will, Samuel was bequeathed a small amount of property. Samuel Turnbull's will names his son, Lattimore Turnbull. Fortunately, Lattimore Turnbull is an unusual name and we also know Lattimore lived on the property that Samuel inherited from John Rideout."

"How do you know that?"

"Lattimore sold a portion of the same land in 1846, proven by the boundaries stipulated in John Rideout's will, which are replicated in the 1846 deed."

"Go on."

"Lattimore's will, dated 1852, named his son, Thomas Turnbull. In 1850, it becomes easier to follow descent because as of that date, the United States Census recorded not only the head of the household but also the names of any children in the household. The 1890 U.S. Census shows that Thomas Turnbull's son was Herbert Turnbull and a much later census shows that Herbert was Henry Turnbull's father."

I offered the documents into evidence. Judge Greene granted my request but looked reluctant to do so.

"Do you wish to cross, Mr. Sevier?"

"No, your Honor."

The defense calls Dr. Simon Boule to the stand.

The bailiff swore him in.

"Dr. Boule, please state your credentials for the court."

"I received my Ph.D. in Chemistry from Yale University in 1995 and I've worked in the area of forensic research and science ever since. My company, GeneTech, provides private criminal defense consulting services."

"Dr. Boule, have you had the opportunity to test Mr. Turnbull's DNA?"

"Yes, I've taken a DNA sample from Mr. Turnbull."

"Did you take a DNA sample from anyone else involved in this case?"

"Yes, also from Mr. Rideout."

Sevier turned red. "Relevancy!"

"Overruled. You may continue, Mr. Alexander," Judge Greene said.

"Dr. Boule, please tell us about your analyses of those samples."

"For both men, I generated a 15 locus autosomal DNA profile, then a 16 locus Y chromosome analysis."

"What were the results of those DNA tests?"

"The tests reveal that Mr. Turnbull and Mr. Rideout share a common male ancestor within the past five to eight generations."

"Is it possible to determine the identity of that ancestor?"

"According to your prior expert's testimony and the historical documents just entered into evidence, the only possible candidate is John Rideout, the man who built the Blackhall estate."

"Why is John Rideout the only candidate?"

"Your expert testified that John Rideout was the only adult Rideout male living in Maryland at that time and that John Rideout owned the house slave named Jade, who was Mr. Turnbull's ancestor."

"Do you have an opinion whether it is reasonable that the 9 Core Loci the FBI was able to isolate from the semen sample is a match to both Davis Rideout's and Henry Turnbull's DNA?"

"I do. It is quite reasonable."

"Please explain why."

"They have some common DNA. The FBI had only a partial DNA profile to work from. However, the relationship between the two men is quite easy to determine when full Y Chromosome DNA profiles are developed."

"Some people would wonder if your DNA analysis could be accurate because," I pointed to the defense table, "it's easy to see that Mr. Rideout is Caucasian and Mr. Turnbull is African-American."

"Yes, it's accurate. Mr. Turnbull's DNA is mostly African-American."

"Is this the first time that an African-American man and a Caucasian man have shared a similar DNA profile?"

"No. President Thomas Jefferson's case is a prime example. He owned a slave by the name of Sally Hemmings. Her descendants' DNA proves that her children were fathered by a Jefferson male."

"Please explain why the FBI didn't make the same determination that you did—that Mr. Rideout and Mr. Turnbull share a common ancestor?"

"First, it's my understanding that they didn't test Mr. Rideout's DNA. And even if the FBI had tested Mr. Rideout's DNA, they had 9 loci to work with instead of the more comprehensive DNA profile that I developed, so they would not have seen the full extent of the match."

"So, they would not have seen the full extent of the match. But if they'd tested Mr. Rideout's DNA, would they have picked up the difference in the DNA of the two men?"

"No."

"Why is that?"

"It so happens that the loci involved in the FBI's DNA sample all match to both Mr. Rideout and Mr. Turnbull, including the rare allele at D3."

"But that means, does it not, that if they'd tested Mr. Rideout, they would've realized that Mr. Rideout could've been the contributor of the semen sample?"

"Yes, if they'd tested Mr. Rideout, they would've realized he could've been the source of the semen."

"Dr. Boule, could you please explain how the term *cold hit* is used when referring to DNA evidence?"

"Yes, a cold hit is a term for when a search process matches the DNA of the evidence sample profile with the DNA of an offender profile stored in a state or federal database."

"And is that how law enforcement matched Mr. Turnbull's DNA to evidence from the crime scene? Through a cold hit?"

"Yes."

"And please tell us, when law enforcement is dealing with such a small DNA sample as they have in this case, is it possible to have more than one cold hit from a DNA database?"

"Yes, that's been my experience."

"That seems troubling to me, and I would imagine that would be troubling to all innocent people everywhere, since DNA is considered infallible science."

Sevier popped to his feet. "Objection your Honor, Mr. Alexander is testifying!"

"Sustained. The jury will ignore the comment."

"Dr. Boule, please tell us, if a partial DNA profile matches more than one suspect, how does law enforcement decide which suspect to charge with the crime?"

"Generally, law enforcement uses a partial DNA profile as corroborating evidence in charging someone who has the motive and the opportunity to commit the crime."

"So, a partial profile supplies law enforcement with a potential lead?"

"Yes, a partial profile can supply a potential lead but not an infallible match."

"And what about the DNA in Eden and Echo Hines's car? Was that also a partial DNA profile?"

"Yes, that DNA had also degraded. Nine loci were also isolated."

"Did you have the occasion to run the DNA found in Eden and Echo Hines's car through Maryland's DNA database?"

"No, sir. I'm not allowed general access to samples and analyses not developed specifically in connection with this case."

"Okay. Well, can you tell us whether you've had past experience with a similar case?"

"Yes. I began my career in the Arizona State Crime Laboratory where I was working with a partial DNA profile in 2002, when DNA analysis was in its infancy. I ran the profile through the state database and came up with two felons who matched at 9 of the standard 13 loci. The FBI estimated the odds of unrelated people sharing those genetic markers to be one in one hundred and thirteen billion. I was shocked not only because statistically, the match was thought to be impossible but also because their mug shots showed that one was black, the other was white."

"Did that cause you to take a closer look at the Arizona database?"

"It certainly did. At the time, there were about 65,000 DNA profiles in the Arizona database, yet I found 122 pairs of people who shared the same genetic markers at 9 places and some even shared markers at 10, 11, or 12 places."

"And how many DNA profiles are currently in the Maryland state database?"

"Literature from the State of Maryland gives the figure at 280,000."

"And CODIS?"

"About 13 million."

"Is there any way to extrapolate the likelihood of a random match statewide and also nationwide for the DNA obtained from the semen sample in question?"

"That's a difficult proposition because of Mr. Turnbull's allele at D3. However, both he and Mr. Rideout share the same rare allele so there are probably other men in the general population who also match."

I raised my eyebrows. "I notice that you've used the word *probably*. Why can't you say for sure?"

"It's an unknown."

"Please explain why."

"The DNA of the entire population of the United States is not available for comparison. Only the DNA profiles in CODIS."

"Does that affect the chances of a cold hit, such as the one to Mr. Turnbull's DNA?"

"Yes. In the case of a cold hit, CODIS is the database against which forensic DNA evidence is compared, whereas the DNA of the general population is not taken into consideration, even though someone in the general population may have committed the crime that law enforcement is investigating."

"Are you saying that once a person is in the DNA database, they are more likely to be accused of a crime simply because their DNA profile is available to law enforcement?"

"Yes, and the negative impact especially falls on minorities since there is an overrepresentation of minorities in the criminal justice system. That results in a disproportionate number of partial matches that implicate them in criminal acts. In effect, the DNA database, if not used wisely and carefully, can become a revolving jail door, especially for the African-American community. They become, in essence—the usual suspects."

"Just to be clear for the jury's benefit—earlier, a government DNA expert testified that Henry Turnbull is the source of the DNA in the evidence sample *to the exclusion of everyone else on this planet.* Are you saying that the expert was wrong?"

"Yes, and many prominent population geneticists have been criticizing the FBI for years for making claims of source attribution. My work with the Arizona database showed the chances of two randomly chosen people having the same DNA profile are very small. Nonetheless, when you take all the comparisons that could be made between millions of people in a database, matches aren't that surprising, especially between relatives. I don't know why the FBI hasn't changed their source attribution policy. They should."

"One last question. In your opinion, was the DNA that was deposited in the car left there the night of the murders?"

"It's impossible to know. It could've been there for a long time. As I said, it was partially degraded."

"Your Honor, I offer our DNA analysis and report into evidence as defense exhibit # 5."

"Your witness," I said as I sat down at the defense table and smiled at Henry, who was shaking, tears of relief trailing down his face. I patted his back and whispered, "Don't break down, now."

"Cross, Mr. Sevier?" Judge Greene asked, looking pissed.

"Judge," Sevier whined, "we need time to examine the defense's evidence."

"Court adjourned!" Judge Greene slammed his gavel and stalked off the bench.

The next morning, Sevier declined to cross-examine our expert.

We asked for a dismissal of all charges. Based on Judge Greene's reaction yesterday, I thought he might grant our request, but he denied it. Henry's fate would be decided by the jury.

CHAPTER 53

Reed was ecstatic. Daddy had called and said Henry's chances were good for acquittal. And how amazing that Henry and Davis were practically brothers! Who would've thought it?

Henry. She smiled. She missed him. She couldn't wait to have him back at Blackhall. The poor dear had been through so much. She would baby him when he returned. An idea flashed through her brain. She should extend her renovation plans to include the Little Cottage! Henry would like that. She'd been in the Little Cottage when they'd been waiting for the police and she cringed remembering how grimy it had been. Talk about needing a renovation! Yes, it was time to do something about that hovel that Henry called home.

And now that she was going to be living at Blackhall permanently, maybe she should hire a chef to prepare meals for her and Henry. And a man to take over Henry's duties. Daddy was right. It was time Henry retired. Come to think of it, she was going to need quite a few staff, like she had in the city. And now that Davis wasn't around, maybe she'd even hire a nanny. She sat down at the desk in the library and began making a list of positions to advertise. First on her list was hiring a curator to compile an inventory of Blackhall's contents and value them for insurance purposes so she could move everything into storage and the renovations could begin.

****

Henry had aged during the past few weeks. His hair was whiter, his wrinkles were deeper, and his back was locked in a distinct seventy-five-degree angle. He shuffled into the attorney-client conference room, escorted by a U.S. Marshal. "Here you are, Mr. Turnbull." The Marshal smiled at him, held his arms, and gently lowered him into a chair.

Jake helped Henry scoot his chair in.

Henry covered his face with his hands and sobbed. "I want to go home."

I put my arm around his shoulders. "You have a good chance. Just hang in there a few more days."

"I'm sorry, Justice Alexander. I won't cry again."

My heart broke for everything this frail old man had gone through. "I just talked with Reed. She sends you her love. Davis, too."

He wiped his face. "I can't get over that Davis and I are related and we didn't know it."

"I wonder if Davis's father knew," I mused. "He donated those papers to the State of Maryland."

Henry grunted. "Probably why Old Paul wanted to get rid of them!"

I nodded. "You're right. A lot of families hide history when slavery is involved."

"Do you really think I'm going home?" Henry asked.

"I think there's a good possibility," I said, gently patting his back.

He slumped into a heap. "I don't understand why the FBI didn't test Davis's DNA."

"The FBI can't take DNA without an arrest or a search warrant and to obtain a search warrant, they need probable cause, which in the case of DNA, is a high standard. The FBI has to show a judge that it is *more likely than not* that the DNA will yield evidence of the crime. In Davis's case, the security footage from the airport had already exonerated him."

Henry stirred in his chair. "I wish Davis had given you that sex tape earlier," he said.

"It wouldn't have mattered. With the FBI attribution claims and without a way to explain the DNA in the twins' car, you would've gone to trial. Davis knew that and when he handed the tape over, he said he didn't think it would do much good, but by that time, I'd consulted with Dr. Boule and knew that we could also cast reasonable doubt about the DNA in the car."

Henry looked blank.

I put my hand on his. "What it all boils down to is that I can stand up in court and argue until the jurors' butts turn to iron. However, when they saw the sex tape with their own eyeballs? I think that was a turning point."

Henry nodded. "I knew I could count on Davis."

Henry stood for the Marshal to take him out of the room. I could see by the Marshal's face that he'd taken a liking to Henry. I was glad Henry had someone looking out for him. Henry had gone through hell for absolutely no reason and I was furious at the U.S. Attorney's Office and even more furious at the FBI.

CHAPTER 54

We continued to closing arguments but by then, the prosecution had the wind taken out of their sails. They did the best with what they had but it was clear to me their reputation for honesty had been sullied in the eyes of the jury. Bill Sevier looked nervous, knowing the jurors were no longer in the palm of his hand.

"Ladies and Gentlemen of the jury." Sevier smiled hopefully as he approached them. "Echo's blood was found on the library rug. The twins' car was found in Blackhall's stable. The twins' bodies were found buried on Blackhall's property. Blackhall is where these young women were killed! That's a proven fact. So what if Henry Turnbull didn't actually have sex with the Hines twins. Mr. Turnbull's DNA was found in their car."

"You may ask—how do we know the DNA in the car was Mr. Turnbull's? After all, the defense says it was only a partial profile. We know because Eden and Echo Hines were murdered about 3:30 in the morning, long after Mr. Rideout was in the air heading to China but when Henry Turnbull was at the estate. It was Mr. Turnbull who killed the twins, buried them on the estate, and hid their car. Use your common sense. Killing Eden and Echo Hines was the only reason someone would bury these women and hide their car. And Mr. Turnbull was the only one on the estate at that time with the DNA profile found in the car!"

"The facts speak for themselves. Mr. Turnbull is the only person who had the motive, the opportunity, and the DNA profile to commit and cover up these heinous crimes." Sevier steepled his hands, like he was praying. "Ladies and gentlemen of the jury, don't be fooled by the defense's slight-of-hand tricks. Don't leave your common sense at home. Please, think for yourselves, apply the facts to the law, and return the only verdict that is possible in this case—a verdict of guilty of Murder in the First Degree."

My turn. I jumped to my feet. "Ladies and gentlemen of the jury, the only evidence the Government has in this case is DNA evidence." I held up the FBI's DNA Report. "The FBI's DNA analysis is what this entire trial hinges upon." I tossed the report into a wastebasket where it landed with a loud thunk. "Completely discredited! The prosecution said the DNA proved that Henry Turnbull had sex with Eden and Echo Hines. Wrong! The FBI said that Henry Turnbull's DNA was found in the car." I held up my finger. "How can they know that for sure? You heard Dr. Boule say there must be other men fitting the same DNA profile, even with Mr. Turnbull's rare allele, but these men are simply unknown to law enforcement because their DNA is not in CODIS."

Some members of the jury openly bobbed their heads in agreement.

"The FBI should be ashamed." I frowned. "They focused on Mr. Turnbull from the beginning and tailored their evidence to fit their theory. Their DNA match was only a partial profile. That's equivalent to an eyewitness saying, 'I only saw the murderer's chin but don't worry, I can ID him in a lineup.'"

Some of the jurors chuckled. *This was turning into a lawyer's dream.*

"Think about it. It's only because of our research and Mr. Rideout—not the FBI—that you know the FBI's DNA analysis points to the wrong man. Mr. Rideout came forward with a tape of himself having sex with the President's daughters. Did Mr. Rideout want to present that tape to the jury? Of course not. He didn't have to do that. He has a business to consider and a wife and a child he loves and you'd better believe that tape has caused some serious problems for him on both those fronts. But Mr. Rideout couldn't stand to see a man wrongfully convicted of murder. If it weren't for Mr. Rideout, you may have convicted Mr. Turnbull. God knows, men have been convicted on less."

I paused for effect. "So, who did kill Eden and Echo Hines? Blackhall is an easy target. Mr. Turnbull is the caretaker and he is an old man. In fact, the estate had a number of burglaries over the past year, so break-ins were frequent and you heard the testimony from the Anne Arundel police. There was a burglary at the mansion the same week, perhaps the same night, Eden and Echo Hines were killed! Gee, I wonder if that was related? But no, that's too commonsensical. And the FBI didn't follow up. Instead, the FBI claimed that Mr. Turnbull had a stash of Scopolamine handy in his cottage, just waiting for the day when two beautiful women came along so he could rape and kill them." I shook my head. "That's ridiculous."

I pointed at the prosecution table. "Instead of looking for other suspects, the FBI blamed Mr. Turnbull for the murders. But I ask you to look at Mr. Turnbull closely. The man is seventy-eight years old. He's stooped. His bones are arthritic. Do you really think he's capable of killing the Hines twins, then carrying the weight of their dead bodies through the brambles of a dense forest to a spot a mile away, dig a grave and bury them?"

I held up a finger. "You have to question that. All of it. Because we have true suspects who had a million reasons to kill the twins. Remember General Fontaine's appearance on the witness stand? Eden and Echo Hines were blackmailing General Fontaine and several other men with sex tapes, threatening to ruin marriages and destroy lives. If that isn't a motive for murder, I don't know what is. Yet, did the FBI follow up on those leads? Again, the answer is no."

I held up my hands. "However, the prosecution is right about one thing. Someone killed the President's daughters. Those young women were brutally killed without any mercy. An animal slaughtered them! And that's a horrible fact. Mr. Turnbull would like to see justice for Eden and Echo Hines. We would *all* like to see justice for Eden and Echo Hines. And as members of the jury, it is natural for you to want to solve this crime, find someone guilty, and put him behind bars so that President Hines can have closure and go on with his life. But the sad fact is that we may never know who killed Eden and Echo Hines."

I shook my head. "Do not think that leaves you powerless." I pointed a finger at the jury. "It doesn't. You can still right a terrible wrong and that wrong is the Government's unwarranted charges against Mr. Turnbull. So, I appeal to you to exercise your power, right this injustice, release this crippled old man back to his little home and family. Let him live out the rest of his life in peace and quiet. Return a verdict of—not guilty."

As I returned to my seat, soft sobs rippled through the courtroom and I knew I'd done my job.

CHAPTER 55

All in all, the trial had lasted two months. I was worried about the lesser charges as we settled in for a long wait. To everyone's surprise, the jury came back in less than an hour, blowing away the record for a verdict returned in federal court. I knew it was good when I saw the jurors smiling at Henry between dabbing at tears.

"All rise."

Judge Greene strode to the bench. "The jury foreperson may read the verdict," he said.

"We, the members of the jury, find Mr. Henry L. Turnbull not guilty of all charges."

Judge Greene banged his gavel. "The defendant is free to leave."

Henry wept.

We were going home.

✶✶✶✶

President Hines opened and closed his fist, felt the straight edge of the knife as he flicked it back and forth, staring straight ahead at the Washington Monument, stark white against the coal black night. My God. What had he done? He'd approved the death of Turnbull based on faulty DNA analyses. Only a massive U.S. Marshal's presence had prevented Fontaine's men from killing Turnbull. Only Justice Alexander, a man he'd detested, had had the balls to step in and save Turnbull from a fate the old man didn't deserve.

The President ran his finger along the knife edge, retired to his bedroom, set the knife on his nightstand, and pulled on a pair of blue pajamas.

He sat down heavily, sinking into the feather mattress. He picked up the knife again, examined the sharp edge of the blade glinting under the lamp, knowing he was no better than Fontaine and Fontaine was a monster.

Fontaine had been desperate to have the investigation into Eden's and Echo's deaths shut down, their deaths pinned on Turnbull before his own crimes could be discovered. The President had fallen for it, compromised himself, and that had left Fontaine free to kill Arnett, something the President never would have condoned.

The President drew the knife over his head and plunged it! Into the bed, stabbing the mattress repeatedly, slashing it until white feathers filled the air. His daughters, gone ... Arnett, dead ... his own integrity, shattered.

✳✳✳✳

Henry not guilty! Reed was overjoyed but also annoyed that Harrison was there to share the news. She turned off the TV and faked a smile.

"Good, news, huh?" Harrison said, giving her a hug.

"Yes." She crossed her arms and pulled away. Harrison was always at Blackhall. Came over every night, now. Invited or not. She should never have given him the gate code and a house key.

When she'd questioned what he did during the day and why the necessary demolition hadn't been scheduled yet, he said he was finishing a job in Baltimore so he could devote all his time to her. She wasn't sure whether he was referring to her, personally, or to the renovations. Because trying to get Harrison to focus on the renovations had proven to be difficult.

And it had been even more difficult to keep him from staying overnight. She was determined not to sleep with him again, and that put her in the uncomfortable position of trying to turn their relationship back into a professional one. She wanted this boy genius to make her house one of the most beautiful in the country but enough was enough. She was tired of fighting him off. And she'd noticed a few ceramics were missing from some of the guest bedrooms. Harrison was the only other person in the house.

After that, she also suspected him of pilfering her phone. When she'd lost her phone again, she'd bought another one, had her old phone disabled, and attached the new phone to a small pouch around her waist. Just before Harrison had arrived, she'd found a message from Davis. "Please, Reed, give me another chance. I love you."

She wanted to call Davis. She wanted to see if they could put their marriage back together. It would be a long, difficult road. Yet, despite everything, she loved him and she'd come to see that he was trying to save Henry's life by getting on the stand and allowing the sex tape into evidence. That showed character. Of a sort, anyway. And then there was Samuel. Did she really want Samuel to grow up without Davis around? She needed to think about that. Except for the other women, Davis was basically a good man. And her own father had been heartbroken about his father's absence.

"Harrison, I need to call it a night. I have a headache." She wanted Harrison to leave. Right now.

"You want me to go?"

"Yes." She was going to take charge. She'd kick Harrison out if she had to.

"Oh, dear," he said, "I can't do that."

Reed stammered back, "What do you mean? You have to!"

CHAPTER 56

Davis, Henry, Claire, Jake, and I celebrated with a dinner of steak and mashed potatoes, prepared at Henry's request, and three bottles of Davis's most expensive wine, served at his suggestion and brooking no argument from the rest of us. Good cheer and laughter filled the dining room until we noticed that Henry had passed out, sound asleep, snoring loudly, his head flat against the dining table. The poor guy had been through hell and back, and without Davis in his corner, would now be a convicted felon in sandals and a striped jumpsuit, spending his first night in a maximum security federal prison. The idea made me burn and I had a feeling of profound satisfaction in establishing his innocence.

Jake, Claire, and I took our leave, quietly tiptoeing out of the room and saying goodnight to Davis.

We stood for a moment on Davis's driveway as the cool summer night embraced us.

Jake smiled. "Goodnight, Justice A., Mrs. Alexander."

I choked up and gave him a hug. "Jake, I couldn't have done it without you."

He smiled. "I'll stop by and pack up those litigation files for you."

"Thanks. Goodnight."

As he walked towards his car, Jake turned on his heel. "Justice A., don't you wonder, if Henry didn't kill Eden and Echo, then who did?"

Exactly what I was thinking.

Claire and I hurried home. She had an early morning flight to San Francisco for a tax case. I stayed up and googled Harrison Smith again, took a closer look at his website. The twins' killer was still out there and Smith's financial troubles were weighing on my mind.

Harrison Smith's website touted his professional credentials in renovating large, historical estates. I clicked through several photos of projects he'd completed in the Annapolis area. No wonder Reed called him a genius. His renovations were spectacular and he'd retained the historical integrity of the homes while transporting them into the current century. The homeowners had heaped on rave reviews. I could see why Reed wanted him to work on Blackhall. And she was his type of client. It was obvious Harrison didn't come cheap.

I noticed a small icon embedded in the website. Harrison had given a talk about his philosophy of architectural design. I clicked on it but couldn't get it enlarged. I called Ruth.

"Hey, sorry, I know it's late but I need a favor. I'm going to forward you a link to Harrison Smith's website. I want you to run this video and do a facial recognition analysis, see if this guy is who he says."

"Wow. You're really worried, aren't you?"

"Just being cautious."

"Maybe overly cautious, Papa Bear?"

"Okay, I admit it. I'm worried about Reed's involvement with him."

Ruth sighed. "His face isn't gonna be in the system."

"I know. It's an off-chance. Humor me."

I hung up the phone, exhausted from the trial and found myself dozing off.

Harrison leaned over Reed and almost yanked her arm out of its socket. "Goddamn it," he growled.

Reed shrank in fear. "You're hurting me!"

Harrison put a paper in front of her and slammed down a pen. "Here! Write your suicide note." He let loose a hideous laugh. "You tried to commit suicide when you were nine years old! Everyone knows you're mental. Your kidnapping last year pushed you further into psychosis and you isolated yourself. You became unbalanced, obsessed with this old house, its history of Josephine Rideout and her baby. You identified with her. Just look at you! You're wearing her ring!"

He glared a burning hole through her. *"When the President's daughters were murdered, the entire world found out about Davis Rideout and his sluts! It humiliated you—at first—then, it made your psychosis worse and it eventually drove you insane. And now, just like Josephine, you're going to jump off that cliff with Samuel!"*

"Why are you doing this?" Reed sobbed.

"Because you found out that I killed those women!"

I woke up in a cold sweat. I was still in my study. My arm was asleep. It was two in the morning. I couldn't call Reed fast enough.

She didn't answer.

I started pacing the floor, finally deciding that everyone was right, I worried too much about Reed. She was a grown woman. It was just a bad dream. I went back to bed.

****

The phone woke me at 8:00 the next morning.

"We ran the video like you wanted. Harrison Smith is who he says he is, so stop worrying."

CHAPTER 57

In a mansion outside Philadelphia, Pennsylvania, Theodore Manville IV held two 18th century silver candelabras up to the light and turned them over, examining them, congratulating himself on the purchase price. A mere $50,000 when they were worth several times that, maybe as much as $300,000. He examined the hallmarks again, just to reassure himself. Yes, the four hallmarks identified the work of Paul de Lamerie, the famous London silversmith. The only other known candlesticks like this resided in the Victoria and Albert Museum in London. The pieces were beautiful, chased in the Rococo style, the body of the pieces depicting Neptune rising from the sea.

He looked around his living room, trying to decide where to place the candlesticks in his vast ten thousand-square-foot stone mansion. It would have to be a place of prominence. The dining room was the obvious spot, or perhaps the French console he'd just purchased. But both seemed too pedestrian for such important pieces. He carefully set the candlesticks down on a nearby table, stood back and framed them with his hands. Manville fancied himself an artist and he liked to surprise the eye. But they didn't look right there. Maybe he should contrast them with something modern, perhaps position them near one of his Rothkos. He'd have to think about it.

He strolled out onto his terrace that overlooked the grounds of his forty-seven-acre estate. Cherry trees lined a pond at the bottom of the hill and he sat down and admired his pet swans floating in the water, stirring up little bubbles as they glided along. He shook his head, thinking about the candlesticks again, wondering where in the world his contact got this stuff. The man had access to all sorts of antiques. He'd said the candlesticks were inherited from his grandparents. Could be. The age of the pieces was right.

And the man had the pedigree. His family had been wealthy and extremely prominent.

Not that Manville cared as long as the pieces weren't listed in the databases of stolen art maintained by Interpol and the Art Loss Register and they weren't. He'd checked. He was safe. And he was so rich, no one would ever suspect any of the furnishings in his mansion could be stolen. Well, there was someone interested in where he was acquiring pieces, a fellow collector named Glenn.

Manville threw back his head and laughed. Glenn was jealous. Manville enjoyed the jealousy, loved to show off his prizes. Manville couldn't wait to flaunt his candlesticks.

"Thomas!" he yelled over his shoulder. A house servant stepped onto the terrace.

"Yes, sir?"

"Let's plan a party. Right away. Put Glenn Howard at the top of the list and send the invitations today."

"Yes, sir. Right away, sir."

✶✶✶✶

I called Ruth. I was still convinced the murders were all related, but my theories were starting to swirl in my head, turning into a mishmash of nightmares and wild deductions. I needed her feedback.

"Are you sure you want to get into this again?" Ruth asked.

"I don't have a choice. My daughter refuses to budge from that Goddamn house! I'm afraid she's going to be the next to die."

"What makes you think that?"

"How about three women turning up dead at Blackhall? Damn it! These cases have to be related and the killer is using Blackhall as his killing ground. But Reed's too stubborn to see that!"

"I don't see it, either. Forensics hasn't come up with anything to link the crimes."

"Listen to me. I think Harrison Smith may be involved. He has financial problems. Maybe he was trying to steal the decanter when he happened upon the twins. And, of course, General Fontaine had a motive to kill the Hines twins. They were blackmailing him. The cop who found Arnett told me that Arnett clutched at his uniform like he was trying to tell him something. Get it? Uniform? General Fontaine? Maybe Fontaine ran him off the road and that's what Arnett was trying to say."

She sucked in her breath. "Good Lord. Are you okay, Warren?"

"I need your help sorting through everything. And I have only three weeks before the new Supreme Court term begins."

"Why are you so focused on Harrison Smith? I see why you're suspicious of Fontaine. On the other hand, Fontaine has an alibi."

"Who's his alibi?"

"His wife said he was home with her."

"Not much of an alibi," I muttered. "Can I look at your files on him? See if anything pops out at me?"

Silence. She was considering it.

I cleared my throat. "Hello? The President authorized my involvement in his daughters' investigation and no one officially took me off the case."

Within minutes, I was on the road to Quantico, down I-95. It was an hour-long drive of large semis jostling for position, crowding the road and whizzing by me at ninety miles an hour. I was happy to land on the Quantico Base.

I tapped on Ruth's door, surprised to receive a hug from her. "What's that for?" I laughed.

"That's for you."

"Jeez, don't embarrass me, Ruth."

"I'm worried about you. You sounded like you'd lost your fricking mind." She smiled and pointed to a massive pile of boxes. "Those are the files. Dig in."

"Let me see your background on him."

She scrapped a box off the floor. "Here you go."

A few minutes into the box, I was transfixed by a sheet of paper in my hand.

"What is it?"

"One of Fontaine's relatives is a Mrs. Olivia Trego. Fontaine is her nephew," I said.

"So?"

"Mrs. Trego owns the home across the alley from Lilly's bedroom window."

"She does?"

"Fontaine knew I was helping the FBI. I always thought taking Lilly might be retaliation of some sort. I'd like to get a search warrant for Trego's house but I don't think a judge would sign off." I had an idea. "You know what? Mrs. Trego is ninety years old. She didn't answer the door when I knocked. Let's do a welfare check on her."

Ruth's eyes crinkled into a smile. "I like that. Let's do it."

An hour later, we were at Mrs. Trego's house. I rang the bell. No answer. The door was locked tight. I kicked it in and blanket of dust swirled into the air. Ruth pulled out her Glock.

"Mrs. Trego!" I motioned to Ruth. We'd agreed I would take the upstairs while she looked around the first floor. On the second floor, I cautiously made my way from room to room and creaked each door open. The upstairs had been stripped bare.

I bounded down the stairs. "Find anything?" I asked.

"No."

"Are you thinking what I am?"

"What happened to Mrs. Trego."

"Let's see if there's a basement in this place."

We found the basement door off the kitchen and switched on the light just inside. It didn't work. I heard something scamper across the floor. Could be a rat or could be someone down there. We crept down the stairs. The basement was dank and smelled like standing water. Faint yellow sunlight filtered through half-windows covered in cobwebs. My eyes adjusted to the feeble light and I could see gleaming stacks of furniture and decorative objects piled on tables. The room was crammed with dazzling, high-end items that you'd see in a fancy antiques store, many of them gilded bronze and the rest, silver objects of all sorts.

I picked up an elaborate sterling silver candlestick. "What's going on here?"

Ruth holstered her gun. "I'm not sure. I guess these antiques belong to Mrs. Trego."

"A damp basement is an odd place to store valuable antiques."

Ruth held up a small but extraordinary-looking silver pitcher and scrutinized the bottom. "P. Revere," she said awed, her eyes rising to meet mine.

"Paul Revere?"

"We'll have to get it authenticated." Ruth pulled out her iphone and did some quick research of government databases. "I don't see any of these items listed as stolen. Of course, there are so many of them. We need to do a full inventory and get appraisals." She scratched her head. "But first, I think we need to talk to Fontaine."

I started taking photos with my iphone. "Think he'll talk to you?"

"Maybe I can offer him a deal. If he has the right information."

✶✶✶✶

Fontaine met Ruth at his attorney's office downtown. "I haven't been in that house in years," he insisted.

"I'm concerned about your aunt, Mrs. Trego."

"She's in the Grand Oaks Nursing Home. I've kept quiet about moving her there." He hesitated. "Do I have immunity for anything I tell you here?"

"Unless it's a felony," Ruth said.

"And that plea deal you mentioned?"

"If you have the right information, I might be able to do something."

Fontaine's shoulders rose and fell. "I guess I have nothing to lose. My aunt became an invalid and I had to put her in a nursing home. A caretaker looks after the house and stays there a few nights a week. The District slaps huge taxes on vacant property so I have to make sure it looks lived-in."

"Why not sell it?"

"I'm getting the house in my aunt's will. Georgetown property has sky-rocketed in the sixty years since she bought it. If I sell it now, I'll have to pay $175,000 in capital gains. If I wait until after I inherit it, I'll pay zero because of the stepped-up tax basis."

"Did you leave anything of value in the house?"

"I went through every room, made sure that nothing expensive was left behind."

"We found antiques in the basement," Ruth said.

He looked confused. "All I left down there were some old tools no one would want."

"What's the name of your caretaker?"

"Auggie Custis."

"Auggie Custis who lives on R Street?"

Fontaine snorted. "Do you know anyone else named Auggie Custis?"

"Why did you hire him?"

"He put an ad on Craig's List, offering to look after houses in Georgetown. I met with him. He seemed like a decent chap and he lived right across the alley. It seemed perfect."

****

Ruth reported back after her interview with Fontaine. "It's suspicious but we don't have enough for a search warrant of Auggie's apartment. The antiques could be an inheritance from the Custis family. We need to question Auggie and see if he'll explain the fortune in Trego's basement. But first, let's find out more about him."

CHAPTER 58

An FBI agent rushed into Mortich's office. "Sir, the lab results on the screwdriver we found at Justice Alexander's house are back."

Mortich scrambled to his feet and grabbed the paper. "About time. Let's see." He scanned the information. "Get an arrest warrant drawn up. Now!"

"Yes sir." The agent scurried out the door.

Mortich rubbed his chin. Damn. The President had been right about Alexander. The bastard had killed his own law clerk. Mortich called Ruth's cell phone. "Do you know where Justice Alexander is?"

Ruth was standing outside Branham's Coffee and Beans with Warren but something told her to say no. "Why?"

"It's a yes or no answer."

"No."

"You'd better not be lying to me. We've done forensic testing on a screwdriver we found in his fireplace."

"What?"

"It had been taped to the flu and fallen into the grate and it has Lilly McCleary's blood on it. I'm going on TV to announce that we're issuing a warrant for Alexander's arrest."

"When?"

"Right now." He hung up and smirked. Alexander had made a mockery of the FBI in the most important trial of the century. Payback would be sweet.

****

Ruth turned to me. "Did you hear that?"

"Someone's trying to frame me. I need to call Claire."

"No. We're closing in on the killer. Smash your phone and we'll buy a burner and call her. C'mon, do it before they find you."

"Are you crazy? I'm not going to run from the law. I'm going to turn myself in."

"You'll never get bail and I need your help." Ruth started laughing wildly. "Did you hear what I just said? I need you to clear you."

"Unfortunately, that's probably true." I took her arm and we rushed across Wisconsin Avenue, just above R Street in Georgetown, and entered Branham's Coffee and Beans. Inside, the walls were red brick and dark wood beams crisscrossed overhead. The smell of dark roast hung in the air. A TV was turned to CNN.

I approached a polite-looking young woman. "Can I take your order?" she asked.

"We're looking for your manager."

She smiled. "You're looking at her. What can I do for you?"

"Do you have an employee named Auggie Custis?"

She turned dark. "I haven't seen him for weeks. He just stopped coming in. Didn't even bother to call."

Ruth flashed her badge.

"FBI, huh? What did he do?"

"This is just a security check," Ruth lied. "Do you have a personnel file on him?"

"Not here."

"What about a locker room? Do you have a place where employees can lock up their valuables?"

"Yeah, it's in the back. Locker number 7 but he cleaned it out."

Ruth and I went into the back and examined the locker.

"Call a technician," I said. "Let's see if we can get some fingerprints."

"You'd better wait in the car. You're a wanted man."

As I left Branham's, the manager looked from the TV to me and yelled, "Wait a minute. Aren't you that judge who killed his law clerk?"

****

The results of the fingerprint test were immediate. Augustine Washington Custis had never been born, had never been issued a birth certificate or a social security number. His fingerprints revealed that Auggie was a convicted rapist named Brad Swanson who had been raised in a wealthy old Baltimore family.

Ruth and I were now at Brad's grandmother's mansion in the countryside near Baltimore. Alexandra Swanson had the young body, face, and brilliant silver hair of the winsome grande dames of Mary Petty's New Yorker Magazine covers. A liveried butler stood at attention nearby. She invited us to sit down in a room filled with antiques, baroque curtains, and Flemish tapestries. Clearly, Brad Swanson would know what antiques were valuable enough to steal.

"Brad's parents died in a fiery automobile crash in 2000," she said. "New Year's Eve. A great tragedy for everyone and Brad came to live with us." She looked down at her hands. "I'm afraid that we don't see him anymore. Brad got into some trouble and my husband insisted that tough love was the only way to get through to him. So, we cut off his funds and sent him on his way, hoping that would force him to get his life together. He's in trouble again?" she fretted.

"No, ma'am. We're just investigating some burglaries in the general area."

Her eyes grew wide. "Oh! I thought this was about Brad. I guess I just assumed ..."

She seemed relieved and turned to the butler and smiled. "James, please bring us some tea and refreshments."

I handed her some photos I'd taken of the antiques in Mrs. Trego's basement. "Have you ever seen any of these items?"

She slid on diamond-studded reading glasses, took the photos, and glanced up at me and back at the photos. "Well," she said, "I can tell you these are period pieces and are very valuable, indeed. And this small Rococo mirror," she tapped the photo with a fingernail, "is early 17th Century French. There are probably two other Rococo mirrors like this in the world. And this one looks just like one I saw at Blackhall a long time ago."

Blood rushed to my head. "Blackhall?"

She looked perturbed. "Surely you've heard of it! It's been in all the newspapers as the place where the President's daughters were killed!"

"Yes, ma'am. Do you have an association with Blackhall?"

She took off her glasses and looked off into the past. "Old Paul and Lorraine Rideout owned Blackhall. I guess the son owns it now. My mother and Old Paul Rideout's mother were best friends and I used to go to parties there when I was a young debutante. Blackhall was such a wonderful house at that time, although it looks a bit rundown now from the photographs in the newspaper. Old Paul had debts and then I think the son let it go."

"Please, ma'am, tell us what you know about the estate."

She sniffed. "Well, I know about all the estates in this area. I was quite the party deb in my time and everyone wanted me as a guest. Of course, that was when people still entertained. Not at all like today. No one entertains or dresses anymore. My word. I don't know why people bother to spend money on clothes. Everyone looks so awful in tee shirts and jeans."

"To get back to Blackhall."

"Oh, yes. The Rideouts. Old Paul and Lorraine raised thoroughbreds, raced them all up and down the East Coast. They were doing quite well with the enterprise. Then, there was a fire one night in the stable. A cigarette started the blaze. There was some tittle-tattle about Old Paul and Pauline Winston taking a roll in the hay." She laughed. "Literally. Old Paul didn't smoke and everyone knew Pauline was a chain smoker. It was awful because most of those fine animals went up in flames. Old Paul tried to save them but hay burns quickly and the fire station was so far away that by the time they got to Blackhall, the Rideouts had lost hundreds of thousands of dollars. After the fire, they withdrew from society, stopped entertaining, and slid deeper and deeper into debt. If it weren't for that son, they'd lost their estate entirely. As it was, it was awfully close."

"To get back to that silver mirror."

"Why, here is James!" she exclaimed.

An enormous tray, filled with scones, cookies, and cream and sugar was set down by a silver tea service.

"Please pour, James."

"Yes, ma'am."

She handed us steaming cups. "Where were we? Oh, yes. The Rideouts were like so many old families, never selling anything, storing old things away." A devious look crossed her face. "I have to confess that I loved to sneak up to the attics of those estates during parties. I've always been interested in antiques and the things I saw!" She lifted her cup and daintily crooked her little finger.

"Are you saying you saw antiques hidden at Blackhall?"

"Well, I don't know if they were exactly hidden but there were hundreds of them in Blackhall's attic, all covered in dust. Most of them were in bad shape although they could be fixed. I never did understand why Old Paul didn't sell some of them to pay his debts. I don't think he knew how valuable they were. Some people don't."

"Did Brad know about the antiques?"

"Of course! I used to tell him tales all the time."

Her hands began trembling and her tea cup clattered so hard she had to set it down. "You don't think Brad stole anything, do you?"

"No ma'am, we're just questioning anyone who knows anything about these estates."

That seemed to appease her and we continued the questioning, never saying anything that would make her alert Brad.

****

On our drive back, Ruth read the background report on Brad Swanson that had been e-mailed to her phone.

"He's classic Ted Bundy in the way he was able to fit into society and thrive in his social and school life. Then, he raped a girl in college. His grandparents came to his defense and hired an expensive attorney who got him a light sentence, one year. But he became notorious in his social set. I guess not even the Swanson money could protect him from being ostracized because when another girl was raped, this one a member of his grandparents' country club, Brad's family was shunned and their country club membership withdrawn. That's probably when they cut him off."

"I guess not being able to hit the links was simply too much," I said.

"Brad was also suspected in the rape and murder of another girl although there wasn't enough evidence to arrest him. The killer wore a condom, and probably gloves, and cleaned up the crime scene. And get this. The girl had a trace amount of Scopolamine in her system."

"The same drug used on the twins." I looked at Ruth. "Before his grandparents stopped the cash flow, Brad probably had money to go to South America or Europe and pick up some Scopolamine on his travels."

"So now we have Brad without his grandparents' money, and as a registered sex offender, it would be difficult for him to find a job. Could be why he moved into Washington. From this information, it looks like Maryland notified the central Sex Offender Registry in D.C. of Brad's move. The notification fell through the cracks, and Brad seized the opportunity to change his name and start a new life."

"But without papers to back up a new identity, how was he going to find employment?" I asked.

"That was the problem and probably the consideration behind adopting the name Augustine Washington Custis."

"His theory being—who wouldn't trust a Custis?"

"It would be a good theory. Remember that Branham's manager said she'd hired Brad on the spot, and when she'd asked for his driver's license as an ID, he claimed he'd forgotten his wallet at home?"

"And she probably didn't follow up because she trusted him," I added. "Like I did. He lied about everything."

"Including his social security number or maybe he stole one. The law prohibits employers from asking tough questions, even when they suspect fraud. But Branham's wouldn't pay much and I bet Brad began stealing to supplement his income. Blackhall was an easy target. His grandmother told him that the place was basically abandoned and the layers of dust in the attic told him that the antiques had been forgotten. He's no dummy. I think he was treating Blackhall like his own personal piggy bank."

CHAPTER 59

Since I was a wanted man, I couldn't go home. I had no place to eat or lie my head. My house in Georgetown was surrounded by FBI agents. I'd managed to place a call to Claire in San Francisco where she was in the middle of a tax case. Claire would be questioned but she was a smart lawyer and a strong woman. She could handle the FBI. I had no worry about that.

Having gone down the path of *wanted criminal*, my only refuge was with Ruth. After meeting with Brad's grandmother, Ruth drove me to her house on Edwards Ferry Road in Leesburg, Virginia. It was dusk and we scouted the block for FBI agents. We didn't spot any although we both knew it was only a matter of time before they showed up.

Ruth's house was an old colonial, dark grey with yellow wood trim. Two chimneys jutted into the sky, one on each end, high over dark grey shingles. Trees shaded the yard and a red berry wreath hung on the door. Very attractive.

Inside was just as tasteful. I'd expected wild leopard rugs or maybe a sofa with leopard spots, like a large animal crouched in a corner. Instead, old quilts covered overstuffed paisley chairs. On either end of the long room was a stone fireplace. A raft of wood beams spliced overhead. It was like going back in time to a more genteel way of life.

"Very homey, Ruth. All you need is a cat in the window."

"I wish I had time to take care of one," she said wistfully, pulling a rubber band from her thick bundle of brown hair and letting it fall around her shoulders.

Silver photographs lined the mantels.

"Jeffrey Pennypacker," I said, picking up a photo.

"He's my man," she said proudly, looking over my shoulder.

"He's good looking."

"You met him at your swearing-in."

"I remember. Scotland Yard Detective. You must have a lot in common. Have you set a date?"

"Probably sometime next year."

I put the photograph down and looked around. "I can see Jeffrey being happy here. Your place looks like it could be in the English countryside. Very old school, clubby."

"Jeffrey likes it, although we might sell to be closer to Quantico." She walked into the kitchen and motioned for me to follow. The kitchen also had a wood-beamed ceiling. Woven baskets lined the top of shelves. Another stone hearth and comfortable chairs made up a keeping room, an extension of the kitchen. I felt right at home. She put a kettle on the stove.

"Tea? I'm going to have some."

"Sounds good." I deposited myself into a kitchen chair and tried to shrug off the idea that every law enforcement officer in the country was looking for me. I had to turn myself in. Soon. It was only a question of how and when.

She stood at the kitchen sink and washed her hands. "I want to thank you for agreeing to walk me down the aisle and give me away." She laughed. "Funny thing to say, isn't it? Give me away."

I chuckled. "Makes you sound like chattel."

She dried her hands. "It goes back to that idea."

"I'm honored to do it … assuming I'm not in prison."

"I'll spring you if I have to. You're the closest thing I have to a brother or a father. Both of mine are dead."

I nodded. "I remember. That's too bad."

"Your mom's still in assisted care in Jackson?"

"Yes. She's doing well."

She poured two cups of tea, stuck her nose into the refrigerator. "Cream?"

"Sure."

"What about your father? In all the time we worked together you never mentioned him. It was always mom did this or mom did that." She slid into a chair and sipped her tea.

It was a relief to talk about something other than my wanted status, something other than the case. I felt protected here in Ruth's home, almost like I'd never have a problem again unless I opened that front door. I relaxed.

"My mom was the only parent I had any interaction with. That is, any I can remember."

"I always felt like your dad was off limits."

"My dad left us when I was three. I barely remember him."

"I'm sorry. I had no idea."

"It's no longer important."

She shook her head. "I would think that would always be important." She stood, walked to a cupboard and returned with chocolate chip cookies on green paper plates. "I hope these won't spoil your dinner."

"Hardly. I could eat a bear." I chomped into a cookie. "Wow, that's good," I said, wiping crumbs from my mouth. "Homemade?"

"Yes." She laughed and her brown eyes sparkled. "Ravenous?"

"Sure am. Jeffrey's going to be a happy man if you whip these up for him."

"So, what did your dad do?"

"He worked in rodeos. Out west, in Wyoming, Nevada, all around."

"Oh yeah? Doing what?"

I took another cookie. Although I wasn't finished with the first one, I wanted to get another one lined up. "He was a bronco rider, roped calves, steers, anything that was dangerous, he'd jump on it." I hesitated. "But I'm proudest of his work as a rodeo clown." I saw her face, a flash of surprise.

"It's not what you think," I said. "A rodeo clown is the most dangerous job in the rodeo. I guess nowadays, they're called bullfighters. They divert a bull's attention when a rider's thrown. If a bull runs into you flat out, it's like being hit by a Mini Cooper going 25 miles per hour. Bullfighters are in the mud and the blood and the beer. And my dad was the best. I have an old newspaper article about him. In his career, he was speared nine times, had numerous broken bones, and kept going back in. Ultimately, he saved lives more than a thousand times. I check periodically. He still holds the record."

✳✳✳✳

That night as I lay in bed, looking at the stars from Ruth's guest bedroom window, I wondered what my dad was doing now. I also wondered what prison would be like. We had enough information on Brad that Ruth could take it from here. We'd agreed that she would call Mortich in the morning and say she'd talked me into surrendering. That would give her some cover with the Bureau. Being at Ruth's house was a good way to spend the last of my freedom and that night, my sleep was filled with peaceful dreams. I feared nothing. I was my father's son.

CHAPTER 60

The party at Theodore Manville's mansion was gearing up. Laughter and chatter filled the vast rooms. Manville was eagerly anticipating Glenn Howard's arrival. Manville was dying to goad the rival collector, show off the amazing candlesticks he'd just purchased. Glenn would never be able to find anything comparable on the market because they were virtually unique in the world of decorative arts. Manville couldn't wait to see the look on Glenn's face.

The doorbell rang.

Ah. There he was now.

Glenn entered dressed in a houndstooth jacket, black trousers, and a black silk ascot at his neck.

Manville stuck out his hand. "Glenn! My friend, welcome." Manville motioned toward the bar where uniformed bartenders stood at rapt attention, awaiting orders. "Please, let my people serve you a drink."

A beautiful red-haired woman, wearing a skintight green dress, came up behind Glenn and slid her arm around his waist.

Manville's eyes bugged out. "Well! Who is this?" he said, leering at the lovely creature. "You must introduce us, Glenn."

The redhead smiled shyly and held out her hand. "You must be Mr. Manville. Glenn has told me all about you." She lowered her head, looked up at him and batted her eyes. Manville felt electricity sizzle through his body. Manville was a collector of more than just antiques.

"Let me get you a drink, Miss …?"

"Colville … Crystal Colville."

"Crystal. What a lovely name." He hesitated, turned to Glenn. "Would you mind if I showed your lovely friend my private bar?"

Glenn smiled warmly. "Not at all." He pointed his index finger and cocked his thumb like a gun. "Don't forget to bring her back," he said playfully.

What an idiot, Manville thought. He turned to his newly found prize-to-be. "Right this way. Your name reminded me of something wonderful that I just acquired." Manville leaned in and placed Crystal's arm through his. "May I get you a drink, my dear?"

She giggled. "A gin and tonic sounds divine."

He patted her arm and ushered her into his library. "Perfect. You read my mind. Please have a seat."

She sat down in a tufted leather chair and tucked her purse beside her. Manville opened a cabinet and took out a sapphire and diamond-encrusted Revelation Baccarat Crystal Decanter. He glanced over his shoulder. Her jaw was hanging open. Good. She was appropriately awed. It wouldn't be long before he had her in the sack. "You have good taste, my dear. These are real sapphires and diamonds."

"My God!" she gushed. "The jewels are like flashlights!"

Manville grimaced. An awkward simile. This girl didn't have a lot of class. But when he looked at her body, his trousers tightened. He'd show her a big length of class soon enough.

He lifted the decanter, poured some gin into a glass and reached into a small refrigerator under the bar for some tonic water, talking with his back to her. "I wanted you to see this crystal decanter, my dear Crystal, because it's almost as beautiful as you are." That ought to get her softened up for what was to come. From him, a compliment would be like a pat on the head from God. He turned around.

A Glock was in his face.

"Hands up," Crystal barked. "FBI. Put the decanter down and get on the floor. You're under arrest for possession of stolen property."

Manville peed in his pants. "Jesus Christ. Who are you?" he blubbered as piss ran down his leg, flowed over his handmade shoes and onto his priceless Aubusson carpet.

"FBI Agent Ginger Baker." She slapped cuffs on him and shoved him up against the wall. "Remember that name the next time you're tempted to buy stolen goods." She kneed him in the groin for good measure. He dropped to the ground and moaned in pain, rolling around in his own urine. "And that's for those dirty thoughts. You're disgusting."

CHAPTER 61

Early the next morning, I woke to a telephone ringing in the bowels of Ruth's house. It was still dark outside and I quickly dressed and made my way downstairs to see what was going on. The aroma of fresh coffee pulled me into the kitchen where Ruth was on the phone. She glanced at me and put a finger to her lips.

"Sir, I just got off the phone with Ginger Baker. That's right, Ginger is part of my team on the Hines case. No, no. What matters, sir, is that we're closing in. Warren is with me and it seems he's been right all along. Warren and I have information that should link Auggie Custis to the decanter stolen from Blackhall and Custis was the Super in Lilly McCleary's building. I think we can wrap this up when we question Manville."

Mortich pondered Ruth's words. He'd seen Ginger's report a few hours ago. The decanter could be important and they hadn't recovered any prints from the screwdriver recovered from Justice Alexander's house, an indication it had been planted. Mortich looked at the other suits around the table and back at the giant screen they were all watching. Night vision showed FBI agents as they surrounded Ruth's house. Mortich could see Ruth and Alexander through a window. All he had to do was say the word and Alexander would be cuffed.

But when Mortich had called the President with the news of Alexander's impending arrest, Hines had been strangely disinterested, instead launching into a furious tirade about the FBI's mistakes with the DNA evidence in Turnbull's trial. If Mortich made another mistake and wrongfully arrested a Supreme Court Justice, it could be political suicide.

"I'll give you forty-eight hours," Mortich said. "If you don't have an arrest by then, Alexander agrees to surrender himself. If you double-cross me, I'll have you both arrested." He hung up.

Ruth turned to me. "We have forty-eight hours."

I sat down at the kitchen table. "What's going on?"

"There was a sting last night at an art collector's house, a Theodore Manville. An agent found the decanter that was stolen from Blackhall."

"Are you sure it's the same decanter?"

"There are five of them in the world. The other four are in Europe."

I rubbed my stubble of beard. "Has Manville lawyered up?"

She smiled. "He'll talk if he knows what's good for him."

"What made you look at him?"

"An antique collector thought Manville was buying stolen goods and when he mentioned a Revelation Baccarat Crystal Decanter, Ginger decided to move in. We'd kept the one stolen from Blackhall off the Art Loss Register to see if it would surface. And we got lucky. It did." She grabbed a windbreaker and headed for the door. "C'mon. I'll start the car. We don't have any time to waste."

****

At FBI Headquarters, agents eyeballed me aggressively like they were dying for an arrest but stayed their distance as I positioned myself behind the one-way mirror.

Manville had a thicket of grey hair carefully styled and dutifully sprayed into a helmet. His clothes looked expensive, but crumpled, like he'd slept in them. I also noticed a large stain on his trousers. I didn't know what Ginger had done to him but he'd pissed his pants.

"Mr. Manville," Ruth said. "And Mr. Jordan, is that right?" she asked of his attorney who wore a custom-made navy blue suit and red tie.

"Mr. Manville," Ruth began again. "This interview is not just about a stolen decanter. It's more serious than that."

Jordan snapped to attention.

"The decanter in your possession, Mr. Manville, implicates you in the murder of the President's daughters."

Manville caught his breath. "What?"

Jordan put his arm on Manville's shoulder. "Theodore, don't say a word."

Ruth smiled. "Mr. Manville, you are in serious trouble."

"I don't know anything about the President's daughters!"

"Mr. Manville, we suspect your decanter is stolen and we're not after you. We're after the man who sold it to you. So, we have a simple proposition for you. Give us his name and you can leave. And if your story checks out, you won't be charged with anything."

"Auggie Custis!" Manville screamed. "His name is Auggie Custis! He's the man who sold it to me. Is that good enough for you?"

Ruth smiled in my direction. "Yes, that's good enough for us."

I wanted to bang on the glass in celebration. Now, we had more than enough for a search warrant of Auggie's apartment.

✳✳✳✳

Within the hour, Ruth and I were at Auggie's door, search warrant in hand. It turned out that Auggie's apartment was in the building's basement, right under Lilly's apartment. His walls were covered with photos of Lilly he'd stolen from her apartment and disturbing photos of Reed asleep in her bed at Blackhall. I wanted to kill him. "This guy is sick."

I rummaged through a desk drawer. "I found something. Flash drives. The same brand as the ones at the twins' house. They could be the twins' videos of themselves and the blackmailing victims."

Ruth started toward the door. "I'm going upstairs to Lilly's apartment. Stay down here. I want to see if noise transfers between the two spaces."

I looked up at the ceiling. There was no overhead insulation and the wood floorboards were clearly visible. I heard Ruth walking above me. I called her cell phone. "Okay, say something at normal level," I said, holding my hand over the receiver.

"I can hear mumbling," I said.

"What about now?" Ruth said.

"Better."

"And now?"

"I can hear you perfectly. What did you do differently?"

"I'm sitting on Lilly's bed and right beside it is an air vent that must connect to Auggie's place. Look for it. I bet Auggie could hear Lilly in bed."

I scrapped my hand along the floorboard, located the vent and a square piece of wood that fit over it. "Found it and Auggie made a wood cover to close it off when he wanted to," I said.

"That's why Lilly never heard Auggie talking."

A chill ran through my bones. "Unless he made a mistake one night."

CHAPTER 62

"Really, Daddy, I'm fine!" Reed said over the phone. "Honestly, Claire and Davis are right. You do worry too much about me. I'm the one who should be concerned. What about that arrest warrant? I've been frantic! I couldn't reach you and even though Claire said not to worry—"

"That was a misunderstanding. It's been resolved."

She wasn't so sure. Her father had a way of minimizing problems and she didn't want to bother him with her latest troubles so she didn't tell him about the scene she'd had with Harrison. How Harrison had insisted on staying at her house. How she'd finally gotten rid of Harrison by calling the police. How the police had found her old phone in Harrison's pocket. It was awful. Harrison had turned out to be some sort of lunatic!

The police had suggested filing charges but she just wanted Harrison out of her life. She'd hired a new architect, who said he could implement Harrison's plans for the house. Since she had paid for the plans, they were hers to do with as she pleased. She hadn't known that! What a relief. And now, the demolition work was on track, the renovations about to begin, and she was glad to be moving on. She was proud of handling everything herself and not relying on her father for help.

"Davis and I are back together and I'm moving into Washington until the renovations are done," Reed said. "We're going to work on our marriage. You'd be proud of me because I laid down the law with him."

"Good!"

She laughed. "I haven't told you what I said, yet."

"I'm glad you're standing up for yourself."

"I said I'd return only if he entered counseling for sex addiction and I couldn't believe it, he actually agreed."

"That's great. And you're right, I am proud of you. I'm proud of you and I've always been proud of you."

She gave a little sigh of contentment, looked around at the scene all around her, people rushing everywhere. "Sotheby's is here, valuing antiques and hauling them off to storage so we can start the demolition."

"Sothebys?"

"They've been here all day. And the strange thing is that Sotheby's curator is a dead ringer for Auggie. Of course, I've only seen Auggie at night with his cap on."

"Auggie?"

"Auggie is one of our security guards."

****

Auggie a/k/a Brad had been fortunate the FBI had focused on Lilly's body and not on the antiques in the attic. The damaged condition of the antiques and caked-on dirt had disguised their true worth. Earlier in the day, he'd even convinced Reed that some of the more damaged pieces were worthless when, in fact, they were extraordinary specimens of the earliest American furniture ever made. The total value of everything in the attic after repairs? At least fifteen million. Easy.

When Reed was in Washington, he'd hacked into her computer and had all her e-mails sent to him. That's how he knew she was about to start demolition and hire a curator. The little twit thought she was contacting Sotheby's! What an idiot.

He would store most of the antiques to avoid suspicion, just in case she checked on them, but cart away a few of the more valuable prizes, including the match to a Louis XIV ormolu-mounted, ebony cut-brass, tortoise shell, horn and pewter marquetry armoire that had recently sold at Sotheby's for four million. Manville would be thrilled. It was a large piece and Brad could never get it out of the house by himself, but now, he had movers doing the lifting for him.

He was sad about one thing, though. *Reed.* A week or so ago, he'd slipped away from the other security guards and circled up to the mansion. Reed had completed the arrangements for the antiques to be moved and had informed the guards of her plans. The truck loads of antiques would go through without interrogation. And the day guards had no idea what he looked like. His plan was brilliant.

It was time to rape Reed and kill her and the baby. Reed was practically a hermit. She wouldn't be missed for a few days, maybe even a week. He could hide their bodies in the woods while the antiques waltzed out the front door. After their bodies were found, no one would think to question him because she'd given her permission for the antiques to be moved.

He'd thought of everything. Finally, it was time for his chocolate dessert with the cherry on top! He'd crept to the library window, knife in hand, ready to spring, but Harrison Smith had been in the house, then the police had arrived. And after that, he hadn't had another chance.

That damn Harrison Smith. *A few months ago, Harrison had almost caught him crouching under Reed's window, watching her breast feed.* That had been a close call. But Brad had been wearing his guard's uniform and had stood up before Harrison saw him, murmured, "good evening," and acted like he was on patrol. Once again, acting like he fit in had saved Brad's ass.

✦✦✦✦

The pilot brought the chopper down on Blackhall's lawn. Movers were scurrying in and out of the house, and Brad was supervising the removal of a large mirror. He spotted the government seal on the chopper and took off.

"Brad!" I ran after him, threw my body forward and caught him by the legs. He slipped through my hands, struggled to his feet, and ran down the lawn toward the cliff.

"Brad, stop!"

He was nearing the cliff's edge. I stopped running and walked toward him. I didn't want to spook him again. "Let's talk this through."

He had his back to me, looking out over the Bay. He glanced over his shoulder. I could see his mind spinning, trying to figure a way out, but going over that cliff would be suicide.

He put his hands in the air. Cowards always do.

****

We found traces of Echo's blood on a knife Brad was carrying. After that discovery, Brad admitted to killing Eden and Echo yet denied killing Lilly. Nonetheless, our theory was that Brad listened to Lilly when she was in bed with men. Although Brad fantasized about her, he couldn't risk his position at the apartment building by acting on his fantasies. A few nights after he raped and killed the twins, something happened, we're not sure what. Maybe he started talking to himself about what he'd done, realized he'd forgotten to replace the vent cover, came upstairs and let himself into Lilly's apartment with the master key.

He would've taken Lilly to Blackhall because it was an isolated place he was familiar with. We theorized he killed her in the attic, covered her body with powdered lime, and as an additional measure, applied Smelleze, a product used in morgues. But his efforts hadn't been completely effective, and gaps in the floorboards let the smell linger and permeate through the house.

Over the course of the next few weeks, Ruth questioned Brad, who said he'd found flash drives in the twins' Gucci bag and had spent hours watching them screwing half of Washington. He also bragged about sneaking into Blackhall and masturbating by Reed's bedside. Thank God I wasn't in the interview room to hear that. I would've killed the bastard. He was the lowest form of scum.

But, strangely, Brad continued to deny killing Lilly and that troubled me. Because despite the soundness of our theory about how Brad killed Lilly, there was something about this case that was still bothering me.

CHAPTER 63

Claire and I had been summoned back to Blackhall for some sort of big announcement. Davis escorted us into the library where Reed was sitting, Henry standing next to her.

Davis poured some expensive wine into crystal glasses and passed them around. He held up his glass. "We asked you all here because we wanted our family to be the first to know that Reed and I are expecting another child."

"That's wonderful," Claire gushed and rushed to hug Reed. I shook Davis's hand. Henry patted Davis on the back. "Congratulations, son," he said.

"That calls for a toast," I said. "To the new baby."

"To the baby," everyone echoed.

"How far along are you?" Claire asked, excited.

"A few weeks. It's hard to tell." She stole a glance at Davis. "That's what the doctor says ... that it's hard to tell."

"And I have another announcement," Davis said. "When we learned the antiques in the attic were valuable, we hired a curator, this time a legitimate curator, to go through the items, catalogue them and return an inventory. While going through an old desk, the curator found the rest of Josephine Rideout's suicide letter."

"Really?" Reed jumped up and threw her arms around Davis. "You found the letter? Oh, my God. You didn't tell me!"

"I wanted it to be a surprise," Davis said, kissing her on the cheek.

"Have you read it?"

He smiled. "Let's go into the library. Henry, you read the letter." Davis took a red box from the desk drawer and pulled out a yellowed piece of paper. I immediately recognized the box. It was the same one I'd seen them with in Henry's cottage.

Henry put on a pair of reading glasses and began:

John had to attend to business in Philadelphia City and after he left, I decided to take the children to Blackhall where the breeze cools the air. I sent my maid ahead with the children to prepare the house, and at the last minute, it being an unusually beautiful spring day, I decided to travel by horseback, something John thought gentlewomen shouldn't do. I didn't care. I wanted the wind in my hair and I urged my horse onward. I traveled so fast that I was at Blackhall hours before my maid and the children were to arrive in the carriage.

As I galloped up to the house, night was falling and I saw John's horse and a carriage I didn't recognize. John should've been in Philadelphia and I was suspicious. I tied my horse behind the stable and quietly slipped to the library windows. The Governor's daughters, Theresa and Thomasina Gilbert, were on the floor with my husband, rutting like animals. I ran to the barn and hid, keeping my horse quiet, waiting, deciding what to do. I must have lost track of time because I saw John ride away. I thought about riding after him but instead I went into the library and confronted the women. I told them to leave John alone and never come back to my home.

They rolled around on the sofas and laughed at me. I don't remember what words were said, but Theresa shoved me and I shoved her back. She fell and hit her head on the fireplace. Thomasina turned on me, enraged, and I grabbed a knife from the desk and stabbed her in self-defense.

Jonah, my old and trusted slave, heard the ruckus and ran into the room. He saw the women, naked and dead sprawled on the floor, and the knife in my hand and understood immediately what had happened. I didn't have to say a word. He took the bodies somewhere. Where I don't know. Jonah returned and shooed off Theresa and Thomasina's horse with their carriage, then he cleaned the library, sopping the blood from the rugs and rolling them up to be washed, which he did himself.

Two months later and no one seems to suspect anything. John established an alibi of being in Philadelphia and my maid told the sheriff that I was with her. But I can't live with myself. I have nightmares and I can't sleep. Every night, Theresa's and Thomasina's faces come screaming at me from the dark. They haunt me and I'm afraid of the night.

I can't rest until Governor Gilbert knows where his daughters are, until they have a proper burial. But I can't face the hangman. And I'm fearful my own sons are destined to be philanderers like John because that's the example he sets for them. That's why I'm taking them with me. My babies will be better off in heaven, with their Momma.

I was surprised at the letter's content, but mostly because of its implications. Henry and Davis had known about the letter early in the investigation and kept quiet about it because it evinced why the police should question Reed in the twins' disappearance. And that meant I owed Henry because despite being faced with the death penalty, he had never pointed to Reed as a possible suspect. He'd protected her every step of the way. The man who had my sympathy at trial, now had my gratitude for life.

CHAPTER 64

Henry, Reed, and I were gathered around the breakfast table at Blackhall. Henry swiveled a coffee cup in his hands and blew steam off the top. "I started reading about DNA last night," he said.

Reed perked up. "You did? Because of the trial?"

Henry nodded. "Yes ma'am. And guess what I found? Did you know that we all receive energy from our ancestors through our DNA? After our ancestors die, their energies are still present in us and their traumas are also imprinted on our DNA and because of that, people often re-enact the trauma!"

I rolled my eyes.

Reed flew off her chair, her eyes glistening like wet marbles. "Henry! That's it! It was Josephine trying to right a wrong! Remember what she said in her suicide letter? She couldn't rest until the Gilbert girls had a proper burial. What's the likelihood of the President's daughters driving out to Blackhall to meet Davis just like the Gilbert girls came out here to meet John Rideout? My God, it wasn't a coincidence after all. It was Josephine trying to make sure the Gilbert girls were finally found!"

I tossed my newspaper on the breakfast table. "Oh, for God's sake. That doesn't make sense."

Reed crossed her arms. "It does. You're the one who always says there's no such thing as coincidence."

"Events centuries apart? They're completely unrelated and anyway, taken to its logical extreme, your theory lets Davis off the hook for having sex with Eden and Echo."

"Not really. He has free will," Henry said.

"That's part of the theory?" I looked at Henry over my reading glasses. "Trauma is imprinted on DNA but everyone still has free will? Where are you getting this stuff, Henry?"

"It's on the Internet. Good as gold."

"Hmmm." I took a sip of coffee and leaned back in my chair. "Let's see ... Josephine's trauma about her husband's infidelity compelled Davis to re-enact the episode, all to the delight of Josephine who wanted Blackhall to be searched and her old murder victims found?" I shook my head.

"Something like that," Henry said.

I folded my newspaper. "I have an entirely different idea why Davis had sex with Eden and Echo and it has nothing to do with trauma."

"Oh, Daddy," Reed sighed.

"And anyway," I said, "the Gilbert daughters were found before Eden's and Echo's bodies were located so under your theory, Josephine had no reason to sacrifice the twins, did she?"

Reed cupped her coffee. "You don't understand, Daddy. I don't have Josephine's DNA and I was the one who arranged the dig that found the Gilbert women."

I groaned and shoved my chair back. "Anyone want more coffee?"

Henry turned back to Reed, unable to contain his excitement. "And did you know there's such a thing as ancestor cleansing? You can actually cleanse an ancestor's trauma so it won't affect their descendants' actions."

Reed's eyes grew even bigger. "Oh my God! I wish we'd known that earlier!"

Henry nodded solemnly. "Me too. Could've saved us a lot of problems. *Yes sirree.*"

"Oh, for God's sakes," I muttered, lifting the coffee pot from the stove. Had everyone gone nuts?

"The Bible talks about bad times passin' down from generation to generation," Henry said, nodding at me as though that capped the discussion.

Reed smiled and turned to me. "See? And anyway, what's the difference between DNA transferring trauma and being able to identify someone by DNA?"

"Being able to identify someone by DNA evidence is proven science. What you're talking about is not science. What you're talking about is nonsense."

Reed frowned at me. "Just because it hasn't been proven doesn't mean it's not true. DNA carries genetic characteristics like eye and hair color, so why can't it transfer trauma as well?"

I refreshed everyone's cup. "I'll wait for the science to come in."

Henry grew excited. "There is science! On the Internet, I read all about a doctor in New York who's found that children of people who experience severe trauma have low levels of somethin' called cortisol."

"That may be," I said, "but that's a lot different than saying that Josephine's trauma transferred to Davis's DNA, which compelled him to re-enact John Rideout's scenario while Josephine cheered from the wings."

"Well, I know one thing," Henry said, looking in my direction. "There's good people who know nothin' about the spirit world."

Reed set her jaw and glared at me. "Henry's right. People are afraid of the unknown, so they claim there's nothing to it. That's why you're so close minded."

"I'm close-minded because in all my time in the FBI, not once did I discover a dead person committing a crime." I gathered up my newspaper. "I'm going to read in the library," I said. "I'll try not to sit on a dead ancestor."

As I left the room I heard Reed whispering, "He doesn't understand."

"Yeah, I know," Henry said. "Best not to bother him. But I've seen Josephine, yes I have."

"Me too," Reed whispered. "And I've realized that when we renovate the house, Josephine isn't leaving because she's not in the house."

Henry whispered something back, what I didn't hear. I wasn't interested. I knew gobbledygook when I heard it.

CHAPTER 65

Late that night, Reed slipped a sheer negligee over her head and walked to the fireplace. Red flames shot high and maple logs cracked and spit.

Davis walked into the bedroom, saw Reed's nude body backlit by the flames and whistled low. "You look gorgeous."

Reed beamed.

Davis slipped his arms around her, rocked her back and forth and kissed the back of her neck. "You are the sexiest pregnant woman I know."

Reed laughed and touched his hand. "I don't like the qualifier."

"Okay, I take it back." He smiled.

She pivoted in his arms and playfully hit him. "I should've known not to marry a lawyer."

"And I should've known not to marry a woman every man wants. But I did and I'm glad." He took her hand and led her to the canopied bed. "Come here, gorgeous." He pulled her down on the soft bedding.

She fell into his arms and he kissed her.

She drew back. "Davis?"

"Hmmm?" He kissed her neck.

"I wanted to ask you a question about Harrison."

Davis smiled. "Who?"

Reed pouted. "You heard me. Harrison, our architect."

Davis sighed, ran his hand through his hair. "What about him?"

"He said his uncle, Lawrence Smith, was an interior decorator who worked here a long time ago. Do you remember him? I think you would've been about eighteen or nineteen at the time. Harrison said his grandfather was in the Kennedy administration."

Davis sat up in bed. "My God." Davis's face drained of blood. "Mary."

"Who's Mary?"

Davis lay back down, uncharacteristically still, staring at the silk folds of the canopied bed. When he spoke next, his voice sounded odd in a way Reed had never heard before. "You haven't gotten involved with our architect, have you?"

Panic lit her eyes. "Of course not!" She grew quiet. The fire took on a false crackle. They both lay there, neither one saying a word, neither one moving. After several minutes, Reed turned her head toward Davis. "Why do you ask?"

"No reason," he said.

She leaned on her arm, the fire playing over her face. "Tell me. I want to know."

Davis sighed. "Mary was Lawrence Smith's niece who worked on the house with him. She got pregnant and claimed the boy was mine."

Reed shot straight up in bed. "Harrison is your son?"

"It's possible and with my reputation, everyone believed her. She was a few years older and wanted to get married even though we hardly knew each other. Jesus. It was only an afternoon in my bedroom. I was eighteen and heading off to college. I was a boy for God's sake."

"You didn't recognize Harrison's name?" Reed asked, stunned.

"She named him Michael. Maybe Harrison is his middle name. I don't know. It's been so long. God. I never connected the two." Davis stood up and walked to the fireplace.

Reed lay motionless on the bed.

"Are you okay?" Davis asked.

"Well, it's sort of a shock." Bile rose in her throat. "Oh God, I'm going to be sick." She ran for the bathroom and vomited into the toilet, gagging until tears ran down her face. Finally, she was able to lift her head. Davis was standing behind her. He put his hands under her arms and pulled her to her feet. "Are you okay?"

"Yes. The pregnancy has been rough." She stumbled to the basin, ran some water over her face, and rinsed her mouth.

"Let me help you back to bed." He led her back into the master bedroom, fluffed some pillows, and pulled the sheets back. He lay down beside her and held her. "Has Harrison been bothering you in some way?"

"No, everything's been okay," she said, her eyes fixed on the peak in the canopied bed where the folds of blue silk were sewn together. "Although, he never scheduled the demolition. It seemed like he was never all that serious about starting the project."

"I'm not surprised."

"Why?" Something about Davis's voice disturbed her.

"Do you really want to know?"

"Yes."

"Mary died from a gunshot wound. The family claimed it was a hunting accident. At that time, suicide in a family was a disgrace. But it was common knowledge that she killed herself."

"But you had nothing to do with that!"

"No, although Harrison probably doesn't see it that way." Davis sighed. "I was a boy but I wasn't blameless." He looked tired. "Reed, there are things in my past that I'm not proud of. I've made mistakes and looking back, I see that some were serious and I wish I could change them."

"I've made mistakes, too," Reed said, her voice cracking. She thought for a while. "Do you think Harrison is after your money?"

"He doesn't have a legal right to it, if that's what you mean," Davis said, the fire reflecting in his eyes.

"Why not?"

Davis propped a pillow under his head. "Mary couldn't prove I was the father. At the time, there was no such thing as DNA testing. But her family was prominent and started making trouble. I'd been accepted to Stanford, my first choice, and Mary's father threatened to have my acceptance revoked. He could've done it, too. He was a good friend of the university's president. So, my father offered her family a deal—a substantial amount of cash in exchange for her signing a document that I wasn't the baby's father."

"So, your father paid them off. What was he like? You never talk about him."

"He was bitter about his business going under and he took his anger out on me. Frankly, I hated him."

"But he must have loved you."

"I guess so. He went into debt to pay Mary although his business had collapsed years before. At the time, I thought he owed me and years later, when he asked me to bail him out of financial trouble, I wanted to spit in his face. Then, Henry made me realize I would eventually regret not ... well, anyway, I gave my father two million for Blackhall, which was a lot more than it was worth at the time, just to give him some cushion. So, I guess in our own way, we were there for each other." Davis stared at the fire, a sad look in his eyes. "I know that doesn't sound like much of a connection to hang on to. But it's all I have. The sad thing is that no matter what your parents do, deep down you still love them."

Reed nodded, tears forming in her eyes, moved by the rawness of his emotions.

Davis shifted toward her. "Reed, it's time we started being honest with each other. Both of us."

Tears ran down Reed's cheeks. "I was lonely and upset. Later, I found out Harrison was hiding my phone and erasing your messages. I fired him. The whole thing was awful."

Davis wrapped his arms around her and buried his face in her hair. "Jesus Christ," he said.

She began sobbing.

He lifted her chin and wiped away her tears. "Don't cry. It's my fault. I hope you can forgive me." He pulled her closer and kissed her cheek.

"I don't understand. If Harrison wasn't serious about renovating the house and he doesn't have a claim to your money, why was he here?"

"My innocent sweetheart…" Davis held her tightly. "Why? He saw an opportunity to get back at me. So, he decided to fuck with us."

CHAPTER 66

I had some concerns about the case and I asked Ruth to meet me at Clyde's Restaurant in Georgetown. It would be good to talk to someone other than Henry and Reed ... someone sane.

Inside the restaurant's hunting-lodge interior, leather booths were surrounded by idealized paintings of beautiful people from the 1920's engaged in society sports—skeet shooting, rowing, horse racing.

A waiter brought us burgers. I dipped a fry in ketchup and scarfed it down. I felt a tug on my sleeve and looked down to see a little tow-haired boy about ten years old gripping the edge of our table, peering up at me with big brown eyes. "Sir, are you Justice Alexander? From the Supreme Court?"

"Yes."

He handed me a pencil and scrap of paper. His parents were smiling from the next table. "Can I have your autograph, please?"

I almost fell into my ketchup. The media had done a one-eighty, praising me for risking my reputation by representing a wrongly accused man ... but this? "Of course, son." I scrawled my name. "What do you want to be when you grow up?"

"A law man, like you."

Damn. The kid knew how to get to me. I ruffled the boy's hair. "There you go," I said, handing him my signature.

"Thank you, sir." He trotted away and his parents mouthed "thank you" to me.

Ruth laughed.

She was annoying. "Eat. Your food is getting cold."

"What were you saying about Brad?"

I pushed my plate aside. "Okay. Our theory wraps everything up and I was ready to slap a bow on it. Brad killed the twins and a few days later, he killed Lilly. But there are remaining problems. Why would Brad kill Lilly and hide her body at Blackhall if he'd left the twins' bodies there and knew the FBI might search the place? Someone covered Lilly with lime so we know the killer was trying to hide her body. What makes sense is that Brad wore a condom to rape Eden and Echo so his DNA wasn't detectable. Or maybe he didn't rape them at all. Maybe he just killed them. What doesn't make sense is that he left the twins' bodies on the library floor, yet a few days later, tried to conceal Lilly's body in the same house."

Ruth stopped munching on a fry and stared at me. "I don't believe I'm hearing this."

I moved closer to the edge of my seat. "I've been thinking about some of the problems you raised yourself. The MO. If Brad killed Lilly, why didn't he use Devil's Breath on her like he did on the twins? Lilly was a fireball. Without the Devil's Breath, how did he get Lilly compliant enough to climb those old cliff stairs? The stairs were the only way he could've gotten into that estate and if she wasn't drugged, I'm sure she would've found a way to escape."

She shrugged. "Maybe Lilly was unconscious when he carted her out there. We found ligature marks on her throat so she was strangled before she was stabbed."

"Listen to yourself. That would prove my point. If she was unconscious, it would be impossible for Brad to carry her up those old stairs. You said yourself they were in terrible condition and missing several rungs."

Ruth was quiet.

I sat back, thinking about my conversation with Henry and Reed and their wild theories about Josephine Rideout. "Not everything that seems to be related can be related. At first, I thought these murders were connected but now, I don't think so. It's not only the MO, the murder weapon was also different. Why would Brad kill the twins with a knife but strangle Lilly until she was unconscious, then kill her with a screwdriver? Brad kept that knife on him so why did he use a screwdriver? These killings deviate too much to be the work of one person."

Ruth skirted my eyes and examined a painting of a trim young woman skiing in the Alps. "You're never satisfied, are you?" She took a big bite of burger. Her eyes looked heavy, maybe even sad. "For months, you've been taking the opposite argument, saying these cases are related, lecturing me that there's no such thing as coincidence. And when we finally agree with you, when everything finally lines up the way you suggested, you flip on us. Tell me one fact that's changed."

"I don't know. But there's something about these crimes, something else that I haven't put my finger on yet, and it's driving me crazy."

****

"Leave it alone," Claire said.

"I can't," I said.

"Don't you see? The FBI's theory exonerates you." Claire kept picking up a book and putting it down again.

"I'm not worried about being re-implicated. I didn't have anything to do with Lilly's death."

"Damn it! What about what we just went through?"

I put my arms around her. "I'm sorry but I was Lilly's boss and I feel some responsibility for her."

"Why do you care? Lilly lied about having an affair with you!"

"I think Jake asked her out and she tossed that at him, not thinking."

Claire put her hands on her hips. "For God's sake, don't be so naïve. Lilly was spreading that rumor on purpose. She knew it would get back to me. And she connived to get a job with Davis so she'd be firmly ensconced in your life once she drove a wedge between us."

"Oh, c'mon, Claire. That's crazy."

"Honestly, Warren, sometimes you worry me. For someone who was an FBI profiler … I saw the way Lilly was hanging all over you at the Christmas party. Are you really that blind?"

I looked at Claire, chagrined. "Okay, I knew she had a crush on me and I ignored it because I didn't know what else to do. I didn't mention it to you because it seemed like treacherous ground." I kissed her. "I'm glad you trust me."

"I do because I know you're a good man but Lilly wanted to break us up."

"Maybe. I don't know, but all murder victims deserve justice and Claire … I made a promise to her mother."

Claire shook her head. "It's more than that. For good or bad, you'll always be FBI."

CHAPTER 67

"You wanted to talk to Brad," Ruth said, her hand resting on the doorknob to the small concrete room where Brad sat on the other side, handcuffed. "And he wants to talk to you. I just hope you know what you're doing."

The jailer buzzed us in. Brad looked at Ruth defiantly. "I didn't kill Lilly. You have the knife so you know I killed Eden and Echo. So, there's no use fighting that. My big mistake was selling Manville that decanter."

"Don't give yourself so much credit," I said, pulling up a chair. "We were already onto you. Locating the decanter merely sped up the process. But why sell it if you knew it could link you to the murders?"

"With the President's daughters murdered at Blackhall, I didn't think Rideout would be dumb enough to report the decanter and bring the police sniffing around. And Manville was supposed to keep quiet about what I sold him. As for Lilly … do you really think I'd kill someone that close to home and draw attention to myself? No. No way. I did not kill her." He smiled slightly. "Although I have information about who did."

"You're lying," Ruth said.

"The Government wants the death penalty. Do you think I'd offer information, otherwise? But I'm not talking unless the death penalty's off the table."

"That's not going to happen."

Brad laughed. "Don't know why not. My death won't bring the President's daughters back." He grimaced. "These cuffs are tight."

I motioned to the guard and he unlocked the cuffs.

Brad rubbed his wrists. "That's better. Like I said, I get a life sentence and in exchange, you get Lilly's killer."

Ruth and I looked at each other and left the room. Once outside, I said, "Let's talk to the Justice Department."

*****

We were back to see Brad two days later. The Justice Department had conferred with President Hines and a counter-proposal had been offered. The death penalty would be dropped if Brad's information led to the arrest and conviction of Lilly's killer. It seems that the President had some compassion for Lilly's mother and her desire to know who killed her daughter.

On this visit, Brad's cuffs were already off and a cigarette dangled from his mouth. "I heard Lilly with a man the night she disappeared," he said. "They were in her living room and I can't hear much in that room. It sounded like a normal conversation. Then it got louder and at that point, I definitely heard your name." Brad looked at me.

"My name?"

"Yep. I heard the words Justice Alexander. The man yelled your name, like he was angry at you about something. Then I heard a loud thump, like something hit the floor. A few minutes later, I heard Lilly's door open and close. I looked out my window but didn't see anything."

*****

I now had some indisputable facts. Lillly's killer knew that Lilly worked for me. And he had the code to the gate at Blackhall. That was the only way he could get Lilly into that estate. The gate code was in my computers, both at work and at home.

Jake saw me enter my password every day. And he had a huge ego. Maybe he made a play for Lilly. She would let Jake into her apartment. She found out what he wanted and said no. Jake's a big guy, maybe he got a little rough and one thing led to another until something awful happened.

Jake hadn't asked me about Lilly's investigation when he returned from Nepal. It was almost like he knew what had happened to her. And Jake had offered me up awfully fast with Ruth and Chief Brown. He'd been diverting attention from himself.

More importantly, I'd learned from Ruth that Jake had informed the FBI about the screwdriver in my fireplace. Jake had inserted himself into the case the entire time. I'd seen a lot of criminals and the more intelligent the criminal was, the more likely they were to engage law enforcement. That was part of the excitement for them. The game, the adrenaline rush, the danger.

Sort of like mountain climbing in Nepal.

That son of a bitch had framed me.

CHAPTER 68

I knew just the person to help me get justice for Lilly, and oddly enough, that was Chief Justice Bannister Brown. After Brad Swanson's arrest, Chief Brown had profusely apologized and was now going out of his way to be friendly. You see, I was receiving great press from the legal community. I was on the front cover of The Washington Lawyer and Harvard Law Today. Legal experts and talking heads all across the country were extolling my virtues, calling me brave and compassionate, an example of all that was right in America. Of course, they were overdoing it, but I was glad to have my reputation back. It also reflected well on the Brown Court and that's what the Chief cared about.

I was meeting the Chief for lunch at The Palm, our third lunch together at his favorite restaurant, where he loved to relate stories from the Court's past. He'd turned out to be quite the raconteur.

"Warren! My friend, over here," Chief Brown shouted from across the room, standing quickly, spilling a glass of water in the process. A waiter hurried over. The Chief ignored the mess and pumped my hand. "Good to see you," he said. "Get us a different table," he directed the waiter.

"Yes, Mr. Chief Justice."

Several high-powered lawyers in the room clapped and smiled as we passed their tables. Chief Brown waved at them, basking in the adulation. The waiter seated us under a wall stacked to the ceiling with caricatures and cartoons depicting the rich, the famous, and the political elite.

"Great to get together," Brown said, laughing, squeezing his large posterior into a wood chair.

I smiled. "Glad you had some free time."

"Anything for you. Let's have a drink."

"Just ice tea for me. I have some work this afternoon."

He frowned. "Well, I have a one-martini limit. Sort of like a speed limit."

We laughed and spent a few minutes with our noses in the menus. He put his down. "So, what's new with you?" he asked jovially. "I mean, besides being an American hero."

I looked over the top of my reading glasses and set my menu to one side. "Actually, I have interesting news."

He raised bushy eyebrows.

"The FBI has re-opened Lilly's case."

Chief Brown looked confused. "I thought the FBI arrested Brad Swanson."

I lowered my voice and looked around the room. "This is highly confidential. The FBI has changed their thinking. They have solid evidence that Brad killed Eden and Echo Hines but they've changed their mind about Lilly."

"No kidding?"

"At first, the FBI was positive that Brad killed all three women. It made sense because Brad was the Super at Lilly's building and he had a key to her apartment."

"What's changed?"

"What's changed is that I finally realized that whoever killed Lilly had no idea Brad Swanson would be arrested for her murder. There was no reason to plant the screwdriver, otherwise. You see, the FBI determined that the screwdriver was taped to the chimney a few months ago and its weight finally broke the adhesive."

Brown stared at me.

"Lilly's killer jumped the gun. That was his big mistake."

The waiter placed a basket of rolls on the table, and Chief Brown grabbed a knife and slathered butter on one. "My God, you're right," he said, his mouth full, his jowls shaking. "Wait … what if Brad Swanson was the one trying to frame you?"

"It wasn't him."

Brown swallowed a chunk of bread. "Why not?"

"Brad would've planted evidence that connected me to all three crimes."

Brown dug into some more butter. "Man! This is exciting. Do you have a suspect?"

I lowered my voice. "This is strictly confidential. It was Jake."

"Jake Larsen?" Brown almost fell off his chair.

I nodded. "Everything fits. There was tension between Jake and Lilly and he thinks he's God's gift to women. Lilly would've let Jake into her apartment. And Jake had access to my computer where I keep the code to Blackhall's gate. Once the FBI knew who they were looking for, they located Jake's car on a traffic video leaving the District after midnight the night Lilly disappeared. We're scouring the tapes for other possibilities but we're sure it was Jake."

Brown looked skeptical. "I can't believe Jake would kill anyone."

I looked over my shoulder. "That's just it. No one would. He has no history of violence so we think it was a crime of passion or perhaps an accident. We need forensic evidence, and that's going to be difficult because Jake and Lilly worked in the same office and he was in her apartment with me shortly after she went missing. So, we need to find Lilly's DNA somewhere it shouldn't be, like the trunk of Jake's car."

"You think she was in his trunk?" Brown was aghast.

"It's possible."

Chief Brown turned green and gulped some water. "I think I'm going to be ill."

"Bottom line is that we need a search warrant but we need more evidence first."

Chief Brown looked surprised. "You need more?" He shrugged. "I guess you're the criminal law expert."

"If we can get someone to look in the trunk, and if they see blood in there, that would be enough." I smiled at Chief Brown. The waiter came by and I waved him away. "Give us a few more minutes," I said and the waiter retreated.

I turned back to Chief Brown. "That's where you come in."

"Me?" He recoiled in his chair.

"I fabricated an excuse to have Jake stop by the Supreme Court later today. The FBI and I have a plan. We want you to tell him you're having car trouble and need a ride home. You're also taking a painting with you."

Brown frowned.

"Don't worry," I said. "The FBI has supplied the painting and it's been designed so that it won't fit in Jake's back seat but will fit perfectly into his trunk. The painting is in your chambers now. When Jake opens the trunk, just be alert, look inside, and let us know if you see anything. It's a long shot, but worth a try."

The Chief snorted. "Sounds like a rinky-dink plan for the FBI."

"The best plans are simple."

"Why don't you do it?"

"You live in Jake's neighborhood so it makes sense you would ask for a ride. And, you have to understand, Jake's hyperaware of everything I do because he framed me. I gave Jake an extra key to my house in case he needed a litigation file when I wasn't home and he used it to plant the screwdriver. He tried to throw suspicion on me from the beginning. And Jake partnered with me to represent Henry so he would know every move I made. Jake is like a chess player. He moves when I move but he would never suspect you of trying to trap him."

Brown continued chewing. "What if I don't see anything?"

"You might not, even though there may be blood in there. Sometimes, it's so microscopic you can't see it."

"You're kidding."

"Blood is nearly impossible to get out of fabric. For example, the rug at Blackhall had all sorts of dried blood that was invisible to the human eye." I laughed. "You've heard of luminol, haven't you? And we know Lilly was strangled before she was killed with the screwdriver. When someone is strangled, tissue around the trachea and larynx can hemorrhage and the victim aspirates blood. It can be a miniscule amount. Can't even see it with the naked eye although it's enough to put a killer away. Of course, a carpet can be replaced and that gets rid of the evidence but most criminals are too stupid to think of that. And that hangs them more often than you'd think."

The Chief put his head in his hands. "My God," he mumbled, "if Jake is guilty, what will happen to my Supreme Court? Just when our reputation is soaring, this could be a disgrace we may never recover from."

"Chief, if you help us nail Jake, the Court's reputation will not only remain intact, you'll be a hero. You'll be a man for the history books."

He nodded thoughtfully. "I'll do it."

CHAPTER 69

Although Chief Brown had not seen any blood in Jake's trunk, Ruth and I were keeping vigil in Jake's neighborhood on Capitol Hill, an area favored by Supreme Court employees because of its proximity to the Court. It was a cold, breezy September morning. Red leaves tumbled across dormant lawns fading to yellow and a faint sun lolled behind dusty clouds. I huddled deep into my brown leather jacket as I kept lookout from the front seat of a white van with the words *Pete's Plumbing* stenciled on the sides.

The door to a house opened and a head emerged. I trashed my coffee cup and elbowed Ruth. "There he is."

Ruth shifted the van into drive. "Here we go." She pulled a leopard print baseball cap low over her forehead. The van purred as it accelerated and followed a late model Audi through the streets of Capitol Hill and over the Potomac River, grey spits of water angry in its basin.

"Where's he going?"

"Looks like he's on his way to Alexandria."

Twenty minutes later, the Audi pulled into a car dealership outside Alexandria, Virginia.

Ruth broke into a huge smile and pounded her hand on the steering wheel. "Jackpot!"

I reached in the back for a video camera. "I need to record him going into the dealership."

"Got it?" Ruth asked a few minutes later.

"Yep."

****

A few days later, I went to Chief Brown's chambers to thank him. I smiled broadly. "Congratulations. Thanks to you, we caught Lilly's killer."

The Chief's eyes bugged out. "You arrested Jake?"

There was a loud noise at the door as Ruth and several other FBI agents stormed in.

"Bannister Brown," Ruth said, "stand up and put your hands behind your back. You are under arrest for the murder of Lillian Stella McCleary."

Chief Brown looked bewildered. "What? No! You're making a mistake!"

"Sir. Come quietly."

He retreated behind his desk. "I'll have your Goddamn badge! You can't fuck with me, you little bitch!"

Ruth smiled. "We're not … sir. You did that to yourself when you took your car to the body shop and asked them to replace the carpet in the trunk. Lab results show that Lilly McCleary's blood and hair are embedded in the fibers."

"You can't use that in a court of law! You didn't have a search warrant!"

"We didn't need a warrant. When you dispose of property, we're free to take it as evidence." She smiled. "You of all people should know that."

Brown scuffled with the agents. He was a big man. "Goddamn it!" he screamed.

"Calm down, sir," Ruth said, looking at another agent who had a taser ready. "We don't want anyone to get hurt, not even you."

"You can't do this to me!" Brown screamed. "I'm Chief Justice Bannister Brown!"

Ruth smiled. "Don't worry, sir. We'll be sure to get your name right on the indictment."

✳✳✳✳

"Wow," Claire said. "What made you suspect Chief Brown? I mean, I still can't believe it."

"At first, I was convinced it was Jake but the man Brad heard in Lilly's apartment referred to me as Justice Alexander and Jake would've called me by the name all my law clerks use, Justice A."

"Good catch," Claire said, approvingly.

"Jake did report the screwdriver. He was packing the litigation files for storage when he saw it in the fireplace. As an officer of the court, he was required to report it as potential evidence. I would've done the same thing."

Claire shook her head. "What I don't understand is how Chief Brown got the gate code."

"Dorothy told me that he can access the other Justices' computers in case there's an emergency and needs to retrieve a document. Ruth had the FBI do a forensic examination of my computer and it showed that Chief Brown had accessed several of my files, including the file containing the gate code, from his home the night Lilly disappeared. But by itself, that didn't prove anything nefarious."

"Suspicious, though."

"Definitely. So, I asked Ruth to look for Chief Brown's car on traffic videos. Brown was recorded after two in the morning leaving the city. That's when I was positive he'd killed her. Unfortunately, the video showed him alone in the car. We needed evidence that Lilly was in his trunk and to get it, we had to set a trap. It was our last hope because we had no forensics. He'd committed the perfect crime. But, it didn't look like he was going to take the bait."

"So, if he hadn't had the carpet in his trunk replaced, you wouldn't have caught him."

"Not in a million years."

CHAPTER 70

Davis was worried that he'd be indicted for lying to the FBI, something he confessed to when he took the stand at Henry's trial. Davis could've gone away for a long time but we heard through multiple sources that neither the FBI nor the Justice Department wanted to rehash Henry's trial and their humiliating DNA debacle.

The Supreme Court was in turmoil after the Chief's arrest and the other Justices were anxious to put the horrific episode behind them. The Justice Department offered Chief Brown a deal that I thought was too lenient—life without parole in exchange for a guilty plea and a full confession. The Chief was considering it.

General Fontaine was never tried. Not for money laundering, not for criminal conspiracy. The President gave him a full pardon before a jury could be convened. That convinced me they were somehow involved in Jerry Arnett's death because if that wasn't quid pro quo, I don't know what was. It was the way of Washington and something I was determined to change.

****

Within days, Chief Brown had agreed to accept the plea deal and give a full confession to Ruth.

"You planted the screwdriver in Justice Alexander's house, didn't you?" Ruth asked.

Brown nodded. "Alexander leaves his jacket on a chair at work. I took his house keys out of the pocket. It only took an hour to drive across town and return the keys before he knew they were gone. You see, the screwdriver was my insurance in case anyone suspected me. One phone call and I'd be in the clear."

He tugged at the sleeve of his government-issued orange jumpsuit. "As for Lilly ... I was in love with her. Everyone says she was a flirt but we had a special connection—we were both brilliant. I'd never met a woman who could argue so cogently. And she liked me. We'd even gone to dinner a time or two. I was making headway. Then, after working with Alexander for a few weeks, she didn't want anything to do with me. But when she waltzed into my chambers for my help with United States v. Clark and said *Chief Brown, you are a brilliant man*, my heart jumped out of my chest."

He grinned, little white teeth stretching ear to ear. "You see, she was telling me she wanted me." He let his hands rise and fall. "She'd changed her mind and why not? After all, I'm the Chief." He smiled smugly. "So, I went to her apartment and she let me in. She didn't seem happy to see me but I thought it was an act. Y'know, playing hard to get. Then, I tried to kiss her and she ordered me out. I didn't understand and I got angry. The little bitch had led me on! I yelled something like—You're fucking Justice Alexander, why not me?"

Brown grew quiet, a tear running down his cheek. "I know. That wasn't the right thing to say. I've never been good with women."

He slammed his fist on the table. "But then she laughed at me and called me a disgusting slob! She shouldn't have said that." The Chief choked back a sob. "She was like all the other women! Shallow bitch. Suddenly I was on top of her, strangling her with a lamp cord."

He hung his head. "Looking back, I see that I was taking out all the years of rejection on Lilly. She went limp. I thought she was dead. I couldn't believe what I'd done! I've never done anything like that before. I was terrified out of my mind. I put her in the trunk of my car and drove around, trying to decide what to do. I logged onto Alexander's computer, hoping to find the code to the gate at Blackhall. I didn't think Lilly would ever be found in that Godforsaken place and if she was, he'd be blamed for her death because of all the rumors flying around the Court."

"What about the Court's reputation? Wasn't that important to you?"

"It was!" He slammed his hand down again. "But it was a Hobson's Choice. On the one hand, I had to make sure the right people knew about the rumors in case her body was found. But I also had to protect the Court from scandal so I went back later and covered her with lime so no one would find her. I was taking a chance by doing that. I could've gotten caught but I did it!"

Brown glared at Ruth. "If Alexander had simply resigned, it would've solved all my problems. Then if he was arrested, he wouldn't have been a black eye on my Court!"

What a psycho.

"Was she dead when you arrived at Blackhall?"

"I carried her up to the attic and she started coughing. She'd regained consciousness. My God. If I'd just taken her to an emergency room, maybe I could've claimed it was an accident, maybe people would've believed me … but I couldn't explain the attic. It was too late to let her go. I'd lose my position at the Court." Brown covered his ears. "She began yelling at me. I can still hear her voice—*What have you done to me? I'm calling the police!* I stabbed her with an old screwdriver I found on the attic floor. I had to! It was my only way out." Brown turned red with rage and he dug his fingers into his face. "That bitch! She's ruined my life! Fucking tease!"

CHAPTER 71

Days turned into months and the Christmas holidays were upon us. Snow was falling heavily, piling deep, drifting high against the wall surrounding Blackhall, cocooning the estate in its own fluffy world. The smell of roast turkey permeated the mansion and Davis and I had just finished setting the table for Christmas Eve dinner. Everything was set. The Christmas tree was twinkling. The fireplace was ablaze. Red stockings hung in a row.

"Where's Henry?" I asked, watching Reed set out chocolate cookies for Santa who would soon be on his way.

She looked at her watch. "He should be here by now. Why don't you go tell him dinner's ready." She leaned down and swooped up Samuel who was crawling madly toward the shimmering Christmas tree.

Davis decided to go with me and we bundled into heavy down parkas and trudged our way through the white drifts to Henry's cottage. "Y'know," Davis said, smiling. "For the first time in a long time, I feel good. Reed and I are in therapy. We're being honest with each other and working things out. Samuel is a wonderful boy. And Henry is safe and can live out his life in peace."

"Life is good?"

He stopped and looked at me, snow piling on his shoulders. He nodded. "It's going to be a good Christmas."

I smiled and we resumed our walk down the path to Henry's door. We knocked and waited, snow swirling around us. Davis tapped again, pushed on the door. "There you are."

Henry was sitting in his favorite chair, dressed in a spiffy navy blue blazer with gold buttons, an early Christmas present from Reed. A wreath hung from the fireplace and presents for little Samuel were piled neatly nearby, wrapped in red Santa Claus paper.

Davis laughed. "C'mon, Henry. Santa's waiting for you."

Henry didn't move. I pushed Davis aside and kneeled at Henry's side. "Henry ... Henry?" I examined his eyes, felt his pulse. "My God," I said, looking up at Davis, "he's dead."

Davis sank to his knees and wrapped his arms around Henry. I'm sure I heard him say, "Don't leave me." Raw emotion, so vulnerable it was unsettling, like seeing someone naked and alone in the world. I stood back to give Davis some time. Several minutes went by before he could compose himself and we could return to the mansion to break the awful news.

****

Henry had died from a sudden heart attack. The doctor said his arteries had been hardening for some time and the strain of the trial had caught up with him. Davis was swept away with grief and guilt. Grief because he loved Henry. Guilt because when he met Eden and Echo for sex, he'd set into motion a horrible chain of events that eventually destroyed the only father he ever knew.

Personally, I thought the FBI was just as much to blame. My beloved FBI, the Bureau I'd always been so proud to serve, had bitterly disappointed me. No one should go through what Henry had.

****

Snow had been falling all morning. It was a deep white blanket that covered the road as we traveled to the tiny country church for Henry's funeral. Everyone attended—Claire, Reed, Davis, little Samuel, Henry's church friends and all his neighbors. And I was there, too.

The small chamber was packed, people sitting shoulder to shoulder as the minister read several passages from the Bible. Davis rose, his face contorted with grief as he began the eulogy. "It feels almost impossible to convey how much I loved Henry, but I will try. Henry lived a simple life of quietly doing what he thought was right ..."

When Davis finished, sobs lingered well into the next hymn, *Rock of Ages*, specifically chosen by Davis for his memories of Henry—*let me hide myself in thee*. At the last minute, just before the lid was closed, Reed stepped forward and placed a small bundle of white sage in the casket. I heard her say, "This will keep your spirit safe, my dear friend."

Davis and I and several other men carried Henry's casket to the hearse for his last ride to Blackhall where we would lay him to rest. A small mausoleum overlooking the water had been erected for Henry and Susannah, whose body had been moved a few days earlier to lie beside that of her husband.

The hearse led a string of black cars behind it, headlights peering through snow whipping across the road, piling into drifts along the miles of fencing leading to the house. We cleared the iron gate, stopped at the top of the long hill and walked behind the casket as it was rolled along a cleared path to the crypt at the cliff's edge.

Large flakes fluttered everywhere, onto our hats, coats, faces. And sudden gusts of wind stirred the white fluff into swirling diaphanous clouds before dying down again. The scene was otherworldly, everything a pure white—the willow trees bowed by snow, the ice on the Bay, even white clouds shrouding the sky. And in the hushed silence, the casket was rolled into the mausoleum, the only sound, the soft crush of wheels on the newly fallen snow. We stood reverently, our tears falling silently, as Henry passed by.

CHAPTER 72

Five Months Later

Reed takes Henry fresh flowers every day, sits with him for a few moments, tells him about her day. She misses his company and she's become the keeper of the flame. She's put in a new lilac and crepe myrtle path that leads to the mausoleum, and it's become her favorite spot and a place where Samuel loves to play.

Reed said that she and Davis are excited about the new baby, that Davis said families are like the willows at Blackhall—the trees can readily take root from cuttings or broken branches lying on the ground. I was startled by Reed's choice of words and wondered what she meant but from the tone of her voice and the way she said it, I decided I didn't want to know. She and Davis are on their own, as it should be. I'm left with my suspicions, which I pray to God, will never be verified. A parent can only take so much.

Reed asked Davis to cut back on his travel and he agreed. Will they be able to make their marriage work? I don't know but they are much more affectionate with one another. Davis says it's time to start being a father and much of his time is now spent at Blackhall. Samuel is walking and follows Davis everywhere, much to Davis's great delight. Davis even plays hide-and-seek with the boy, something I had to see to believe.

Time has gone by. The renovations are done. Reed and Davis poured massive amounts of money into the estate and she reports that the house is spectacular. We're seeing it for the first time today. We're returning to Blackhall to meet our new grandson who was delivered just last week.

We clear the gate and round the bend, our car growling low on the long, hard climb up the hill. It's a beautiful blue day. Red-breasted robins hop across the green grass. Pockets of purple violets and yellow daisies